THE OGHAM CONNECTIONS
BY: D. BAUGH ROY

PROLOGUE

New Orleans-February 1998

  His job was to work the midnight shift at one of the large industrial warehouses on the docks flanking the Mississippi River as it perpetually curved the mighty waters around the port city. He jumped out of his position on the forklift and stepped outside into the cool night air for a short cigarette break. It was 1:45 am. Having rained earlier, the fishy waterfront smells blended with the scent of fresh rain, combining into a unique, if not obnoxious odor. Sam, a 16-year veteran, lit his cigarette, took a long tug on it, blew the match out and tossed it to the ground. The early morning fog began its slow entrance into the area and covered the match almost immediately, leaving the darkness once again in front of him. Taking another drag on his cigarette, he leaned against the building to ponder what he would do on his next day off. Fishing was out since it was still too cold. Maybe he would hit the casino this time since the last day at the track had been financially too disappointing.

  Sam's attention was diverted from his casual thoughts as out of the fog a shape of a car without headlights came slowly up in the darkness toward his location. The sight was usual if not ghostly. The warehouse road ran the length of the row covering a span of ten long warehouses, mostly unoccupied this time of night. Sam thought it was a bit unusual for a car to be driving up this time of night and without any headlights on, especially in the fog. He straightened up to see what may be going on in the darkness.

The driver's side was opening, and a man stepped out of the door. Slim in build with long hair combed back into a ponytail, he was dressed in a yellow rubber suit, similar to that of a dockworker, and wearing tall black rubber boots. Sam tensed a bit as he watched the man walking rapidly toward him. The building's only security light dimly glowed on the driver's face. He was making short nervous glances behind his car, but there was nothing there except the black darkness and the thick fog. There was obvious perspiration on his face even though it was a cool night. As he walked closer to Sam, the man looked as if he was pulling something out of his pocket. Sam got more nervous because there were many crazy things that could happen in this area of town at night. The kind of things that people in the daylight hardly ever knew about, and if they knew, they didn't talk about. The man moved up close to Sam, then reached out and grabbed him by the arm just when Sam decided it was time to go back to the safety of the warehouse.

The man's raspy voice startled Sam as he spoke. "I don't mean to scare you, sir. I know you don't know me, but I need your help. Please."

Sam shook his arm free from the touch of the man and said, "Go away, man! I'm busy working. Try somewhere else."

Sam started back inside the warehouse, hoping the guy would disappear. The man grabbed his arm again and as Sam turned with his hand forming into a fist ready to throw a punch, he saw that the driver had desperation written clearly on his face as he said, "I haven't got any more time. Listen, I have $3,000.00 cash for you if you will just keep this for me for about an hour."

This dollar figure definitely got Sam's undivided attention. Maybe he should listen a few seconds more. The man showed Sam a round metallic disc and then nervously looked behind him again.

"You see, there are some people following me that want this. They were right behind me, but I don't see them now. I lost them in this fog. Man, as soon as I have dealt with them, I will be back. What do you say? Deal?"

Now Sam just so happened to be in need of some extra cash. There was that bad bet at the track and all. Plus, it looked to him like the little disc object was something he could keep safe for a little while. Sounded like a good profit for a small favor to this stranger. Without thinking anymore about it, he said, "I don't know about this. But I don't make that kind of money in a whole month on this job. Have you got the cash like, ah, up front, so to speak?"

Looking relieved, the man counted out hundred-dollar bills. He handed Sam the money and the small disc object. Sam just began to regret his decision and wondered if he should just give the money back and go back to work, but he didn't get a chance to do that because the man quickly turned to go back to his car saying, "I will be back in about an hour. And, thanks."

Sam liked the feel and the smell of money and as he recounted it, he thought that maybe he had taken advantage of the guy. Maybe he should have asked for a little more since the $3000.00 came so easily. Thinking that it must be his lucky night, he counted the money again while smiling.

The man's car started out again slowly and quietly, still with no headlights. He was obviously trying to hide from someone, Sam was thinking. Since he was headed toward a dead-end, Sam watched the car as it turned around and then it quickly disappeared from his view. Sam threw what was left of his cigarette on the ground, still smiling slightly. He was baby-sitting a little round disc for an hour for three thousand bucks. Luck was finally with him again! He opened the door to enter the warehouse and was about to shut it again when he heard a screeching noise in the direction the man just drove. Under another small security light approximately 150 feet from the doorway where he stood, he saw the man's car and it only made it a short distance before another car blocked it. The fog was breaking up under the light so he could now see the two cars. He wasn't sure what was about to happen, so he stepped back into the doorway, with his curiosity making him leave it slightly open. From there, he couldn't see but he could hear what was going on. There were sounds of several doors opening and closing. A man with a foreign accent, definitely not a local boy, Sam was sure, said, "Get out, you." Then, "Where is it?"

Sam recognized the raspy voice that answered as the man who just gave him the money. "Go chase someone else. You got the wrong guy." Of course, from the sound of things, Sam was hoping that his answer wasn't going to be: "Well, you see there's a warehouse worker over there who has it now. You can get it from him."

Another heavily accented voice said, "You will give it here or you will tell us where it is, Raven. Surely, this is not worth dying to hide it, is it?"

"No, you are right. I do not wish to die. But you still have the wrong guy. I don't have whatever it is you are looking for."

Suddenly a muffled noise rang out. It was the same sound Sam often heard when gun silencers were used on TV. That was followed by a groan and then there was laughter from several men.

The first accented voice said, "Now you have no weapon, and you have a bullet in your leg. The next one is for your head. I think you should give it up now, don't you?"

Another accented male voice said, "But, Sir, we cannot kill him! We have no other leads."

"I know he has it. There's no way he could have hidden it in this short period of time. He hasn't been out of sight but for two minutes since he arrived here. Do you see anyone else here that he could have given it to?"

The other voice replied, "No, Commander. But he could have tossed it in the river for all we know."

Once again, the apparent leader said in an even tone, "Give it here now and your life will be yours to live out, even if with a slight limp."

"Like I'm sure, it would. But I don't have it," was the calm reply.

"Too bad, Raven. You were given a chance. We will find it whether you live or die. Dying for a secret. How gallant and heroic. I hope it was worth your life." Another muffled shot and then the sound of footsteps. There was what sounded to Sam like a lot of guttural sounds and then a distinct "Shit! He doesn't' have it on him." Followed by, "Search the car! Better yet, here's his car key. Load him in it and we'll dump him in the big Ponchatrain Lake. Then we will take the car and search it very carefully." There was a short pause and then, "You think you have tricked us, you piece of shit! Let your last words give us the location of the disc now and maybe you can go to heaven. Yes?"

With no response forthcoming, the leader again expressed his frustrations with a long line of what must have been choice curse words in his own foreign language, Sam thought. Close to being terrified, he was almost hyperventilating. He was also experiencing some wetness in his pants. "Jesus H. Christ!" he said in an inaudible whisper. He heard one of the cars leave, felt the money and disc object in his pocket and nervously tried to close the door very quietly.

Unfortunately for Sam, the sound of the door closing caught the attention of one of the men in the road as they were entering one of the cars, and he looked down toward the warehouse door. It was dark and no one was there. No one had been there because he would have noticed. But then he saw the glow of the recently smoked cigarette through the foggy surroundings. He quietly got on his cell phone and rang the leader now in the dead man's car. "I think a pigeon might be here. I'll take a take look around and contact you by cell if I find this pigeon."

Now normally, even in the worst of times, Sam didn't consider himself a wimp. But he was experiencing a real primordial fear. Shaking uncontrollably, he wondered if anyone noticed the door, or for that matter, the earlier exchange. All he did know was that what sounded like true criminal professionals had just obviously murdered the man who trusted him. Sam, a lowly forklift-driving warehouse employee, to keep something very valuable was unthinkable. That meant he was the new man with this obviously mighty important disc object in his pants pocket and he realized he was in just as much danger with it. He thought about what he would do, and after a couple of hours of hiding in a locked closet, and letting his pants dry, he eased out. The checkout clock showed 6:15 am

Looking carefully around and seeing no one in the dawning light, he sauntered down his usual path to the bus stop. That's unusual, he thought to himself as he noticed two men at the end of the warehouse drive with fishing poles and fishing tackle. Not likely to be fishing in these cold toxic waters. He looked the other way and continued his walk casually. He glanced back and saw the two fishermen were now walking toward him. His heart jolted a second and then began to race. He looked in front of him where there were two more men walking toward him. These guys were dressed in dark suits, the kind that he saw on cop shows where the FBI was the good guy. Somehow, he knew that these were not good guys here! They were not bloody likely to be taking a morning stroll here either! I'm dead meat, he thought. He was being boxed in from both front and back.

Since Sam worked in the warehouse district for almost

sixteen years, he knew the area like the back of his shaking hands. He made a quick dash for an alley running in and out of it quickly and then toward the busy area of the district. Over the streetcar tracks and down the sidewalks, turning and weaving through foot traffic like a professional pick pocket. He did not look back. He knew they would be there, whoever 'they' were, so he ran as fast and as far as his scrawny legs and his fear for his life would take him.

CHAPTER ONE

Scotland, January 2000

  The sun was beginning to peek through the darkness on the horizon where the ocean met the sky. It was a glorious light that began to brighten the whole sky. It started filling the breaks in the clouds with a pinkish hue, then grew slowly into a bright orange, and finally burst into a vivid golden fireball. As she looked at the day's beginning, the calmness of the scene seemed to work a magic on the tightened nerves she had been living with for the past months. It was almost as if she was being wrapped warmly inside and a maternal voice was saying "It's all going to be all right now."

  Yes, she thought, I am going to be all right now. She reached beside her lounge chair for her mug of hot coffee. The cup jerked in her hand and then fell to the ground. Her hands were still trembling. Well, maybe she wasn't all together all right, she said to herself.

  She began to let herself review in her mind the last months of danger, trauma, fear and strangely enough, love, that finally led her to this moment of pure peace. It had been far too dangerous for her to reflect on things until now, so the doctors told her. But she felt safe and insulated from the whole world here. Many a day had now passed after those awful events. No more feelings of being watched and followed. No more jumping at the sight of every strange face. No more fear of the torture or impending death.

  The therapist encouraged her to replay her 'ordeal' in calm moments such as this. She said, "It's a healing exercise.

Recall it slowly and it will help you to discard it mentally." Well, it was not so easy to do. It was even hard to remember what she was doing when the first phone call came that day which started these complicated events in motion.

Dorsey County Courthouse, Mississippi
March, 1998

"Leigh? An ADA wanted in the courtroom!" That voice was the Circuit Court bailiff. Almost at the same time another voice from the second floor was calling, "Leigh! Telephone and they say it's urgent!" That was the District Attorney's Office manager/secretary/mother-hen, Cheryl.

Leigh Ann Reid, the only Assistant District Attorney in the courthouse, just exited the courtroom hoping for a five-minute break since there hadn't been one in three long and monotonous hours of a criminal plea day. She was trying to head to her office to check her mail and calls and maybe even return a few, if only the important ones. She thought for a moment when she heard both the bailiff and her secretary calling out for her. Hmm, which way shall I go? Such a choice! Back to the courtroom where the Judge would be sitting with little patience, as usual, since he wanted her instantly when he called for her. Or, should she go up to the sanctuary of her office for the supposed urgent call and possibly a chance to at least relieve herself of the morning coffee? Well, if she went back in the courtroom, she would probably be there for three more hours without a break. After all, it was Friday, and the Judge did not take a lunch break on Fridays since it was also his Royal Highness' All-Stop Golf Day. She decided to keep walking toward her office when the Judge's administrator, Alene, grabbed her by the arm and said, "Leigh. The Judge is calling for you again!"

"I know. He always is every time I lose sight of the courtroom! Could you tell him that I have an emergency call and need about five minutes?" she asked pleadingly.

"Sure. He can wait, it's not like there are several other ADA's after all, right? Besides, I haven't told him yet that two of his golfing buddies cancelled out for this afternoon's activities. When he hears that, he might actually take a real lunch break."

Good girl, Alene. She understood the demands of Leigh's job. "Thanks. I owe you," Leigh said, and then she ran quickly up the stairs to her office with the sound of her heels clicking on the marbled stairway. On her way into her office, Cheryl yelled into the hallway, "It's that good-looking ADA from the 34th District."

Well, that would be a nice break, she thought. She got to her desk and picked up the phone. "Hello, Kevin. How are things?'

"Leigh. I hope I didn't interrupt too much in court. But this can't wait," he said in a very serious tone. Especially for Kevin Johnson, whom she had known for six years. He usually had a happy-go-lucky voice no matter what.

"Well, I am up to my ears in pleas and sentences today, Kev. The Judge is trying to get out early for golf and I am the only one here, as usual. Other than that, I only have one murder trial to get ready for over the weekend. Of course, he may plead on Monday. You know how it goes, don't you?

"I'm going to be in Hattiesburg tonight at the Blue Parrot. Can you meet me at eight o'clock?' Kevin asked almost in a whisper.

Hesitating at the brash request out of the blue, she said, "I really don't know. Like I said, I'm going to be--"

Before she could finish, she heard, "Please, Leigh. Make the time. I need your advice on a delicate matter." Kevin was desperate sounding.

Okay, Kev. Can you give me an idea of what kind of a delicate matter? Personal or business?" Kevin had been in more than one "delicate" personal matters in his not-so-recent past and Leigh did not want to spend Friday night driving two hours to hear about some fling with a married woman that was going sour. She was a friend. But she advised him before on that score before, and she hoped it was the kind of advice Kevin followed.

"Business, Leigh. But that's all I can say. I am at my desk with lots of peering glances right now. See you tonight." With that he was off the line.

Leigh sat and looked at the phone. Business? Interesting. He always thought himself much more the skillful lawyer than she. What could he want? Maybe he wants to run for Judge again in his district. She had been there for him before when he wanted to take a shot at it. She lined up some campaign donors and helped plan a kick-off rally. Unfortunately, he backed out at the last minute. He didn't tell her the reason. Apparently, he was too embarrassed. She found out through a mutual friend later. It was the married woman thing! Oh! Well, like it wasn't a surprise, but maybe he learned his lesson. So had she. No way would she get involved in another political race for Kevin again. Or with him on a personal basis, for that matter.

The phone rang again. Cheryl's voice said over the intercom, "A lawyer from Jackson. I think he said Levon Smith. Know him?"

"No, but I'll take it. Maybe he has another one that wants to enter a guilty plea. Let Alene know I'm trying to hurry, okay?"

The criminal court term had been so overloaded this time that anyone with a reasonable defense was getting a good offer from her. She couldn't try all of the cases on her plate, and the Judge wanted all of them disposed of by the end of the term, which was next Friday.

"Hello. This is Leigh Reid. Can I help you?" she asked in her crisp and professional tone.

"Levon Smith, Ms. Reid. I represent Carl Knight charged with—"

"Conspiracy to Sell Cocaine," she interrupted and finished his sentence for him. "I know him. You should have gotten your plea offer since they have been faxed or mailed to all defense attorneys. The Judge wants all pleas entered by Monday. I offered the best deal possible considering the evidence." After her usual spill, she waited for a response.

"I am aware of the offer and it is reasonable. We plan on pleading on Monday. However, I am not calling directly about Carl. It is about a friend of his that has some information on a case or two in your district. I have not been retained by this friend, but Carl insists that you, and only you, need to talk to him. Shall I give you his pager number?"

"Let me get this straight. You don't want to haggle over Carl's offer? I'm shocked! But, then again, this is Judge Beasley's court and you know how he sentences if one goes to trial and is convicted on a drug charge. Let the Court Administrator, Alene, know you want to plead, and she will set up a time on Monday. As far as talking to this friend of Carl's, what is his name and what information does he have?"

"I don't know his name. Carl says you will know him and that it's better that I don't know the name or the information. In fact, Carl says that he wants to invoke the attorney-client privilege on me even giving you the phone number and he doesn't know the information that this person needs to talk to you. It must be something sensitive. Maybe an unsolved murder lead, huh?" Mr. Smith must not have any clue, thought Leigh. She would have given his client a little better deal. Every defense lawyer worth his salt would try to negotiate with a prosecutor for a better deal! The fact that Carl wanted nothing else other than for her to contact an anonymous friend regarding possible criminal activities perked up her interest, too,

"Well, okay. Give me the number, and I'll call him next week after my murder trial."

"Carl is here with me while we are on speakerphone and he is shaking his head. He says you need to call right now, Ms. Reid. I don't know why, but Carl's very anxious about this."

"Yeah, must be a matter of life and death," she said sarcastically. "Okay. Tell him I'll try the number now. See you Monday at the plea hearing." She hung up and immediately dialed the number. A serious of beeps sounded and then the prerecorded female voice said, "This is a digital pager. Please enter your number now." Leigh did so and hung up again. There, Carl, I tried the number, she said to herself. Probably another dope-dealer since one of their notorious tools of the trade was digital pagers. Well, maybe some useful bit of information may be gained if he calls.

She looked at the other unreturned message slips on her desk. Below them were several letters and correspondence to be dealt with. Damn, she thought. I'll never catch up!

"When's the new ADA coming?" she asked herself aloud as she tried to shuffle a few of the papers almost gathering dust.

"I'm still trying to get the boss to answer that question, too." Cheryl said as she walked in with some pleadings for Leigh's signature. "You know, I get the same response each time I ask him. 'I'll let you know when I know' he says. So, what's up with your ADA friend, Kevin?"

"I don't know. I'm going to meet him tonight in Hattiesburg. We'll see." She signed the pleadings and was just handing them back to Cheryl when Alene came in saying, "Leigh! I thought you were in the motion hearing in chambers!"

"What motion hearing? There was not one scheduled, was there?" Leigh started to look for her court schedule for the day in the pile of papers on her desk.

"No, there was not one scheduled, but it is going on. The DA is in there. It's on the murder case set for Monday. I'm sorry. I thought you were in there." Alene looked distressed. She was obviously upset at the spontaneous hearing going on that she was not privy to. "I think it's a Motion to Dismiss," she added.

"What?" Leigh almost screamed. "You are kidding me! The Judge never lets the defense pull that one at the last minute! I better go down. Funny, you say the DA is in there? I didn't even know he was here. Oh, well, I am always the last to know anything around here."

"No, that is actually me. Well, after you." Cheryl mumbled as she took the signed pleadings out the door.

Leigh was getting more than a little upset. The murder case set for Monday was hers to try. The DA made it plain he did not want to be lead on it; although he told her he would assist. No doubt it was because this was a high profile case.

But, why was he down in chambers with a dispositive motion on the case without telling me, she wondered. She almost stomped out of her office toward the Judge's chambers. She glanced in at Cheryl who was back at her desk. Cheryl shrugged her shoulders and said "Hey, don't look at me! I didn't know he was here either and that is the first I've heard of any Motion to Dismiss."

Leigh tossed her messages to Cheryl's desk and she headed to the stairs. "Call these people back and tell them it'll be late today or Monday before I can talk with them. Also, before you take lunch, I left my number on a pager. If it's returned, it's a friend of that attorney, Mr. Smith, and I need to take it; so, I'll request a quick break." Leigh and Alene walked down together.

Alene whispered to Leigh, "You know, it is none of my business, but I can't believe you didn't know this was going on. The DA should have waited for you on this motion. Something's really up. I don't trust that defense attorney, James Fields. He's a real piece of work. Let me know what happens, okay? This trial has a lot of community people upset and the Judge can't afford any bad publicity over it."

"Neither can the DA. Yeah, I'll let you know what happens."

Leigh did not bother knocking on the Judge's door before opening it and waltzing into the room as if she had every right to be there.

The Judge was talking and stopped with Leigh's entrance into the room. The DA, Mike Ross, a normally cool respectable-looking prosecutor was visibly upset in casual clothes like he was summoned here at the last second. He was red in the face and had clinched fists. Leigh walked over to him, leaned down and whispered, "What's going on here?"

"It is a Motion to Dismiss." He answered back at her slowly and quietly without turning to look at her.

"That's crap! Fields hasn't served this office without any such motion and there's no reason to hear it without notice. Surely the Judge isn't going forward on it! Not at this late date!"

"Yes, he is." Mike still did not look at Leigh but added quietly, "Sit down."

"Is everyone ready to proceed?" Judge Beasley looked at her first and then at the DA.

"Your Honor," Leigh began by standing up.

Mike grabbed her arm and said, "I'll handle this."

Leigh sat down again. She couldn't believe he had said that! He had never interceded on her cases. What was going on here? She tightened her lips and folded her arms on the conference table and stared at the defense attorney.

"Mr. Fields, I believe you have a Motion?" The Judge looked at the defense attorney. Leigh leaned over and said to Mike, "You notice there is no court reporter? Move for the court reporter to come in, Mike. This needs to be put on record!"

"I said I'll handle this, Leigh," Mike said again and then promptly sat back again without making the motion.

Leigh was astounded! She sat and listened to the Motion to Dismiss and made herself be quiet. Boy, this better be good, she thought.

"Your Honor, Sir," Fields began clearing his throat and looking too important. He was a defense attorney with a lot of flair, Leigh had to admit. He dressed in expensive Italian suits, usually brought a team of associates and books into the courtroom and made large fees for representing the higher profile defendants in Dorsey County. He was knowledgeable of the law, but he also took advantage of situations and bullied his way in trials. Where most Judges wouldn't allow it, Judge Beasley, a long-time friend and associate of Fields, would give Fields slack every time. Whenever Fields was in front of him, there was usually something like this going on. A last-minute Motion, a behind-the-door conference without the prosecutors, or sometimes even a little 'ear-wigging', or talking to the Judge about the case, in the open courtroom but at the bench 'off the record'.

"I have to apologize to the Court for this late-hour Motion. I have just, however, been advised by my associate that there exists an audio tape of one of the prosecution's witnesses that we have not been privileged to hear. It seems that since we have not provided it, and we believe it is exculpatory in nature, we have to move to dismiss this case. It is an egregious discovery violation that the District Attorney has committed since the information was vital to the defense's posturing and preparation for this trial. We, therefore, ask on the behalf on our client, Roger Halford, for the dismissal of the indictment against him with prejudice."

Leigh was furious at this meager excuse for a Motion to Dismiss. It was a lie that the defense attorney had not been notified of any such tape. Fields had been given a notice by letter of the existence of all taped statements, a transcript of the tapes, and permission to listen to any of them at the Sheriff's office at any time. Leigh's copy of the letter that was sent to Fields was in her file upstairs. Plus, a faxed copy. And he is trying to base a Dismissal with Prejudice on this lie? That was preposterous. If anything, it should have been 'without prejudice' since that would allow the state to recharge Fields' client and proceed again.

"What says the Prosecution?" The Judge looked at Mike.

"I have informed the Defense of the existence of the tapes, Your Honor. I also have given them the transcript of the tape. The fact that Mr. Fields chose not to retrieve the original and review this particular one is not my fault. The case should not be dismissed on these grounds."

"Do you have a copy of the letter?" The Judge asked.

"Yes, sir. I believe I have it upstairs."

"Well, your Honor, I never received such a letter," said Fields.

Leigh leaned over and whispered to Mike, "I have the fax confirmation where we faxed it to him also."

Mike leaned up and said, "We sent it to Mr. Fields, your Honor."

Tell him we have the fax confirmation, Leigh said to herself and waited for Mike to do just that, but nothing else came out of his mouth,

He sat stone-faced.

After a second of what looked like feigned concern, the Judge said, "Well, I will look at some cases, but I think unless the District Attorney can provide me with further documentation that the Defense was provided this information, I'm inclined to grant the motion. Let's recess for five minutes."

With that, everyone got up. Mike and Leigh left, but Fields was still in the room with the Judge. Leigh stood at the doorway waiting to let Fields exit, too. She raised her eyebrows as if to question why he was not coming. Finally, he looked at the Judge and excused himself leaving the room with Leigh with a grand gesture of offering his arm so she would leave at the same time. She jerked away and exited in front of him into the hallway.

Outside away from the group, Leigh grabbed Mike and said, "Why didn't you tell him we have the confirmation of the fax, Mike? Why didn't you move for this to be put on record? If he dismisses this case, the public will be up at arms! What I'm saying is not even an understatement! You know this vic was well-liked by the community. You can't let this happen, Mike. I don't care what prior relation the Judge had with Fields before he got on the bench, friendship should not rule the law!"

Mike looked at her and said nothing. He just paced back and forth,

Leigh was beside herself. The snarling glare she gave Fields was enough to cut him into two. The very audacity to try something so underhanded and at the last minute. He sneaked away from where she was standing and huddled in a corner with his entourage.

She went back to Mike and tried again to talk to him, "Mike, what gives here? You know a discovery violation like this doesn't warrant dismissal! Let me get you the cases that say even a violation such as this only warrant a continuance of the case, not a dismissal. I can get the faxed transmission copy and present it when we go back in."

"I know the law, Leigh. We can't win this one." He looked helpless then.

"We can, Mike! Let me go back in and put everything on the record. There won't be a chance of resurrecting this case if it's not preserved right now! You know that, Mike."

Mike Ross turned looking directly eye to eye with Leigh and said very slowly and deliberately, "You don't understand. We cannot and will not win this motion."

That is when it hit Leigh. The realization hit hard, too. This was something that was not supposed to be won by Fields! She realized this with eye-opening clarity. She looked hard at Mike and then asked cautiously and quietly, "As in 'preordained', Mike? You agreed to this? You are going to let this just happen and not do something about it? How can you?' She was calm on the outside, but near boiling mad inside.

"One day, Leigh, we will want the Judge to do something for us in return. Let it go. I am going to take care of it."

Damn straight you are, Leigh almost said aloud. She threw up her hands and went out of the hallway to the stairs back to her office. Her heels clamored so loudly that each click sounded like a pistol being fired. She slammed the office door behind her.

Pacing back and forth with a slow-building fury, a sickening nausea began in the pit of her stomach with the realization of what was happening. As she tried to calm down a knock came at her door.

"Come in," she screamed loudly to the door.

In walked the old-man Bailiff who was a virtual fixture at the courthouse since he'd been there for years. He apparently was in the hallway and heard the earlier exchanges and he looked like he had something serious to say since he closed the door behind him. She had never seen him come to her office before, much less need to close the door.

He walked over to Leigh and said, "Miss Leigh, I have been working in this courthouse for fifteen years, but you have only been her a year. It is not my place to say this, but I have seen a lot of things go on here that many people would call, well, not right, underhanded or corrupt. But what I just think I saw downstairs was worse than anything I've ever seen. Pretty bold, I'll say. You're upset, but there is not a thing you can do about it. The Judge and Mr. Fields go back a long way, you know. They practiced together on many cases. You probably don't know how much that very large contribution was from Mr. Fields to Judge Beasley's campaign. It is not common knowledge. I thought you would want to know that. It might help you understand if the DA is going to let the case go. It is the sad reality here you know, tit for tat." He looked sympathetically at Leigh and smiled, patted her on the shoulder and then turned around and walked out closing the door quietly behind him,

Leigh stared at the door as it closed. She had just witnessed her first taste of true 'good old boy' politics at its worst and the corruption that is intrinsic with it. She was experiencing a system shock and she didn't think she could go back out and face the culprits she was used to working with again.

Before she could do anything about her dilemma, Alene called through the door and said, "Leigh, the Judge is ready for sentencing hearings."

"The DA is down there, isn't he?" Leigh sarcastically sneered through the door,

"No. He's gone, Leigh." Alene sounded sympathetic, too. Did everyone but Leigh know this was going to happen? Throwing a murder trial for a political payback?

Leigh sighed resolutely and gave in. "Okay, I'm coming." Leigh decided she would finish her job at least for the day. There were a lot of sentencing hearings scheduled for the afternoon and she, apparently, was the only one to do it.

Back in the courtroom, a flurry of noises accompanied a series of prisoners dressed in inmate stripes, handcuffs and leg irons being brought in. They were awaiting sentencing by the Judge. Some looked at her with distaste and others were smiling broadly, one without teeth and another with all gold teeth in the front. Leigh looked at the sentencing docket at her counsel table and sorted through some files to make sure she had them all. The Judge began his calling of the docket. "Cause No 5532--State v. Chambers. Leroy Chambers, you have previously entered a plea of guilty to the crime of Burglary of a Residence. Is that true?" the Judge asked the inmate coming to stand in front of the Judge's bench. Judge Beasley was a relatively young Judge with normally a real laid back attitude. Leigh's normally good working relationship with him up until today, made the routine days go by quicker. And, until today, she never saw any actions on his part that would be necessarily termed underhanded or unfair. After what happened today, though, she would never trust him again. His political paybacks certainly changed her respect for him unconditionally.

Leigh's inner sixth sense seemed to warn her about people and situations. It always proved to be true to her, too. Right now, it was going off the meter, and she knew it would be best to be on the alert when dealing with someone as powerful as a Circuit Judge with voters and backers who want something in return for their contributions and support. Too bad she had to learn this the hard way today.

Judge Beasley continued, "I have carefully reviewed your Pre-Sentence Investigation Report, and I see that there are no serious prior offences. However, I want you to know that I cannot stand for burglaries since my own home was broken into within the last month. What is the District Attorney's recommendation?" the Judge asked looking at Leigh.

My turn, she thought. Like he did not know what the

recommendation was. Like the Defendant and the Defense Attorney did not know what the recommendation was from her. It was for the record mainly, she knew, but it sounded so silly to her sometimes to have to repeat what everybody that needed to know already knew. She stood and faced the Defendant and then looked at the Judge. Trying to swallow her disdain at this point for him, and quite deliberately, she looked a moment before announcing her recommendation. "The State of Mississippi recommends a three-year sentence with the Mississippi Department of Corrections, plus restitution to the victim in this cause." There, the big secret was out, she thought wryly. The other inmates with sentences coming up took the words in slowly and began to compare in their minds their own charges and recommendations. The Judge looked at the Defendant and took his deliberate moment before saying, "I'll accept the State's recommendation. They have good attorneys that know their cases. You sure have been offered a good deal, though. Don't take it lightly. You would be serving the maximum sentence if it was up to me and had you been convicted by a jury in this case. Do you understand?"

The defendant, a black man with the toothless smile said "Yessuh, Judge."

"Anything else by the State'?" he asked Leigh.

"Nothing by the State," she answered robotically"

"Anything else by the Defendant?" he asked.

"Nothing by the Defendant," said the Defense Attorney.

"That will be the sentence of the court," said the Judge. "Next case."

The Defense Attorney, a public defender, and the Defendant both gave audible sighs of relief. One never knew what the Judge will do in sentencing. Most of the times he took the State's recommendations, but to keep the suspense up, he would sometimes buck the plea-bargaining powers of the prosecutors and make his own sentence. That was, of course, unless he just dismissed the case because he owed the defense attorney a payback, Leigh reminded herself.

The next Defendant came up and the same procedure was followed. Then the next one, and the next one, and so on, until 3:00 pm. They sentenced twenty poor souls in one day. It was the wrapping up of a long week of plea negotiations and plea hearings. Not to mention three trials. A murder, another on a drug charge, and a third on a child abuse charge. Leigh, completely exhausted from the week and the day of monotonous ritualistic procedures, was glad to see the Judge showing signs of anxiousness to get the courtroom cleared. No doubt so he could vamoose it to the Great Golf Green. After engineering the throwing of a murder case, she wondered how good his game would be today

Finally, the last Defendant was sentenced, and the Judge asked to an almost empty courtroom, "Anything else for the Court?"

Leigh stood and gathered her books and her files and said without looking at the Judge, "A long weekend."

Judge Beasley was smiling and said, "Yes, I think we all could use it. Good job this week, Leigh. Looks like the docket is almost clear. Let's get out of here before something else comes up"

With that, the remaining courtroom staff, including the court reporter, the circuit clerk, the probation officer, and the bailiffs all beat feet it to their respective offices. The Judge walked beside Leigh through the back-escape door leading into a hall where the Judges' chambers were. Beyond this area, Leigh was about to take the stairway to the second floor and to her office when Judge Beasley stopped and touched Leigh's arm and said, "I hope Mike knows what a good job you are doing here. He missed your three convictions this week. Have a good weekend, Leigh."

"Happy golfing." was all she could muster to say to him through her teeth. Her stomach was tied up in knots from her witnessing the earlier hearing. His attempt at thanking her for not causing a stir by praising her did not go unchecked. He probably hoped that even if she didn't understand, maybe she wasn't too mad. She left him and wondered how he and the DA would be able to sleep that night.

Up until now, Leigh handled most of the felony crimes of Dorsey County, and she was only expected to go to the other two counties in their court district on trial days to assist the DA. She was happy doing just that. Besides, the DA always let her make the discretionary decisions he would have normally make, unless it was a truly high profile case. One that attracted reporters. She felt at her best when he showed the confidence in her that he obviously had by letting his biggest populated county be hers. Her only want had been a new assistant to help with the paperwork and pre-trial motions. She had previously procured a grant for the salary of a new assistant and she had advertised for the position. However, the DA kept the applications that made it in before the deadline. He was supposed to be 'reviewing' them for a month now. She couldn't understand why he hadn't narrowed the applicants down and asked her opinion on them.

Cheryl greeted her at her office door and said, "Is that it for the week?"

"Yes, thank God! By the way, the murder for Monday is off the docket in case you haven't heard."

Cheryl looked at her in shock and almost shouted. "What? I was just typing jury instructions for it. What happened? Is it continued?"

"Guess again. It got dismissed." Leigh went to her desk and before Cheryl could close her mouth to respond, Leigh asked, "Did I get that return call from the pager earlier?"

"No, but there is a message for you to page Levon Smith's friend after 6:00 pm. Gutsy for him to ask that, huh? I told them I didn't think you would be able to call after working hours, and the guy said just tell her it is regarding the 'Carl Knight' matter. Now, what's going on with the dismissal? Why was the DA here for that hearing earlier?"

"I'll tell you about it later." Leigh took the phone slip with the pager number Levon Smith had given her and without looking at it, put it in her purse.

"So, no murder trial Monday? Well, I guess you can now focus on like what you are going to wear tonight to meet Kevin?" Cheryl was smiling with a sly look in her eyes.

"Oh, I almost forgot!" Leigh had forgotten and was really too tired to think about it now. Looking at her watch, she said, "I have time to go look through the correspondence on my desk, get home and search my closet and take a nice warm bath. You can go early, too."

She looked at Cheryl. "I see that smile! I wouldn't get my hopes up if you think you're going to see me matched up with Kevin. You know we're"

"Just friends. I know. Like, sure!" Cheryl was chuckling to herself as she went back to her desk. Leigh heard her also mumbling to herself, "Damned DA! He thinks he's too good to do anything but come in and get a high-profile case dismissed. No, couldn't help us out here with our docket. But could just waltz in and create chaos for us."

Leigh smiled almost for the first time that day listening to Cheryl's mumblings and she went to her desk to shuffle through some papers, dictating some replies for about thirty minutes. The phone rang several times, but Cheryl was insisting to everyone that Leigh was still in the courtroom.

On her way out the door, Leigh popped into Cheryl's office and asked if anything else needed tending to.

Cheryl's face was still showing her ire at the DA. "Just have a good time and good weekend. I'll leave in a few minutes. By the way, Mister Big-Shot called back and asked if everything was going okay in the courtroom. I told him must be since you hadn't been up here since sentences started."

"He didn't happen to ask for me, did he? Too bad. I could have kept him on the phone a while." Leigh was still smarting from the dismissal and thought if she talked with Mike now, she'd get herself fired. She looked back at Cheryl and said, "I better run. See you Monday."

"Yeah. Have a good one."

Leigh left the courthouse. Taking a deep breath as she got outside the building, she thought to herself, one more week and the close of another busy term. Her three trials resulted in three convictions. At least a few of the criminals were once again held at bay by the system. She was a part of seeing justice served for a few of the many victims of crime in her district. That was the rewarding part. Juries were always so quick in their verdicts when the evidence was there. People were so tired of crime and especially tired of drug-related crimes. The two became almost indistinguishable. Over ninety percent of the property crimes were committed by drug users trying to support their nasty illegal and quite costly habits. Violent crimes were also more times than not committed either by a dealer or an 'under-the-influence' type.

Leigh built a solid reputation among law enforcement officers and agencies for being tough on the violent offenders. They respected her and there was nothing they wouldn't do for her when she called them for assistance. With her undergraduate degree in Criminal Justice, her attachment to law enforcement and prosecution was understandable. While working her way through law school, she worked as a crime analyst. She solved several felony crimes using plain old deductive reasoning and using her people abilities. And studying forensic science with the Office of the London Coroner gave her one up on many criminal investigations undertaken by untrained or understaffed rural law enforcement agencies. She made a stand on helping to get more funding for training officers and agencies and she had been successful in doing just that. So, she felt good about herself and what she accomplished.

But the ironical conclusion to the week had been the dismissal of a murder case, her murder case, for political reasons. Leigh found herself thinking of the victim of the murder as she got in her GMC Jimmy. Mac Reeves was a nineteen-year-old black youth. He just came home from college for a weekend. He was a straight 'A' student with a great future ahead of him. Leigh had seen pictures of him in his local high school graduation clothes. He was apparently a very likeable guy too. Raised in a slum area with a drug addict for a mother and no father, he was one of the many commonly-termed 'welfare babies' from Mississippi rural areas. He and four other siblings were conceived for the sole purpose of increasing monthly welfare payments to the mother, for which many mothers knew the pay scale and increasing weekly benefits by heart. Leigh knew from preparing the case for trial that Mac's mother had government payments that were often turned into cash to support her drug habits, drinking habits, and sexual whims. The children are always the victims in these sad scenarios, Leigh knew. They had no life to call their own, hung out in the streets and eventually turned to crime and drugs themselves so that they could have more of the consumer goods constantly shown to them by the drug dealers. New cars, cell phones, designer clothes, gold jewelry, all within reach with cash from drug users.

Mac was one of the few that used his desire to succeed in life in a positive way and got out of the stench, filth, and sadness associated with the others. He had an actual future and he was a role model for the entire community. That is, until he was shot down with a sawed-off shotgun three months ago. While visiting from college with his high school buddies, he witnessed a major drug exchange at a local bar. They were followed home and in the front yard of Mac's home, he tried to tell them to leave them alone. He was unarmed and had no quarrel with the crazed crack dealer and his stupidly following henchmen. He did not even try to defend himself as they blew his chest right out of his body. The shooter that night was Roger Halford, a sixteen year old black youth with a juvenile record a mile long. He had the money to hire Fields and now he would walk away from this terrible murder of Mac Reeves. Such a miscarriage of the justice! Prior to today, Leigh had a certain amount of pride to be a part of this county. No more. Not now.

Leigh's eyes watered as she found herself driving by the crime scene where Mac was basically slaughtered like an animal. The pre-autopsy photos ran through her mind. Such a nice kid with no chest, just a whole where it had been. She pulled up and stopped. Leigh sighed and whispered out loud. "Mac, you were a good kid. I am sorry that your death will not be avenged by our so-called justice system. I can't understand why it happened, but I want you to know that I believe that Halford will meet his fate sooner or later. I have to believe that. I know you won't rest in peace. I hope that all the idiots who let Halford go free will not rest in peace. Ever."

She felt better somehow as she drove away. Maybe it was because she just wanted Mac to know that she was not guilty by association with the DA and Judge and by being there, he might have heard. Crazy me, she thought.

Her mobile phone rang. She was not in the mood to conduct anymore business. Ready to snap at whoever was on the line, she picked up to hear her son's voice on the line. "Mom?" It was the best thing she heard all day!

"Hi, son. What's a good-looking kid like you calling your old mom for on a Friday evening?"

"Just checking in to see how you are and to let you know I'll be coming home this week for spring break. I'm bringing a friend from Australia who is really homesick. Can you help cheer him up with a little home cooking and clean country living?"

"Sure. I can't wait. I'll get Della to make up the guest room. Oh, yeah, Joe will be spending a few days with us, too. Maybe we can all go to New Orleans for a day of two."

"Great. Sounds like a plan. I'll see you Tuesday evening. I love you, mom." With that, the line clicked off.

Leigh's spirits lifted even more at the thought of having her one and only child home for a week. She had been missing him so lately. He started his second year at Harvard with plans to take after mom and become a lawyer. She could see herself fifteen years before with the 'great unknown' luring in front of her! She wanted then to excel at being a lady lawyer. Remembering that feeling, she couldn't fault him for his choice of career paths. If he wanted to be rich, she had told him to enroll in pre-med. Jarrod was now nineteen. Hard to believe that she could still remember the feeling of joy in knowing she was pregnant.

She had been married then to the 'cute and nice' husband from her local rural high school. The perfect words that described him in the high school annual! But, he developed a not-so-nice personality when he drank. She found out that the hard way. She let him hit her only that once. And she was pregnant then. That was also the last time she saw him. She immediately moved into a safe haven shelter, filed for divorce alleging cruel and inhuman treatment, proved her case by her doctor's report, and the Judge granted the divorce with full custody given to her of the child along with a termination of parental rights. Sonny, her cute, but not-so-nice husband, she had never seen again. She heard that he was still busy drinking and being a typical 'good old boy'. The marriage lasted a grand total of thirteen months. Unlucky number. Unlucky marriage. But she never looked back. She redirected her life at that point. Jarrod knew about his father since he was small and yet he never expressed any interest in knowing anymore after hearing that he had been cruel to his mother.

When Leigh found herself a single mom, she vowed to make something of the rest of her life and have financial security for her and Jarrod. She received her undergraduate degree with honors from the University of Southern Mississippi, majoring in criminal justice. Small wonder that her interest lay there, since she was already familiar with criminal assault, in a very personal way. But she always wanted to try to get into law school and fight for the underdogs. There wasn't much support from her small lower-middle class family. So, borrowing money to do so, she took the law school entrance exam and passed. With great will, a lot of determination and the advantage of a night law school so she could work in the day to keep food and clothes for both she and Jarrod, Leigh plowed her way through law school and passed the bar entrance exam on the first try.

Jarrod grew up a loving and considerate young man. Leigh's older brother, Joe, had been there for Jarrod as he was growing up, providing the necessary 'guy' kind of things like fishing, hunting, boating, and shooting guns. They were very close.

Joe was a bachelor. He was in law enforcement, too. As a special agent with the US Department of Customs, he said he witnessed too many divorces among law enforcement officers, so he would not ever marry. At least, Leigh always told him, not until he found the right one! Well, judging from her experience in failed relationships, she was not the one to argue with him on that subject.

It was 5:00 pm when she pulled into her driveway. Ah, Marlowe! Her home was her greatest accomplishment outside of raising Jarrod and her building her career. She rescued and renovated the historic home when it was truly about to tumble down. It was once a grand Greek Revival house built just before the Civil War, and only survived Sherman's burning rampage because it had been owned by a 'Yankee' family from Chicago. The family that purchased it after the war saw hard times during the depression and the house had never really had an opportunity to see its own potential until Leigh bought it. With a few surrounding acres, she took the plunge about six years before and spent all the money she made from a large personal injury settlement on the redo. After getting the home almost perfect, she then purchased the Arabian horses that grazed peacefully on either side of the home now. She just now felt an instant peeling off sensation of the week's stress when she saw her home and horses.

"Miss Leigh!" a voice called from the long white front veranda. It was Della out sweeping and straightening up. "I didn't know you were coming home early. I haven't finished cleaning!"

"Della, don't you worry about that right now. Come on in with me and let's make us a cappuccino and sit for a spell, ok?"

Della put her broom and dustpan down. She looked at Leigh quizzically and said, "Miss Leigh, just what are you up to?"

"Just come with me. We have to make some plans. Joe and Jarrod are coming home to stay for the weekend. Jarrod's bringing a friend from school with him."

"Well, lands sakes! It has been way too long since both Mr. Joe and Jarrod were here at the same time. I'll just have a ball getting the meals together. And, that means Mr. Joe and Mr. Jarrod's favorites." She smiled with such delight that it warmed Leigh's heart.

"1 was just going to suggest that we plan a few meals. Let's make those cappuccinos first." With that, they headed into the long hallway that spanned the depth of the home. The home was gleaming in the late evening sunlight. The polished hard wood floors were reflecting the light and a glow was Leigh felt she could sit and rest a bit while visiting with Della and the day's bad events would melt into her memory banks.

Della came into the breakfast/conservatory room with a tray of coffee and cookies. The view out on the back pastures and horse barn was therapeutic and Leigh felt a little resurgence of energy in her system. They planned for the weekend for a few minutes, discussing changing linens, planning menus and making grocery store list. The fresh flowers now blooming in the spring plantings around the house were sufficient to brighten up the rooms with arrangements.

Della's husband, Charlie, was the farm groundskeeper, plus he helped with the daily barn chores. He was also getting skilled in the grooming and exercising of the horses. Della took care of the house and meals. They were quite a team. Leigh found them just as they were retiring from the federal government in Washington D.C. five years earlier. They wanted to retire and return to their home state but were not ready to stop working. She felt about them like she would any family member. They endured the extensive renovations with her, helped with the initial breeding and foaling of the horses, and were always happy to do anything that would make the place run smoother or look better. They were never demanding. In fact, she paid them a pittance of a salary for the number of hours they both put in. They were a very happy, bright, and contented couple with no children of their own. They made Marlow, the house and farm, a home. Leigh smiled at the satisfying feeling she had every day living here. She had no doubts about her happiness at home and with her horse business. Her only problem at the moment was the unsettling feeling that was easing into her stomach at the thought of the corrupt practices with her boss and the Judge. Just how far would they go for political paybacks?

CHAPTER TWO

It was after 6:00 pm when Della left Marlowe. Leigh and Charlie made sure the horses were back in their stables for the night, fed and watered. Back in the house, she started her bath water. The bubbles were growing in size, and she was already imagining the relaxation from a long hot soak. As she was just about to step in the bath though, she thought about the call she was supposed to make to Levon Smith's office.

She put her robe on, cursing under her breath and reluctantly went to dial the pager number. She wasn't really expecting anyone to return the page at 6:15 on a Friday night, but the phone rang almost as soon as Leigh hung up, startling her. Leigh heard a male voice say, "Ms. Reid?"

She responded, "Yes, this is Leigh Reid. To whom am I speaking?"

"This is Garrison Roberts, Ms. Reid. Perhaps you know the name?" Perhaps! She definitely heard of him. Most everyone in central and southern Mississippi had heard of him. He was one of the wealthiest men in the state. He also was reputedly one step ahead of every law enforcement agency's investigation into his financial holdings. He was truly rumored to be a Dixie Mafia crime boss. Just great! Not exactly the type of informant she was expecting to talk to nor wanting to talk to.

"I have indeed, Mr. Roberts. Your name is frequently heard in my circle of acquaintances. However, I don't think it would be appropriate to discuss any, shall we say,' activities' of yours, without one of your lawyers being present."

"The purpose for my calling is not for my benefit, Ms. Reid. It's for yours. I've made arrangements for us to meet and discuss a highly sensitive matter. Your office wouldn't have been suitable under the circumstances, and I've used the pager number to make sure you won't be traced back to being in contact with me or any of my enterprises. If you have a few minutes, I am only five minutes away from the closed cotton mill on Old Station Road. I believe it would be an appropriately quiet place for us to meet. Before you say no, I have to say it is very important that you are aware of something involving your office. Can you meet me at the mill as soon as possible?"

Leigh thought very quickly. She certainly couldn't afford to be seen with this man and she knew he ordinarily was accompanied by a team of associates, AKA 'bodyguards'. The place he wanted to meet was very close to her house, though. "Are you alone?" she asked already surmising this unexpected call may be the result of something else underhanded going on at her office, especially in light of the day's prior events.

"Yes, I'll be in an '84 white Ford pickup. There is no one else with me and I've made sure we can have a private chat."

"Mr. Roberts, from what you have prefaced our 'chat' with you make it difficult for me to decline your offer. So, yes. I'll see you there in a few minutes." Leigh sighed a long deep sigh as she hung up. Goodbye, hot bubbly bath! She got redressed, let the water out of her tub, and grabbed a small makeup bag. There would be no time to dress for her meeting with Kevin in Hattiesburg. She had to be on the road no later than 7:00 pm in order to meet him at 8:00.

She was on Old Station Road in a jiffy, but she looked cautiously at the old mill building before turning in. She wanted to make sure she was not followed. It was almost dark. She didn't see a white pickup, but she drove in anyway and parked on the back side of the abandoned overgrown mill.

She got out and quietly closed the door, waiting. The sound of the night insects started melodiously in the dark of the woods surrounding the old mill. The smell of freshly sown earth was almost fragrant. Leigh liked this time of day the best. When the dark creeps up on the sun and the earth cools down there was almost a magic to the time, she thought. Even under the unusual circumstances, Leigh enjoyed just breathing in the country air. The honeysuckle vines growing over the doorway of the mill caused a whiff of their sweet perfume to permeate the air and Leigh took deep breaths enjoying the scent.

The pickup pulled in quietly within a few moments of her arriving. She felt a tight grip in her stomach and her breathing quickened. She hadn't even heard it coming. She would not have normally agreed to such a meeting with any criminal suspect. Especially one with such a wide-range criminal reputation. The thought crossed her mind that it might be some sort of set-up, but her inner stoic, if not mostly correct, sixth sense told her it would be a safe enough encounter with the infamous Mr. Roberts.

"Ms. Reid. Thank you for coming." The voice came from the driver's side of the truck as the tinted window came down. Yes. It was the real Mr. Roberts. No one else was in the truck, she observed. He got out and offered her his hand. She did not take it, but said, "You're welcome, I think. Let's get to the point. What is all this about?"

He leaned up against his truck, crossed his hands and smiled. "Well, I sure will, Ms. Reid. No small talk with you, I see!" He smiled and she relaxed a bit. "Let me say I know you are in a position to have some knowledge about my enterprises. I won't pretend that I haven't been in some, shall I say 'not-so-above-board' deals, but I am here to let you know first-hand about what's about to go down at your office. You probably won't believe this, but you can trust me. I believe I can trust you, too." Leigh just looked at him. He seemed to be acting honestly enough. Years of examining witnesses and jurors had made her a good judge of non-verbal communications and their effect on a person's veracity. But this is an infamous crime lord, she reminded herself. Trust was something she did not just give anyone in her business or in his, to be sure. Especially after the shocking incident she experienced earlier. But he surely didn't appear to be a gangster. Not that she knew what one should look like. He looked approximately sixty years old, was dressed like a typical Mississippi farmer in a plaid flannel shirt with overalls, and even had a Mississippi Cattleman's Association baseball cap on.

"Go on," she prompted him with a skeptical eye and ear.

"You've handled the prosecutions of some of my, well, 'associates' in the past. I've always found you to be fair-minded in your dealings with them. You don't pull any punches, and, as we all say in our line of work, jail is always a likely 'risk'. I have seen many DA's with chips on their shoulders. Some who try drug cases just to set an example and show voters they can win. Others don't even offer pleas. You, on the other hand, try only those that refuse to take your reasonable plea offers. I have seen that you actually try to make certain the addicts get treatment while serving time. I admire and appreciate you for the job you do, even though we are on two different sides of the fence." He smiled at her. Well, go figure! She felt he was genuinely praising her accomplishments!

He continued, shifting his stance against the truck. "And, I have no doubt that you are not the kind to appreciate corruption in public office. So, well, here goes. The man you work for has just hired a new assistant district attorney to work with you. I doubt you are aware of this yet. It happened this morning. What you also won't know is that the new assistant is a known cocaine addict with ties into the interstate transporting and distribution of drugs, particularly methamphetamine. Normally I wouldn't be too upset with that arrangement, mind you, if the ties were with my organization.

However, he is inextricably tied with a competitor that is moving into this area and several surrounding counties.

"This group does not play fair. They are ruthless and bribe many a political 'patsy'. Unfortunately for you, I know that the DA knows of this new employee's habits and connections. In fact, the DA has offered protection for the new crime organization in return for campaign funds in the next judicial elections."

Leigh shook her head as if to shake off what she just heard.

"You did know that the DA was running for Judge?" He paused to let this sink in. Leigh's feelings were moving from skepticism to downright nauseating. This, too, was unbeknownst news about Mike, but after what she already witnessed today with the murder trial, it was not very surprising he would want to run for Judge. "By the way, the Judge, Beasley, is aware of all this. He has joined in the menage-a-toi of bought officials due to the fact that his next political goal is Congress."

Roberts stopped and looked carefully at Leigh who was trying but hadn't found her voice yet. "As a result of this new hiring, I expect you will experience a new attitude toward you as of Monday. The official plan is to make your job unbearable so that you will seek employment elsewhere. They consider you a threat to them and their plans. They believe you wouldn't go along to get along, if you get the drift. The DA will not fire you. He is too shrewd for that. He knows he will lose popular votes in the district if he fires you."

"How do you know these things?" Leigh asked as she began to feel this whole setting and conversation was becoming a bad dream. Her throat was dry. He obviously had 'inside' knowledge of these facts.

"I have someone high in the chain of command of the new competitor organization." He smiled and shrugged, "It's a business and spying is part of it. Anyway, he works solely for me, and he is in because we needed the layout for the new organization's plans. He found this information out quite by accident last night. He doesn't know I am letting you in on the information. His life is in enough danger as it is. The money involved, plus the vast amount of resources they have—well, he wouldn't be treated kindly if they knew he worked for me."

Leigh was understandably speechless. He waited and when she did not say anything, he continued, "I have in the recent past began several truly legitimate businesses that have no financial or otherwise connection to the illegitimate ones. I have amassed a small fortune. But, I am ready to try to live my life without the constant need for bodyguards and surveillance. I tell you this because I am offering you a job with any of the legitimate businesses I have. You can leave the DA's office before this group has a chance to execute their plan of infiltration which includes getting you out. I know you won't be able to stay there. They will make it intolerable for you. I offer this to you because of my respect for your honesty and fairness. I know, go figure! I also know that giving you a heads up on this will possibly give you an incentive to help me somewhere down the road."

Leigh's mind was whirling through the information she had just heard. She knew what he was saying might possibly be true. She also knew she was in a bit of a shock for the moment. She couldn't say anything. There was another noticeable silence. Finally, she said, 'I appreciate your candidness with me. I appreciate the forewarning. And I do certainly appreciate the confidence you have in me to offer me employment. I have a question though that burns in my guts at this moment. Why for God's sake are you risking your security and career by confessing these things to me of all people? After all, I could go launch my own prosecution of you and your dealings. Why does my welfare truly bother you?"

Garrison Roberts laughed loudly. "Well, missy, that's the easy part to understand! I have more than altruistic motives. I have good reason to believe I'm going to take a fall in the near future. A large fall. That's the reason for the creation of the legitimate businesses. The feds have gotten too close to me this time. However, I'm now in the position to offer them something they may use. In turn, my immunity will be required. It has to do with what I have just told you. I will be a 'snitch' for the feds, quite simply. I'm starting the process as soon as possible. That is another reason why I thought it best to let you know these things tonight. Next week, I will turn myself in to the feds to avoid the hassle of a long drawn out and public arrest. This way, I am going to be one up on them."

Leigh just numbly stared into nothingness. There were no words to sufficiently describe her feelings. Before today, she would have never expected the DA to be involved in the type of corruption that goes with protection payments and the 'throwing' of significant murder cases. Nor would she have thought the Judge would be in the thick of these morally and legally wrong antics. More astounding though, she never would've dreamed that the one to warn her would be an infamous local underworld figure like Garrison Roberts! Her last bit of skepticism was gone. She believed he was being truthful. Whether or not things played out like he expected was anyone's guess, though. She would be very interested in what would happen next week.

"Well, thank you again, Mr. Roberts, for your thinking of me. I shall take your offer to work under consideration; however, with the amount of investigations that may be launched into your finances, I would feel like I would be going into something that would be under extreme scrutiny by the feds, if you know what I mean. And, for the moment, at least, I am still employed as an Assistant District Attorney."

"I understand. However, I do admire your legal skills, and in the future if things get bad for you, well, you will always have the offer." With that, he started to get back in his truck. This time, Leigh offered her hand and he shook it.

"Good luck to you. Mr. Roberts. Being on the good side won't be easy after where you have been. The Feds will probably deal with you. But don't expect to walk away. Some jail time and a hefty fine, even with your revelations. And, once you get out into those legitimate businesses, please let me know. In the meantime, I can vouch for your willingness to cooperate, if need be, but off-the-record."

"Figured some jail time. But, with a little luck, it won't be too bad. Federal prison, I hear, is not so bad if your stay isn't long." He was smiling as if he could knock out a jail term without any effort whatsoever. Probably could.

She was beginning to feel a mutual respect for Mr. Roberts. He had come to her without high-powered lawyers or henchmen and had given her some apparently risky information and helped her by warning her about her boss. He backed his pickup out slowly and eased down the dirt road into the darkness. Nothing but the night insects were heard as Leigh walked back to her Jimmy.

Leigh got back in and just sat and stared ahead. She couldn't absorb everything at once. Looking at her dashboard clock, it was now 6:55. She sighed heavily and started back on the road. She would still make her trip to Hattiesburg, although she felt a heavy weight settling in on her. Kevin had sounded as bad as she felt right now when he had asked her to come to meet him. Oh well, she thought. What other nifty surprises are in store for the remainder of this long Friday?

Leigh entered the Blue Parrot, a typical university town student bar and restaurant a little after 8:00. She hoped she wasn't too late. It was dark and loud music from a live country western band was almost deafening. She couldn't make anyone's face out even though there seemed to be no shortage of shadows there. It wasn't her kind of gig. Never had been. She found a stool at the bar and ordered a gin and tonic. She looked in the mirror behind the bartender to see if she had applied her makeup in the right places in the car as she had pulled into the parking lot.

"Glad you could make it, Leigh." A familiar voice almost whispered in her ear. Kevin. She turned around and he grabbed her by the elbow, kissed her on the cheek, and with his most charming smile, said, "I have a table over here for us. You look absolutely like a ray of sunshine to me! How do you do it with the demands of the jobs we have?"

They sat down in a dark corner booth opposite each other.

"You know I won't fall for all that misguided flattery, don't you?" She couldn't help but appreciate it though after her day so far.

Kevin was every girl's dream of the perfect man. He had a handsome face, with dark, wavy hair, green eyes, and the build of a professional athlete. His face at the moment looked at her very seriously and he said, 'I meant every word of it, kiddo. You know how I've always felt about you. Unfortunately, I have something else in mind for tonight." Kevin looked a little out of sorts to Leigh. He had his usual charm, but something wasn't quite right with his mannerisms.

"Kevin, cut to the chase, will you? You won't believe what an extremely hard day, week, and court term I've had and I'm quite frankly too tired to play games now. I want to know why you needed to see me and why it couldn't wait." Leigh's face gave her away to Kevin, too. She knew there was edginess in her voice and Kevin would want to know what was causing her anxiety. She couldn't afford to say anything to him regarding the latest news about her DA. Not yet, anyway.

"Right, well, I know I have kept this from you far too long, Leigh. I'm very sorry for the delay in getting it back to you. It certainly was a lifesaver to me on a major case." Kevin reached beside his chair and pulled up his briefcase. He opened it up and handed her a group of papers. It was a legal brief she had done and given to him several months ago.

Frowning, Leigh said, "Kevin, I told you before that I didn't need that, I have copies, you know...."

Kevin interrupted her by placing his hand on her arm and said "I know you told me you weren't going to need it then. But I know how important research time is to all of us ADA's and this is some top-of-the-line work on hearsay. I haven't ever found it so concisely put like this. I know the original is valuable to you. So, here, and my thanks for letting me keep it so long."

"But, Kevin, I don't need...." She was going to say she had plenty of originals she could reprint from her laptop. But Kevin knew this too. Something definitely wasn't right with him. She looked closer at him and saw that there were beads of perspiration on his face. He had a beer on the table in front of him. That, too, wasn't Kevin. He never drank anything with alcohol in it. He began looking nervously across the dark room. Okay, she said to herself, I'm in the middle of something here that I obviously don't understand. Calling her here like this just to give her back something she did not need was apparently something Kevin had to do for some unknown reason. She told herself to follow Kevin's lead and get away as soon as possible.

She continued, "Well come to think of it, that brief would have come in handy in a murder trial I tried last week. I couldn't find the cites I needed to effectively argue that Rule 801 (25) exception. Lost that motion, too. So, thanks for getting this back to me. Anything exciting going on in your life, Kev?"

"I have been extremely busy and I'm looking forward to a nice long out-of-term break in April. Other than that, not much. What about you?" Kevin said quite nervously and then he looked again around the room as if expecting to see someone he knew.

"Nah, same old thing. You know how it goes. Trial dockets, motion and plea days, grand jury days. So, you think you will stay in this district a while? I know you had said last year you thought you would like a change of scenery."

"I'm satisfied where I am." Kevin then looked around the room again and jumped up suddenly. "Come here, kiddo and give me a hug. I'm really glad you came down!'

Leigh was just about to ask what in the blazes was wrong with him. But she saw the anxiety in his eyes and did what he asked. He put his arms around her and said in her ear, "I've gotta get going. I will be back in touch soon. Take care." He released her and then walked right out the door without another word.

Well, for heaven's sake! So, this is my day for surprises, Leigh thought. I wonder why I really was asked here. What purpose did it serve him for me to hug him in this place? Whose eyes needed to see that'? Leigh sighed it seemed for the thousandth time that day. Go figure! Has everyone gone absolutely stark-raving mad?

She gathered her purse and the brief he had given her and headed out herself. No reason to hang around this joint. Odds are the problem Kevin was having had to do with some woman. Maybe it was the old 'make her jealous routine'. He knew better than involve her in that game, she was sure. Who knows? I'm going home, she said to herself. What a wasted trip!

She was outside getting her keys out of her jacket pocket when she felt something different inside the fabric. She got inside her car and started the engine before she pulled it out to look at it. It was a white envelope taped close. There was no writing on it. She turned her overhead light on. There appeared to be something small and round inside and she opened it to see. It was a metallic disc that looked similar to a small CD. It was something she obviously had not put in her own pocket. Where did it come from? Being just a little too tired to even venture a guess; she folded it back up and put it in her pocket again. I'll worry about that, like Scarlett says, tomorrow. Putting the Jimmy in the direction of Marlowe, she drove home with nothing but disturbing jumbled thoughts guiding her.

CHAPTER THREE

Saturday morning greeted Leigh with a pleasant breeze and an abundance of sunshine coming through the lace curtains in her bedroom. The smell of coffee brewing and bacon frying made her smile. She got up and lazily meandered through her home with a mug of coffee and the morning newspaper Della had left on the breakfast table. She knew she had to deal with the information that she had gotten from Roberts, her career choices, her strange evening with Kevin, and getting ready for company, but she could not help postponing dealing with problems as she decided to just enjoy being home and relaxing with her morning brew and paper.

Her home had been transformed on the inside to resemble what it might have looked like in 1860. She had added the necessary user-friendly updates of two baths with old fixtures, wall lighting, and gas-starting fires in the four large brick fireplaces. The drapes were her favorite, though. She had researched the period styles, shopped for the perfect fabrics, and found an ingenious seamstress to measure, make and install them. The large dining room had a banquet size table with Jacobean chairs. The fabrics on the windows matched the chair seat covers. All the colors, from the walls to the oriental carpets were historically accurate. She liked her sunroom and her study the most, though. They had the heart of Leigh in them. She was sitting in the sunroom watching the day get started when Charlie knocked on the back door of the sunroom to let her know the horses had been let out for the day.

"I'll be here the rest of the morning if you need anything.

Then I help Della with the grocery in the afternoon. It'll sure be nice to see Mr. Jarrod. Been way too long."

How nice to have him around, she thought, closing the door.

She got dressed about 10:00am and headed out toward her pond. She stocked it with bass and trout. The grounds around it were just beginning to grow into a nicely landscaped area. When she bought the house, she asked for fifty acres. The grounds around the house were severely overgrown at the time. The acreage behind the house had been used for crops for years. It too had been neglected and had ended up with lots of brush patches and few trees. Leigh immediately cleared the area for pasture space and seeded the land with Bermuda grass. The pond area was replanted with willow trees and other trees with foliage that would burst with fall colors in the autumn. She now had a green rolling-hill panorama with a footpath through the pastures to a large section of virgin timbered woods.

These woods were a place of solace to her in the spring and fall. Other times of the year, they were either too wet or had too many poisonous snakes and biting insects for a pleasant walk. But right now, they were perfect for hiking through. After looking over the pond area, she headed in the direction of the footpath deciding a walk would help clear her head. After a few minutes' walk, she came upon the sandbar on the rock bed creek that ran right through the middle of the wooded area. Leigh could always sit on this sandbar and not hear anything from the outside world. The sound of the water flowing over the stones was relaxing. It was rumored that General Grant's most trusted cavalry men had spent a couple of days on this very sandbar while planning the Siege of Vicksburg. Leigh hadn't brought her metal detector down to scope out the possible treasures left by Yankees or Confederates, but it was on her list of things to do before the weather got too hot again. She sat on a fallen tree log and just listened for a few minutes, absorbing the relaxing sounds of the wind in the trees, the water in the creek and the sound of the birds in the forest. Quiet, nice calm quiet.

While she sat, her thoughts drifted to the throwing out of Roger Halford's murder charge and the conversation she had with Mr. Garrison Roberts. It seemed as if three days had actually past since last night. What is it about traumatic events that make time go by as if each second was a minute? One thing was for sure. She wasn't staying at the DA's office, come Hell or high water! She would leave as soon as she could secure alternative employment. She couldn't give up her home no matter what happened. She'd put too much into this property and it would always be her home. It was Jarrod and Joe's too. She had to remained employed to finance the maintenance and staff. If she were forced to leave, she needed something she could go immediately into and draw a salary. That left private practice out. It would take too long to build that up to a profitable stage.

She thought of Mr. Robert's offer, and she felt a sickening sensation in her stomach at that prospect. No, the best thing for her to do would be to call her contacts with other DA's offices Monday to see what the hiring climate was like in the districts closest to her home. She also still had academic connections with her undergraduate criminal justice department. She did not think teaching would be something she would like, even though she previously taught many seminar classes to law enforcement officers and enjoyed it. Well, she concluded, I'll just have to turn over some stones and see what is out there for me. While reflecting on her chosen plan of action, she casually picked up a stone in the creek to see what was under it. Nothing but sand. Well, she thought, smiling wryly, I hope my calls turn up more than just sand. It was time to get started so she headed back out of the tall woods into the pasture area.

As she emerged from the woody area, she spotted her stallion whom she raised from birth. In fact, she helped him into the world when the mare had a tough time delivering. Cerces was a magnificent chestnut with the classically sculpted Arab head and a long neck that many a show horse owner would die for. He was a big baby to Leigh. He was as much a pet as any dog or cat, even though he was also a top performer for Arab shows nationwide. He trotted over to greet her when she emerged from the woods. His gleaming coat reflected the morning sun and his velvety nose blew warm air into her hair as he waited to be stroked.

"What you up to, big guy?" she gently patting his neck and back. He answered with a soft murmuring sound. He was taller than most Arabs and his legs moved him like the wind when he ran. This morning it was still a little cool and she could tell he wanted to play in the crisp air. She grabbed his halter and loosened the strap and released him. This was always his signal that he was free to run with the wind and live it up. It was called 'freestyle' in the show world. He had the form, gait and personality for blue ribbons each time out. He reared up and whinnied in response to just feeling plain good. He ran until Leigh was breathless from watching him. When he had tired, he trotted right back up to her and stopped. He knew the rules. Leigh pulled out an alfalfa cube from her wind breaker pocket and gave it to him. "OK. You deserve a treat." She placed the halter back on him and turned and walked toward the house. Most everyone who saw her with the stallion admonished her for trusting him so much. "He'll turn on you. You won't even know it when it happens," they had said. She looked back at him. He had gone back to the open pasture area and was grazing happily. Well, she thought, I guess I'll just live in my stupidity then.

The barn phone was ringing as she passed the doorway on the way back to the house. She had installed a phone line there since she spent so much time out with her horses. She was either bathing them, feeding them, foaling or lunging them. She went into the barn office and answered, "Leigh Reid, Can I help you?"

"It's me." Cheryl's voice. Odd for her to call on a weekend, Leigh thought. She sounded upset.

"Hey! What's up, girl?"

"Well, I thought you ought to know this." Cheryl's voice was flat. Not a good sign. "After you left yesterday, we had a visitor. Looks like we have that new associate you needed. But I didn't think you knew this yet. Have you heard?" Leigh's heart skipped a beat. They hadn't wasted any time, had they?

"No! I haven't heard. Who is it?" Leigh hoped her voice did not give her fears away.

"Oh, you'll love this! You've tried cases against him before. I think at the time you called him the 'epitome of a lowlife slick-haired sleaze ball criminal defense lawyer' if I am quoting correctly. Mason Mueller from Jackson. And, he stopped by to introduce himself. That's how I got to know. No one bothered to tell me either."

"Oh, just great! I cannot believe this. I don't get consulted after I wrote the grant for his position, sent the advertisement out, and weeded through the applicants for Mike! And look who I have to work with? I guarantee you Mason Mueller was not in the applicant pool. A fine note, I'll say." She wanted to scream out that he was a cocaine user, into drug trafficking, and would start the downfall of the whole office. Instead, she just said, "I guess I'll have to think about this. I appreciate you letting me know. How did he seem to you?"

"Oh, he was sugar and spice. But he wanted keys to your office. He said you would be sharing the office with him. I told him that there were only two sets of keys. You had yours and I had mine under strict orders not to give them out. He acted very nice about it and said he would just ask the DA about it again. Then he said he would begin working midweek next week, but he would not be around a lot since he had to close down his practice in Jackson. That's about it. What are you going to do about this? I was ready to give Mike a big piece of my mind and I even tried to find him. But, I called everywhere and couldn't locate him. He should have told you first, is all I can say. I am furious, but I know that it is you that should be more offended. After all the work you have done for Mike, and to hear it this way? Well, I never!"

Me, either, Leigh said to herself. Most assuredly never. "Look, don't worry about it, Cheryl. I'll be in early Monday and we'll take it one step at the time, okay?" Leigh wasn't going to let Cheryl in on anything. She couldn't afford to do at this point. The plot had just been confirmed in Leigh's mind, though. Roberts was right. Looked like she would have to follow through on her plans to get out and get out quick.

"Sure, Leigh. And, I still want to hear about what happened with the Halford murder trial being dismissed. That didn't smell right to me. I'll see you. Don't let it get you down too much." Cheryl clicked off.

Leigh felt like she had a ticking time bomb in her stomach. She could feel the seconds marching by one by one. By Monday afternoon, she better have some good results from her employment search or she might have to implode or explode on someone! What she was really pondering at this point was who would she explode on? The DA, the new ADA, the Judge, or all three?

CHAPTER FOUR

Monday Morning-Dorsey County Courthouse

It was 8:35 am when Leigh walked into her office. As she expected, she beat everyone there. She wanted to get in early enough to catch the people she wanted to talk to about her forced employment change. Most of them she called by 9:30 am, and they all agreed to check on the status of open slots and told her they would get back at her at her home number. The only one she did not catch at his office was Todd Weems, her former criminal justice professor at her undergraduate university. His secretary told her he just recently retired and could be reached at home in the afternoons. Leigh called his home and left a message for him to call her at work or home. She hoped she would be through with court by lunch time; she was planning to clean out her desk after lunch and prepare her resignation letter.

Cheryl came in, made coffee and brought Leigh a cup, "How ya doing?" she asked and sat down in front of Leigh's desk.

"Ok, I guess." She looked at her friend and sighed then said, "Look, Cheryl. I have always been up front with you, you know."

"Yeah, well, you are the only one that has been. I can't count on anyone else in this office for that!" Cheryl was tough, but she was obviously hurt because of the snub to her and Leigh.

"Well, I have thought this out very carefully since you called Saturday. I don't wish to work with this, this new associate. He is unethical, manipulative, and deceptive. And that is just in the courtroom! And, I cannot work with the DA when he hasn't got enough confidence or trust in me to even discuss the hiring of this guy. I've always been loyal to him in every way, and the insult to me is too much to ignore. So, I have made a decision to leave. Leave before I get so mad that I get fired!"

She saw the look of shock and panic on Cheryl's face. "Look, Cheryl, you and I go way back before this job. I don't want you to be influenced by my decision, though. I know how you need your salary. I have no idea where I am going, so I can't promise to take you with me. After all we've been through over the last few years, I am afraid you will be soured on the job here and end up getting too mad to stay, too. This isn't what I want for you. You can stay and bear it. I know you can, but, you'll have to watch your back with this Mueller fellow, although he probably will have to be nice to you. After all, he won't have a rat's chance of knowing how to do his job here, since I won't be around to guide him and you know the DA won't either. That will leave you to help him. So, when I say 'watch your back', I mean don't let him ride herd on you. If you think he's up to something, the best thing will be for you to keep a journal at home for future references. Ok?"

Cheryl was red in the face. "No! Not Ok! I'm not staying here without you. This office will fall apart without you. Besides, I don't have a clue about the administration of the grants. No one else will either. I was your secretary before we came to this place, and I go where you go…" Cheryl crossed her arms in front of her as if her decision was final.

"I'll be glad to take you with me if I can find a place that is suitable. But don't count on it, Cheryl. I want you to keep your chin up and keep doing the great job you do. I don't like this anymore than you, so help me out here. I want to know you won't give this up until you have a good replacement position. You have a family to feed, OK?"

Cheryl uncrossed her arms and dejectedly she said, "You're right. I can't just up and go without something to go to. Well, I guess I'll try. That's all I can promise at this point. But you really think I might need to keep a journal on him? That sounds like you anticipate he's going to screw with me!"

"Trust me and don't let on to anyone that you are keeping one. With that sleaze ball snooping around here, you never know what can happen. I don't think he has a decent bone in him. Just write down the things you fundamentally think he might be doing wrong. It'll be better than having nothing in case you ever need to defend yourself against him." She did not want to alarm her, but she knew the Feds would not know immediately who was or and wasn't in on any wrongdoing.

Cheryl said, "So what is the bad news about why we lost the murder case Friday in a motion hearing?" Before Leigh could answer, the phone rang. Cheryl got up to go to her office to answer it. "I'll be back to hear your answer."

Leigh turned her radio on to hear the morning news and weather. She bought a mini stereo system as her one luxury item for the office. Mike always refused to buy anything in the line of comfort items. He hadn't even purchased a copy machine until Leigh procured a grant for one. Cheryl and she had been borrowing from the Circuit Clerk's office for the couple of years prior to that.

Cheryl came in with another cup of coffee for Leigh and said, "That was His Highness, your future ex-boss, who said only that he would not be available today. No mention of the new 'assistant', so I asked him just when he was going to let us know about it. He said he figured I already knew since I was asking. What a jerk!" Cheryl shook her head and walked back out to get the phone again. The day was getting started quickly now.

The voice on the radio was into the statewide news. Leigh had a half ear to the news as she flipped through her disheveled desk, but her head turned toward the radio when she heard the following statement: "There apparently was no body found, only various blood stains on the walls in the hotel room where sources say Kevin Johnson, Assistant District Attorney for the 34th District, had checked in for the night. The blood samples have been taken to the State Crime Lab for examination. Sources in the District Attorney's office have refused to comment, and the local Sheriff, Rodney Thompson has indicated that he believes foul play is involved. He indicated that they are launching an area-wide search for Mr. Kevin Johnson. More on this as the story develops. In other news...." But Leigh heard nothing else.

CHAPTER FIVE

She sat frozen in her seat and thought her heart had truly stopped beating. She knew she wasn't breathing. I'm going to faint, she decided. No, I'm not. I'm going to throw up! Jesus! I don't know what I'm going to do, she finally concluded after a few seconds passed. There was just nothing but pure shock running through her system.

Cheryl came in again saying, "Here's a revised docket for the day's circus in arena one, also known as the main courtroom." As she put it on her desk, she took one look at Leigh and said, "My God, Leigh! You look white as a ghost. What is it? Who died?"

Leigh said, "Ironic you should say that. Apparently, you haven't heard the news this morning, have you?"

"What? For God's sake! From the look on your face, it must have been someone close."

"Well I guess you could say that. Kevin Johnson is missing. They found blood in a hotel room he supposedly checked in over in Columbia and they're saying foul play is involved."

"Kevin? Your Friday Night Kevin? How? What? Oh, my God, Leigh! That's horrible!" Cheryl sat down and looked sick too. After a few seconds, she asked, "What happened when you saw him Friday?"

"I met him at the Blue Parrot and we had a short, if not strange, conversation about work. That's it. He stayed only a few minutes and then left in a hurry. I left not long after him," She sighed with sadness creeping in slowly as the initial shock was wearing off. "I surely didn't think it could be the last time I would see him. He certainly didn't give me any idea that he was in any sort of trouble. He just acted kind of strange, like really nervous."

"That's really weird. Then he mysteriously goes missing the next night? Wow, Leigh. Can you call and get some details from the DA's office down there? Or do you want me to?"

"I'll see what I can find out. But I don't think I better make it an official inquiry since I may have been the last one to see him." Leigh thought quickly of her media contacts. Some of them knew more about the goings on than the local law enforcement. She rang up the radio newsman from the largest station in Jackson.

"News room. Brock here," came the familiar voice.

"Leigh Reid here. How's it going Brock?"

"Leigh! What a nice surprise. I haven't talked to you since that uh, the Caraway child abuse trial. What's shaking in your area?" Brock and she had been business acquaintances for years. He always got the first scoops from all over the state and he had quite a clientele of sources to call on when he needed inside information.

Leigh simply spoke the words, "Kevin Johnson."

"Oh, yeah! Isn't that wild? He was a good prosecutor. Weren't you two were in law school together?" She noted and didn't like the past tense reference. After all, Kevin had not been found dead. At least, not yet.

Brock added, "Oh, I do have some AP reporter's notes here on the desk. You need some unofficial information?"

"1 sure do. I thought you would have the latest and I didn't want the run around from the locals."

"Gotcha there, and that's for sure what you'd get. Bet they are tight lipped on this one! Let's see here; I'm reading this thing now. It says that Kevin apparently rented a room at the Centennial Hotel in Columbia on Saturday night. The note says he checked into a single room about 9:00pm and no one was apparently with him. Someone from close by his room in the hotel heard what sounded like gun shots about 2:30 a.m. Sunday morning. No one bothered to check in or call anyone. That's typical, isn't it? Must be one of those no-tell hotels. Anyway, let's see, the cleaning crew found the room in shambles early this morning and blood stains on the wall and lavatory. No one saw anything else out of the ordinary. Kevin's car was recovered at the hotel with his briefcase in it and nothing else. That's about it. This reporter's source is anonymous don't you know. You got any off the record ideas on what might have happened?"

Leigh knew she shouldn't give away the fact she met with him Friday night even if it was to a trusted media friend. "No. I'm just shocked, that's all. We've been comrades in the prosecution field for a while. Thanks for the report. It helps knowing a little more. I'll return the favor if I find out anything else."

"Sure, Leigh. Anytime. Say, wasn't your office supposedly trying a murder case today? I heard it was postponed. Pretty big case, too. What's the scoop?"

With something like vile creeping into her throat over the question and what the answer was, along with her worry over Kevin, she said, "You'll have to talk directly to the DA on that one, Brock. I just haven't got a clue." Leigh wanted all the heat that could be fired up sent directly to her corrupt boss.

"Well, can I get a quick tape on the other murder conviction last week? Wasn't that the one where the guy killed another one with a bar stool over a game of pool? I haven't heard if the Judge sentenced him yet, so I'll get the clip and run it with the sentencing news."

Leigh agreed and gave a quick synopsis of the evidence, verdict and potential sentence on a pre-recorded tape. You scratch my back; I'll scratch yours. That's the name of the game in media relations as she had learned from experience.

She hung up and gave Cheryl the details of the conversation. Cheryl then said, "I 'm so sorry. I know he was your friend. Maybe they'll find him soon." She left the room and Leigh turned the radio off. She sat and thought about her meeting with Kevin again. At least, she would not be an immediate source of information for the investigators. Her meeting had been on Friday night. He was very much alive at that point. His checking into the hotel occurred on Saturday, so she thought she probably wasn't the last person to see him alive. At least the hotel clerk should have been the last one other than those who caused the blood stains. .

She was horrified at the thought that he might be dead. What a shame to lose someone so good at his job and with such a bright future. Not to mention their relationship over the years. It was true that after her divorce from her husband, Kevin was the one who was there for her. He was a kind and gentle man and she had cared very deeply for him. She hoped for a stronger bond between them at the time, but Kevin was not ready for anything serious. He told her he felt she needed more time and he wouldn't be her 'rebound' choice. Feeling like he was essentially using her when he said that, and thinking he was just coming up with excuses to not be serious, she cut if off suddenly after that. She was hurt, but she got over it after hearing of his various affairs with married women following their breakup. For a while, they didn't talk with each other. However, he finished law school first and asked her advice on his first job offer, that of Assistant District Attorney for Hinds County in Jackson. She remembered telling him to go for it because it suited his personality to a tee. He took the job and had loved prosecuting. Just as she learned to love it once she took the Assistant DA position. They stayed in touch, but only on 'friendly' sort of terms. Like during his campaign for Judge.

In fact, Friday night was the first time he mentioned his feelings for her since she broke off with him. For that, she was touched, especially in light of the fact that he may be dead now. She realized that he really was the only man she had even had the time of day for since her marriage dissolved. Tears pooled in her eyes as she thought he might really be gone. Sure, she dated a few attorneys and a few cops, but there had never been any feelings develop for any of them, except Kevin.

She was always too involved in bringing up a child and in her career to let herself get involved with anyone since Kevin. She liked it that way. Sometimes she told inquiring minds that her horses were better suited for her than a man. They did not lie, did not drink, and did not beat up women.

It was close to 10:30 am and there was a plea set in the courtroom. It was for her newfound friend, Levon Smith, and his client, Carl Knight. She started down to the courtroom with a heavy heart and tried to put the news of Kevin out of her mind for a few minutes. She wanted to make sure that his plea went according to plans. The underlying information she learned through Carl's friend, Mr. Garrison Roberts, gave her an incentive to gut it up and move forward.

Entering the courtroom, Leigh took a second to notice who might be in the audience. There were several people in the spectator chairs waiting. She always scanned the room before sitting with her back to a crowd. It was a habit that went with her law enforcement background and her sixth sense. She took a second glance at a guy that looked like one of the Banditos motorcycle gang members. This was somewhat out of place she thought. Donning dark glasses, he had long brown hair pulled back in a ponytail, sported a mustache and beard, and wore the requisite black leather jacket and pants. He didn't have the usual beer gut, which was a little strange. She wondered what connection he might have to Carl or Carl's friends. He turned in her direction lazily and then back to the front of the courtroom. Other than that one person, she knew the rest were just the usual court watchers who came in hoping to see something to liven up their normally dull lives. She was more interested in getting the matter at hand over with so she could go back to her desk, the Kevin mystery and her new job search.

The case was called by Judge Beasley, whom she now looked at in an entirely new light. She tried very hard not to show her distaste for him and began reciting her proof in the case of *State of Mississippi vs. Carl Knight*. The plea went according to plan and Judge Beasley finished by sentencing Carl at the same hearing. Thank you for that, Judge, she said to herself. She did not want to leave Carl in the hands of the new ADA for sentencing and she did not plan on being in the courtroom in this county again after today if her job search went well.

When the hearing was over, most of the courtroom audience emptied, except for the biker as Leigh took a casual note of. The Judge asked if the State would be ready for three more sentencing hearings in the afternoon, and Leigh looked at her docket and frowned. There were no other sentencings scheduled on her revised docket.

She stood up and said, "Judge, the State was not aware of additional hearings this afternoon. I am sorry. I cannot be ready for them since I was not aware of them."

Judge Beasley looked up at Leigh with what looked like open hostility and said loudly for all the courtroom staff to hear, "Ms. Reid, I cannot tolerate postponing sentencings. I don't care what your excuse is."

That was so uncharacteristic of him, she thought. Leigh was a bit bewildered at first, then like a light coming on in her head, she got the message. And, she was not going to let him insult her like that. She said curtly, "Perhaps his Honor would like to inquire on the record of his administrator regarding the preparation of today's revised docket, and I will put my copy into the record, and," she paused as she started toward the court reporter to hand her the docket, "I will be happy to place it in as an Exhibit to my testimony if you would like to officially swear me in?"

The Judge, obviously not expecting such a rebuttal, looked at his administrator, Alene, with a dark glare, said, "No, Ms. Reid that will not be necessary. Perhaps some wires were crossed. Court adjourned until 1:00 pm for civil motions"

Leigh left the court room without saying a word. That was obviously the beginning of the Judge's part in the play about to be acted out according to the big plan to make her life miserable enough to quit! With this realization, she quickened her pace as she couldn't get back to her desk soon enough.

The letter of resignation was dictated in less than one minute. It was short and to the point. She gave it to Cheryl who refused to type it at first. Then she did it anyway. She reckoned she couldn't talk Leigh out of resigning, and she really didn't want to now because of the way she was being treated. Leigh told her to fax it to the other two county courthouses in their district, special attention to the DA. Then the time would start running on her giving him adequate notice. Leigh figured she had enough unused vacation time to leave that afternoon and be paid for two weeks. Plus, she would still have additional vacation and compensatory time to be reimbursed. And, she also had a nice lump sum in the state retirement plan that she could draw out and live on until something else came up for income.

Enough with staying and waiting for a sure flogging. It was oh so obvious to her that Garrison Roberts had been right about everything.

At 2:30 a call came in from Todd Weems, her former professor in criminal justice. Leigh answered hoping he would be the one to pull her out of the dilemma she found herself in.

"Leigh! What a nice surprise to hear from you! It's been way too long." Todd's voice was as soothing to her as it had always been since her first class with him at the university.

"Todd! Thanks for returning the call. I've been meaning to call you, but the schedule here has always been too heavy to allow for many calls to old friends. I was shocked to hear you had retired! What made you finally do that? I thought you never would."

"My lovely wife of 25 years put her proverbial foot down and said we had to live a normal life since our kids were all safely away from home. I still consult for the University, but I am traveling a lot, too. Enjoying picking and choosing the jobs I want these days. Really, life really couldn't be better. How are things going with you?"

"Well, I am very glad you asked that, because I am in need of a change from my present job. Like really quick. I know you have a lot of connections with contacts all over and I hoped I could get some advice."

"Sure, Leigh. But the last I heard you were doing a fantastic job there. In fact, some of your colleagues and I were discussing you last month at the Criminal Justice Planning Agency meeting. You could be in for the next DA. Maybe even higher, you know. I have always thought you would be a political whiz kid. So, what has brought about such a drastic decision?"

"Well, you heard about Kevin Johnson I'm sure since he prosecuted in your district." The University of Southern Mississippi was in Hattiesburg, the same district that Kevin had been prosecuting in.

"Yes. Really sad news around here about that. In fact, I have been called on to consult with the Sheriff's office on the forensic aspects of the investigation. As I recall, you and Kevin were in law school together, weren't you?"

"Yes. I'm still shocked at the moment. We just talked recently. I can't believe something violent has happened to him. The Crime Lab will be able to do a rush job on the blood stains, I would assume, but that won't solve the mystery as to where he is, dead or alive. He hadn't indicated to me that he was in any sort of trouble."

"Those type of hit jobs are rarely forewarned, Leigh."

Hit jobs? That sounded really foreboding. But she had to face the possibility since prosecutors carry risks in taking on some professional organizations. "I know, Todd, I would appreciate it if you could keep me updated on the investigation." Leigh knew he loved forensic mystery solving and loved to share his work. He also would monitor the case for her out of friendship.

"No problem, Leigh. I'll let you know what I find out. But, back to your employment question, for lack of a better term. What does Kevin's possible demise have to do with you wanting to leave prosecuting? Or does it? I know how you love putting the bad guys away." Leigh really did not know what to say, to that question. She sure couldn't tell him what had transpired with Garrison Roberts or with the Judge and DA. Before she could answer, though, Todd said, "Never mind. Maybe I don't want to know. It doesn't really matter right now. I'll put my sources to work and try to come up with something that would be challenging enough for you. Something comes to mind already, but I'll need to check it out before I tell you about it. If it is a probability, it is damned good timing, I believe. I'll call in a day or so about that, okay?"

"Thanks so much, Todd. Someday, I'll clue you in on all the reasons for this career change request."

"No need to bother with that until you're ready. Call you in a couple of days."

Leigh hung up and smiled. Todd was her favorite professor from her undergraduate courses and since then had become a good friend. He made a habit of following her career moves and checked in with her often. If anyone could help her at this point; he was certainly in a position to do so since he networked nationally and internationally with criminal justice gurus on a regular basis.

"Cheryl?" Leigh asked while pressing the button for the intercom on the phone. "Have you heard from the DA or the new associate today?" She tried not to sound trite when saying 'associate'.

"Nope. I think they're hiding out from you, quite frankly."

"Thanks," Yeah, I am sure they are plotting and planning their next big "Get Rid of Leigh" move, no doubt. "I'll need you to contact the State Office of Finance and Administration to start the paperwork for my leaving office. Can you do that today?"

"Ok. Still don't want to. But, I will."

Leigh then seriously began the process of getting her desk cleaned out. She packed up her meager personal belongings and put them in several boxes. Then she went through her laptop computer and deleted all correspondence and research she had generated. She left the grant files where Cheryl could at least contact the grantors and explain her leaving. Most of the grantor contacts had been close business acquaintances of Leigh's. They, more than likely, would not wish to continue funding the grants unless an adequate explanation from Leigh herself was made for her leaving. She planned to not let them know anything. They could surmise the obvious: That she must have left unhappy. It gave her little satisfaction though in being forced to leave the job she loved before she was ready.

By 4:00 pm, she was ready to leave. She had her boxes loaded up in her car and came back to tell Cheryl goodbye. It wasn't easy, and there were some tears from both of them. She assured Cheryl she'd stay in touch and keep her informed of where she was. Then she walked out of the courthouse for what she thought would be the very last time leaving the place she thought she'd be for the rest of her career.

CHAPTER SIX

Monday evening at 8:00 pm

Leigh, in an effort to focus on something other than Kevin's disappearance and her being jobless, was in her study trying to read through some of her magazines and plan a spring redo of the master bedroom. Her classical music was playing throughout the house and a glass of chilled Berenger White Zinfandel was on the table beside her. Folded up into the large upholstered chair, she realized that the world was somewhat topsy-turvy for her right now, and she could use an escape from reality. No sooner had she begun to unwind, then the phone rang. Let the machine get it; there's not anyone in this world I'd want to talk to at this moment, she said to herself. Let them all be damned! The machine clicked on and Leigh listened to the message of the caller begin: "Leigh. It's me. Leigh! Pick up, please!"

Hearing the familiar voice, she thought, oh my God! Running at breakneck speed to the phone, she picked up the receiver and almost screamed. "Kevin, I'm here! Is it you, really you?" Her voice broke as she asked the question.

"Yes, Leigh. It's me. Listen carefully because I have only a few minutes. Let me tell you quickly what's going on." He was talking fast and in a low tone.

"Kevin! Everyone thinks you're dead! I thought you were, too, for heaven's sake! How are you? Where are you? What in God's name has happened? Do you know I've been sick with worry? There's a manhunt going on all over Lamar County!"

"Leigh. Please, Leigh. Slow down. I'm so sorry to put

THE OGHAM CONNECTIONS

you and everyone through that worry, but it was absolutely necessary. It truly is a matter of life or death. Mine. But I'm very much alive, I assure you. I staged the incident at the hotel. I've gotten myself into something that's extremely dangerous. I had to let some not- so-nice chaps think I'd been kidnapped and/or murdered You are the only one I could turn to that they wouldn't be able to figure on. Let me try to shorten this so you can understand, since I don't have much time. There was a man from New Orleans that was chased by the state troopers on Highway 59 last week outside of Hattiesburg for speeding. When he was pulled over, he said he wanted to get caught, and he wanted to talk to a lawyer. The troopers of course brought him to the prosecutor, being lucky me, and now I'm in this thing up to my eyeballs. I managed to get this man on the road out of town to a safe place until the authorities need him for a murder that he said he 'kind of' witnessed. That is, if they ever find the body. The person that was killed had given this man something right before he was killed, telling him to hold it because some other people wanted it. This poor man said the murder happened at the Fram Warehouses in the warehouse district while he was hiding behind the door of his job place. He was given this object to supposedly safe keep until the guy that gave it to him came back. The guy was murdered, apparently killed with guns with silencers, even though, my guy didn't see it. He heard it and some explicit language about doing away with the body. Apparently, there are no other witnesses other than this man who wanted protection. What he had, he very gladly gave me so he wouldn't be a 'target', he said. He had been chased by what he terms 'bad guys in black suits' before the troopers got him. It was something I knew nothing about, but, I knew he feared he would be the next victim by keeping this object. Before I could do anything with it, I mean, like checking it out with the Feds, I started being followed by who knows how many people up until I staged my vanishing act. All because of this "item" that apparently someone wants very badly and will apparently kill to get it." He stopped long enough for Leigh to jump in.

"Kevin. Why didn't you turn over this 'item' into the authorities in New Orleans? It sounds like that would have solved the problem posthaste."

"Yeah, I know but, I didn't because, Leigh, there is a likelihood that the Feds may be a part of this whole thing. The man told me that the people chasing him had dark suits and extremely high tech equipment. He said some of them looked official to him. And, quite frankly, you know how some of government operations are run. There are some very bad eggs in the chicken shed sometimes. And some of the men had foreign accents, which means there could be some international involvement. He spotted the men several times before he got out of New Orleans. That, to me, sounded a lot like it could be 'Fee-Bees' (FBI). The supposed murderers hitmen, whatever they were, may be the same as the ones chasing me. He never saw them up close, so he can't ID them. He can, however, ID the killer's voice. He says he definitely would remember that tone or accent."

Leigh was speechless. It sounded incredulous to her that this could happen over some 'item' that could be easily ditched immediately by whoever possessed it. But a murder may have occurred over it, so it would be evidence if a body was ever found. Quickly trying to figure how she could help, Kevin was continuing, "Leigh, you have the same sense I do about things when they don't smell right. It just didn't smell right to me and I didn't think the right thing was to give up the item without knowing why one man died trying to hide it and putting me in the position where I had to fake my own demise for it. That's where you come in, Leigh. I know you must have thought I had lost my mind Friday night at the Blue Parrot. I had to let them believe our encounter was strictly for returning a favor by giving you back that brief. I didn't want them to think I'd given you their all-important item and then they start following you.

"Gee, thanks, I suppose I should be given a medal, huh?"

she said wryly thinking she'd helped him once again out of a jam. "What about the blood they found in your hotel room? Is it going to turn out to be yours?"

"Yeah, I cut myself intentionally to give them something to analyze."

"What are you going to do with that item now, Kevin?" Leigh was so relieved he was okay that she was beginning to feel so much better just hearing his voice.

"It's not me that is going to do have to do something with it. Sorry, kiddo, but it's you, since you have it now. You see, I really did give it to you."

CHAPTER SEVEN

Leigh thought she had not heard him right. Clearing her throat, she asked, "I'm sorry, what did you just say, Kevin?"

"I know you won't believe this, but I meant what I said when I said you were the only one I could turn to. Hear me out, Leigh. I know you have your brother, Joe, at U.S. Customs. He could take this item and turn it over to whomever he thinks is trustworthy. I didn't have time to make any confidential connections with the Feds. These guys seemed to be everywhere I turned! You wouldn't be in danger once Joe has it and I could stay below surface for a while. Those goons that want this may decide I was killed by some other faction that wanted it too. I don't know, but I am sorry, Leigh that you are now in the possession of the item."

"What?" she said loudly wondering if she'd had too much wine. "I am not! You gave me my brief back. That's all I got from you!" Leigh could feel her face flushing with anger and fear at the same time.

"No, Leigh. When I hugged you, Dear, I placed it in your coat pocket. I was trying not to let them see I transferred it to you."

Well, that's two times she was going to be sick today because of Kevin.

She thought for a second and then remembered the disc-like object in the envelope she had found in her pocket when she was driving home from Hattiesburg. She hadn't given it another thought since that time because of all the upheavals at the office and Kevin's disappearance and now, reappearance. Oh, just great! Just great!

"Kevin, you didn't! Oh my God! What am I going to do with it?" Her heart started racing and she was beginning to feel that nauseous feeling again that seemed to be the order of her days recently.

"Leigh! Like I said. Call Joe, please, and quickly. Let him see what he can do. It's dangerous enough for me to fake my own disappearance. It's the logical solution, though. Call Joe tonight and get yourself rid of that thing. I wouldn't be able to live with myself if something happened to you because of me. Promise you'll do it. I am already regretting giving it to you, but I was really scared." Kevin's voice was breaking up on the other end.

Leigh did not know what to do or say.

"I am on my way, as we speak, out of the state to who knows where to lay low. It will be a while before I will contact you again. I'll be in touch though somehow when I'm resettled. I am looking at this as an opportunity for a whole new life for me, too. I sense these people are apparently cunning as well as ruthless, though, Leigh. Be careful."

"Kevin, I ... Kevin?" No answer. A dial tone and it was obvious he was gone.

CHAPTER EIGHT

Leigh was motionless for a few minutes trying to absorb her new situation. Her music had stopped and the quiet seemed to envelope her with a dark dread.

I've got something one person has died for and another has just faked his death over. I know nothing about it, don't want to know anything about and I am placed now in the position of getting it to somebody trustworthy. Who was involved in the murder? Was it a Federal or local law enforcement cover up? Who was the victim? What was so important about that item she'd been handed off? She was thoroughly upset. Then she thought, at least I think I have that something. She jumped out of her chair and briskly walked to the armoire in her bedroom. She found the suit jacket she had worn Friday night when she met with Kevin. She checked the pocket to make sure that the odd object was still there. Yes. Of course, it was! She couldn't be so lucky as to have lost it, misplaced it, or accidently trashed it. Nope. There it was. She pulled it out and looked at it. Opening the white paper envelope it was in, she pulled out the round metallic disc. "What are you about?" she asked as she examined it. Some sort of cd it seemed to be, but it was smaller. She quickly grabbed her laptop and placed the disc into her cd rom drive of her laptop and closed it. Then she felt a cold chill run down her spine, and she stopped. What was she doing? Whatever was on this thing, obviously, there were many reasons she didn't need to know. She was not on the 'need to know' list yet! This knowledge could cause her to be in as much danger as Kevin. Then, curiosity getting the better of her, she looked anyway at the screen in front of her.

There was a large number of symbols covering the screen. They were what looked to be in complete confusion, no order or sense to them. Whoops, she thought, as she removed the disc. It was some sort of code, she was thinking, maybe. Something she really didn't need to know nor would she know without some sort of decoding software. That was certainly out of her area of expertise. It looked like no language she had ever seen. Perhaps ancient looking symbols, but from where, she wondered. What mystery did these symbols hold? What secret did they have that put her suddenly in a potentially dangerous situation? Shouldn't she just, like pretend like it did not exist? Maybe she should trash it, or even better, burn it? It was, after all, just a small thing that could be disposed of easily, maybe put it in the fireplace and burn it down to nothing? It was something that could easily be misplaced, lost, or destroyed by accident. After all, no one knew she had it yet. She hoped. But, then she thought of Kevin. He probably could have done away with it too, but he had gone to a lot of trouble to rid himself of having anything to do with it. He trusted her to get it to the proper authority so they could pick up the investigation into the murder (if one did occur). One lost soul had apparently died trying to hide it. It must have something on it that was so important that once anyone had it, they were associated with the contents and were at risk. So, throwing it away, burning it, etc., probably wasn't going to keep her from being charged with the knowledge of what these stick-like symbols meant, now was it? Kevin apparently thought one murder investigation was worth his fake death. No, she thought. And, it wasn't worth her life, either.

Putting the disc back in the paper, she wasn't sure of what to do with it. But she was sure of one thing. Her life did not need this type of complication right now. Today, she just left a job she loved because of corrupt officials. She had a son to support at Harvard. Her horses, her home and staff needed her, and she had no clue what she was going to do for income. And now, well now she just was placed in the middle of who knows what kind of sinister plot to hide some stupid metal disc with what looked like ancient stick-like symbols on it at the risk of several lives. Oh, boy, she thought as she took all that in, and then she went promptly into her bathroom and threw up.

CHAPTER NINE

"Joe. It's me." Leigh had dialed his cell phone in Atlanta. It was nine in the evening there.

"Leigh. Hi, Sis! I was just finishing up some paperwork. I'm catching a ride on a Customs helicopter in the morning over to your place for that nice, long upcoming weekend. Is everything okay for the trip over? You don't have to work this weekend, do you?"

"Are you on a secured line, Joe?"

"Yes, always on this phone. I can encode too. Why? What's up?" His sister was strangely remote sounding.

"Encode, Joe."

"Okay. Geez, Leigh." She heard a couple of buttons being pressed on the other end. "We're scrambled, now. Tell me what the heck is going on." Joe knew when Leigh was serious, and she sounded extremely serious now.

"Look, I've been given some information about a hit-type murder in New Orleans. There's some evidence in the form of a metal disc, like a CD, but smaller. It has some sort of what looks like ancient symbols on it. I think it is a code, but not sure. Supposedly the man murdered over it was in New Orleans recently. One of our Federal enforcement agencies may or may not have dirty agents involved in the murder or the cover up of it. I doubt its public knowledge even to your own intelligence resources. I don't know anything about who was murdered; only that it happened at Fram Warehouse in the warehouse district in February. The body may have been disposed of by throwing it in Lake Ponchatrain. You think you might be able to find out anything about it discreetly?"

"New Orleans has its own office and world, Leigh. It also has a lot of murders. You know there's as much corruption there as in Chicago or New York. And, if a federal agency is involved, it may be near impossible to track any lead on this. I could make a call or two. How do you know about this? What about this evidence? Where the evidence is now?"

Leigh hesitated. She already decided not to tell Joe she had it herself. If there were federal agents involved in this somehow, cover up or not, she didn't want Joe to be accused of being a co- conspirator trying to hide something from his agency either. "Don't know who it was, but there is a witness who can identify the shooter's voice, since he heard it, but didn't see the murder. The disc is safe for now and I can put my hands on it when need be."

"Don't get involved in this, Leigh. It sounds too deep and potentially dangerous. Let me handle this. I'll call and make some off the record inquiries. Okay? Then I'll check our intelligence sources for any movement like that in New Orleans. If there's anything that can be found, I'll find it and then you get that evidence to me posthaste, okay?"

"Keep in mind if there were Federal agents involved in the murder, Joe, you may get the runaround."

"Hey! That smarts! You wouldn't insinuate government agencies would keep something like their involvement in a murder from the public, would you?" Joe asked in an insulting tone.

"I don't really know what to think, my brother, but I do know that sometimes even the best laid plans can go awry. You know, snitches, informants, etc. do end up missing or dead and the public is never made aware of those deaths, Joe. Can you check and let me know when you get here in the morning? Will that give you enough time?"

"Okay, Sis. Don't worry. If there's something topside to be found out about this murder and the evidence you spoke of, I'll turn it up by tomorrow. After all, I wouldn't want to show up and to be deprived of Della's pancakes!"

"See you in the morning, Joe, hopefully with some good news."

Tuesday, 8:00 am

The whirling and chopping engine sounds of a helicopter coming very close to the house made Leigh jump out of bed and go to the window. Her horses were neighing from the barn and she thought they must believe the world was ending with all the clamor of the engine noise.

She hadn't slept at all. Another couple of minutes passed, the noise wound down, and then she heard the sound of her brother clamoring down the hallway.

"Where's my pancakes and my little sister?" came the booming voice as Leigh stepped into the hall from her bedroom.

"Joe! You are a sight for sore eyes, big brother!" Leigh jumped into his arms for a bear hug.

"Now that's the kind of greeting a man likes when he is hungry. Say, my pilot has heard of the legendary pancakes here and I offered to feed him, too, if that is okay?"

"Glad you are here. Yes, we have plenty of food for your friend, but before we eat, tell me, what did you find out about that matter in New Orleans?"

"Nothing, nada, zero. Dead end everywhere. Guess it is something that is officially swept under the carpet or unofficially not being investigated. You tell that informant to be careful, though. If it was a sophisticated 'hit' over coded information, they could be in danger or a target themselves."

"Thanks, Joe. I expected you wouldn't turn up much. But I hoped you would." She felt the knot in her stomach coming back in in spades. "Okay, I'll let that informant know. Don't worry about it a bit anymore."

Yes, Leigh thought, she apparently would be the informant and target of the moment. She also knew professional hitmen keep knocking down doors until they find what or who they are looking for. She really had no clue what she should do or even who to tell. But she thought about it over her long sleepless night. She didn't want her brother involved in anything that might cause him undue office pressure, either. One in the family was enough to be out of a job at the moment. She decided right then and there not to do what Kevin had advised. She wouldn't give it to Joe. If there were people on Kevin's trail, maybe some time had been bought by his staged disappearance. Maybe no one suspected her at all, should Kevin had been under surveillance at the Blue Parrot. Yes, she thought. The disc was in her hands for now and she would hold on to it for the time being. Who knows, maybe she could try to investigate its importance secretly and with caution. Things weren't truly as bad as they seemed all night in the dark. Today there was sunlight and she brightened herself as the prospect of having house guests.

"Ms. Leigh. Did I hear Mr. Joe come in?" Della came out of the kitchen with a kitchen towel in her hands. Leigh would break away from her serious thoughts and tried to enjoy her day.

"Yes, fix two extra settings. He's bringing one extra mouth, his pilot, to sample your wares."

Della laughed, hugged Joe, and then went about busying herself with breakfast.

Joe headed to the helicopter to inform his friend he could stay and eat.

This old house needs more people in it, Leigh thought. It seemed to smile when there was a gathering. She rushed to her bathroom to finish dressing for the day. She anticipated having her son, Jarrod, home in the afternoon. Della had agreed to be available for all the meals and clean up while Joe and Jarrod were there. Bless her!

Joe's pilot, Tom, was a comic at heart, and by the time breakfast was over, he and Joe had Leigh's mood swung totally. Della was busily cleaning and starting a good southern lunch. Fried chicken, mashed potatoes, collard greens, corn bread and chocolate pie. The aroma in the house prompted Joe to ask Tom to stay for lunch, too. Being a pilot with Customs had its advantages, she was told. No one ever looked for you until there was a major crisis.

Plans were made at that point for Joe and Tom to go down to the lake and throw in a line or two. Joe asked Leigh to join them, but she politely declined. She liked having the stocked lake. But she did not like fishing herself.

She helped Della with the lunch preparations and then headed to the barn to check on the horses. It was time for their morning turn out. She took one at a time to different paddocks to graze and enjoy the day.

After lunch, the party was complete. Jarrod arrived with his Aussie friend, Jacob. Leigh's heart was full at seeing Jarrod, even though it had only been a month since he'd been home last.

She ran out and hugged her son, as he was getting his backpack out of the Jeep Wrangler.

"I'm so glad to see you! But I thought you were going to use some of Joe's frequent flyer miles and fly down, Jarrod," she said to him after meeting Jacob.

"I didn't want to leave you in a lurch for a vehicle while I'm taking Jacob around, Mom. Besides, we had fun taking turns driving. It only took eighteen hours straight through. We are no worse for the wear."

Jarrod had Leigh's looks with his auburn hair and hazel eyes. He also had the sharp facial features and darker skin tones. He was very handsome. Almost devastatingly so, she thought to herself. She knew he would come home one day with a female friend rather than a male. She couldn't bear to think about losing him to someone else. They had been so close. He was her pride and joy. But it was inevitable. She couldn't keep him all to herself forever. Every mother's woe!

"Eighteen hours? Oh, is that all! You shouldn't be staying up all night driving like that, you know." Leigh knew Jarrod wasn't one to take chances. He was a stickler for details and mapped out his future plans to a tee. She wasn't really worried about him making a bad decision.

"Mom! I wouldn't let anything happen to me, you know, if I can help it. Boy, I'm so glad to be home. I saw the helicopter out back. Is Uncle Joe here already?" He was obviously looking forward to spending some time with his uncle, too.

"Yes, he and his friend, Tom, are down at the lake. Why don't you take Jacob and go on down too, or do you want some leftover lunch first? Della can re-heat it."

"Lunch sounds great. I'm starving! I'll go up and get Jacob, change clothes, run down to say hello to Joe and then eat." He stopped and looked closely at Leigh. "How are you, Mom? You look awfully tired. Is everything going ok?" That was her sweet son. He had already noticed what the strain had done to her in the last week.

Leigh did not want to go into the job situation or the 'cloak and dagger' mystery she'd found herself in, so she just said, "Later, I'll tell you all about it. Go have fun for now."

About 4:30 pm that afternoon, Todd Weems was calling back to Leigh. With the guys all out still fishing, Leigh was in the study by herself when the call came in.

"Are you sure you're ready for a drastic change, Leigh?" were his first words.

'I'm not only ready but sitting on 'go'. Why? What have you found?"

"'Sitting on go' is where you need to be for sure. As in, get your passport ready. You have an offer overseas."

"Okay! You have definitely got my attention." Leigh thought that overseas sounded like an answer to all her problems, well, depending on what exactly the job was. As she listened carefully, Todd gave her the details. It was a research fellowship with the University of St. Andrews in Scotland, for approximately 9 months. She would be reporting to the Director of the Criminology Department there in three weeks if she wanted the job. It would entail a salary plus living expenses. They would hire her on Todd's recommendation since he formerly conducted several international seminars there over the years. The research project she would be working on would involve helping to set up and monitor cross bordering criminal intelligence divisions within the United Kingdom and the commonwealth countries. If the pilot project was successful, it would be adopted by the Scottish Parliament and on into the European Union.

"Leigh, you really need to think about this. It is a prestigious but labor-intensive project but it will probably lead to another very good position. You can't wait too long deliberating. It'll give you the break you need and it gives you some international criminal justice exposure. You can use that to your advantage career-wise. I'll need your answer by Thursday, since I told them I would get to them by then, okay? It really is a great place, Scotland, The Highlands, Edinburgh, Loch Ness and some nice people, too. I would love to go back permanently myself."

'Wow! Well, I did say I needed a career change, didn't I? I have to figure out how to put some personal things in order in that short period of time, Todd. But I can tell you right now that I'm very interested. You remember how much I loved England when we went in undergraduate school and studied with the London Coroner's office twenty years ago. You know, I've always wanted to go back and visit Scotland. It does sounds great. Hey, you know you're a pretty swell guy. I should think you had to cash in some sort of favor for this, and I'm very grateful."

"On the contrary. The hiring committee chairman thought your experience and education suited you well for the job. They want a fresh perspective from someone in the field, not in a classroom. Not to mention the fact that you're American and our IT advances in criminology are somewhat advanced compared to the Scots."

"Okay, I can decide and call you by tomorrow Todd with confirmation on everything. Thanks again." She put down the phone and went to the window to look out. Surveying her property and her horses grazing peacefully, she thought how hard it would be to leave under normal circumstances. Then she slowly looked around the room while she played her new option over in her head.

Was there really a choice? Scotland? Stay and risk my life over something I know nothing about other than I may be a target for murderers? Scotland? Stay and job hunt for how long? Scotland? Stay and watch the local corrupt officials take over the entire political arena? Well, that settled it. Scotland is it.

CHAPTER TEN

Leigh officially accepted the offer the next day. She called Todd and set the process in motion. The contact name and number of the professor she needed to contact about the job was obtained and Todd assured her again that it was a good move for her to make.

Alan Flackerty was the department chair at St. Andrews. After a minute or two of not understanding his words over the phone with such a Scottish lilt to it, Leigh began to make out what he was saying. He was having the same trouble with her accent and for a while, 'pardon me?' and 'I'm sorry, what?' were said over and over. But, after a bit, she understood enough as did he. He advised her that she would be given a prepaid airline ticket to Edinburgh and he would set up accommodations for her close to the University. He told her he would meet her as soon as she recovered from jet lag and they would go over the project. He wished her a great flight and looked forward to meeting her. The conversation was upbeat but to the point and any doubts she had about the decision were gone after hanging up. In fact, she was beginning to feel pretty great about the decision. It gave her an option that would involve her going to a country she had wanted to visit all her life. It also involved leaving the aggravating circumstances she had found her career suddenly flung into. And, it gave her an opportunity to stay in law enforcement if at least on the fringe. Most of all, she would be away from the fear of being found with the disc that Kevin had politely dumped on her. She hoped being in Scotland would buy her enough free time to check out the symbols that were on the object and possibly solve the mystery surrounding the reason it was so important. Tidy, she thought. A true answer to her prayers for help.

The job of telling her family was not one she looked forward to, though. Since Jarrod and Joe were still there for their visit, she first sat Jarrod down and explained the offer she had. Then she told him why she had left her job. Leaving out the corruption aspect, she explained the fact that someone had been hired to work with her that she couldn't work with because, quite simply, she did not like him, and that she had not been consulted on his hiring. Jarrod was understanding, but visibly upset that his mother was going so far away for such a long period. But he thought the opportunity was a certainly exciting sounding and felt that the research was something that would be most respectable, especially coming through the University of St. Andrews. But he wanted her to promise to come back home as soon as she could and also insisted he would have to make a trip to visit her there since he had heard her talk about her former trip to England for so many years. He deserved that much out of this, she knew.

Next, Leigh told Joe about the job problems, the shortened version again, and her new opportunity in Scotland. After fully discussing the security issues surrounding a lady traveling by herself in a strange country, he only wanted to know if they would arrange for her to carry a gun in Scotland and he told her he would be happy to expedite getting her passport for her. Joe was never one to mince words, but Leigh could tell he was worried about her leaving on her own. He volunteered to come with her to see that she made it there safely. She, of course, insisted he was being too much of a doting big brother and reminded him she had always taken care of herself.

The last of the news breaking was for Della and Charlie, who took the news pretty hard. They both had tears in their eyes. She assured them that she still needed them to take care of things while she was gone. In fact, she could still pay them one-half their salaries for part-time work. Della said that she and Charlie were part of Leigh's family and they had enough monthly income from their respective pensions that they could afford to work for free if need be. That brought tears to Leigh's eyes. She only told them she was going to study in Europe in different areas. She did not want her ex-employer or anyone else for that matter, trying to try to track her down for anything. And, she really wanted to have some anonymity for a little while. So, she asked them, as well as Joe and Jarrod, to keep her whereabouts to themselves. However, within a few days, it became crystal clear of the need for discretion in keeping her destination a secret. In fact, it became a dire and absolute necessity.

It was one week to the day that Kevin called to report he was still alive that she began to feel as if eyes were on her. Jarrod and Jacob were back at Harvard, Della and Charlie took a few days off at Leigh's insistence, and Joe caught an official ride to New Orleans, presumably to do some more snooping before heading back to Atlanta. Alone again, it slowly seemed everywhere Leigh went she felt there was someone there: watching, listening, and waiting. Although she was out and about shopping daily and getting details for the trip tended to; when she was home, it was as if anywhere in the house she was being watched or listened to. She felt the eyes even when she was out in the pastures with the horses. In fact, she felt an odd sense that even her phone calls were being listened in on, even at the barn. Instead of giving in the creeping paranoia that was beginning to seep into her mental sensibilities, her thoughts and movements, she called her local "bug" expert law enforcement friend, a state drug investigator, to come check her house for any listening devices that may have been planted there.

When he finished the sweep, he told her that her telephone switch box was untouched and if anyone had bugged her house, they would have had to get past her security system. He checked the house, barn, and car. Nothing was found. But she was sure she was being watched. So, she stopped conversing about her trip plans unless it was in a room with loud music on. She knew what "boom" mikes could do. Even if her phones were not bugged, her voice could be picked up from two city blocks away with the latest technology in listening devices. It was scaring her enough to cause her to ask Joe for another passport under her maiden name. Not easy to do, he had told her, but then Joe liked challenges. She told him it was just a precautionary measure she wanted to have in case she needed it for safety purposes since she would be in a country without a gun. Now that he understood.

Two weeks later, with all her last-minute tasks completed, Leigh was on a flight leaving New Orleans to Newark, New Jersey. She gave Jarrod and Joe the barest of details of what her flight plans were. She told them she would have to contact them when she had a phone number and/or address and she swore them to secrecy from anyone asking where she was going to be. She did not think her family would ask any more questions if she gave them the partial truth about her not wanting to be found by her ex-employer.

Newark International Airport-APRIL 1998

Leigh exited the aircraft and headed straight to the nearest ladies' room. Dressed in a tan and white professional two-piece suit with low heeled shoes, her dark shoulder-length hair was pulled back and styled professionally, and she carried a tan crushable overnight bag on her arm. Inside the bathroom, she pulled out a bright flowery sun dress. Then she replaced her flat shoes tall heeled skinny sandals. She added a couple of extra layers of makeup, in bright colors. She then donned a red wig with a straw sun hat and glasses. She put the suit in a cosmetic tote that was in the overnight bag and then she tossed the bag in the corner of an empty stall. When she left the ladies' room, she was L. Solomon, heading for a different gate than Leigh Reid's ticket showed. L. Solomon's destination was Paris, France. As she sat in her first class seat on the jet that would carry her across the ocean for the second time in her life, she found herself smiling for the first time in two weeks hoping the disguise threw off those wandering eyes that she knew without any doubt were still following her.

London—Victoria Train Station

It wasn't easy to find her way around Pairs, but she spent a night there in a low-budget hotel under yet another name, paid cash, and then caught a small quick flight to London. She took a train from the airport and rode the inner-city 'tube' until she got to the Victoria train station. Constantly watching for signs that someone was following her, she went out on the streets of London to see the city she had not seen in twenty years. Back then, when she was still in school, the city was so much bigger than life. Her school responsibilities were negligible, and she had so much free time that exploring in and around London was fun and exciting. Now, she couldn't afford to stop long enough anywhere to even shop in case someone was still looking for her, so after only three hours, she reluctantly boarded the British Railway train to Edinburgh.

Spending the first several hours staring out the window of the fast moving train, Leigh wondered at the amount of people and cars on the busy English roads and towns. When she had been here before, there certainly hadn't been near so many of either. She had almost forgotten about the quirky roundabouts and the driving on the 'wrong' side of the road. As the pleasant images of the countryside whisked by her window, she began to nod off into a nap.

When the train steward approached Leigh dressed in the traditional British conductor's uniform, he nudged her gently, asking for her ticket. Startled, she jumped, then apologized and handed the ticket to him. He looked at it with a smile and said, "Miss, I think ya would enjoy the sleeper car, too. Ya have Berth 28 and I'd be happy to show ya where it is, if ya want." He spoke with a chipper Scottish accent. She was exhausted, so she headed behind the steward to a small, but tidy sleeping cabin with a toilet. She thanked him, and he commented, "Ya know, Miss, I could have supper sent in to ya. It won't be a bother." She thought she must have been a sight to him in the cold Scottish weather with her sundress still on.

"Thanks. I would appreciate it," she said and checked off her choices for her supper off a card he handed to her. After he left, she fell onto the cabin bed and sleep soundly until the knock on her door was followed with her supper. She found she was starving and ate everything on her plate. After supper and a shower, she was Leigh Reid again in another professional suit, with longer sleeves and heavier fabrics, preparing for the cooler temperatures.

Her flight to London from Paris had added a little over two extra hours to her original schedule. Hoping the flight to Paris had thrown off anyone that may have been watching her after her identity switch in Newark, she wasn't planning on staying in Edinburgh but a couple of days. She would then move on to St Andrews and into whatever accommodations that had been arranged for her, but she was still paranoid. The annoying little disc object was in her laptop carrying case. After watching her step for a couple of days, and making sure she didn't have that feeling of being watched like she had back home, maybe she would feel better about her safety and the disc's security enough to allow her to focus on the project she'd been hired to complete. It was dusk outside and Leigh's sleeper cabin window beckoned.

Her eyes fixated on the landscape whipping quickly by. Here she was on a train to Scotland, she began to actually realize. She wasn't really familiar with Scotland or its history, but as the train weaved its way on past the industrial landscapes of the Midlands and northern England, she was in Scotland before she knew. There was a gentle change in the view, but she truly wasn't expecting the sight of the Scottish countryside to be so beautiful. She could tell the country was more sparsely populated than the heavily populated cities of northern England.

Remembering a lawyer who came from Mississippi to hunt frequently in Scotland, she recalled his remarking that one day he would come hunting here and never go back to Mississippi. He loved the area and told her if she ever got the chance to go, the best part of Scotland was the Highlands. God's country, he had called it. She hadn't even a clue as to how to get to the Highlands, but she promised herself to arrange a tour into that area as soon as she was comfortable with her surroundings and new job.

Her new job. Well, okay, that was beginning to sound exciting. In a way. She smiled thinking about having a chance to see the country and to do something that sounded like a worthwhile project for law enforcement, and it was certainly in her comfort zone. If she could be shed of the foreboding that her nagging sixth sense gave her about being followed because of the disc, she could be happy to be on this train heading for a real change of pace. No adversarial courtroom skills required. Just a calm research project. That sounded almost yummy.

The sleek silver bullet-shaped train slid quietly into the Edinburgh station about 3:30am. Leigh exited looking carefully around before leaving and felt a little excitement at the prospect of being there. The station was brightly lit but very few people were traveling this time of night. She asked for a taxi to the hotel booked by Alan. Since it was very dark upon pulling out of the station, the streetlights gave a surreal glow to the old architecture of the city. As the taxi headed through the downtown streets, she almost nodded off trying to watch where they were going. Being truly affected by jet lag and the stresses of the last few days, Leigh quickly checked into her room at the hotel, an older one with only one check-in person at the desk and then, without taking time to see what her surroundings really looked like, and without taking a shower or even changing into bedclothes, she turned down the covers of the bed and crawled in and slept like a baby for ten solid hours.

    The sun peaked through the crack in the heavily draped windows of her hotel room and Leigh slowly woke to some very unfamiliar surroundings. A momentary mental block of where she was confused her until she realized she was in Edinburgh. There was an instant renewal of energy hitting her with the realization she had made it there. She had traveled quite a way in the last couple of days and now she had a whole day until she had to take another train into St. Andrews that night. She jumped up and showered. She was excited to think about wondering about the streets of Edinburgh. Her limited research on the city left her breathless prior to her trip. So much history and so much to see. Only one day was not near enough, she knew, but she had a few hours to at least browse a bit. She would be back for several trips, she truly hoped. After dressing, she went to the hotel restaurant for a short continental breakfast and then headed onto the busy shopping streets. She stopped in a small clothing store and purchased several woolen sweaters, a couple of woolen caps and scarves for her wardrobe. Then she visited a couple of museums on her way back to the train station. She picked up a few tourist brochures to read on the train that night. She would hopefully learn a little more about the area she would be living in for the duration of her project at the university.

    It was evening before she knew it and boarding time for the city of St. Andrews. It was to be a short trip and the last leg of her trip to her new beginnings. As she entered the train and found her seat, she had a sudden sensation of someone following her again. She looked behind her and saw nothing unusual. Of course, what are bad guys supposed to look like, she wondered? And just what was 'usual' in Edinburgh? There were a group of senior citizens sitting together with a tour guide fussing over them on one side of her car. In the back, there was a businessman in a suit with a laptop out. There was another couple of teenagers with backpacks on. Nothing too out of the ordinary, she figured. Trying to not get too antsy, she sat down and began reading a magazine. But as she thumbed through it, she felt eyes on her back again. Without turning this time, she got her purse and the laptop carrier and headed to the ladies' toilet. While in there, she contemplated her situation. Was she imagining things? She had never actually seen anyone following her or watching her back home. Was she just paranoid? Or were these people just that good at blending in? Whether she was imagining things or not, she remembered Kevin's warning and the lengths he had gone to fake his murder. She also remembered Joe's warnings about safety. No. Preventive measures should be taken, she decisively thought, and she exited the ladies' toilet. Heading in the opposite direction to another car, she sat in the first seat that was unoccupied. After just a few seconds passed, the door she had just come through opened with a nicely dressed gentleman coming in and sitting down near her. She hadn't noticed him before. He had a newspaper that he quickly covered his face with, so she could not really get a good look at him, but she sure felt that this was the one who had been watching her. She read her magazine a few more minutes and then got up again and went to the next car. This time, she left a couple of her brochures she had been reading on her seat as if to say, 'I'll be right back'. After sitting a few minutes in the next car up, the same gentleman that followed her into the last car opened the door into the new car. Leigh had her makeup mirror out and saw him looking until he saw her back. Then he casually sat back down in an empty seat behind her. Well, Leigh, she told herself, if there had been a doubt before, there wasn't one now. She was definitely being followed! The question she had to answer now and quickly was: What was she going to do about it?

    She nervously sat and waited until dusk had taken over the outside of the train. She got up and went to the toilet area. She looked to see if the man following her could see her enter or exit and she saw that the angle of his seat to the entrance of the toilet was blocked by the bar and bartender for the car. Inside, she decided she would make another identity change. Not knowing if anyone had seen her enter, she pulled out one of her new woolen sweaters and pulled it over her head. Then she donned a wool cap and threw a sweater around her throat and lower chin. She exited the toilet and, forgetting about her luggage stowed on the train, she took only her laptop carrier. She moved quickly and stood at the next exit door and upon the announcement of the next station, she quickly made a dash to exit the train from two cars up.

CHAPTER ELEVEN

He tracked her to the hotel in Edinburgh. But she had eluded him on the train. She was good at this cat and mouse game. But, fortunately, he was better. Of course, he'd been trained by the best of the best. His was a mission, not a job. He meant to get that disc with the sensitive information coded on it back no matter what. But he also was waiting for certain mercenaries to surface again. There was a payback necessitated by Raven's murder. They soon should smell the trap that they had been lured into by that Mr. Johnson, the prosecutor at the Blue Parrot that night in Hattiesburg. Right now, the mercenaries were probably assuming that the prosecutor wasn't actually dead but was being held by rival 'code' seekers. When they eventually are unable to find the code, he thought as he continued through the crowd looking for Ms. Reid, they will surely begin to look back on that night at that Blue Parrot bar, too. Then the pieces will fall into place for them. They would be on the same trail as he already was, but at least he was ahead of them at the moment.

The information on the leader of this mercenary group was sketchy: A neo—Nazi German, one that took the old ways to heart. His code name was "Kadar" and he was not too shabby on surveillance techniques himself. In fact, it was becoming known in the underworld of hired assassins and objective completion squads that Kadar would kill first and ask questions later, unless he thought he had a susceptible prospect for the various methods of torture that he could exercise with expertise and apparently, delight.

Unfortunately, she would be bait for Kadar since it was

inevitable that he would come. It was not going to go that far, though, he assured himself. It was his intention to make sure that he got to her before there was any rough stuff by Kadar or any of Kadar's employees. He was not the type to engage in Kadar's interrogation methods.

As he checked the last of the passengers exiting the train, he reminded himself that there wasn't anything she would be able to do with the 'code' anyway. It was written in the ancient symbolic Ogham language of the Celts, then it was encrypted by the best in the world, who also worked with his group. The chances of her getting past the encryption was nil. It was obvious her talents did not encompass espionage encryption methods. A smart lawyer, yes, but no spy. She was, quite simply, to him, a target. Okay, it was true she almost lost him in Newark. He figured Kadar would not be so quick to pick up on the passport change or the airline change. But he recognized her gait when she came out. That was something no one could fake. He'd liked looking at that set of legs, too. It was hard not to. Not a bad way to spend his days, actually. He had quite enjoyed tailing her tail, he mused to himself. But she had been a clever one with the disguise, along with having a striking appearance. He had to match wits with her to stay up. He and his men had spread out around the hotel and waited in London. They watched and knew when she boarded the train to Edinburgh. They had followed her in the city and stayed with her on the train to St. Andrews. But they had not counted on her exiting before getting to St. Andrews, which was her final destination. Now the target was lost to them as well as Kadar.

Taking a bus from the seaside town that she found herself in after her hasty exit off the train, Leigh took a bus and made it into the town center of St. Andrews about 6:00 am. As the bus slowed for parking, she thought she had stepped back into another time when she saw the rich ancient stone buildings and the large stone wall that must have once surrounded the seaside of the city. It was built of enormous tan stones with wood gated archways built into it. The main cobblestone street that ran in front of the center of town opened into an historian's dream of architecture. There was a ruined castle, a ruined abbey, and more stone walls that looked imposing enough to the normal visitor, much less the number of conquerors that must have tried to take the city at various times. St. Andrews was a bay city on the eastern shore of Scotland. The blustery North Sea was the only thing between it and the once feared Viking boat warriors as Leigh knew from her reading on the train. The wind was chilly to newcomer, but as Leigh walked around the town, absorbing the place, she warmed and began to get a feel for the enormous history that was here.

As she turned into the shopping area of town, she found there were storefront shops with everything from Celtic jewelry to harsh weather clothes, antiques to Danish modern furniture. The town was just waking up and there was an open air market that included wares of fresh vegetables, fresh meat, and what she really needed, fresh hot coffee. She grabbed a cup from one of the market vendors and then sat on a bench to watch the city begin its day. She could imagine the weather did get cold here, since it was in the 40s and it was April. That was hot time already in Mississippi. She also learned from her reading of the tourist brochures that St. Andrews had been the birthplace of golfing. Well, she probably ought to send a golfing souvenir to the Judge back home, she thought wryly. Wow, that seemed like another world away now. But she could think of several appropriate comments to go on the card that would go along with souvenir. She had a raw anger about her having to leave her job. But the memory of how it had ended was beginning to fade since it seemed as if her life there was far in the past now even though it was only a few short weeks since she left her office. She was beginning to believe she was a different person from the old Leigh, mainly because she was sitting on a bench some six thousand miles away from what had been her home her whole life.

From where she sat in front of a beautiful old church, she concentrated again on her brochures. She was well immersed in the city's history before she looked at her watch. It was 10:00am, and she hadn't even checked in at the University! Looking at her map, she walked quickly to the University gate, an imposing brass monstrosity that exuded class and history. The main reception had stone walls, floors and arched stone ceilings. While marveling at the interior and hopefully not looking too open-mouthed in awe, she did not notice that a young lady came in.

"May I help you?" asked the young lady with the Scottish lilt in her voice.

Leigh turned and saw the lovely young girl with long straight red hair staring at her with a smile of genuine interest. She was dressed in red tartan plaids and looked inquisitively at Leigh. She was most probably a student.

"Yes. My name is Leigh Reid. I'm here to see Professor Flackerty in the Criminology Department. Am I in the right building?" Leigh wasn't sure whether he would be in, since he had no idea when she would actually arrive in town, but she had promised to check in this morning.

"Oh, right! Ms. Reid! So nice to meet you! I'm Gabriella McKennah, Professor Flackerty's clerk for the semester, at your service." The girl held out her hand to shake, which Leigh took and gave a small shake. She continued, "I've heard about your research project It sounds smashing! I'm an architectural history student here, but since I work for the Professor, I have picked up a bit on criminology. I am sorry, but the Professor won't be back in until tomorrow about 10:00am. If it isn't a bother, I can set an appointment for you to see him in the morning. I am sure he will be glad you made it here."

"Okay. That will be fine, Miss, uh, McKennah? I'll see him and you, I assume, then. Back here at this spot?"

"Call me Gabby, Ms. Reid. Everyone does. Yes, here is fine. I will try to meet you again tomorrow if my class schedule does not change. If not, the Professor will have someone here to show you the way to his office. By the way, do you have your lodgings sorted out?" Leigh had already heard the words "sorted out" so much since she arrived that she smiled when she heard them again.

"Y'all sure do an awful lot of 'sorting out' of things out around here." Leigh smiled feeling already comfortable with the jab at the colloquialisms with Ms. McKennah.

"I love your accent! You must be 'Deep South' American, right?" Gabby's eyes were a deep blue and they twinkled as she talked to Leigh.

"Mississippi. Yes, which is about as deep as 'Deep South' gets. I like your Scottish accent, too. In fact, I think it's a prettier accent that the British. Oh, you asked about my lodgings. I plan on booking a B&B not too far out of town. I'm heading there now to check it out." Leigh did not want to give anyone any details about her lodgings because she had no clue where she would be staying, but also, she thought the less anyone knew of her comings and goings, the better. At least until she knew if she had ditched her follower from the train.

"Well, if it's not 'just right, y'all just come on back here now and we'll 'figure somethin' out for you." Gabby said in her best imitation of a Southern drawl.

Laughing, Leigh said, "Nice try, Gabby. Needs a little work, but by the time I'm through here, I'll have you speaking like a true Southern Belle!" They both laughed then, and Leigh said, "See you soon, I'm sure." Gabby smiled back as Leigh left the building.

Finding a car rental agency in town, she rented a car in Todd Weems' name and headed to the tourist information center where she was told she could book her new accommodations.

While waiting, she thought about meeting Gabby McKennah. She had been so bright and cheery. Her mood was elevated from being around her. She hoped to see more of her while she worked through the University.

After a short chat with the tourist information hostess, Leigh secured a suite at a Bed and Breakfast lodge that she understood was rarely booked by the center. The farm surrounding the home had too many animal noises for most of the clients that were referred there. The suite was secured in Leigh's brother's name this time. The bill was to be forwarded to the University for payment.

A couple of stops in a pharmacy and clothes shop yielded Leigh a few things she would absolutely need the next couple of days.

It took a few minutes for her to orientate herself to the driving of the car from the right hand side and on the left side of the road. A couple of near misses and a tense moment at the first roundabout and then she was off and running. Following the directions she had been given, it took her about twenty minutes of driving in the rural countryside before she saw a faded sign on the road that said, "McDavid's Farm, Bed and Breakfast--Turn Here" and she turned onto no more than a dirt road. The drive went off the road until she saw a two-story box-shaped stone farmhouse. It was clean but obviously not a mansion. A working farm, to be sure, but it looked quaint and welcoming.

She drove up and went to the whitewashed door and knocked with the brass knocker. A plumpish lady in a faded floral apron opened the door. She waived Leigh into the reception area and smiled as she dried her hands off with a kitchen towel. "Ya mus be da guest dat called earlier," she said in a thickened Scottish accent. Leigh had to listen closely to understand her.

"Ah, yes. I'm Ms. Reid."

"Very nice to meet you, Ms. Reid!" Funny how the lady tried to pronounce her words more carefully after hearing Leigh's American accent, Leigh smiled.

"I have ya room all ready for ya. It's up the stairs here, if ya will just follow me, please." The stairs were narrow and steep up to the second floor, but once up, the hallway was wide and light shone through windows at each end. Leigh was shown her room and she was amazed at the cleanliness and homey feeling it exuded.

"I've put fresh towels in the loo fer ya, if you need to shower before supper dis evening. We have fresh mutton and parsnips soup. If you wanna eat with us, we serve about 6:00 pm. If you'd rather I bring you a plate up, just let me know. There's a phone on the nightstand, and we ask ya just let us know if you make a long-distance call. And," she added as she opened the lace curtains, "Breakfast is at 5:30am, a bit early, I know, but me and me husband is out and about by 6:00am every morning tending to the dairy cows. Guess, that's about it. If you need anything else, just call me. Oh, I am Doris, Doris McDavid."

Leigh thanked her hostess, and with a trip or two to her car, she picked up her new purchases of clothes and toiletries from St. Andrews. She left her luggage on the train in her hasty exit before, so her wardrobe was a bit scampi at best. Settling in within a few minutes, she looked out her window and felt suddenly very tired. She sat on the bed and it was so soft that she laid down to rest for a little while. Her eyes closed and it was way after supper time before she awoke. Feeling guilty for not eating with her host family, she went down to apologize.

"Awe, ya don't need to worry, lass," said Doris when she saw Leigh still looking sleepy as she wandered into the kitchen area.

"I've got fresh bread, gammon and cheese for a sandwich, if ya like." Leigh knew that meant 'ham' sandwich and she accepted one gratefully with a glass of fresh milk and headed back to her room. After wolfing it down, sleep found her again.

The next morning started with the early breakfast at 5:30am. Leigh was up and feeling very refreshed after catching up on sleep. Hot fried eggs, toast, baked beans, and fresh orange juice were served her after she went downstairs and sat at the large wooden table in the middle of the kitchen. Doris and her husband, Ben, came in to say good morning and then left her to wander about the house. She noted a footpath that wound through the back part of the farm and she got her jacket and headed out for fresh air and a walk.

The wind was brisk again and she walked with a quick pace to warm up her blood. The path headed down hill toward the ocean. The North Sea was calmly lapping against the bottom of the cliff where Leigh stood. She was amazed that she was actually there. The North Sea! A loud and almost angry sounding surf hit below. How imposing it would have been to have seen the great Viking ships that would have been crossing here to reap havoc on the land. Caught up in the moment, Leigh noticed a round building on a point further down the path. It looked old and abandoned. Made of what were massive stones, it reminded Leigh of a castle turret sitting on the ground. She was so absorbed in the view, that she didn't see the two men watching her from a short distance away. They already identified her and called into the Keeper. Relaying she checked into the McDavid Bed and Breakfast, they confirmed that she had not met with anyone that morning.

The Keeper was very relieved. He was on his way to their location to personally stay on surveillance throughout the next couple of days. The men were congratulated for their find and told to wait until he personally relieved them.

At 10:00 am, Leigh promptly entered Professor Flackerty's office. Gabby had not been there to greet her this morning. There was another girl that escorted Leigh in.

"My goodness, Ms. Reid! You don't look like the ol' hag that Todd Weems made you out to be!" The man said laughingly as he came toward her from behind his desk. "Hi! I'm Alan Flackerty. Please come in and join me for tea or coffee, whichever you prefer." Alan Flackerty was a tall man with small intelligent eyes behind wire-rimmed glasses. She guessed his age to be around 54. He was dressed in the classic tweed jacket and dark brown trousers Leigh had noticed on most gentlemen around the University. The only deviation from the standard dress she had been seeing on men was the banded collared shirt. Quite the American style, she thought. He had blonde hair with freckles on his face. She decided he was a genuinely nice guy after a few pleasantries were exchanged.

"Now, then. Let's see. I have taken the liberty of recruiting the local constables that were active in criminal investigations for this and the surrounding counties for your project," he said as they sat in two old brown leather chairs in front of his desk. "Although the crime in Scotland hasn't risen as fast as it is in England; there is a growing concern regarding illegal drug trafficking. It's been increasingly finding its way into our rural landscape, but we do have the normal thefts, mostly petty in nature. The criminal entrepreneurs here are virtually non-existent except for the drug dealers. That's been largely due to the use of the waterways and the canal boats. You'll find all the particulars with the constables." Flackerty smiled as he said, "Ya know, other than the drugs and the crimes associated with them, we've not had too much to worry about since the last of the whiskey steels were dismantled in the Highlands."

That led to Alan launching into the story of Scotch whiskey that first came out of the Highlands at least as far back as medieval times. This story went on as they moved from the University over to a pub near the University for a lunch. Sitting in the small room warmed by a coal fire, with low lights and an Irish tune being played over the speakers, Alan told her that the word "whiskey" had come from a Gaelic term, usige beatha, which meant "water of life". "No one that goes into the Highlands couldn't be affected by its pure air, the quite lochs, so few people, but most of all, by its history. You know, the inaccessibility to outsiders gave it a mysterious reputation," Alan told her as he settled in to tell her the rest of the whiskey story.

"The first English malt tax on the whiskey production

in 1713 gave way to many illicit stills popping up in remote areas. Revenue officers got a taste of the Highlander wit and cunning for years. Smuggling was such a profession that even royalty would indulge in the Scottish whiskey trade because it was so tasty. The illusive Highlanders made well with the illicit trade all the way until 1823 when a new Parliamentary act was passed that made it easier to produce legally than illegally. That was when the distilleries that are famous now were born. The last of the illegal stills eventually phased out. They went from numbering well over 10,000 to as little as six in 1874."

Alan was so well versed in this particular bit of Scottish history that the story was told on past lunch when a hands-on lesson of the best of the Scotch brands now brewed in the country was given. She began to feel intrigued about the people known as the Highlanders. And, after several taste tests were offered, she felt lightheaded.

Alan was explaining that he had an extensive repertoire of Celtic and Viking history, and he offered to be a temporary tutor to her at her leisure on those subjects.

She found that it was 4:00 pm by the time she checked her watch again. In addition to the knowledge gained about Scottish whiskey history, as well as knowledge of the drink itself, albeit too much, she also had enough notes on her research project to start her lecture outline for the first meeting with the local law enforcement designees Alan contacted. Her topic of research and presentation was to be 'Cross-Bordering Intel' for the entire UK. Her starting point would be addressing the constables for the immediately surrounding counties. She agreed to meet with Alan again within the week with her proposed guidelines. Feeling excited, a bit drunk, and pumped up with anticipation for the project, she almost did not notice Gabriella McKennah in the front office of the criminal justice department as she was leaving.

"Ms. Reid, I hope you had a good meeting with the Professor." Gabby came toward Leigh smiling. She was dressed today in a brown knit pantsuit, with her red hair piled up on top of her head and secured with a shining copper hair ornament. She looked quite the lady as compared to the school girl look the last time Leigh had met her.

"Yes, not only did I get a local history lesson in Scottish whiskey, I'm afraid to admit, but I also have enough starting points for my research project here. So, how are you? Do you have classes here in the mornings?"

"Yes, and I try to be in here every afternoon for a couple of hours. How are you faring with your new accommodations?"

"Fine, thanks. By the way, I found an interesting site out by the ocean near where I am staying and I wonder, since you study architecture, if you would know anything about it? It looks to me like it's from the medieval period and its round like a turret. It has only one room in it, though, and I couldn't find any signs of there ever being any more rooms attached to it."

"Sounds like a bathhouse. They were used for several hundred years as places to change clothes in and to have meals prepared while the ladies would sunbathe. Of course, sunbathing here was never like with 'heat'. Never much of that here. But the fresh air and the ocean would also bring out ladies to sit and enjoy picnics. There aren't many left intact, though. They were abandoned after the spa towns started being built. Of course, there are the larger round buildings usually found on the coast and islands. Those are much larger and older. They are known as 'broches'. You like the old architecture in our country?"

"Yes, indeed. I'm an old house lover from way back. I have a restored antebellum plantation house in Mississippi. I love to see old ones come back to life. But, of course, old in Mississippi is only about 150 years. Here, I'm overwhelmed because old is what, 800 years?"

Gabby laughed. "That's close. I live in one built back in the 1100's. It's been kept up over the years very well, though.

My dad has done the last major renovations on it."

"Sounds wonderful." Leigh glanced at her watch again. "Look at the time. I'll be back next week, and maybe we can talk some more. I have to run now."

"Oh, Ms. Reid, I don't mean to pry, but the Professor told me that you have some experience in solving crimes as well as prosecuting them. Is that right?"

"Well, I guess you could say I've had some luck in helping put motives and evidence together where it tells me a story. That isn't really hard when it comes from years of experience in law enforcement and prosecution. Why do you ask?"

"Oh, I was just wondering. Sounds like you have had an exciting career. Maybe you could tell me about it sometime."

"No problem. I'd love to visit some more with you. I will see you next week, then."

Back at the B&B, Leigh called into Joe's secure number.

His voice boomed out, "Where have you been? I thought you were going to check in before now!' Joe sounded upset.

"Well, I'm sorry, Joe, but I'm just getting settled in and I haven't had a chance to make calls, why? You sound really upset. What's wrong?"

"Well, sister, it's your home, Marlow. I'm sorry, there's been a break-in there and it's been, well, ransacked."

CHAPTER TWELVE

"The horses are okay," Joe was saying, trying to reassure her, "but the barn as well as the house has been gone through. I hate to have to break the news, especially when you are so far away and just getting settled. But knew you had to know."

Leigh said, "Yes, you're right to call. I am shocked, though. Give me a second."

"The local deputy contacted Della, who called me," Joe continued. "She says there's nothing really missing other than your VCRs and small radio. The family antiques from Mom and Dad are fine. Must have been a drug addict's way of trying to get something to turn into cash quickly. Don't worry about it. I think everything is under control. Della says she will be staying on a few days to see to the cleanup and file on the insurance for you. I told her to do whatever she thought. That is okay with you, isn't it?"

"Right. Yeah, sure. That is fine. Thanks so much for letting me know about it, Brother."

"You're welcome. So, how are things going over there? Just exactly where are you? You know, I was feeling really disconnected when I couldn't reach you by phone anywhere!"

"Yes, I know you were. I'm not permanently settled yet, but I promise when I am, you'll know first. I'll call you in a day or so to check in again. Sorry, but I just don't know about where they are putting me for the duration, but I should know soon. Don't worry, Joe, I'm fine!"

"Okay, but I'd feel so much better if you were toting, you know."

Me, too, she thought and said, "Talk soon!"

"Oh my God!" she said to herself after hanging up. Now she was sure that they had learned she had the blasted disc. That meant the people following her earlier weren't sure, but watching in case they what? Couldn't find it at her home? Who were these people that they could cross the ocean with her and just wait? What she really wanted to know was: Did they know where she was now at this particular moment. And if they did, where could she go to get away from them before they decided now she had the disc with her? And, most importantly, what would they do to her to get it back?

It was very reassuring that they had found her again. And, still no sign of Kadar's men yet. They are slower than I thought, the Keeper said to himself. He was watching to see who she would be meeting with. He had no clue as to why she was in Scotland. A day or so of following would help solve that mystery. She was getting pretty close to the location identified on the disc, though. Having the disc was one thing. Finding out what it meant was another. Her having it and trying to break the symbolic code on it was the additional risk he did not need. But he was still sure that there was no way she could break the message. It had too many twists and turns in it. He was satisfied that he could just watch for now. Then, if things went according to plans, she would be the bait for Kadar. The Keeper was cold and calculating in this regard, since his operative, Raven, had given up his life for the secrets held in the message. Calculating, yes, but there was something about this woman that nagged the Keeper about her safety as well as her usefulness.

All night Leigh worried about her home. It was midnight in Mississippi. 6:00am in Scotland. She wanted to find out more about the break-in. She couldn't afford the risk of calling home, though, not knowing who might still be watching and listening at home. Besides, she knew better than to think there would be any evidence that could lead to the identification of the burglar. It was clear from Joe's comments that he or they were professionals. They tried to make it look like a burglary. But Leigh knew better than to think it was just a burglary. She figured it was a simple fishing expedition for the disc and that by now they were on to her. They had advanced past the "Kevin Johnson has it" theory. Whoever 'they' were, she knew someone had been following her on the train. A global chase apparently was on and she was the targeted 'it'. Someone was there that night and saw her and the apparently exchange with Kevin that night at the club in Hattiesburg. No, of course there wouldn't be fingerprints from the break in. There wouldn't be any witness. There would be nothing leading local law enforcement officials to them. Realizing this, she decided it would be best if she didn't call. But, it was time that she made new plans about what to do next.

She spent the next two days reading everything she could find in the local library in St. Andrews and at the University about ancient symbolic languages all over the world. She felt conspicuous everywhere she went, and she watched the cars and people behind her, in front of her and all around her constantly. Her head would jerk up every time someone would enter a room. There was absolutely no reason to believe if she saw one of the followers, that she would recognize him/her. But she looked anyway. Hating to risk being out in public for any length of time, she still needed to find out something about the symbols on the disc while she could.

After some hours of pouring into history books, her research found that the closest kin to the symbols were of Celtic and Gaelic origin. These were apparently a part of Scottish and Irish history. She couldn't find a dictionary of the symbols, though. It appeared that there had only recently been a compilation of what was termed the 'Ogham' inscriptions, and they were believed to have been used by Druid priests for divination and secret messaging purposes. There was no translation available from what Leigh could find. After all her efforts of researching, they were still only symbols to her. And, it was apparent she wouldn't be able to explain them on her own.

"Damn disc!" she muttered to herself as she left the library with the realization, she was up that proverbial creek again without a paddle and the long waterfall to her death was just ahead.

CHAPTER THIRTEEN

The second afternoon back at the McDavid's, Leigh was out walking on the beach front again. She had her hood pulled up around her face mainly to hide her face but also because the rain began as soon as she got to the sandy area of the beach. After walking a little while, the rain began to come down in sheets. She ran to the old ruined building she had visited earlier for shelter. The sky darkened even more, and she began to wonder if it was such a good idea coming out for a walk after all. She sat on a flat stone in a sheltered area of the round bathhouse and tried to wait the rain out. It began to get colder and she started shivering from the damp cold.

"Well, a fine mess you are in," she said to herself. There was a dread creeping in about her situation with the disc. What to do with it was the question she couldn't answer. If she called Joe now and admitted to having it, he'd fly over and get it and her. What would that accomplish, really? She'd lose her job for one thing. Joe would absolutely put his foot down about having to protect her from whoever was following her. Well, that would also get him involved and to what end? If Federal agents were involved, couldn't they get to him just as easy as they could her? If the bad guys were not Feds, but some covert group that was hired to retrieve the disc, then couldn't they get to Joe as well as her? His ATF job was not a top-secret job. Well, she thought as she shivered even more from the cold and the anxiety that was building up inside her, she just should toss it in the sea. That would be the end of it, then, right? Not now, silly, she admitted to herself. They know who you are and that you could have the thing. Even if you ditched it, you'd still be a target. For what you may have learned from it or just because you are in the way of finding it. The situation was grim. Not having a clue as to her next move, she began to get up and try to head back out of the bathhouse in the rain.

Suddenly, she heard someone coming in a hurry toward the building. The sounds of the splashes in the standing rainwater made her turn toward where they were coming from and her heart began to pound from fear. She looked up just in time to see a tall man slide into the building without any rain gear on. He was soaked as thoroughly as she. He smiled as he saw her and said in an educated Scottish accent, "Sorry, miss, I thought I was the only one that was brave enough to be out on a day like this! It was actually a nice day a few minutes ago." He looked up as he tried to shake a little of the rain off his clothes. "You don't mind if I share the shelter with you until it slackens up, do you?"

Leigh had been shocked at first by the intrusion, then she began to get nervous that this person was completely unknown to her and could be any one of several that had been following her. She started to leave out the opening when the man said, "I can start a fire in the old fireplace to take the chill off. You really shouldn't get out there in that downpour unless you want to invite a nasty cold. Do you mind sharing the fire for a few minutes?" He looked at her then with a sincere face and a not bad looking one either, she thought.

"Ah, okay, fine, I guess. But don't you think the rain will stop before you could get a fire going? And, I can't linger too long. It is getting late." Leigh looked at the man a little closer. He had on a tan dress shirt, a brown wool jacket, khaki pants and a tartan plaid tie. He looked like someone who had been in an office or a business meeting. Surely, he was harmless enough. Then she saw he had long hair pulled back in a ponytail. She had seen several Scottish men with long hair since she had arrived, so she wasn't unnerved like she would have been in Mississippi seeing the long hair.

He was not looking at her while she checked him out.

He was looking out at the sky and then back at the fireplace. "Oh, I think this rain will stay on for at least another hour. I'll just get some dry sticks from under the overhang right outside. It won't take but a moment to get the fire going." He ran out then and she watched him gather the wood. Seemed nice enough, she thought. If he was going to try anything, surely, he would have already. But, best to always be on guard, she reminded herself.

"Here. These will do nicely," the man said as he came in and busied himself starting the fire. Leigh watched him move with experienced hands stacking the wood and getting smaller limbs under the larger ones. In a few minutes the room started warming up and the light brightened it up so she could she her shelter mate a little better.

He stood up and smiled at her. "There now, a little warmth will do us some good, I should think. So, I detected an American accent, miss. Are you here on holiday?" That was the natural assumption that anyone made when they heard her talk here.

"No. I am working here. Do you live close by?" Leigh did not want to offer too much information on herself. Better for her to find out about him.

"Actually, I live up in the higher elevations, but I come down here quite a bit on business and to play golf. I take walks on this beach ever so often because I don't like crowds. There are very few dog walkers out here normally. What type of work are you engaged in here in our fair country?"

"Nothing special, just some paid research." She was silent again.

"What type of research? Something at St. Andrews?" he asked as he backed up to the fire and then he smiled again. All Leigh could think of was he had a 'drop dead' charismatic way about him. And his charming smile was warm and inviting, almost comforting. Even so, she was still very guarded about her being in a confined area with a strange man, one that could be trying to get the disc.

"Yes, some very boring research. I just took the job to have a chance to learn more about your 'fair' country." Don't give him much information, Leigh, she said to herself, no matter how charming or good-looking he is. Damn, he had piercingly blue eyes.

He leaned down and poked at the fire with a stick. The flames lighted up the corner where he was and when he turned back around, he looked at her with his very blue eyes. She began to feel a little uncomfortable with the silence and the look. In fact, she thought it best to not tarry here very much longer. She got up and looked out the door again.

'I have a car not too terribly far off this footpath if you would like to make a run for it. I could drop you wherever you need." He was trying to be a gentleman, she thought, but she didn't want to get too friendly with him or anyone else for that matter since she knew sooner or later, she would become a an active target again. The freshness of the news about the break-in at Marlow was also fine-tuning her aloofness.

"Thanks, but I think I can manage now. It has let up a little bit." She turned and looked at him and extended her hand to him. "Thanks for the fire. It was nice," she said as he took her hand and shook it gently and held it for a second. No sparks there, she said to herself as she felt her face beginning to redden with a feminine shyness she hadn't experienced in a very, very long time.

"Are you sure you don't want a ride? It wouldn't be any trouble. And, I won't bite,' he said with that smile again.

Feeling the moment becoming too much for her with this stranger, she just nodded politely and then ducked into the rain and ran. She didn't want to look back at him. He'd left quite an impression on her and she wasn't going to encourage anything as she knew it was crazy to even think about such things at this point and particular time in her life.

She was back at the B&B in a few minutes, but she was soaked through and through. She went to her room, stripped down and got her bathtub full of hot water to warm up in.

In the bed before she fell asleep, she thought of the blue-eyed man that was so nice. He didn't even introduce himself to her. Nor did he ask her name. Too bad, she thought. Of course, she didn't volunteer anything either. But, she would have liked to at least known his name. In fact, she found herself strangely wanting to know a lot more about him as she dozed off with his image in her thoughts.

    The next morning with her map in hand, and an eye on the rear view mirror, she traveled around the area exploring the small villages around St. Andrews. When she felt sure she wasn't being followed, she checked out a couple of small hotels, B&B's and a resort. She drove pretty much all over the county of Fife. The picturesque seaside villages were so quaint and well-preserved; she was enjoying seeing more of her surroundings. She walked the streets of Pittenweem, Anstruther, Elle and Leven. They all sprung up with the North Sea fishing industry centuries ago. She walked the street of one of the towns with its whitewashed and pastel colored stores lining up like a picture from a storybook from long ago. The sounds and smells of the fishing populace was oddly calming to her as she stopped in a small pub for lunch. Fresh haddock and chips. Quite the quintessential fare, she thought. It was great.

    The trip helped her establish a working idea of the county's layout for her research project, too. Plus, since she was going to have to stay on the move now, she wanted to plan where her next accommodations would be. It was best to continue to move around, she knew now that she was sure she would be found if she stayed anywhere very long. She was totally unaware that they had already found her. They had more men watching and they were now following every move she made. She was definitely not going to be out of their sight again.

    The next day she was back at St Andrew's for another

visit with Alan. The meeting took an hour. She gathered several books to take back to her room to read. She would spread the materials out with an idea of getting organized for the project. But her guard was still up while she was trying to get her thoughts on the project as she headed from the University.

He went in after she left and asked questions at the reception at St. Andrews. The secretary thought the well-dressed gentleman was extremely good-looking and very familiar looking to her. There was no reason not to tell the nice man about the American lady. She was a research associate working with the Criminology Department under Alan Flackerty's direction.

The phone rang in her room at the farm. Leigh looked at it. It rang again. Only Joe had her number. Becoming a bit paranoid after the news of the break-in, she picked up and listened before saying anything.

"Hello, Ms. Reid? Are you there? It's Gabriella McKennah from St. Andrews." As if Leigh would not have recognized her voice, she thought and smiled.

"Yes, how are you?" How did she know where she was staying, Leigh wondered. She didn't recall telling anyone at the University.

"I hate to bother you. Oh, and I found you through the Tourist Information Centre. I hope you don't mind, but I needed to ask you something." Gabby sounded very serious.

"Shoot! What's up?" Leigh was decidedly curious and concerned too that she left a trail a student could find.

'I, well, my father and I have a proposition for you. I know this is out of the blue, but he asked me just this morning if I knew of any new source of private criminal investigators in the area that he could hire. You see, he has an unsolved crime, a very old one. He says he needs a fresh, qualified investigator to look at the case. I told him about you and your experience. He has asked me to propose you consult with him on the case. Do you have time to do something like this while you are working at the University?" Gabby voice was hopeful sounding.

Well, Leigh was not expecting this! Investigate a crime? How could she get involved in something else with the other matters on her plate at the moment?

"Well, I –," she started to decline but was hesitating while trying to think about the request.

"Ms. Reid, he's been through a number of sources, public and private in years past. He is actually quite desperate to have a new set of eyes on the matter and he is willing to pay very well for it. Mainly because in addition to the crime being a rather old one, it is also one of, how shall I say, a sensitive nature? It involves a family member. Will you consider it, Ms. Reid? I'd really like for you to come to visit our home, anyway. You can see some real Highland historical places where we live. It's a way out of any big cities, but it's really a beautiful area. Please?"

That 'Highland' word again. Hmmm. Okay, that made it tempting enough. She really did want to visit that part of Scotland. Up until now, she had had no plans or reasons to go. Darned if she had insecurities about the request, the idea of traveling won over her hesitation. And, she really appreciated Gabby's interest in asking her.

"Well, first of all, please call me 'Leigh'. You make me feel ancient. Secondly, well, it is an interesting proposal. I'm not a private investigator, though. Thirdly, I probably could use the distraction from my other work here, even though I'm just getting started with it. And, finally, I cannot even begin to promise I could help. But I could try." She liked the idea of a challenge, one that did not involve software programs and reading, ad nauseam, for her current research project. And, it might give her a break away from the seemingly constant need to watch her back.

"You name your fee. My father will cover it and all expenses. He said if you accepted, he would like you to come to our home, though, right away to review his materials he's collected over the years. He travels a lot and thought since he travels a lot and his schedule permitted it, perhaps this weekend? Do you think you could do that? He really is anxious for someone to take a stab at the case." She laughed at herself. "Oh, I'm sorry, but that is so funny! No pun intended since the crime involves a sort of a stabbing. Oh, and he did say it you accepted, that he could prepare your accommodations at our home, since he thought it would be better if you stayed with us rather than travel back and forth from Inverness. Will that be a problem?"

Well, it was Wednesday afternoon, and as Leigh thought about her normal schedule she was trying to establish for the University work and her abnormal schedule of trying to keep an eye on the disc and her life, she thought she could try to go on Friday morning. "A stabbing you say. Well, it does sound interesting from the get-go. Yes, I will accept, and you will have to give me travel directions. How do I get there?"

"Great! Travel is no problem. You can go with me, if you'd like, since I'm going home Friday afternoon as I do on most Fridays. Is there a convenient time for you? It takes about 4 hours from here by auto. Of course, you can also travel by rail on the West Highland Rails. It's a lovely train ride, but you would miss the pleasure of my company!" she laughed again with addictive effervescent quality. "Oh, since you will stay at our place, you might want to know it is actually more than a bit of out of the way. No towns really close to it. Just in case you wanted to shop or anything like that prior to going."

The more remote, the better, thought Leigh. "I remember you said you had a 1100 AD house, Gabby. Sure, I'd love to go with you this weekend. What do I bring to wear? Is it cooler up there than here?"

"Oh, yeah. Quite cooler. Bring a coat, long all-weather boots, some warm gloves and a woolly hat. We hike a lot. It might dip below freezing. It always gets cooler in the mountains. Anything you don't have, though, I am sure we can provide. My wardrobe is quite extensive. I keep more clothes there than here at school. Great, well I'll just let Father know soon as we ring off. He'll be pleased you have agreed to come."

"Ok. I don't know that I'm what he needs, but I'll certainly 'take a stab' as you said earlier." They both giggled at the turn of the phrase. "Can we meet around 3:00 pm at the Green Lion Hotel lobby in town?" Leigh knew she didn't want Gabby making a trip out to the McDavid's Farm when she wasn't going to be there after today.

"Done! See you then." Gabby clicked off.

Leigh's driving on the wrong side of the road skill was improving. She was taking another step toward trying to keep ahead of anyone that might be following her. She took the rental care for a drive down to the nearest city where there was a small rental car return kiosk. On her drive, she took several turns and then stopped a couple of times to check the traffic behind her. She was not sure, but she thought there were a couple of vehicles that kept showing back up in the rearview mirror. Leaving the car at the kiosk, she took a long walk trying to determine if someone was following her about the town. After a while, she ducked into a public bathroom on a street where lots of people were milling around. Some were shopping. Others were eating. Lots of children were being pushed about in strollers. Total mania like she had hoped. In the public toilet, she went with several other women. A few minutes later, after the use of her handy dandy makeup pouch, out she came. This time she looked like a really old woman with wrinkled skin. She had picked up theatrical makeup to make the eyes and neck to appear old. A white wig. A baggy flowered straight shift skirt. A worn jacket. A scarf over her head and Granny shoes to top off the outfit. She was crouched over taking really slow steps with a cane. She had her clothes she changed out of, her computer and research materials in a rolling shopping cart that she had carried in a plastic shopping bag. She would pass for a Scottish lass of say, about 75-80 years old, she hoped. And what a stellar performance on her part to boot as she sauntered by the watchful eyes of the Keeper and his men.

She boarded a bus, tickets prepaid by credit cards in her maiden name, to London Links Hotel, about midway back to St. Andrews and she made a quick change again in the ladies' toilet near the reception area. There were enough patrons in the hotel to make her not so noticeable in her entry and exit. This time there was a pair of tight knit black jogging pants, a turtle-neck ribbed long-sleeved white sweater, her hair was put up in a French twist, and square-toed platform shoes that was apparently an essential item in any respectable UK girl's wardrobe. Into a cab she slid and instructed the driver to take her to Kilconquhar Resort. When she arrived, she waited for an hour in the resort pub before checking in. Apparently, neither of the two vehicles had managed to follow her.

CHAPTER FOURTEEN

Her new home, for who knew how long, was an independent Scandinavian lodge with 2-bedrooms, a bath with a Jacuzzi, a large kitchen, and a den with a large stone fireplace. She pre-selected it under Flackerty's name again and paid cash for the first week. The management ordered and delivered groceries from the local village, and she found she had a nice selection of fresh vegetables, cheeses, wines, coffee, tea, milk and eggs. The village butcher sent several selections of meat cut to Leigh's prearranged specifications. She was essentially prepared to not leave the resort for several days.

She arrived Thursday evening after checking out of the B&B, and thanking her hosts, whom she had ending up really enjoying being around the short time she stayed there, but they had inquiring minds about where she was going next, for which she didn't respond. In case anyone started asking them questions about her, she certainly didn't want them to have any knowledge of her new whereabouts.

Closing all the curtains, she first started a crackling fire, and then went into the kitchen to fix her supper. There was a stereo system in the lodge, and she found a pleasant classical station. She changed into a warm terry floor-length wrap-around robe. As she cooked a small portion of a vegetable medley with a little butter and salt, she found her mind drifting back to her home, Marlow. Had it truly only been a matter of a few days? Wow, she wondered if she was even missed yet. She wondered how her horses were doing and found she missed them immensely. She missed her son even more. She wondered how he was doing back at school. She wanted to call but knew she better not. It would be so good to hear his voice and let him know where she was and how she was doing. But, if those who had been following her before had broken in her home, they probably knew how to contact Jarrod and could trace her location from her calls to him. She cursed silently at the unknowns who were following her. She wished Jarrod or Joe had email capabilities. That would solve her communication problems. But neither of them had opted to spend the small amount of money it would have taken to log into a network. The internet and its ability to connect the world was not more than a few years old, but she knew within a few short years, everyone in the world, including third world countries, would probably be logging in several times a day. But she was not really sure how secure email was or would be. It seemed best to be safe and stay away from any means of communication for the time being.

She knew she had to figure out something soon about the metal disc and get it into the proper hands. If she didn't, she wondered how long it would be before they caught up with her and handled her like they did the man in New Orleans. Murder is the ultimate price for information, she thought. Well, that and the torture that precedes it. The idea of that happening to her unnerved her again for the thousandth time since she realized she had decided she would keep it. She would have loved to talk to someone and get some objective advice on what to do. But as it was, she didn't trust the authorities and didn't want anyone else at risk. She was wearing fast though and even though she had only been gone a few days, she was really lonesome for her home and family. She wanted to be home, back at Marlow. But then she remembered ever so quickly that sharp personal let down she'd gotten from the job she loved. Of course, that made living at Marlow almost a burden because she would be constantly wondering about income or wondering who was watching her.

"Thanks ever so much, Kevin. It's me that has to be on

the run. At least you threw off the damned hound dogs by handing me their bone." As she said this aloud, she took her glass of white wine and toasted her not so good friend, Kevin.

Lowering her glass to the table, she then promised to herself that she would somehow make the people following her pay for her having to be on the run. She also hoped that her corrupt officials at home would be in hot Federal water when Garrison Roberts got through with them. That, she decided, would probably be worth these deeply resentful feelings about leaving her job and her home because of all the underhanded goings on between the Judge, DA, and drug cartel in the county.

After her second glass of white wine, she ate her supper. In front of the fire, she began to feel a little better about things and she thought it would be a good time to pick up her computer and go to work. She previously gathered quite a lot of information and made many notes in her spare moments for her research project. She reviewed the documents she already started on and began to fine-tune them. She loaded her own framework of what she considered to be an adaptive resource for tracking criminal activities, including report forms, search queries, and suggested secured linkups with Interpol, the FBI, the European Courts of Justice, and others, Then she suggested using a pilot scanning program with media sources all over the world. Many other ideas began popping up as she worked, and she felt that the work product was really coming together.

"There!" she said out loud as she finally closed the computer and put her agenda and handouts for her first meeting in her briefcase. The package was ready for the first presentation to the local authorities. She sighed heavily and looked at her watch. The night had turned into morning. She knew she had been at it a while, but must have really gotten into it, because the time had passed quickly to her. The sun was rising outside. She opened the curtains in front of French doors out onto the back patio and viewed a luscious green field. The scenery began to glow as the dew glistened under the golden rays of the early day. It was a breathtaking view. At the end of the field, there was a drop off to the ocean and the water was crystal blue in color. She had to get out and enjoy the fresh air, she thought. In fact, she was hungry, so she decided to go for a walk around the complex, looking for a cafe. There was a footpath that wound into a wooded area and then into the local village. Before she knew it, she was at a small restaurant and ordering a hot breakfast. The locals walking past her looked at her as if they wondered who she was and why was she there since the resort occupants usually stayed and ate at the restaurant on site or in their own chalets. While she ate, she felt a little foolish at being so obviously foreign in the small village and possibly attracting enough curiosity from others that she could be pointed out to anyone looking for her. She did not want to be off the resort for very long, so she went back via the wooded path and back to the safety and security of the lodge. Once in, she ran hot water and lounged in the Jacuzzi, then went to bed and she slept very soundly.

    Kadar personally made the entry into Marlow. It was an elementary procedure for him to switch off the security system. A minor thorn in his side when it came to disabling such simple electronic devices. He was renowned among his mercenary collaborators for his tracking, surveillance, and IT hacking skills. He also was an expert in art of persuasive interrogation. That played an important part in his being hired by Sahib. That's also why his fee was so high. Sahib needed the information coded onto the disc desperately because he was certainly willing to pay dearly. A 2.5 million dollar down payment. Another 2.5 million upon retrieval and de-codification of the disc. Kadar himself had been given only a slight indication of the vast ramifications of having the information on this disc. He would have felt better if he was told the whole truth, though. What he did know was the coded message was one that could enhance Sahib's position as a political leader in the Middle East. Kadar was always mindful of his employer's motives. It helped to determine his fee, but it also gauged the need for the use of his persuasive skills. He needed to know the prerequisite parameters of brute force and/or execution. In this particular mission, the rules he set were clear. He already killed once. And he was not about to let the coded disc escape him again. He was sure now that the female lawyer was planted with the code in Hattiesburg. He had not seen the exchange, although he heard the whole conversation from a mike on one of his employees sitting next to the table where she sat with the Hattiesburg prosecutor they were following since the warehouse worker made his way into that office. The prosecutor was watched for days with no luck. They planned on taking extreme measures with him, but he simply disappeared. Kadar was quite certain that there was another group after the same information on the disc that Sahib hired him to retrieve. He was not sure who the other group was, but he knew that the operative known as the Raven had been working for the other group. Since he chose death over giving up the location of the disc, Kadar knew the other side was seriously into getting the disc for themselves. Most definitely this other group was not government. Kadar was on a constant lookout for any sign of infiltration into his most trusted employees by an adversary. To his knowledge, no such crossing over had occurred, but it was expected.

Kadar just hours before confirmed that this lady lawyer was another prosecutor named Leigh Reid. He believed she had the disc when he found that this Leigh Reid recently left her job and home after the other prosecutor known as Kevin Johnson disappeared. Kadar wasn't giving up on finding Johnson and was certain that the so called apparent death reports were only that, just reports. It could have been staged if Johnson knew he was being followed. But Kadar was already persuaded by the events that had transpired that Leigh Reid had the disc. He didn't know, however, where she went when she apparently just left. That was only a minor setback though.

He was performing a scan on computer records for outgoing flights, buses, and trains from the Jackson, Memphis, and New Orleans areas. It was a lengthy process. There was no Leigh Reid that had taken a scheduled flight. She had not checked in at any airlines in the adjacent airports. He knew she hadn't used credit cards, or they would have nailed her location by now. Thus, the supposed break-in at her home. He went through her home thoroughly with the idea that she could have hidden the disc. But the place was clean. And, there was no indication of her whereabouts. He was sure the staff didn't know where she was. He already posed as a horse trainer earlier in the day and found out they hadn't a clue where she went. His only hope was to wait and see if she contacted any of those closest to her. He couldn't get a tap on the Customs Agent brother, but he had everyone else's phones being bugged: Her staff, her ex-employer's office, and her son's apartment at Harvard. He could wait. She would be in contact with one of them. It was just a matter of time. They always had to make contact with someone from home when they were on the run. Kadar smiled as he enjoyed the anticipation of finding her and getting the disc. And, of course, collecting the rest of his money.

CHAPTER FIFTEEN

It was Friday afternoon, and Leigh felt refreshed after having almost ten hours sleep. Relieved that her work was in a final form, she could now look forward to her weekend with Gabby and her family. Her inventory of clothes was, at the very least, termed 'limited'. After a quick review of what she was in possession of, she decided to go into St. Andrews a few minutes early before time to meet Gabby and shop for new clothes. A small boutique near the market square yielded an elegant but simple-lined black dinner dress. A rather short one, but she liked it. She also found a pair of gold looped earrings and a gold and black metallic scarf to throw around her neck. New hiking boots, thermal hiking pants, a cream-colored sweater, and a matching cream-colored harsh weather jacket completed her new outdoor wardrobe for the cold weather in the Highlands. Unsure of what else she would need; she bought a new long white cotton gown with a matching robe and slippers. Pleased with her purchases, all the while still making sure to look over her shoulders for any suspicious followers, she wondered about her first taste of the mysterious Highlands. The stress of the last several weeks put such a damper on being too excited about much. In fact, the numbness associated with the constant perimeter checks dulled her senses quite a bit.

She met Gabby at 3:00 pm as planned in front of the Green Lion Hotel. Gabby was parked out front in a teal-colored Land Rover, which suited her personality to a tee, Leigh thought.

"Hop in! We've got a bit of a drive and I'm so glad to have

company this time!" Gabby's face was alight with a brilliant smile.

"Thanks!" Leigh said as she placed her suitcase in the back seat and eased into the front passenger side of the car. "I've hopefully packed well enough for the weekend."

Gabby smiled again and said, "Like I said, if you're missing something, you can always borrow from my closet. We're about the same size, I imagine."

They started out the journey with Gabby asking questions all about Mississippi. She wanted to know about everything from the history to the politics to the fashions and architecture. She told Leigh she wanted to go her last year of studying to Harvard University. What a coincidence, Leigh thought as she then told Gabby about Jarrod and his studies there. Gabby was most interested in hearing about when Jarrod might travel to see Leigh. Hmm, Leigh thought. They really wouldn't be such a bad pair! Stop it, she told herself. No match making for the son. That supposedly went away with the feudal system.

They drove on into the higher areas and began to visit about Leigh's home and horses. Then as they got into Perth, Gabby began telling out the Highland country that she had grown up in. She gave Leigh a brief history of her part of the country and Leigh was surprised to learn that the McKennah's were direct descendants of the Celts and Vikings. She learned that after Scotland forced back the conquering Romans from an invasion, the Scottish always defended their boundaries, held their positions and fought hard to keep their freedom. Leigh never paid much attention in World History, so it was like learning about Scotland from the beginning. Gabby said it was only when the marriage of royalties from Scotland and Britain occurred that Scotland finally came under the rule of Britain. And, it seemed, the Scottish Parliament even voted themselves out of the United Kingdom Parliament in London. Gabby intimated that the harsh feelings from the constant attempts by Britain to take control over Scotland left quite a rivalry and bitterness between the populations of both countries.

Pretty much talked out and lolling into a silence, Leigh continued to enjoy the ride by observing the beautiful countryside. Before long the sun began its descent as they crossed over the River Tay on the A9. The majestic mountains of the Highlands began to loom in the horizon. They were breathtaking to Leigh, who never saw mountains around the flatlands of the Mississippi terrain. Some of the blue-grey mountains had the remains of spring snow caps on them.

The frequency in the number of farms and small villages thinned out as they got more into the mountainous areas. It was dark when they came through the city of Inverness and then crossed over the bay of Moray Firth. Gabby was keeping the conversation going, and before they both knew it, Gabby turned into a long driveway off a two-lane road. Leigh was sure she would never find her way here again as it was beginning to seem to be way away from all civilization. It was still mountainous and there were very few lights peeking through the darkness.

Gabby finally told Leigh that they were close to her home. It was 7:30 pm when some lights of apparently a two-story stone house came into view. Beside it was a massive iron gated entrance with some sort of crest visible on each gate in the headlights of the Rover.

Leigh commented, "How pretty. That must be your family's crest. Is it?"

"Yes, it is the McKennah family crest. Oh, there's Leon, the gatekeeper, he'll open the gates."

An elderly man was coming out of the two-story house and waived to Gabby. Immediately a wash of yellow light covered the entry area. Motion censored, no doubt, Leigh thought. The man apparently used a remote for the gate as it opened automatically. He made sure to seem them through and then the gates closed behind them and Gabby drove on past the house. Leigh expected Gabby to turn in to the parking area by the stone house at the gate and when she didn't, Leigh wondered why she kept driving on. Not wanting to appear ignorant, she asked, "So, how far does this drive go on past the house?"

Gabby just shrugged and said, "Oh, I think it's about a half mile from the gatekeeper's house to ours. Not to worry though, we'll be there in a jiffy now." She kept driving down the lane, which was illuminated with spotlights and lanterns as far as Leigh could see. So, if that was not her house, just the gatekeeper's, what would the actual house look like, she wondered thinking it must be bigger or grander, but that would be hard to imagine as the gatekeeper's home was already big and beautiful, at least what she could see in the half-dark area.

Well, wonder no more, she said to herself as they came around a high-banked curve and in the front of the vehicle was a massive structure with outside lighting on the stone walls and in the trees. The building was apparently very tall and at the top squared off with a tall fortified turret. Whoa, it looked very much like a castle to Leigh. She thought about the 1100 AD house Gabby had told her about. She was beginning to wonder what she was getting herself into here as they approached yet another outbuilding with yet another man there to greet them. Leigh decided at this point not to ask any questions because she knew she would look stupid, and rightly so at this point, because she was beginning to feel in the dark, so she just sat and waited.

They stopped and the man came to the car. "Miss Gabriella! So nice that you were able to come home this weekend. Shall I park this for you?" the gentleman in a uniform, yes, a uniform, queried.

Nope, not her father, Leigh thought as she squinted to look at the man. She was feeling a little like a Clampett in Beverly Hills. What exactly did Gabby's family do? Own a multi-million-dollar business?

"Thanks, Simmons. Yes, we need the luggage out and we're a little tired. This is Miss. Reid who will be staying with us this weekend. Where's Dad?" Leigh asked as she gathered up her purse and coat.

"He's in the Hall with the remainder of The Trust's group. Shall I ring the maître d'?"

"No, Charles, we can find him on our own. Please just get our bags and have them brought up."

Leigh was got out of the Range Rover and began stretching her tired legs, when she thought she heard faint musical notes in the air. A beautiful sound was coming from inside the stone walls of what she was sure had to be a castle. She recognized the sound. It was bagpipes! Someone was playing bagpipes! How Scottish was this? She definitely felt she was culturally experiencing the country by hearing the music. The sound seemed to reach down into Leigh's very being. It was mesmerizing to her as she slowly followed Gabby's trail to what seemed like an entrance into something similar to that of what Camelot must have looked like.

"Welcome to Dalroch, Leigh," Gabby was saying as they entered through thick arched wooden double doors into a large entranceway. This is my home and the home of my ancestors for the last 800 years." She smiled and added. "I'm sorry, I didn't tell you that we live in a castle. I hope you don't mind me keeping it from you. I thought you'd enjoy the surprise. It is one of the few of its vintage still up and running by the same family in Scotland."

Leigh was trying to not look as shocked as she felt, but pleasantly so. "A castle it certainly is and a definite surprise! I've not had the time to do much touring since I got here, Gabby, but I really hoped and planned on seeing a few castles. Looks like you have just taken care of the first one. Gee! To stay in one will be a treat, I imagine. This is great!" Inside her stomach started to tighten up as she became aware that Gabby's family must be way out of her class of acquaintances. And, she was all of a sudden very self-conscious about her clothes, her hair, and how to act and converse in this a world of obvious wealth.

Gabby smiled at Leigh and said, "Right, well let's find Dad. He's entertaining a group that comes once a month on a tour. Dad likes to show off his restorative efforts inside." She grabbed Leigh's arm and into the castle they went.

The music was now reverberating throughout the large room they entered, and Gabby lead her through two more large arch-shaped wooden doors in the back of the entry room into what looked like a dining room large enough to feed an army. She was so overwhelmed with the place, she couldn't take it all in, but she could see the two long banquet-sized Medieval styled dining tables were elegantly adorned with shining crystal, porcelain, silver and floral arrangements. The music was almost spellbinding as they must have been closing in on the source of it. Leigh felt a strange sensation all over her body. She didn't know what it was, but it seemed to affect her deep inside her as if touching her soul. The music evoked feelings of hope, desire, pride, and love. Strange how that could happen with music, Leigh mused. She was obviously feeling the effects of the long day. They exited out of the dining room into a grand gold and rose-colored room the size of Leigh's whole house. It had wall sconces all glowing, sofas placed on the walls everywhere, and a balcony above the far end. They were what Leigh would have called 'high-toned' people milling about everywhere.

Gabby was saying, "That would be Dad up in the balcony playing. He likes playing his bagpipes from up there. He says the acoustics are so much better there." Gabby was smiling in a proud way. Leigh couldn't see the man from where she was standing. But, the music came to a stop and down from the balcony on winding stairs came the man with bagpipes. He was dressed in a Scottish tartan kilt. Tall with light brown hair combed back in a ponytail, Leigh thought he looked somewhat familiar as she tried to get a better glance of him, but the group seemed to circle him as he got down to the floor. Really silly of me, she thought. Why would he look even remotely familiar to her? She was almost laughing at the thought. He was still a good distance away, but Leigh could tell he was wandering through the group of about 100 people all dressed in apparent formal dinner clothing. Suddenly someone lifted a silver cup and a toast was announced: "To our elegant and talented host, the Duke of Dalroch!" Everyone turned and lifted their glasses to Gabby's father.

CHAPTER SIXTEEN

The Duke of Dalroch? Oh, just great, Gabby. A secret about living in a castle is one thing. Being in a blooming royal family was quite the other! Her face was losing color fast she knew as she made this realization. Gabby grabbed Leigh and sheepishly took her to meet her dad. Leigh was trying to say 'no, thanks, let me get out of here quickly before someone realizes I am here' but she was pulled through the elegant crowd while everyone's eyes on them. Leigh knew she was certainly out of place in this crowd. And then, suddenly, they were facing the Duke.

"Father, I am honored to present to you, Ms., Leigh Reid, from the states, namely, Mississippi." Gabby took on an air of dignity that Leigh certainly did not have nor could muster at this particular moment. Leigh froze. She wasn't dressed right! She had on jeans and a University of St. Andrews sweatshirt. Plus, she did not know how to talk to royalty. This was a good time to quickly vanish out of the room. But she noticed that the entire room of people had stopped what they were doing and were watching her. She lowered her head and stared at the floor, which was quite nicely done with a mosaic of the family crest surrounded by polished wood. Funny how she noticed it while trying to avoid everything else around her!

"Ms., Reid, may I present my father, Geoffrey McKennah, the 12th Duke of Dalroch."
A hand extended out in front of Leigh as she kept her head down as if she did not really want to acknowledge she was a human being at the moment. "So nice to meet you. Ms. Leigh Reid. Thank you for humbling us with your visit to our

home." Leigh was trying to find her voice as he continued, "These kind people are here tonight sampling Dalroch's cuisine. Would you like to join us?"

"Thank you. I am--," she stopped trying very hard to get on with the art of speaking and sounding human. She finally lifted her eyes to her host and in an instant, she was taken aback with yet another and truly unexpected surprise. It was the man that had been in the shelter with her when it had been raining back in St Andrews! She would know those blue eyes anywhere. Her hand was being taken by his and he gently shook it. Well, shock was really the better word for this little surprise. Small world indeed it must be, as it was quite a coincidence that he was Gabby's father, and a Duke for crying out loud! And, she had already somewhat met him! She was a complete and utter stranger to this country and kingdom, yet he had already made an impression on her! She became even more small feeling and said, "I'm appreciative of your offer, ah, Sir, but if y'all would just go ahead and do what you were doing before I came in, I'd be very grateful. It has been a long trip to your lovely home, but I believe I would be better served to ask your daughter to show me where I might freshen up. Please, excuse me. Oh, and it is so very nice to meet you, your, well, I'm sorry, but what exactly am I to call you?"

Gabby leaned over and whispered while the smiles continued in the group, especially on the face of the Duke, "'My Laird'."

"Uh, My Laird." Leigh finished this time smiling because she was finding humor now in the impromptu protocol lesson. Then she added, "And, I would like to say that the song you just played was a treat to hear. You sure can play it with real style, My Laird."

"Thank for your compliment. The song is a favorite of mine. And most certainly take your leave and make yourself comfortable. We have fires here, too, that should take the chill off," he said indicating he knew who she was from their earlier encounter. "Gabriella, please show Ms. Reid her accommodations while I continue with my guests." The Duke let go of her hand. He had sure held it a long time, she realized. His eyes were still on her too. They were such a deep blue, the color of the ocean and sparkling so. She blushed and felt like she was being summed up again. But she was also staring at him, she knew.

"Come this way, Leigh." Thankfully, Gabby was whispering again and pulling at Leigh's arm. Leigh followed her out of the room with as much grace as she could muster, but she was beginning to chuckle at the spectacle she must have been to the classy looking ladies and gents in the room. Not to mention, her disheveled appearance and utter lack of royal 'know how' must have been the reason for the Duke's amused stare. It was quite kind of him not to point any of that out to the crowd. Although Leigh was embarrassed beyond words, it did not come close to the shock of already meeting the man who was Gabby's father and, of all things, the Duke.

Gabby was grinning from ear to ear as they cleared the doorway out of the room.
"My goodness gracious, Gabby! You are full of surprises, now aren't you? You could've given a girl a warning that I might, just might be meeting royalty tonight. Or for that matter, that you are of royal blood!"

Leigh wasn't upset with Gabby; she was more impressed that Gabby had pulled such a trick on her. She obviously was having fun at throwing out the little factual tidbits about her family.

"Oh, don't worry about us, Leigh. We're really harmless. You know, not many a Scot or Brit would've been able to handle that situation with the finesse you did, Leigh. I'm sorry, but I really didn't remember the Trust group would be here tonight and I thought your learning about who we are would be only between my father, you and I. I surely did not mean to have you introduced like that!" Gabby was very apprehensive about this, Leigh could see.

"No bother, really. And, thanks for the compliment.

THE OGHAM CONNECTIONS

Next time, though, a brush up on royal protocol would be nice! What about your mother, I guess she would be the Duchess of Dalroch? Where is she tonight? Looks like she really missed the show!" Leigh saw a hint of a sad look in Gabby's eyes as she finished asking the question and wished she hadn't asked it.

"My mother and father divorced when I was quite young, Leigh. I don't ever see her and I don't wish to see her. Maybe I'll tell you more about her sometime, but for now, we're both tired so let's get you to your rooms." The plural 'rooms' did not escape Leigh either. What type rooms, she wondered. All she needed was a bed and, yes, a bath.

Gabby lead Leigh back into the large room behind the entry way of the castle. A large, elegant double winding stone stairway was the dominant feature as it encompassed most of the space and volume of the room. Made of white marble steps with mahogany railings and banisters, there was a deep burgundy carpet gracing the middle section of the stairs. The first landing divided the stairs going up into two symmetrical and opposite directions. In the center of the landing as they made their way up, was what looked like a glass display case with various types of armament placed on a green velvet cloth. The impressive array consisted of several knives, swords, body armor, and other things that she clearly had no clue about. She only glanced at it, but as she did, a strange feeling come over her. Not quite sure why. She was too tired, maybe. She looked back at it again. No. She was definitely drawn to something there. Why, she wondered as she truly knew nothing about what she was looking at, the history or the significance of anything in that case. She was sure, though, that she would have to come back and get a closer look at the display after she rested.

She and Gabby continued up to the second floor and into a long hallway that led to a second hallway and then to the left. Everywhere she looked there was a look of well-heeled rich taste, from the outstanding craftsmanship of the moldings, dark paneling, and tall wooden doors to the elegance in the designs, and even from the personal accumulation of what must have been generations of family heirlooms. These included old wall tapestries, obviously expensive antique carpets, marble busts, silver service sets placed sporadically, elegant lamps, and massive furnishings with just the right decorative items placed here and there. Most of these things Leigh truly only had seen in books and magazines. This was a showplace, she decided as she attempted to absorb what she could while trying not to look so much like a child in a candy store. Deciding she would have to be given the proper tour before getting to work here, she continued to follow Gabby until she stopped in the middle of yet another long hallway and opened a set of double doors. She waived Leigh in. "Come in. This will be your suite while you are here. Dad picked it out so you could be close to the study which is down the hall back through the center landing and on the left. I hope this will be okay?"

Leigh took a look around as she stepped into the room. On the direct other side of the entrance was a large lead glass arched window with a cushioned window seat under it. To the left was a massive full tester bed that caught her breath. It was lavishly endowed with delicate linens in peach and cream colors. Lace-edged pillows with monograms of the family crest topped the bed. The headboard and foot board were paneled in dark mahogany and it was so high off the floor that there was a step stool with four steps beside it! Whoa, Leigh thought. A real climb up to that dreamy bed! The curtains around the bed all were of thick tapestry fabrics that coordinated with the window coverings, linens and seat cushions. Two cream colored tall wing back chairs were strategically placed in front of the fireplace, which was roaring heat into the room. Then on the window side of the room there was an elegant peach velvet chaise lounge placed by a large bookcase that surrounded the massive window and was filled with books. Elegant frosted wall sconces were on the wall on either side of the massive bed and above the mantel and were dimly lit emitting a soft glow. The whole room gave an aura of comfort and elegance.

Leigh smiled and told Gabby, "Well, I think it looks like it is fit for a queen! I feel honored your Dad chose it for my stay. Thank him for me. It looks so good to me that I might just jump in that big bed right now and pass out!"

"Come see the rest, first," Gabby grabbed her hand and pulled her in the direction of yet another set of double doors. She opened them, "This is your dressing room. To the right is your bath and to the left is the toilet area." Leigh saw a central room with built-in paneled closet doors, a large cheval mirror, a lady's dressing table with two tall table lamps on either side, and with makeup lights on the wall above it, and what appeared to be a seamstress' figure for clothes to be put over to look at before they are put on, she guessed. At the back of the room was a large marbled lavatory with more lighting and glass shelves with toiletries for even the most discriminating guest. Of course, Leigh was highly impressed, but tried not to 'ooh and aah' too much to embarrass herself more than she probably already had with her shocks of the evening. The bath area consisted of a white marble-enclosed oval-shaped tub with two steps up. Green plants draped the back of the tub and there were more aptly placed toiletries and linens on small wooden tables. Several oil paintings were on the wall around the bathing area with scenes of what appeared to be the Highland mountain areas. *I've died and gone to heaven*, she thought to herself.

She looked over at Gabby and said, "Okay, you got me again! This is fabulous! I'll just take advantage of this bath before I retire. If you are going to join your Dad, please tell him I'll be up bright and early. Of course, at his convenience, we can get started on the case he wants me to review."

"Sure, I will tell him. But you don't want to come down for some food or a night cap first? Dad always ends the day in his study with a glass of red wine, and I'm sure he'd love for you to join him."

"No, thanks. He's got a room full of guests to deal with, and don't think I'll be up too long. Will I see you in the morning or do you have plans?"

"I'm just going riding first thing. My favorite pony likes early morning exercise. He usually doesn't get it unless I am home, but I should be back by breakfast, though. Oh, it is served promptly at 8:30am. So, I'll probably see you then?"

"Sounds fine. Good night, Gabby." Leigh smiled warmly at her new young friend. She really was a likeable person. Even though she sprung a couple of surprises on Leigh, it was obviously all in good fun for Gabby.

"Oh, by the way, any more surprises to spring on me tonight or tomorrow?"

Gabby laughed, "No. But I could come up with some more, if you like!"

Leigh laughed with her and said, "No, no thanks, Kiddo, I've had enough to last a while. Trust me."

"Right, well, I am really glad you came, Leigh. So is Dad. Good night, then."

Leigh closed the door behind Gabby. Taking a deep breath, she looked for her bag in the dressing room. She put her night gown out, and eased into the bathtub once it was full of bubbles. Sinking down and sighing with the luxury of the hot water and the surroundings, she almost fell asleep with the relaxing rush over her. When she came back to the bedroom, she felt so good and excited, she took one look at the bed, ran to it and jumped up in it like a little girl. This, she told herself, is quite the switch from her other accommodations. Pulling the silk sheets up over her, she thought: She was staying in a castle, the home to that handsome and most intriguing Duke, and she had her own suite like she was somebody. It was not lost on her either that Gabby had said her father was divorced. Hmmm, she smiled at that thought. Of course, that didn't mean he was unattached, she reminded herself. Then she pinched herself on the arm to make sure she wasn't dreaming this entire set of events up. Well, it hurt, so it must be real. It was such a stark revelation to her that she smiled herself to sleep within a very short time.

CHAPTER SEVENTEEN

She awoke to a soft knock on her door.

"Ms. Reid?" It was a woman's voice speaking very softly. It wasn't Gabby's voice, Leigh thought as she tried to get her eyes fully open.

"I'm sorry if I woke you, Mam. My name is Leslie. I'm your maid for your stay here. My Laird wants to know if you want breakfast in your suite or downstairs?"

A maid and a choice. What 5-star service! Breakfast in bed sounded lovely, but she had promised Gabby she'd eat with her.

"Downstairs, please. I'll be down in a few minutes. Ah, thank you, Leslie."

"Yes, Ms. Reid. May I come in and serve you coffee or tea?"

Leigh grabbed her robe and sat up in bed. "Ah- yes, that would be just fine. Come on in."

The maid was in uniform with a full silver tea service. She also had a newspaper and a bouquet of fresh peach and cream flowers. Of course, matching fresh flowers! She left the tray on a table near the chaise lounge, opened her drapes so the sun came pouring in, and quietly left the room. Better than room service at the Hilton, Leigh thought!

Leigh had her coffee, with fresh cream, no less, and then found hiking clothes she purchased the day before. Before going downstairs, she crawled into the window seat to take her first look out of the castle in the daylight. The scene took her breath immediately. Below was a panoramic view of a formal garden that was in full bloom. Behind it were the hills that lead into the mountains. But before the hills was what looked like a large lake. It gleamed in the morning sunlight. She felt as if it wasn't real for a moment since it was so beautiful. The lake looked accessible from the back of the garden area down a steep grassy incline. It was almost like someone had painted a lovely picture and placed it in the window. It was hard to describe the feeling that this beauty caused inside Leigh. All she knew was that she had to get out and see more. The castle inside was gorgeous from what she had seen so far, but she really felt like getting out and walking around the grounds to feel the fresh cool air of the Highlands. Oh, well, she was here to work, and she was getting paid, she thought pragmatically.

She headed out of her suite, although she wasn't sure where she was going. She made it to the landing of the stairwell and stopped once again at the armor display cabinet. There it was. She felt it again. That same drawing sensation. The hair on her arms stood straight up. Why was that she wondered. It was as if there was something inside calling out to her. Silly me, she thought. It's the history of the place and the objects inside the display and I must just be truly enchanted with it. Or it is enchanting me on its own!

Just then, someone touched her elbow. It startled her out of her thoughts, and she jumped involuntarily.

"Ms. Reid. I see you found our McKennah Clan Heritage Collection. Oh, so sorry, dear. I hope I did not scare you." It was the Duke. She had not heard anyone come up behind her. She turned and looked at him and smiled. He was dressed as a normal person this morning: Jeans, a blue shirt and tan sport jacket. Thank goodness! She didn't feel like trying to be humbled by her lack of royal know how this morning. His eyes were dancing with life, she noticed. Just like last night. He held her stare for a moment and then looked over at the display case. "Actually, it consists of a memento from every battle my family has fought in. I know the history of most, but it would take a while to go over all of it. However, if you are interested, and if you have time after breakfast and an official tour, I'd be glad to tell you about them." His smile was very warm. Unfortunately for her, she felt her heart jump a beat at that smile.

"I would be delighted, your.... well, what shall I call you this morning?"

"Geoffrey is fine. And, I do apologize for not having time to properly greet you last night. May I call you 'Leigh'? After all, I feel like we should know each other by now." He cocked his head and smiled again. Those eyes again. She could let herself get lost in them. Not waiting for a response, he continued, "I was hoping we could get to know each other a little more though before we settle down to work. Gabriella has a high respect for you, you know. She was taken by the fact that you are such an independent woman with such an illustrious career."

"Whoa, there now! First of all, who am I to tell a Duke what to call me? I'll leave that up to you, Geoffrey. But, I don't mind 'Leigh'. Secondly, I appreciate Gabby's enthusiasm for my status and career, but it's not really anything to brag about. Certainly not illustrious. Thirdly, thanks again for the fire in the rain the other day. I didn't tell Gabby that we had bumped into each other before. That is, I really was still a little shocked that you were the same person I had visited with earlier."

She smiled back at him and he took her elbow and escorted her down the stairwell. "We'll let that be our little secret, then, Leigh. I had no idea that you would be the American crime buster that she told me about, so touché! They walked into the center hallway again as he continued, "Well, I guess we shall see what you can do by trying to assist in our sordid family murder mystery. But for now, let's have breakfast. Oh, I'm glad you dressed for outside ventures since I planned an afternoon in the hills, if that is all right with you.

I thought we could do a short tour of the inside this morning. Then go out to the grounds this afternoon."

As if reading her mind from earlier in her room, she said, "Fine with me, but when do I start work? You know I'm on the clock, don't you?" She really wasn't interested in jumping right in yet either. The tours sounded great, but she wanted him to know the work was important to her. He didn't have to take time for tours for her.

"No worries, Leigh. We'll have time for the work. You need to get to know the place first, I think. It should help you when you settle down with the materials I have for you."

They entered a large dining room but not the one she had seen the night before. The table was full of tall urns with fresh floral arrangements, places set for three, and a buffet set up with hot serving dishes to the side. He took her to a chair and pulled it out for her.

"Please, be seated. We will be served in a moment." Breakfast was indeed served as Gabby had predicted, promptly at 8:30am just as she came running in breathless. She was dressed in traditional English riding jodhpurs, a red riding jacket and boots. Her face was flushed from the fresh air. "Morning Dad and Leigh. Sorry I'm late. I am starving!" She smiled and looked at them both while grabbing her plate and helping herself from the buffet.

"Gabby. Can you not wait to be served? Louise will be right out with fresh juices and she will prepare our plates." Geoffrey was smiling while talking. He had the look of a doting dad when addressing his daughter. Leigh watched them through breakfast as they caught up on the goings on at school. She could tell from their demeanor toward each other that they had an extremely close relationship. She recognized the bond because it was the same as she had with Jarrod. She felt a sharp pang in her chest thinking about how far away he was. Her smile faded and she stopped eating.

As if noticing her mood change, Geoffrey stood up and said, "Well, then Leigh, I think it's time for your tour of Dalroch. Are you through with breakfast?"

"Sure, and I am at your disposal, Geoffrey. Lead on." Good timing. The thought of her getting firsthand personal tour of this massive museum of a home was enough to get her spirits back up.

"What do you mean you haven't found her?" Kadar was getting edgy with his men. They tracked a Leigh Reid from the information center receptionist's computer log in at St. Andrews. Computer whizzes they were, but it was not good enough. He needed them to produce more detailed results. There was no other trace of her from the center, not yet anyway. "Keep digging. That was her first mistake. She will make another." At least they had narrowed down the parameters of her movements: Scotland. He booked his flight from Mississippi and was airborne in two hours.

…………………………………..

Geoffrey McKennah was an amazingly well-informed host. His knowledge of Scottish history and of his family's role in the building of his country was admirable. She was very impressed, if not a little intimidated by the notoriety. Leigh was given a thorough and very enjoyable tour of the castle. Geoffrey, it turned out, happened to have a real sense of humor along with his royal manners and very good looks. Of course, she thought. Pretty well the perfect host, if not the perfect 'catch' for some lucky woman! Then she chided herself for even thinking such a personal thought while trying to make money, or take, money from him on a purely professional level.

There were so many twists and turns and rooms that she had a hard time keeping up with their particular locations. The walls were all of stone, cut almost four feet in depth. There were four levels, including a basement and a rooftop level with a glassed-in conservatory built on it. Here there were Geoffrey's and Gabby's favorite plantings of Camellias. They weren't bushes like Leigh had seen back home. They were almost trees and in twenty different varieties, all towering tall in the room and blooming profusely. Geoffrey explained that the rooftop level was only one hundred fifty years old. It was built after the major Highland wars were over, when there was little chance of being destroyed by weapons.

After a refreshing midmorning tea inside the conservatory, he took her outside the rooftop to the fortifications that held the castle in his family for centuries. He told her of the McKennah Clan's loyalty to the Crown and the quickness in their ability to form troops whenever the needs arose to defend not only the castle but the country. His forefathers were McKennah Clan Leaders for as far back as anyone could remember. He was the present-day leader, but, he told her, there were very few times they needed to assemble troops these days. The Clan met on social occasions mainly. The tartan plaid of his Clan was designed by the Highlanders from the times that they fought and lived barefooted in the hills. Different designs for different clans so one could tell who they were facing on a mountain path, or a battlefield. Yes, they had fought each other in the earlier days for control of different land areas. She could hardly imagine the strength and courage it would have taken to fight and defend as gallantly as the Highlanders had. The battles were very bloody, he explained, especially during the uprising in the 1600s and the fight to make Bonnie Prince Charlie their King in the 1700s.

The hills were rocky and steep, the winters harsh, and the ability to communicate back and forth were tremendously inhibiting factors. Geoffrey was a direct descendant from these warriors. Leigh felt admiration and pride in knowing someone like him. He explained that during the days of war, the Clan would meet here and discuss baffle plans and arm themselves from this very room prior to going out into battle. Below were long wooden tables with framed maps laid out on them. He explained that there was a room outside in the present-day stables that held black powders and other ammunition for the weapons back when battles were imminent. From this room, he took her to the other sleeping chambers and suites in the castle. He explained each room's historical significance and she saw that every miniscule detail had been attended to just like in her suite. All sleeping suites had their private baths and dressing rooms. Hers, she noted, had the most luxurious amenities of all of them. She was beginning to feel special by his singling out the best for her. She felt a little like she was walking around inside a fairy tale book. One, okay she had to admit, she was beginning to hope would not end anytime soon.

  They ended up in what he told her was his favorite room which she discovered quickly was hers too. It was the massive study and library. Darkly paneled with a wall the length of the castle filled with books. It was decidedly a masculine room with dark leather sofas and club chairs, and hunting trophies on the top of the other three paneled walls. But it was also dressed in a lovely floral tapestry fabric that covered the large window in the room. This fabric was on several other cushioned chairs with ottomans in the room. There were also delicate floral arrangements on several tables. A massive fireplace with a roaring fire brightened up the room. Above the mantle of it was an oil portrait of Dalroch that portrayed the castle with the lake water in front and the sun shining brightly down on it. Geoffrey explained that it was painted some 250 years ago by someone that she would hear more about later in the tour. Leigh was impressed with the minute details in the painting and was eager for the tour to continue so she could learn more about the artist. There were several reading lamps aptly placed for those wishing to engage in browsing the ominous number of books. A semicircular mahogany desk in the front of the large oval window was where apparently Geoffrey kept up his business affairs. On it was an antique phone and it, quite frankly, was the only evidence that the world outside was accessible. Otherwise, one could feel that they were in this room literally three or four centuries ago.

Leigh looked at an inviting fireside chair and sat down in front of the fireplace. Geoffrey came and stood by her. "So, other than what I've showed you, and what you've seen in St. Andrews, what do you think of Scotland so far Leigh?"

As if she felt quite at home with this man, she answered, "Well, I'm sorry to say that I haven't had time to really get out and tour your country. It's been a whirlwind visit so far, but I've seen enough to know that this is a truly special place. I find its history rich with heroes and monuments of rich architecture such as this one and those in St. Andrews. There is also the same sort of independent thinking and genuine niceness here in the attitudes of the people not unlike those that started America. I have to say that I am eager to learn more of the Highlands and the mystery that seems to surround the people that came here to settle initially. I am really anxious to learn more about the Celts. They have such an influence on your culture." She paused and looked up at Geoffrey. "You have the luxury of not only knowing the history, but you get to live it daily in this place. I'm envious. You have also had so much done to the interior that makes this place comfortable without losing its historical charm."

Geoffrey had picked up a large silver goblet off the fireplace mantle wile Leigh had been talking.

She went on, "You know, I think your interior designer chose just the right fabrics in all the rooms. Not that I am a professional by any stretch of the imagination, mind you. But, in the bedrooms, especially, the air is one of not snobby royally, just elegant comfort. I love the way that each room captures the mood that it was designed for. It's a feat or talent that is also envious. So many owners don't try to be keepers of historical places back home. They just use them up until they fall down around them. I'm sorry, you didn't ask my opinion, but you got it anyway. You see, I have a true love for old homes. I own an ante-bellum plantation home in Mississippi that I restored and that I sorely miss." She stopped talking and blushed immediately at her wordy response to such a simple question. "Sorry, I didn't mean to rattle on like that!"

"Oh, I can certainly understand your feelings for a place. It is true that you can fall in love with a place as well as with a person. I started boarding schools when I was young, and my visits here were seldom, since my father owned several other residences in the United Kingdom. I was in Oxford, my last year of college when he passed away, leaving my mother very ill and the duties here too much for her. I came home as soon as school was over that year and tried to help my mother. I think she grieved herself to death when my father died, though, and one year to the day that he died, she passed away in her sleep. I was very young to be having to take on the duties of a Duke. However, my youth did give me the energy to tackle the interior restoration of Dalroch. I was in love with this place ever since I was old enough to walk. The interior designer that you referred to is me. I love putting rooms together and I have always been the one to choose the colors, fabrics, furnishings, even down to the dishes. I hope that doesn't sound too gay, to you. It is my way of finishing what my father had started in refurbishing the outside of this place so that the public could enjoy it as much as our family. The National Trust owns so many of Scotland's castles, but we have chosen to keep and maintain Dalroch ourselves. I do allow the Trust, however, to send tour groups here once a month to enjoy an evening like last night. It's my way of giving back to Scotland what it has given my family over the centuries. And thank you for your compliment. It looks like you have the same sort of eye for things that I have."

He stopped and then handed the silver goblet he had been holding to Leigh. "Do you know what this is'?"

She looked at it and turned it around in her hands. There was an inscription of some sort, but it was in what looked to her like a different language. In fact, it looked like some of the same symbols that were on her much sought-after round metal disc, which brought a cold chill to her body. She shook her head and handed it back trying not to show the recognition of the symbols. "No. It's beautiful, though. What is the inscription on it?"

"The wording is in an ancient symbolic language. I am told it means: 'May the hill rise behind you, and may the mountain be always over the crest. And may the God that you believe in hold you in the palm of his hand.'"

"That is a beautiful verse. Where did it come from?" Leigh was interested for more reasons than pure curiosity at this point.

"It was given to the 1st Duke of Dalroch in 1477 when the title was created. It is said to have been owned by the famous Kenneth MacAlpin, who was the very first King of Scots and the King of Picts. He was crowned as such in 843 AD. That would have been the actual birthday of Scotland. It was a ceremonial gift for the 1st Duke's call to arms in the 15th century and the subsequent winning battles that were fought near here. We have never given the goblet to anyone for authenticating it to the 800s AD. It really is a sentimental piece rather than a monetary asset to our family, you understand?"

"Yes, I do. How extraordinary. I'm sure the Trust would love for you to let them have it or at least know about it. I think it's being on the mantle here keeps it looking more like an ordinary piece rather than the unique one it obviously is. That's very clever of you." She was humbled by the fact that he chose to reveal such an obvious family secret to her, a virtual stranger. She smiled up at him.

"That reminds me. You still want to get the Heritage Collection's firsthand accounting?" Geoffrey pulled out a pocket watch. "Well, it is getting around lunch time now. Would you mind waiting until later to finish?"

"I have to admit all this touring has worked up an appetite for me."

Just then the phone rang at the Duke's desk.

Looking agitated at the interruption, he said, "Please excuse me, Leigh. I better get that."

Leigh had a half ear to the conversation from which she heard something about computers and appointments, but she was more interested in glancing at the books while her host was on the phone. She made her way to a section that she spotted earlier on Celtic and Gaelic history. There was one in particular that she pulled out to look at. "The History of the Gaelic and Symbolic Languages" looked like one that would suit her needs quite well. She was just looking at the table of contents when she heard Geoffrey hang up. He started over to her and she quickly replaced the book. Best to leave the reason for her curiosities to herself, she thought. As he approached her, he said, "Have you found something that you wish to read, Leigh? If so, please feel free to take it with you."

"No, just perusing your library. I could never get bored here. There's so much to read and learn about." She smiled and then added, "If you have business to attend to, please let me take care of myself, Geoffrey."

"No, no. It was nothing that requires my immediate attention. Let's go have lunch, shall we?"

CHAPTER EIGHTEEN

He walked with her passing rooms and hallways she recognized until they reach parts that she was sure she hadn't seen, if that was possible. The journey ended in the massive commercial stainless-steel kitchen where there was a man and woman with a chef's uniforms on working side by side on a large table with a large array of pots and pans hanging above from a suspended pot holder.

"Karman and Krista, let me introduce you to my guest, Ms. Leigh Reid," Geoffrey said. "Leigh, these are my chefs and my good friends, Karman and Krista Halga from Estonia. They have been with me for five years and make the finest cuisine in all of Scotland." He turned to them and asked, "Have you got our baskets ready?"

"Yes, My Laird. We fixed them up with a little special dessert, too. We hope that you will enjoy. We are very pleased to meet you, Ms. Reid. Please enjoy your stay here and let us know if there is anything special we can cook for you while you are here." Karman spoke English with a thick accent.

There were two rattan picnic baskets given to Geoffrey. Then he saw her quizzical look and explained. "I hope you don't mind, but I have taken the liberty of having my buggy hitched for our afternoon out. We can eat in the hills. Is that all right with you?"

As if she would refuse, she almost laughed out loud. "I do believe you are trying to spoil me. I can't believe all your guests get so much attention. Much less, your ah employees?" She was elated at the idea really. It sounded like fun and she had had precious little of that lately.

"Only the pretty American ones do." Geoffrey's eyes were dancing again.

She felt her cheeks getting red. Oh boy, she thought, let him see you are affected by his charm, dummy. That's really embarrassing, she told herself, if not too silly! She said, "Spoken like a true gentleman." Flattery must be an art with Dukes, she surmised.

"My parents raised me right." He offered her his arm.

"Well, I would think so, seeing as you would be the 12th Duke of Dalroch someday." She and he both laughed as they headed outside.

Just as soon as they were out, Leigh felt the crisp cool air. They walked into the cobble-stoned stable area. She was feeling more and more like she had walked into a surreal story being acted out with her in it, but not truly happening in live real life.

The tall horse was shiny jet black in color and the metal parts of the harness were solid brass and gleamed in the sunlight. The open topped buggy was also black with the red yellow and blue colors of the McKennah clan crest painted on it. Geoffrey opened the buggy door and helped her up to the driver's bench. She sat down beside him, and their legs touched. She felt a sudden warmth that she had not felt in a long time. She thought about how long it had been since she had allowed herself to be this close to a man. Too long, apparently, judging from the sensation she had as if there was an electrical current sending shockwaves throughout her body.

Geoffrey clucked at the horse and he instantly pranced out onto the driveway. They started out down the long way that she and Gabby had come in the night before. Was it just last night that she came here? It seemed like she had been there for days. Why was that, she asked herself. Was it the time she had been spending with the Duke, the allure of the elegant castle, or just the crisp, clean air that greeted them? Probably all of the above. But, whatever the reason, she felt happy. She wasn't looking over her shoulder constantly either. She felt immune from the outside world here.

'Where's Gabby? I thought she would be joining us." Leigh asked, but not really sure she wanted to share these moments with anyone else.

"Oh, she was going into the village to meet a couple of friends. Said she might go to the theatre in Inverness tonight. We may not see her until late this evening or in the morning. You know how kids are, don't you?"

That's funny, she hadn't told him about Jarrod. Gabby must have.

"They do have their own ideas and friends. I miss my Jarrod too much sometimes."

"And his father?" Geoffrey did not look directly at her when he asked this, and she felt it must have been because he knew it was a little personal.

The buggy was now on a dirt road and the bumps jostled Leigh, but not as much as the personal questions. "I am divorced. I have been for years. Neither Jarrod nor I have seen him since the divorce, which happened when he was a baby." She paused and worked to change the subject.

Watching the horse trot gracefully and toss his head every few minutes made her think of her horses back home. There's a topic, she thought.

"I breed and raise horses in Mississippi. Purebred Arabians. This big guy is an interesting breed. " Geoffrey was smiling then and went with the change of the conversation topic.

"He's a cross of a Thoroughbred and a Peruvian. I like the result and probably will breed one more for a matching pair. They have the Thoroughbred stamina plus the muscle power of the Peruvians. Tell me more about your horses, Leigh." Back to her again, huh? Same game as in the shelter.

More than happy to expound on her brood of Arabs, though, she talked for a while until she started noticing the lush surroundings. Flowers were all over the hillside of the path they were on. The aroma was so sweet. So, this must be the world famous heather she read about. Purple, red, and white flowers literally covered the hills as far as she could see. There were small animals scurrying across their path: birds, hedgehogs, squirrels and even a pheasant. It was a virtual idyllic setting, making Leigh want to do the pinching thing again, but thought better of it knowing she would look plum stupid in front of this ever observant and very masculine person next to her. She sat up a little straighter and smiled to herself thinking how it was not going to last, so she better enjoy every single lovely second.

The clop-clop of the horse was the only sound she heard. The air was so clean and crisp as she found herself taking deep breaths. No humidity! What a difference from the hot humid Mississippi climate.

Before long Geoffrey stopped the horse. "We're here then. Right!" he said as he reached behind the bench and took their picnic baskets out. They made a short climb up a small rocky path to the top of a hill. Once on top, Geoffrey said, "This is my reposing spot. I brought an extra blanket because the wind tends to get cooler even this time of year because of the elevation." He started unpacking their lunch and she thought she heard him humming in low tones. He's enjoying himself with her company. That was touching to her since she was virtually a stranger to him.

She took a panoramic look around. How high they had come! She didn't feel like they had increased their elevation very much, but now as she looked down to the left of the hillside, there was a deep valley that held Dalroch Castle. It was an imposing and impressive sight with the structure that stood down there, even though much smaller looking from so high. Surrounded by hills, she knew it was built in this spot for defense rather than for the glorious view. Geoffrey told her that during warring times, the hills would reverberate with the drums of the Clans and loud screams of the Highlanders would echo so much that it would intimidate even the most ferocious soldier. She could see how that could happen as well as how defensible the location truly was. The castle itself was built with four squared-off turrets on each corner. The windows were few and far between. If there was an imminent attack on that castle, it looked as if it would have taken quite a bit of ingenuity to get in. In front of the castle was the lake she had seen from her room. It was somewhat foggy around the shoreline which gave a mystical aura around it. There were dramatic drop offs to the water from the hills.

Then she spotted a stone structure on the edge of castle side of the water. She assumed it must have been a boathouse of sorts. Watching her glances, Geoffrey anticipated her question by saying, "That is where I keep several seagoing vessels. The Loch is virtually unapproachable by land. It connects to another bay that goes into the North Sea a few miles out. That's what gave this location an additional vantage point during warring times. The enemy would have had to approach the castle either by boat, where we had an advantage because of the elevation around the loch, or by the rocky hills before there were any roads. The Clan usually posted enough lookouts and scouts to know who was coming and in time to prepare a defense strategy. The castle was never taken by any enemy. It is a proud fact for historical purposes, but these days we have not had to worry too much about enemy attacks." He smiled and then asked if she would like to eat.

He showed her what was now spread out a tartan cloth. Of course, it had to be tartan, she smiled to herself. There were several varieties of cut cheeses and breads, white and red wine and wine goblets, porcelain bone-colored plates, bone-handled utensils, a menagerie of fruits, and a bowl of a pasta salad. For dessert, a chocolate mousse that was heavenly. They both ate almost in silence except for her occasional compliment of his chefs. It got almost too quiet before Geoffrey broke the silence and said, "Have you ever felt that your son was cheated by not having a father around?"

Startled by another such personal question, she said, "What do you mean by that?"

He was looking thoughtfully at his plate, not meeting

her eyes, "I have brought Gabriella up on my own. Her mother and I divorced not long after she was born. I've never had anybody around that filled that mother-daughter need that I'm sure every girl has." His eyes looked so saddened as he brought them up to meet hers. Leigh felt a twinge in her heart.

    Knowing full well the feeling he was expressing, she said, "Gabby is one of the most well-adjusted and personable girls her age I have ever met, Geoffrey. From what I have observed, you have nothing to feel guilty about. She has apparently not missed anything by not having a mother around." Then she could not resist asking him, 'If it's not any of my business, of course, and you can tell me, but since you mentioned Gabby's mother, may I ask what happened? I mean, it seems your life up here would be everything a girl could want. Look at all this! And, you have such a darling daughter. Why did it not work out?"

He smiled and said, "Oh, she never saw the beauty here. She referred to it as the Ice Hall. She rarely came to stay here. She stayed in London most of the time. We were married when I was just taking on my duties as Duke. We met at Oxford and I suppose now I can say I thought I was in love. I definitely know now though that she was absolutely not in love with me. She left me as soon as Gabriella was home from the hospital. I found out later that she went straight to the bed of a French merchant millionaire. She was always into social climbing and spending. She was beautiful, but only on the surface." He paused an extra-long time and then glanced back toward Leigh and looked deeply into her the eyes with such an intenseness it gave her a very strange sensation for a second.

Feeling uncomfortable again, she rose to walk a little and shake off the sensations his gaze produced. He got up and came beside her. Apparently, he sensed her uneasiness in the conversation for he changed the subject this time.

"Do you see that round building almost covered with vines on the edge of the water near the boathouse?"

She looked and barely saw the building. It was almost

hidden from the camouflage of the vines. "That must be older than the shelter we were in near St. Andrews, is it?"

"Slightly. Bathhouses date anywhere from medieval to the Victorian era. That building is Celtic and pre-Christian. It is known as a broche. They built them for shelter and defense. It preceded the castle and my family. Not much is known about the family it must have housed for a while. There is only one door and no windows. Most of the top of that one is gone. I'd like to show you the inside when we get back. It is never on the official tour." He paused.

"Why is that?" she asked intrigued by it now.

"It is where the murder occurred that brought you here, Leigh."

CHAPTER NINETEEN

The combination of paid for men and 'talk' money now finally produced someone in the hotel at London Links that thought she saw the lady in question. He had a computer printout photo from the Mississippi Highway Patrol driver's licensing bureau which he acquired through his hacking skills again. Yes, she was very similar, the lady told them. In fact, she remembered that the woman she saw had come out of the ladies' toilet in the hotel, but she never saw her go in. She thought it odd since her check-in desk was in clear view. There were many people in that morning she remembered, though, so could not be absolutely certain. Yes, and she said the lady used the pay phone and then got into a cab. No, she wasn't sure which cab company it was. Paid very well for the information, the lady was pleased she was such an observant person.

"Well, now, it is just a matter of hours, Ms. Reid. We'll have you on our playing field," he said to himself as he practically skipped to his car. Kadar's pulse raced at the thought of meeting this clever target.

Leigh was still a little uneasy at the personal nature of Geoffrey's conversation and more so at her own reaction to that intense look he gave her during the picnic. She was sure he must have just been trying to figure her out to see if she was trustworthy of her job. Yes, that was it. She threw it off as just being plain silly, enamored with the turn of events putting her with him at this wonderful place and home. She really needed to remind herself that he was the Duke of Dalroch. That was royalty and all that goes with it. Better for her to focus on the next tour she was going to take rather than get caught up in some fantasy that had not one prayer of being in the real world. Remember, Silly, she said to herself, you are here on business and it was definitely time to get down to it, before you give in to that fantasy.

After they left the buggy at the stables, Geoffrey said, "Maybe you'd like to ride sometime. The stables have several excellent riding ponies. Just let Simmons know what you need, and he'll fix you up." Geoffrey walked on and turned and said, "If you would come this way, Leigh. We'll look inside the broche, and then I'll give you the materials I have for you to read on this case. Is that all right?" He seemed more aloof now or was she just imagining things? Well, best to remember her place, she thought. After all, again, she was an employee, he the employer. Good. That was a place she was much more comfortable in.

They went inside the large round building. It had a stone interior wall and floor. It was cold and damp inside. It smelled of mold and musky mildew. Leigh crossed her arms and tried to see the interior as Geoffrey took a lantern off a shelf and struck a match to get some light. There was an eerie glow that began to dance on the walls.

"This building has been here unused and unrepaired since the murder of Princess Melinde from Spain in 1746," he started.

Well, Gabby had said 'old' case. But 250 years old was a little over the top, Leigh thought quickly figuring.

She laughed out loud saying, "Geoffrey, I was not expecting a case that is centuries old! I guess you realize that evidence would be a little hard to come by after 250 years!" But she added quickly, thinking Geoffrey would feel she wasn't very interested in pursuing the case, "However old it is, I still want to hear all about it."

They sat on a stone bench up against a wall and

Geoffrey proceeded to tell her about the case she was there to work on.

"There are several journals that have been written by members of the family about the incident. There are a few old newspaper reports and even a personal diary the Princess kept during this time. She was 24 years old, very beautiful and well-loved by her family and country. The 4th Duke of Dalroch, who at the time was the Marquis of Dalroch, was very much in love with Melinde. They previously met on board a ship from Spain to London. She was a very talented artist and the Marquis inquired about commissioning her almost instantly after meeting her and seeing her work. She came to paint the castle and the Marquis' horse. She apparently accepted the offer because she herself was a bit smitten by the Marquis. They were apparently in love by the time she arrived here. Their respective families gave their respective blessings to a proposed marriage. She was here with her parents in preparation of the wedding when she was killed. She was found here the morning of the wedding day in a pool of blood. The Marquis was the one who found her.

Geoffrey stopped and stood. He walked back and forth in the room while he continued, "There were some, ah, little known additional facts that were not written down or published. They have been handed down Duke to Duke. One of these was that the Marquis suspected Melinde was here with a lover the night before the wedding. The lover, rumored to be the Marquis of Perth, was a cousin to the Dalroch Marquis. He was very infatuated with the olive-skinned beauty, and she was definitely that--a beauty. There's a portrait of her I will show you. Now the Marquis of Perth was engaged to another and was set to be married the following month. He told his father he wished to break off the engagement to his fiancée, but there were certain rules in those days that had to be followed when it came to uniting properties, wealth, and families.

At any rate, the Marquis of Perth's marriage did take

place and they lived happily ever after. The 3rd Duke of Dalroch faced a public scandal because the rumors were so great in the country that his son had murdered Melinde. Rather than let his only son face murder charges, he fabricated the facts. He invented a story that Melinde was walking along the shoreline and attracted a local pirate, were, fortunately for the story, numerous in the day, who raped and then murdered here in this building. The locals really had no choice but to believe their Duke's accounting and his son's reputation went unspoiled. He eventually took his place as the 4th Duke of Dalroch, as expected. There hasn't been any scandal since then in this family, but a question still remains as to the truth about Melinde's murder. Even though the murder was covered up, there was never a real attempt at ascertaining what really happened to her that morning. We do know that the Marquis of Dalroch denied being down here that night and the family said he was visibly heart broken, saddened and gloomy the rest of his life whenever Melinde's name was mentioned. Obviously, he eventually married, or the Dukedom would have been carried on by another line of my family. Now the Marquis of Perth was indeed in residence here that night since he was to attend the wedding with his family within the next few days."

"So, the family has always tried to keep the truth from coming out. Whatever the truth is, it has been a 'skeleton' in my family's closet ever since. I've engaged several criminal investigators, as did my father, to look into it. The answers have always been the same, though. No witnesses, no suspects, other than both the Marquis of Dalroch and the Marquis of Perth. And both of them had too much to lose to ever speak of the night again. They obviously didn't, and, in short, the murder has been unresolved. I need answers, though, to give me the personal satisfaction that the 3rd Duke was right in helping his son back then. If he covered up the guilt of his son, then I plan on making right the wrong that the Princess and her family suffered even after all these years. It's as simple as that, really."

A few moments of silence passed. Leigh was touched by his intentions and she instinctively stood up and placed her hand on his arm. She jerked it back immediately and kept her eyes from his. Then she turned and said. "Even if it means the truth would cause a public scandal after all these years for your family name?" She shouldn't have touched him. She only meant it as a sympathetic gesture, but it was much more to her after the burning sensation she had felt go through her body. Boy, was that a warning sign or what?

No answer from him. She turned and looked into his eyes. He was looking at her again intensely like he had at the picnic. The room was almost spinning around from the reaction she had this time. She felt like running right out of this place, from him and the feelings that he was arousing in her. His face was almost devastatingly handsome here in the candlelit room. She was almost distracted totally from her thoughts and yes, from the job she had just listened to! Just jolly good! Not what she needed right now. She was not going to let herself feel anything. She just wasn't. She had to get a grip!

She took a deep, if not jagged, breath and gathered her thoughts quickly. She began looking around. "Ah, I would need to know where she was found in here. Oh, and is that in the materials you're going to give me?" She managed to keep from looking at him this time. Best to avoid those piercing blue eyes.

After a few seconds as if he was summing up some sort of thought or theory, he said, "Yes. You will find answers to probably quite a few questions in these. But remember the cover-up and the reasons for it. I have tried to put myself in the Marquis' position and if it was true and she was with a lover, I know I would be inflamed, but I don't know that I would resort to killing. He, on the other hand, may have felt differently. Well, there you have it. That's the case I need you to analyze and give me your opinion on. Still want to tackle it? Or do you want to tell me now that you would rather not tackle it? It is quite all right if you don't wish to accept the job. Really, I would certainly understand, Leigh."

She still refused to look into his eyes, but said, "I accept the offer to delve into the Princess Melinde's unfortunate demise. Without much evidence, I cannot promise or guarantee any more than what you already know. If you'll let me see the materials you have, I will take them to my suite tonight and give them a thorough going over. I assume you don't want them to leave the castle with me?"

"No, of course I trust you to take and bring them back if you like." Geoffrey was smiling again as she glanced at him. "I'm very glad you have accepted."

Still trying not to look directly into those eyes, she said, "Well, if I need to, I'll take them back with me. However, I can tell you this. Although I will review them thoroughly, if this long since happened murder can be solved by me, the answer will come from a combination of things. Mainly, and you may find this amusing, I trust my almost never wrong nagging gut feelings. I don't really want to call myself paranormal or anything close to it but I sometimes experience strange sensations on which way to draw conclusions. So, if I can draw a reasonable conclusion based on that, would you be satisfied?" This time she looked quickly into his eyes and smiled up at him.

"Well, I would have to say it's a deal because it's more than I have now. Thank you again for agreeing to try. It means a lot." He turned and walked to the door.

"Geoffrey?" She spoke his name quietly and he paused before turning.

"Yes, Leigh?" His voice was ever so soft.

"Ah, without having to read the materials first, where in here was she found?"

Geoffrey walked toward her looking her in the eyes again. He reached his arm toward her face. She did not move a muscle. What was he going to do? Touch her face? Oh, God, she thought as her pulse started to race and her breaths became shallow. The closeness and the darkness were obviously playing tricks on her mind, because he reached beyond her face and her head and grabbed the lantern off the shelf to blow it out. But just before the light was out, he said, "She was supposedly found where the blood stain is right exactly where you are standing."

CHAPTER TWENTY

As they left the broche doorway, Leigh saw Gabby running down the hill toward where they were.

"Dad! Leigh! What have I missed? Did you tell her about the case yet? I knew I should have left those silly friends of mine earlier." She was ever the enthusiastic one, Leigh thought as she watched with amusement. Gabby looked from one to the other with an excitement that was evident on her face.

"Well?' she asked expectantly.

Leigh spoke first, after all her vital signs calmed down from the near miss of another touch from Geoffrey. Forget the murder mystery, she thought. The heat from the close encounter with him was enough to cause physical reactions beyond those generated by the facts of the crime she was here to investigate.

She cleared her throat and said, "Your father has shown me the murder site and I'm just now going to go through the reading materials he has given me. We had a lovely day touring the house and hills. I think, though, I have taken far too much of your father's time today. I'll just go on up and freshen up." She turned back to Geoffrey and said in her very businesslike tone, "Where shall I meet you and what time?"

His tone in return was aloof again, "Supper is on the agenda first. Then we can retire to the study to go over those materials, Leigh. I will need to explain a few of them because the family passed on the materials with oral representations that aren't so clear by just reading."

"Great, well then, thank you again for the lovely day

and for asking me to assist in this case. I will see you later. Gabby, are you going back out tonight?" Leigh asked Gabby as she fell in step beside her as they headed up the hill ahead of Geoffrey. Before long, they were out of earshot.

"Well, I thought I might go to a show. It's probably going to be boring, though. So, what do you think of Dad?" Leigh was not sure why she asked that, but she was actually scared to say anything in response. She thought she better say something though before Gabby in all her astuteness picked up on her uneasiness.

"Well, now, he's the perfect host for sure. And you have a wonderful father who adores his daughter very much. Other than that, I really don't know how to rate him on the Royal Scale of One to Ten seeing as he is the only royal person I know, of course, other than you." She laughed at Gabby's smile.

"Hey, I think you ought to stay over some more while you're working, don't you? I mean, you could work easier here, couldn't you? Oh, I didn't ask, but assumed. You are going to take the case, aren't you?"

"Gabby, I have more than enough other work to do back in St. Andrews. This is kind of out of the way for my research project there. Besides, I have a special meeting set for next week. Your boss man, Flackerty, has made all of the arrangements." Gabby looked defeated; Leigh wondered why she wanted her here more. It couldn't just be because of the case, could it?

"I mean I am taking the case, I just need to get back to the job at the University. Well, I guess I could try to come back in a couple of weeks. By that time, I may have a clue on the 'whodunit' here. OK?" With that, Gabby brightened up again and said, "Swell! I am sure that Father would be as pleased as I that you could visit again." Then, she fell back in with her Dad behind Leigh and when Leigh glanced back them, they were arm in arm and smiling.

Leigh went on up to her room, finally finding her way through the many corridors. Without letting herself even think about her personal attraction she was beginning to feel toward Geoffrey, she went and took a long, luxurious hot bath.

While soaking with her hair piled up and almost drifting into a numb state, she let her mind take her to Marlow, to her sanctuary. She was missing her horses, her house, and her work again. And, after watching Gabby and Geoffrey, with their obvious close relationship, she was missing her son - something really awful. She was also finding herself missing the day-to-day hustle-bustle of the courtroom. Too bad that had to end. She was good at her job, too. So much for her promising prosecution career. She didn't know if she would ever darken the door of a courtroom again. It was highly unlikely. She was obviously on a new path now. One that could probably lead to an academic life. Ugh! Now, that was just a little too boring for her!

She was having trouble deciding how to dress when a knock came to the door.

"Yes?" she called from the dressing room.

"It's me, Gabby. Can I barge in?"

"Sure. Come on in, I'm in the dressing room."

Gabby came in and plopped down on the floor beside the big lounge chair Leigh was sitting on still in her robe.

"Father said to tell you that if you don't mind, supper would be in about 30 minutes. Oh, and he dresses for supper. Like every night if you can believe that! I mean, well, if you don't know what to wear, a dinner dress would be fine. And, if you didn't bring one, I have some that you could pick from." She was a real dear, this Gabriella McKennah!

Smiling, Leigh said, "As it so happens, I just purchased one that might do. Want to see if it'll pass inspection?" She pulled out her black dress.

Gabby just smiled with a bit of a gleam in her eye and nodded yes. Then she just shot up and raced out, "See you in a few!" she called out as she was closing the door.

"No show tonight then?" Leigh called after her.

"Oh, yes, but not until after supper." She had another sheepish gleam in her eye. What was she up to now, Leigh wondered? She couldn't help but think Gabby was trying to maneuver her to spend more time with her Dad. Maybe she was too young to realize the class differences between them. When all was said and done, Leigh was still a Mississippi middle class girl with no royal protocol, no family ties in aristocracy, and certainly no wealth. But the thought that Gabby might be hoping her Dad would be interested, and visa-versa, was amusing to Leigh. Not to mention, Leigh was doing everything she could to keep from going down that road!

Finishing dressing in a hurry, Leigh thought about the rigidity of what must be the Duke's life. Dressing every evening! Not to mention she only had thirty minutes and that did not give a girl much of a chance to look dazzling. And she did want to look her best tonight. Maybe she wanted Geoffrey to see that she was capable of looking like a lady despite her profession. Now wasn't that perhaps acting out some sort of fantasy, she thought. Did she really want him to think that she was a woman, not an employee? In her dreams, she thought. Oh, well, she took a little extra time for a special touch of makeup, put hair up in a twist, don her new scarf folded over the low cut of the dress, and put on her new Celtic jewelry from St. Andrews. There. Not too shabby for a girl from rural Mississippi, she thought.

As she looked--really looked with a discerning eye, for the first time in a long time, into the cheval mirror at her reflection, she saw she still had curves in the right places, her weight was not too much, her face still had a smoothness that stress and age hadn't taken too much of a toll on, and her legs still had some shape to them. She really didn't feel too matronly even though she was the ripe old age of 42. Damn, she thought. I am ancient! Too old to be thinking about looking good anymore for any man! But, then, as she turned to leave the image in the mirror, she winked, and smiled. "Right!" she said as she closed the door.

As she approached the dining hall, she heard the sound of the bagpipes again. She followed the sound up to the gallery that Geoffrey played in last night when she first arrived. Yes, as Gabby had predicted, he was dressed formally in a black suit, white shirt and black tie. The music was so beautiful and really got next to Leigh as she came up the stairs. He was so intense in his playing that he did not notice her. The gallery had oil paintings of past residents of the castle. They were all aglow with the portrait lights shining down on them. One in particular had a very striking resemblance to Geoffrey yet was obviously not from this century. She wondered who it was. She made a note to ask him but got so moved by the song that she just stood and watched Geoffrey play until he finished the song.

"Please tell me the name of that song. What an enchanting tune!" she said to him
obviously startling him, as he jumped slightly at her voice. He looked up at her. The sound of the bagpipes was still echoing down in the large room below, but he was very quiet. Had he heard her question? There was that look again. She couldn't be imagining it. It held her in an almost trance-like state for what seemed like a long time. She managed to pull her eyes away from him before he did.

Finally, he broke the silence, "It's called 'To the Gallawae Hills'. It was written long ago. I'll tell you the words sometime. I think you would like them." Then, he spoke very softly, "I think you look very lovely, Leigh." His voice was controlled but he looked out of sorts. His eyes traveled the length of her body and she was enjoying the attention so much that she completely forgot to ask again about the portraiture. In fact, she just about forgot who she was, what century she was in, or anything else, but the almost raw feelings of attraction for Geoffrey.

"There you guys are! Let's eat, already! I am starved. And, I am on a schedule tonight. The theatre starts at 8 sharp!' Gabby was coming up in the balcony. She was dressed in a red satin dinner dress. She looked so pretty in it; Leigh was struck again by her dazzling looks with her red hair glistening as much as the dress.

"Wow, Leigh! You look outstanding! Doesn't she Father?" Leigh was blushing after Geoffrey's looks and now the compliment from Gabby.

Geoffrey put his bagpipes down and came over, bowed and offered his arm to Leigh and Gabby. "You are both beauties to behold, ladies. Now, if you lasses would allow me, may I escort you to our table?" He was so gallant, and they all grinned and went down to supper.

After what could only be called a grand feast back home, consisting of roast pheasant, mashed potatoes, steamed asparagus with lemon sauce, dinner rolls to die for, and a custard covered apple cobbler for dessert, Gabby excused herself and said she was heading back to meet her friends.

"Don't wait up, Father. I'm going to the show in Inverness and will be late." She looked over at Leigh and winked.

Then, she went and kissed Geoffrey on the cheek, "And, I'll be very careful."

"Good night, dear. Have a good time." Geoffrey watched her go and then got up and said while pulling Leigh's chair back, "Would you like to join me in the study now for a glass of wine? I have everything ready for you to look at on the murder."

"Thanks for such a superb supper, I enjoyed it. Yes, I am ready to see what you have." Geoffrey brushed her arm as he pushed her chair back under the table. Electricity again, thought Leigh. I wonder if he feels the same thing? Silly girl, she thought. Work is all that he is studying right now. Besides, employer--employee, remember Leigh?

They went into the study. He poured her glass of white wine and then showed her to a library table that had several old documents covered in plastic covers. She started looking through them one at a time. It was hard to understand the handwriting at first on some of the papers, plus there were a lot of the older Scottish words like from a completely different language. She asked Geoffrey to translate a few of them. The most impressive document was the Princess' journal itself. It had a typed-out translation of Spanish to English attached to it. Although there were no entries for the day of her murder, there were some comments in the prior days leading up to it that were somewhat strange for a bride to make. Leigh noted these in her mind. But Geoffrey was sitting close to her and his masculine smell was beginning to distract her again. He looked rather dashing already and being close to him was clouding her thinking again. Or was it the wine?

She decided it was best to stop this again before it got started and got up saying, "Well, I will just take these to my room and read through them now. I have my laptop here, so I can make a few notes before I leave tomorrow. Then I will be able to work without taking these with me." She walked over and put her empty wine glass on the mantle and stood with her back to the fireplace and Geoffrey came to stand in front of her.

"Oh, Leigh, by the way, I have the portrait of Melinde that our family kept taken down and miniaturized for your review. I don't know how it could help, but maybe seeing her face puts a more personal note on the investigation." Geoffrey opened a drawer and pulled out a small portrait of Melinde and handed it to Leigh. With a quick glance, Leigh felt almost an immediate recognition of Melinde, but she did not know how or why. It must have been from the case documents and reports that her personality and life seemed to match the picture. Whatever the case, Leigh saw she was a beautiful woman. She had black hair up in a beautiful arrangement on her head with a dark blue hat with feathers topping it off. Her suit was blue and had pearl buttons and lace trimmed edges. She appeared to have dark blue eyes and a mischievous, if not, all-knowing, smile on her face. The background was obviously a lush green forest; Leigh looked at it so intently, that she forgot Geoffrey's presence next to her. That was saying a lot after the last few hours of not thinking about much else.

He cleared his throat and said, "May I ask where I can reach you if something should come up that I need to discuss with you, about the case?" Was he really wanting to discuss the case, or was there a personal reason behind this request? She had not let anyone know where she was staying, not even Flackerty or Gabby. Something told her that Geoffrey could be trusted, though. Besides, her heart was telling her to let him know how to find her anywhere or anytime,

"I'm staying at the Kilconquhar resort, Lodge 21. Do you know where that is?"

"Yes, and I'll be in touch if we should need to talk. If you have any questions after reading back through these things, please let me know. I'll be going out of town early tomorrow morning, so I'll say goodbye tonight. I have enjoyed your company, Leigh. I look forward to seeing you again." He offered his hand and she shook it. He held it a little longer than she expected again just like he had the night before. His gaze was so strong, that she was overcome with the sensation that she wanted him to kiss her. What a stupid reaction, she told herself. But just then he pulled her to him by her shoulders. Her heart was racing, and she felt flushed. He looked down into her face and then lowered his mouth to the side of her face and lightly brushed his lips on her cheek. Well, that was as close as it gets without being the real thing! Clearing her throat and trying to breathe, with all the force she could muster, she pulled back and turned and left the room.

She was so caught up in her emotions at the point of leaving the room that she forgot some of the papers. She went back to her suite and just paced. She was mad at herself for overreacting to Geoffrey's attentions again. He was just being polite, she told herself. You know, European hellos and goodbyes. They all kiss on the cheek. What was it about this man that she could not even think straight when he was close? Was she so deprived of physical closeness with a man that she was just overreacting? Or, was this something that was going to drive her bananas? When her pulse began to subside and she finally talked herself out of her fantasies about him, she had gone and taken another long but cool bath. It was not until several hours later that she decided to go back and retrieve the papers out of the study. She had her long white gown and robe on. It was 2:00am. She didn't want to run into him again. Not the way she was feeling inside. She tried to wait until Gabby came home, although she had no way of knowing if she had or not. She eased into the study door and seeing the only motion in the dark was the remnants of the fire crackling in the fireplace, she went to the library table and picked up the papers. Just then a stream of light flooded the room followed by a clap of thunder. She jumped and almost screamed. Then she walked to the large window behind Geoffrey's desk and stood gazing at the sky. She hadn't noticed the weather looking so ominous before. As she stood there, she felt a strange sensation come over her. It was as if she was feeling the presence of someone in the room. She looked around again, but there was no one there. How strange! Maybe the castle was haunted? She took her papers and eased back out of the study and went back to her room. Behind her he watched her intently and then he eased back out the same secret way he entered.

CHAPTER TWENTY-ONE

    In the dark information storage and communications room, the Keeper sat. He was alone, but his thoughts were racing. The place usually was his solace, but the pressing matter at hand was his focus and even the flicker of the monitors and screens couldn't take his mind off it. He knew that Kadar and his men were in the London Links Hotel just a few hours ago. Leigh Reid was staying at Kilconquhar, a little more than 30 miles from there. How soon would they find her? The Keeper had not searched her room, but he would do so tonight personally since he knew she was due to be back there tomorrow. He called for his helicopter. Then he went to a computer and acknowledged the note about Kadar to his operative at London Links. If the Keeper got there before Kadar's men, he could plant the dummy disc that had a few appropriate changes made in the coded symbols. That would give them something to focus on for a while. He was not sure that Kadar knew what he was getting into. The ramifications of the code being broken was global in nature because it held sensitive information on the location of their central data source and document storage location. They had strict security measures, but Kadar might luck up and get past these barricades in the code, too. If the secrets of the Society were revealed, the security of many operatives and certain ongoing projects would be at risk. It was the Keeper's opinion Kadar was too close for comfort. And, what about Leigh Reid? He did not want to admit it, but his feelings had gone way beyond the initial respect he had felt. He feared for her if Kadar got to her before the Keeper's Society could capture him. Kadar would not treat Ms., Reid very graciously after he had followed her, lost her, and now was almost on her again. He was also well paid, sources said. But a matching payment was due on delivery. Leigh Reid was in immediate danger. Could he let her still be the bait he needed to capture Kadar? The answer was now a definite 'no', He planned to try to get her back out of Kilconquhar as soon as possible. He did not know how to accomplish that, but he would. She was becoming too important to him now. He wouldn't let her get caught. She was an innocent bystander in all this. And, it was his fault he had let her continue to be bait. A buzzer went off and a voice across an intercom said, "Chopper's up and ready, Sir." He went up from the underground location to a landing that appeared out on the rocks with landing lights and a black helicopter. He got on board and told the pilot to put down in the fields to the north of the Kilconquhar resort. Time was of the essence.

....

Around 3:30 in the morning, Leigh's sleep was disturbed, and she awoke and sat up in her bed. Strange, she thought someone had been in the room. Had she dreamed it? She looked around quickly, although she saw nothing out of the ordinary. Her fire had died down and the coals were burning bright leaving an orange glow around the fireplace. Leigh was not frightened by what or who she thought had been there. She stayed awake though and replayed the information she had on the Princess's murder back in her mind until she finally dozed back off about 7:00 am.

She was back up and at breakfast at 8:30 sharp. Gabby was there and packed to go back to St. Andrews. She was full of conversation about the movie she had seen the night before, an American film. She went on and on about some American male star. Then she asked about Leigh and Geoffrey's evening after supper, and Leigh told her they had worked on the case materials. She couldn't tell her how her night had really gone. She had spent most of it vacillating back and forth on the murder and on the strange feeling she had that someone had been in the study and in her room. Most of all, her thoughts had been racing about Geoffrey and the feelings he had stirred up in her all day culminating with his light kiss on her cheek. All in all, it had been a long, long night for her.

Gabby asked as she finished her plate of eggs, "Will you be ready by 11:00am to head back to St. Andrews?"
"Sure, Gabby. I am already packed up, too." Leigh was more than ready. She was anxious to get away. Well, actually she wanted more to run away from her growing feelings for Geoffrey. Someone she could never be with. She finally concluded this during the long night of no sleep. He was way out of her league. He could have any number of women in his 'class', she figured. If he was miraculously attracted to her, the only possible relationship she could have with him would be that of a short fling. She felt that she could never be good enough to be a permanent fixture in his life. Oh, she knew of such relationships, but they were few and far between. Besides, they were 'far between'. Not likely that there would ever be anything between them but the Atlantic Ocean, she mused. No, although she did feel a fling would satisfy the growing feelings and desires he had stirred up in her, she was not going to let herself get into a hopeless situation. So, she had made her decision to finish her work for him, send a report in writing via Gabby, and never ever darken the doors of Dalroch again. Yes, it was better to cut ties now. That way, there would be no unrealistic expectations and certainly no more opportunities to have those expectations magnified.

CHAPTER TWENTY-TWO

She arrived back at Kilconquhar via Gabby's escort service late in the afternoon. It was never brought up again on the long drive, the questions about Leigh and Geoffrey. That was comforting to Leigh as she had no answers to give Gabby, even if she was trying to do some immature matchmaking. As far as Gabby knowing where she was staying, she thought it safe if it was safe with Geoffrey. As she got her bags out of Gabby's Rover, she told Gabby she would see her later in the week at the University when the first meeting on the project would take place.

"It was really swell of you to go home with me and to agree to work for Father, Leigh. I'll see you soon, I hope!" With that, the fiery-haired girl put the car in reverse and headed back out of the resort.

In the lodge, by the time she organized her notes on the murder from the reading she had done the night before, it was late when she went to bed. While she was sleeping, she dreamed about the Princess Melinde. It was distorted, but it was a compilation of some notes in the Princess' personal journal that had haunted Leigh since she read them. They were brief notations referring to her new life at the castle of Dalroch. The notes about her new life were referring to 'a new life' and the dream interpreted that phrase as meaning just that 'a new life' was referring to a baby, not just living there with the Marquis. Leigh saw the Princess in the broche rubbing her stomach. It was as clear to her as if Melinde was in the same room with her. Leigh woke up with a start. That was the gut feeling she was having and egged on in her dreams. Melinde was pregnant when she died! That must have been part of the motive for the killing. Whose child would it have been, the Marquis of Dalroch's or Marquis of Perth's, or someone else she did not know about? It was her nagging gut feelings again, but she placed a high reliance on them. Just how would she prove the pregnancy? She thought about it and developed a plan. But it would entail another trip to the broche, and that meant seeing Geoffrey again and she had just made up her mind to not see him again. Maybe she could get in and out of Dalroch without running into him. Of course, who was she to believe he would make the effort to be there even if he knew she was coming? It was too important to her to get the information she needed, though, and then to complete her working arrangement with him. She noted on her computer her ideas while they were still fresh in her mind. Then she got out her computer and came up with a short summary of her conclusions. It was 4:00am when she finally put her notes down and closed her laptop. All she needed was the proof of the pregnancy and then she could narrow down the list of likely suspects.

Monday morning at 6:00 am she called Jarrod. She hadn't slept since she had been awakened from her dreams at 11:00 the night before. She really hadn't slept the night before that, either It had been weighing heavy on her mind that she hadn't talked to her son since she had arrived. Seeing Gabby and Geoffrey together made this seem so much more important. She was very tired and didn't really realize she wasn't thinking very clearly. She placed the call not heeding her groggy sixth sense warning her not to.

"Hello." It was her son's sleepy sounding voice. How wonderful he sounded.

"It's me, Pumpkin. I know it's late over there, but—"

THE OGHAM CONNECTIONS

"Mom! I can't believe it! Finally! It is so good to hear your voice. I have been worried sick about you for some reason. Are you OK over there? Where are you?"

"I'm in Scotland working on my research project. I've also been hired by the Duke of Dalroch in the Highlands area to consult on a criminal case. It's all going pretty well, son, but I guess I'm missing you so terribly much that you must have felt that all the way over there. I'm all right otherwise. How are classes? Isn't it about exam time? Are you ready for them?"

"Yeah. I am so tired of studying, but I think I'm going to have some really good grades barring no real screw ups on the exams. Tell me more about Scotland, Mom."

"Well, if you do have really good grades, would you like to come over here after exams? I have enough money to get you here and stay for a week or so."

"Scotland? You bet, Mom. I'd love it! Call me back next week and I'll have the exam results and if they're good, we can make the arrangements. That's great, something to really look forward to." He sounded so happy and so good to Leigh. It was good for her soul to hear his voice.

"Well, son, I better go. You go back to sleep. Talk to you next week, OK?"

"I love you, Mom. Thanks for checking up on me. Oh, before you go, what's the news on the break-in at Marlowe? Have you heard anything?" Jarrod, bless him, was worried about it too.

It was dawning slowly on her that she was talking too long should someone be trying to trace her call, so she said quickly, "No news, but it's under control. Don't worry about it, dear. I'll talk with you next week. I love you very much!"

Leigh was so elated that she had made that call. She went to sleep again happily and slept soundly finally.

The numbers came up on the screen with a small alarm sound within minutes of the call to Jarrod in Boston. "Bingo, bitch! Contact to your son was your second mistake." Kadar smiled. Now he knew where she was by the number she dialed from. It had been easily discernible. With a little more effort, he had her location. Kilconquhar Resort, lodge number 21. Now, it was only a matter of time before he got what he needed. His instructions were for one team to follow her for now, while he led the search of the lodge. He planned to go in right away.

CHAPTER TWENTY-THREE

In the lower depths of the Society's headquarters, the Keeper looked at the latest intelligence report. He cursed at the fact that they had yet to determine the location of Sahib's latest weaponry. It was a hi-tech chemical weapon that was capable of mass destruction, a WMD. If they could find its location, they had the technology to send their robot roach in and it would be able to dismantle it. They knew what type of chemical compound made up the base of the weapon and even where the weapon had been bought and how much had been paid for it. The only vital piece of information they needed now was, unfortunately, its hiding location. So, Sahib thought his power would be increased and he could begin to build a small empire with leadership based on threats. The threats would come from his new weapon capability and from what he could find in the coded information that he had hired Kadar to retrieve. Kadar, however, was going to be the leverage the good guys needed once they captured him. They would be able to buy off the counterintelligence from Kadar and his men and have hopefully the location of the weapon within 24 hours. At least that was the plan. That would take the roar out of Sahib's master plan.

The Keeper's organization, known as the Stenness Society, or the Society as it was called amongst the members, was named after a ceremonial meeting place of the prehistoric Orcadians, the forerunners of the Celts and Scots. The organization was formed by his father back during WWII. It was a highly secret organization that prided itself not only on its secrecy but on its global peace goals. There was a need back in the mid-1940s, as there had been ever since, to keep a private eye on the comings and goings of all world leaders and terrorist groups. Hitler's rise and fall, and all that it cost, was proof that the international watchdogs of terrorists were not adequate. There was no centrally organized group that shared information. Politics worldwide kept each powerhouse government from giving any more information to others than was absolutely necessary. Thus, financing for the society was originally through a few private member donations. The money had been carefully and artfully invested into a multi-million-dollar return, which gave them the necessary technological equipment, the staff, and the ability to recruit operatives from the best intelligence organizations in the world. Their operatives came from the FBI, CIA, Ml5, Interpol, and other covert organizations. Recruited from these organizations, though, the operatives were effectively 'off the grid' once they joined the Society. They were never in contact with family, friends, or former organizations once in. It was a vow of secrecy that kept them operatives. The price for giving any information about the Society was death. Although paid well for their services, they had to be the best at what they could contribute. The Society was also charged with the duty of knowing all the major physicists and scientists all over the world, their achievements, their career paths, and any new weapon developments. They knew more secrets on political leaders throughout the world than any of the so called world class police intelligence organizations. They also knew every major terrorist group and mercenary for hire. They found and had data on every weapon of mass destruction that was in existence, except for Sahib's latest. Their operatives were placed in locations that allowed them to monitor politically hot areas when needed and they could infiltrate most groups and disarm any weapons before they could be fired. The Society also invested in a satellite defense system that had the coordinates of all the weapons and if all else failed, the satellite could detonate any airborne weapon from missiles guided by the satellites. The chemical weapons and airborne viruses were the more problematic ones for the Society, but they had their own team of chemists and scientists that worked to counteract particular agents that were known. These Society employees were in several countries hidden deep in undercover positions in hospitals, University labs, and industrial settings. All in all, the Society was doing what it was designed to do. It had only one major problem at this moment. The Keeper, as he was known and was his code name, who was the leader of the Society, was having a hard time concentrating. He had ostracized himself from the real-world years ago and had rebuilt the headquarters in its present staunch, sturdy and secure caves below the water. He had totally immersed himself in his work for years. He had little time for living a normal life. The rooms were accessible by entering a landlocked cave on top. Then there was a series of preset security clearances that allowed one to get into the hidden elevators down. The location of this operational and information storage headquarters was top secret even to most of the operatives. They only were in contact via coded electronic communications. The Keeper insisted on the secrecy of this location due to the ever-advancing information technology world and the need to know the location. If the word ever got out about the Society, every world government power would go to extreme measures to know this location. They would also want to know what the Society knows. This would not be healthy in a world full of unrest. The Society had set rules and the Keeper was the rule keeper and the leader. He and he alone was responsible as the Keeper of the coded information. He and he alone decided when the information would be acted on. He and he alone was at the present allowing personal feelings to cross over into business. Leigh Reid. He had personally involved himself in this operation after the Raven was murdered in New Orleans. The information on the disc was highly sensitive and it had to be retrieved at all costs, including unfortunately, Raven's life.

The Keeper found the coded disc in Ms. Reid's apartment at Kilconquhar a couple of hours earlier. He took possession of it and replaced it with a very similar look alike. He thought that would give Kadar what he needed, and he would leave her alone for a little while, at least, until the lady had been neutralized as a target. He was getting a sickening feeling in his stomach, though. Although the chase had started out with him wary of her, he now had seen her enough and watched her enough to know she was not a spy or government plant in all this. To top it off, he was facing a growing attraction to her to a point that she had touched him in a place that surprised him. A heart that he didn't remember he even had since he never allowed anyone to touch it in many years. He was beginning to care for her so much that he was hating himself for allowing her to be put in harm's way. Now he hoped by making the exchange that the immediate danger was gone.

The Keeper watched from a short distance away Sunday night when Kadar made his entrance in the lodge. It was minutes after the Keeper planted the dummy disc. He knew Kadar found it. The Keeper and several of his men were in strategic locations ready to move in if need be. They watched through thermal infrared cameras which showed where she was sleeping. They watched him search and they watched him find the planted code. The Keeper watched with what he realized was an uncharacteristic jealousy when Kadar stopped by her bed and watched her sleep. He stayed there a long time, considering he knew she could have awakened at any moment. The Keeper felt that Kadar was probably committing the act of voyeurism. Uncomfortable watching, he hesitated and looked away trying to get a grip on his uncharacteristic feelings. Just in that moment, they lost him as he literally disappeared from the lodge. He was a slick operator with many tricks to throw off followers. He obviously knew someone was tracking him. Their plans were to take Kadar down as soon as they had a position on him and his men again. The pleasure would be all the Keeper's, too. He thought though that he would now have to make sure Ms. Reid get somewhere safe before Kadar realized he had a fake disc. Because at that point, her life would be in danger then, yet again.

....

     Oh, she was tempting, he had to admit, as she was lying there naked in her bed fast asleep. Kadar was amusing himself watching her breathe after he eased the covers off and enjoyed the view. If he hadn't already found the coded disc in her closet, he would have tried to have a little more fun with her. Too bad. He could have come up with several innovative techniques to try on her. But now he could get the information decoded and get it to Sahib and collect the rest of his bounty. The thought that she may have told someone else about the code here in Scotland made him hold up on leaving the country right away though. He informed his men to keep following her one more day to see who she was in contact with. If anyone looked suspicious, they would decide what to do with them. For now, though, he was sure she was only a mule, a carrier of the message. He knew there was another group that had been watching her too. Sahib had told him they would be after him when the Raven was murdered and that he needed to leave no one alive that had access to the information on the disc. He knew that they would be close behind him. But he thought he could outsmart them. Of that, he was fairly certain.

CHAPTER TWENTY-FOUR

"Leigh?"

It was Tuesday morning. The voice on the phone was Geoffrey's. It had only been two days since she had talked to him, but her traitorous heart began to uncontrollably start racing. Great, she thought. How childish of her. Think of something to say quick, she told herself and she tried very hard to not sound as excited as she apparently was.

"Hi, Geoffrey. What's up? I hope you don't want a report so quick. I do, however, have some pretty strong leads that I need to follow up on." That sounded good. Calmer. Not too nervous, maybe.

"Yes, well that is why I am calling. I have another document that I found just after you left. It may or may not be important, but I thought if you did not mind too terribly much, I would have someone pick you up about lunch time and bring you here to see it. I know it's asking a lot since I know you have other work to do at St. Andrews, but I think you may need this before you go any further on the case. Can you come?" Geoffrey sounded so anxious and serious. Surely one little document could wait a few days!

"Well, I planned on trying to come back over the weekend. You could fax it to me, maybe? I think the office here or even at the criminology department at St. Andrews could receive it for me."

"Right, I would do that, but it is a very sensitive and old document, Leigh. I don't trust to have it handled to even fax it. I can have you picked up quickly and then you can see it for yourself here, and maybe stay a couple of days?"

Well, since he was offering a ride now and apparently insisting on her looking at the document, maybe she should go ahead and go. It would help to finish her work for him quicker. Her ideas about the case were forming fast and she needed the benefit of all the information available. If she did not need to go into the broche again to look for the evidence she thought she might find, she would have asked Geoffrey to just let someone deliver the apparently important document to her at her lodge.

She sighed into the phone, "I guess I could. If it is that important to you. I will need to make some calls and arrange to put off the work I was going to be doing today. I'm sure I can come after that I'll be ready by 12:30 pm if that's convenient." Her clock showed it was 9:00am.

"My pilot will pick you up at the front of your resort. Thank you for coming I know this is most inconvenient. I will, however, adjust your compensation to show my appreciation."

Well, that was very businesslike. 'Adjust your compensation' certainly sounded like an employer to employee phrase, did it not? All well and good with her, then. It made her believe her decision to keep things professional had been right. She meant to stick with it, too. Laughing to herself, she wondered what ever made her believe he wanted anything more than that either.

After she hung up, she called the University and told Alan Flackerty that she needed the first meeting with the local law enforcement contingent set up for Friday. She planned on launching her research project guidelines for them then. Then she asked Alan to find her the name of a private forensic specialist in the area, preferably one with serological expertise. Would do, he had told her. He had plenty of forensic contacts and would have a name in a jiffy. Sure enough, he called her back within a few of minutes with a name and phone number.

She called the number and spoke with a gentleman who had just the advice and answers she needed. He was hired immediately for the analysis she would need when she returned from Dalroch.

When the Duke said 'pilot', it did not dawn on Leigh that she would be escorted to Dalroch via a helicopter. The pilot was very nice but quiet, so she sat and enjoyed the views of the countryside.

The flight was short compared to that of the drive with Gabby so when they crossed over the mountains and started descending, she was surprised. There it was! Dalroch Castle in all its medieval glory. Her spirit lifted automatically at the sight of it. How regal it looked to her. His castle, she thought. That guy who she couldn't quite shake out of her system. Work, Leigh, work! Don't let your emotions for this place and that Duke rule you. She couldn't help feeling a little excited about seeing Geoffrey again, though. Her traitorous heart was pounding, and she was feeling very weak. But she promised herself again to be strictly professional.

Louise Daniels, the Castle housekeeper, opened the front entryway to Leigh. "Ms. Reid. How are you, my dear? I was told by My Laird to let you know your suite is ready. He apologizes that he will not be able to join you here until in the morning. He had business that would keep him until late tonight." She looked at Leigh's empty hands. "Did you not expect to stay? You don't have any overnight bags."

"Actually, Ms. Daniels, I planned on going back this evening. But I guess I could stay, though, if the Duke has gotten detained." She felt a twinge of disappointment but then threw it off as being unprofessional under her new plan of Emotional Detachment that was being implemented immediately now that it was strengthened by the news, he wasn't there to greet her.

"You know your way to your suite, then, I trust. There's a warm fire going in there and if you need anything, just dial 4 on the phone. Supper will be served in the Dining Hall, if you wish. But since you are alone, you might like to have it served in your suite?"

"That would be very kind, Ms. Daniels. Thanks, that is a good suggestion. I will eat in my room." The cooler air outside had given her a slight chill and the thought of a warm fire was inviting to her.

"Oh, and My Laird said the document you need is on the library table in the study." Ms. Daniels said as she was turning to leave the entryway.

"Thanks. I'll go there first. " Then, she forgot she had no night clothes. "Ms. Daniels! I am sorry, but do you think I might be able to borrow something to sleep in from Gabby's room?"

"Heavens, yes! Please, follow me. I'll take you to her rooms and you can pick what you need. Miss Gabby has lots of clothes and she wouldn't miss anything." Ms. Daniels chuckled and rattled on about Ms. Gabby's endless wardrobe all the way to her room.

Inside Gabby's suite, there was a definite 'princess' look to the room. Leigh smiled as she looked around. There were French provincial pieces everywhere with predominately pink and cream colors on the walls, floors and windows. Leigh was touched to see a large photo of Geoffrey and Gabby that must have been taken when Gabby was four or five years old on her dresser. He had been as handsome then as he was now. She went into Gabby's large, if not gargantuan, carpeted walk-in closets. There were the typical blue jeans, sweatshirts, tennis shoes, and scarves. A separate closet held formal dinner and cocktail clothes, and yet another held her night clothes and everything else. Leigh finally decided on a long white satin gown with a ruffled low-cut neckline. It was very feminine and pretty, like Gabby, and it looked like a perfect fit.

She then went to the study, after having Ms. Daniels show her the way from Gabby's suite of rooms and retrieved the document that was on the desk as promised. She glanced at it first. Hmmm, a maid's journal from the week of the murder. Interesting. She took it to her suite. Funny how she felt like it was 'her' suite. So silly of her to think such a thought, she knew, but she did feel that way. She sat a minute on one of the wing back chairs, then she picked up the phone and rang the stables. There were a couple hours of daylight left, and since this would be her last time here, why not take up the Duke's offer to go riding?

CHAPTER TWENTY-FIVE

Kadar's team worked much faster than even he anticipated. They had proven the code was worthless within a 12-hour period. Not unexpected, but definitely a kink in his plans. He checked in with his tag team at the resort, "A helicopter? Find out its destination. What? No flight plan? Where could she have gone? Did you check the registration numbers, you imbeciles? No numbers? You must have been mistaken."

I'll just wait here, he thought. She has sealed her fate with me. Planting a dummy code was brilliant on her part, but she will pay for it. He now believed she was an operative of the cleverest sort, living a double life. One as a prosecutor and another as an espionage agent. First sign she's back, she's all mine, he thought with the quick flash of a smile. The look on his face gave little doubt that he meant every word in every way.

English saddle riding was many years in her past. She only rode western pleasure with her horses. She was a little hesitant to get on board a high spirited animal like the one that was saddled in front of her. He was full blooded Thoroughbred from his looks. Tall, black and shiny. Of course, he was Geoff's favorite ride; she was told by the groom. She borrowed the riding clothes from Gabby's room prior to heading to the stables. Thanks, Gabby!

"Ne'r ya mind, lass. Dis one is as sure-footed as dey

come. Name's Lomond, it is. He responds to de slightest touch, yeah?" The groom was a jolly looking man with a twinkle in his eye.

Sure. The last horse she rode that responded to the 'slightest touch' was the last one she took a spill from. Well, she would give it a go in the stable yard first and then make up her mind. Getting a leg up from the groom, she sat up on Lomond and adjusted her stirrups.

"Okay, Lomond. Let's try a walk first." Kicking him with her heels slightly, he eased out at a walk. Good. Now a slight trot. Kicking him again with a little more pressure and giving a little on the reins, the big black eased into a smooth trot. Good. Then she pulled the reins back slightly and Lomond responded with an instant stop. He knows 'stop' and 'go' and 'go faster'. He'll do, she thought and signaled to the groom to open the gate to the outside of the paddock area.

She took him out at a canter and headed up the hill in the direction she and Geoffrey had gone in the buggy. It was slightly overcast, and the wind whipped into her face, blowing her hair back. She felt so very much alive as she and Lomond raced up the path. There was nothing like the feel of being on top of a running horse and feeling the bond that exists between rider and animal. Before she knew it, she was back on the top of the hill where she and Geoff shared the picnic earlier. She stopped and dismounted. Why was she drawn here again? She was not going to go back over her feelings for Geoffrey again. That was an unacceptable topic to dwell on. She had a new beginning here that included her work with Flackerty and her work for the Duke only insofar as the case was concerned. Which, she hoped would be through with a few more hours of work. Then she could get this whole place, and the man that made it so wonderful, out of her mind. Move on to the rest of her work here. She looked down at Dalroch. Lomond was grazing happily, so she sat and just stared letting her mind not concentrate on anything at all.

What is that, she asked herself as she watched the lapping of the white tops of the water in the lake. There was a dark shape in the hill where it met the water. Perhaps a cave? There probably were a lot of caves in this area, she thought. But she had not seen it before. Then she thought about the tides changing. The lake did empty into the ocean. She figured there must be a few inhabited caves that dated back to prehistoric times. She thought that the cave would be a fascinating place to tour. Pirates had existed before and could have hidden in caves all around here. It looked like a really good hiding spot, too. Too bad she did not have time to go boating on one of the Duke's boats and go cave touring, as well as riding on his horses, staying in his luxurious accommodations, wearing his daughter's clothes, and eating his prize chef's preparations. Smiling sardonically at that thought she started to get up to head back to the castle, but then the words 'hiding spot' hit a nerve. The disc. She hadn't even thought of the dangerous information that might be on the disc that she had been hiding for days!

    Well, maybe just hours. But being up here with nothut the sounds of the wind whipping through the hills, she could almost imagine the damned thing did not even exist. She tried to scan it into her laptop in a well-hidden file so she would be able to bring it up if she needed to. The original she had placed in her suitcase in the top of her closet. Maybe she could get that book out of the Dalroch library she saw earlier and try to decipher some more of the symbols on the disc. The Duke wouldn't even see or know what she was doing since he was gone. She would never want to put him and Gabby at risk by them having any knowledge of the disc or the fact that professional killers were looking for it, as well as her, she reminded herself. Well, that spoiled the moment and cutting her outing short, she grabbed Lomond's reins and jumped up on his back. A brisk gallop back to the barn as the sun began to set gave Leigh a renewed feeling of true giddiness and she felt less worried when she handed the reins back over to the groom, smiling.

"Thanks, he's a real sweetheart!" she said as he clucked to Lomond to follow him back in the stable.

As she came back in through the kitchen entrance, she nodded to the chefs who recognized her with a big smile and waves. Karman and Krista, she remembered, and said thanks for the dinner being sent to her room.

She made her way back to the castle and into the library. She wandered around the bookshelves until she found and grabbed the book on symbols and took it back to her room. She was feeling so good after her ride that she decided to get her laptop out and try her luck with the book and her downloaded disc symbols. She was way into the book, reading mainly, as there was no real new information on the Ogham marks other than what she already learned, by the time there was a soft knock at the door. She looked at the clock on the mantle. It was 8:30pm on the dot. Must be supper, she thought smiling. So ritualistic, these royal servants.

Her room service meal was a fantastic pasta dish with a dreamy tasting cream sauce, a side of green beans and a small loaf of garlic bread. Marveling at the luxury of her being served by servants in a castle, she once again, settled back into her work. After a feeble attempt at trying to decipher the symbols on the laptop as compared to those in the book, she gave up again. Maybe Flackerty's contacts included a cryptologist? She was a novice, and a bad one at that. She never really had much luck with any cryptic puzzles in the newspapers even. Out of her league again, she decided. She was tired and decided to take a nice soaking hot bubbly bath in the ritzy marble tub and then go to bed. She was asleep by midnight.

She woke up. It was dark. What time was it, she wondered? How long had she been sleeping? She turned on her nightstand lamp. The clock on the mantle said 2:00am. What woke her? She wasn't aware of the same presence she felt the last night she had slept there. She got up after a few minutes because she found she couldn't go back to sleep. She looked at the book from the library. Maybe she should take it back before morning. Not bothering with the borrowed robe or slippers, she eased down the hallways to the study. Inside it was cold. There was no fire going in the fireplace like before. She went to the bookcase where she replaced the book. Feeling that she should head back, she thought about her visits with Geoffrey in this room and a warm sensation flooded her chest. She decided to go to Geoffrey's desk. She traced softly the top of the desk with her fingers as if it would make her closer to him than she could ever be. She turned and looked out the large window. The moonlight was so bright that the outside drive and stable area could be made out. She stood and just drank in the quiet and peaceful feeling. She then thought about that fateful night so many years ago that took the Princess's life. It was a shame that her murderers had gone to their graves without confessing. Her thoughts went to the task she needed to complete. She would take care of getting what she needed from the broche early in the morning. Getting colder, she wrapped her arms around her and as she was just about to turn and leave, she suddenly had the feeling that she was not alone again. Oh, no. She did not want an encounter with the ghostly kind tonight. That would certainly top the visit off! She turned slowly around and this time there was a figure of someone standing by the mantle. She jumped and almost screamed. The figure moved into the light of the window. The sight took her breath instantly and she grabbed her chest.

Geoffrey!

CHAPTER TWENTY-SIX

He was dressed in a pair of sweatpants and an open shirt over his chest. The moonlight caught him as he eased out of the shadows. His chest was tanned with dark hair and muscular. His long hair was down loose around his shoulders. As long as she lived, she would never forget the sight and the feelings it stirred in her. He looked like a Highland warrior. He made her heart skip several beats and her breath short. He must have just gotten up from bed, she realized. But where did he come from? She hadn't heard anyone come in.

"Geoffrey. I--well, I wasn't expecting you. Not until tomorrow morning," she said shyly, realizing she had no robe on and her feet were bare. She felt very much like she had no clothes on either when she saw his eyes looking straight through her gown.

"Nor I you, Leigh." His voice was husky, and the words were slow and deliberate. "But I cannot tell you how glad I am to see you." Then he slowly walked up to her and placed his hands on her shoulders. She froze in her position. Without saying another word, he pulled her to him, then he gently lifted her face up to his. She did not resist, and she knew she couldn't even if she wanted to. His fingers slid across her eyes, her nose, her cheeks, then his hand cupped the back of her head and pulled her face to his. She couldn't think of stopping him. She looked into his eyes and was spellbound. Then ever so softly he placed his lips on hers. Time had stopped, she lost all consciousness of her surroundings and only knew she was Geoffrey's and for the moment, he was hers. Lost in an ebb of desire for him, she let him kiss her long and the sensations were rising. There was absolutely no rational thoughts passing through her mind. She knew after tasting his mouth, she wouldn't ever try to stop him from doing anything he wanted with her. The kiss ignited a fire that had been smoldering in her since she had seen him the first time. She responded to his mouth and their tongues answered each other with a longing that was almost primitive in nature. His mouth left hers and he then he lightly kissed the bridge of her nose, then her face, then her neck. She almost made a whimpering noise for she wanted him to continue, and she ran her hands through his long soft hair. She was pressed up against him so hard that she thought he would squeeze her into him. His mouth returned to hers. They were breathless in their exploration of each other's mouths. There was no turning back now. She would be his and he hers, if only for tonight. He grabbed her off the floor and carried her over to the wall with the bookcases. He pressed a button somewhere and one of the bookcases moved back into the wall. She looked questioningly at him. He said, "All castles have secret rooms, didn't you know?' Then he slid her into a room with one wall light on. That room turned into a hall and then into a winding stairwell up into the inner recesses of the castle.

    When they emerged, she saw a massive wood paneled bed draped in fabrics in the glow of a large fire going in a fireplace. It must have been his bedroom. It was fit for a King. This room had definitely not been on the tour he had given her for some reason. He laid her gently down on the bed. He lay beside her on his side and propped his head in his hand. His look had that same intenseness as he had given her before several times. Was this really happening, she wondered. No pinching this time. She touched his face as if to see if she were dreaming. She smiled. Certainly felt real enough. His face was full of emotion. He finally broke the silence, "Leigh. I have to tell you something." He paused as if trying very hard to tell her something very important. Too frightened of what it might be, she put her finger on his mouth. She did not want this moment to be ruined. She knew it couldn't be anything good. She felt his feelings could very well only be lust, this is what she did not want to hear or a lie that he cared for her. She just knew silence would be better. Right now, all she needed from him was to satisfy the desires his body and his mouth had lit up inside her. She leaned up to kiss him. He responded with such a passion that she felt she had never been thoroughly kissed before, not even in the library moments before. When he released her, his hand traveled to the shoulders of the gown. He pulled them down quickly while looking into her eyes and then looked at her breasts. Then he placed his mouth on them and slowly sucked and kissed the nipples until they were hard, and she began to ache for him with such a wanting that she felt herself getting very warm and moist between her legs. Her pulse was racing to an almost deafening roar inside her chest. She felt she would just die if he did not make love to her immediately. Through the gown he slowly traced her body down the curve of her waist and stopped at her thighs. Then he stood up and took off his pants with his gaze never leaving her body. He was full of desire she saw, and she wanted nothing more to have that desire tear through her own body. It seemed an eternity before he pulled her gown off and was on her and in her. He broke through the fiery wetness and she felt an immediate climbing sensation. A long wave of ecstasy jolted her as they both joined each other in a realm that only lovers can know. The feeling was so overwhelming that she thought she was flying. After she caught her breath, he slowly began again, this time he mounted her and with something she could only describe as a feeling of belonging, and they moved together in harmony. And she gave herself to him once again. She lost any capacity to think at all. When he finally came inside her, his groan of pleasure made her reach another climax instantly. He slowly exited, kissed her mouth so sweetly and then lay beside her. They both were very quiet. All that was heard was their contented breaths and the wood crackling in the fireplace. There was no describing the bond that she had with him now. She would be his, she realized, forever. No matter what happened now, it was would never change, this attachment to him. She knew that she was in love with Geoffrey McKennah. She had never loved any man that had brought out such sensual feelings and love. She was satisfied with this revelation and she felt like it was the same for him, although he had not spoken a word since they ended up in his room and bed.

Some time had passed then, and her mind descended back from the sky. He was still quiet, so she finally rose up on her side and looked over at him He was staring into the top of the bed with his arms crossed behind his head. She knew now she had to talk to him about what had passed between them. "Geoffrey, I know you were trying to tell me something before. I want you to know there is nothing that you can say to change the way I feel about you. You obviously know by what just happened I care very deeply for you." She was shy about these words, but she had to continue as he kept his eyes focused on the top of the bed. "But, I am not asking anything of you because of what just happened. You don't have to declare yourself one way or another. I am in love with you and I realize now after this that I always will be. There's no doubt in my mind. I didn't plan on this, this happening at all. It just happened. But, I have never felt like this about anyone, ever. You now know how deeply I can love you and want to love you. It is not because you are the Duke of Dalroch, Geoffrey. That is impressive, sure, to a little redneck from Mississippi like me. Of course, it would be to anyone, but I would have fallen in love with you had you been the stable boy here. It is because you are the most virile and attractive man I've ever known. You temper that with a gentleness and sensitivity that is a rare quality in a man."

She stopped to catch her breath and looked at him again She expected some response, surely. But he was not looking at her yet. She noticed though he had somewhat of a pained expression on his face. She waited to hear his response. He did not even look at her. She waited. And waited. He finally looked at her with no expression on his face whatsoever. He didn't speak. She said, very attuned to his silence, "Maybe I should not have expressed my feelings to you, but I have. I am not sorry for it either. Nor am I sorry I am in love with you." There, she had declared her feelings again. Maybe he did not want the serious type relationship. She was quiet again. Then she lay back down and waited for him to say something, anything! Dammit! She deserved some sort of response. Well, she had said he didn't need to declare himself. Well, I guess he's taking me to my word, she thought. But he was too silent. Had he made a mistake? Was he sorry for this situation he had led her into, making love and expecting him to return it? No, there was something more wrong than that. He was not that kind of man to do this to her. Was he?

"Geoffrey?" she asked almost in a whisper. He then broke his glance away and stared back at the top of the bed. She waited a few seconds longer and then it began to dawn on her that his silence could only mean one thing. This fact hit hard. She could only assume the worst at this particular moment. Assumptions would abound without some sort of explanation. Is that what he wanted? For her to assume? Not believing how incredibly stupid she had been, she wanted to run away from him. She began to get up. He's not saying anything because he got what he wanted, she surmised with a tightening sensation starting down deep in the pit of her stomach. A roll in the proverbial hay. I must have satisfied some physical need only. He's used me. She almost said aloud, "Well, I deserve this, now don't I? Getting some big idea that you cared a smidgen about me before taking me to bed!"

She grabbed her, well, Gabby's gown. Without another word more and before the tears in her eyes began to fall, she ran to the nearest door, hoping with all hope that it wasn't a closet door. She opened it saw a hallway and ran as fast as she could down what she prayed would eventually be the way back to her suite. She couldn't stop the tears as she ran. Finally, she saw a familiar turn in the castle. In what seemed like an eternity, she was back safe and secure in her room. Door locked. She began to tremble uncontrollably and then she fell into her bed and cried for what seemed like ages.

CHAPTER TWENTY-SEVEN

When she felt she could raise her heavy head again, she looked at the clock on the mantle. It was 5:00am. Had she been with him that long? It seemed like only a second in time. The sky was beginning to lighten outside and stream into the room. There was no doubt in her mind that she knew what she must do after the revelation that she had declared her love and he had not. She called the railway office and requested the time of the next train from Inverness to St Andrews. Then she called a cab all the way from Inverness and begged to have them come and pick her up in an hour. Promising a huge tip and doubling the normal fare, they sent one. She had to go and go quietly and quickly. She put on the clothes she had worn the day before, took Gabby's clothes she had borrowed back to her room and then eased into Geoffrey's study and lay a note she had written to him on his desk. Leaving in a hurry though, the note caught the draft from the doorway and blew off the desk and eased down to the floor under the desk. She left the castle as quietly as a mouse through the kitchen side entrance where the chefs had not yet arisen to start on breakfast. She quickly went down to the broche, lit the lantern, and scraped several darkened samples from the floor stains where supposedly the Princess had been found. Then she placed the samples in a Ziploc bag and looked around once more. She said to the empty space, "Goodbye Melinde. I hope to help you rest in peace very soon now."

She left the broche just as the sun started its morning

climb and the darkened areas slowly began to take on the light. She walked around the castle and then down the long drive to the iron gates at the entrance. She was hoping that the sun's light would come and wash away her turmoil from the bitter-sweet ending of her personal little fairy tale story. She was shivering in the cold and from her tumultuous emotional upheaval. The gatekeeper was surely asleep, and she did not wish to disturb him, so she eased around in the woods until she found a place to cross over to the roadway. Stepping over the underbrush and getting scratched on her face a couple of times, she finally got to the pavement when just down the road she could see the cab was coming. Just in time. It pulled into the side of the road when she waved it down. She got in, thanked her driver profusely with a broken voice and sat back, sighing heavily. She was on her way out of this part of the country, a part she had come to love, and out of this part of her life. She didn't look back. She knew not to. It was painful enough to look forward as the tears raced down her face again.

The West Highland Railway commuter train opened onto a large platform at St Andrews. It was 12:30pm. She hailed a cab. She got out at a special little jewelry store downtown. There she bought an antique Celtic pin that she had admired the first day she was in town. She had the clerk wrap it up and she asked that they deliver it to Ms. Gabriella McKennah at the University. The note stated simply, "I borrowed some of your clothes while at Dalroch. Thanks. Please wear this and think of me. I thought it would look great on you. Fondly, Leigh Reid".

The cab dropped her at the reception desk back at the Kilconquhar Resort and she went in to check out. This time she had no set plan on where she would stay, but she wasn't going to be where she could be found by Geoffrey, if he even tried, she thought smiling wryly at the stupid thought.

As the check-out process was going on, the lady at the desk asked, "Did that nice German gentleman find you, Ms.

Reid?"

Her heart skipped a beat. Who knew she was here? She knew no German man here or anywhere else for that matter.

"What German gentleman, mam?" Leigh did not expect the answer she got.

"Why, he was in here just this morning. He said he was a friend of your family and he was inquiring as to whether you had left a number where you could be reached. I assumed he was German, mam. He had that type accent. And, you know we have lots of Germans visit here. More than you would think--"

Leigh wasn't up to babbling by the receptionist, so she cut her off asking "Did you give him my lodge number here?"

"Why, I thought he was a friend, mam."

Leigh was turning as the lady was trying to continue, "He said your brother, Joe, was a good friend of his."

She was out the door and heading to her lodge at a fast pace. No, he wasn't a friend of Joe's. She knew better. Her sixth sense was going off the meter. The ones who had been following her earlier were close! Bastards! How could they, whoever 'they' were, have found her? She had tried to be so careful! Fear was growing in her stomach. Then it hit her like a slap in the face. The call to Jarrod! How could she have been so stupid? They must have traced her location from her call to him. They would've been able to track her from the resort number. Stupid woman, she told herself! Then she felt the eyes on her. Her fast walk turned into a run and she got in the door just as the phone was ringing. She locked it and answered the phone.

"Leigh. It's me, Kevin." Great timing, buddy, she thought. She was frightened and the reason for her fear had started with Kevin. "Listen, I have to talk fast," he continued. "The FBI found me in Wyoming. They are looking for that disc that is supposedly so valuable. They found the body of the man my informant described being shot in the bottom of Lake Ponchatrain a few days ago. I put them in touch with the informant and he spilled all he knew. I called Joe and he's pissed off that he didn't get it from you, and so am I because you didn't give it to him like you said you would! Dammit, Leigh, you were supposed to do that. Why on earth didn't you?" Before she could say anything, he continued, "Never mind that now. The FBI didn't give me any reasons for their need for the thing, but they said that they suspect a militant group. Damn, Leigh! I'm on a secured line, but you've got to get to safely quick. These people are dangerous and if I can find you, they can. Leave where you are now and get to the American Embassy in Edinburgh. Joe's already on his way there. He told me to tell you to hurry and watch your back. You've got to find safety before they get to you. They won't be messing around, you know. Already killing one person for this disc, they won't hesitate to do it again. I'll never forgive myself if something happens to you, Leigh." He waited but there was a strange silence on the line. "Leigh? Are you there?" he asked.

Kadar had already grabbed the phone from her as another man took her with his hand over her mouth and forced her down on the floor and then shot a tranquilizer into her arm. They already carried her out the back door to a car parked out of sight of anyone in the resort area. Kadar was listening to Kevin go on and then laughed into the phone, "Leigh is a little out of it at the moment. Could you call back later?" He laughed and hung up and then added, "Much later after I am quite done with her." Smiling with a terrible twinkle in his eye, he closed the lodge door knowing there were no fingerprints or other trace that they were ever there.

CHAPTER TWENTY-EIGHT

Geoff was furious with himself. How could he have let her go like that? He had deliberately hurt her. He was a fool. It was the meanest thing he had ever done. He hadn't even treated the one night stands he'd over the years like that. He allowed his damn reality check to intercede when his heart had been in control. He tried to stop himself before they had made love. But he couldn't think with her standing there in that gown in his study, then all he had wanted was her in his room, and most of all, in his bed. She aroused his innermost sexual desires together with a trusting love that he had never known in his life. She was the one he obviously had been waiting for, after so many years. She had the brains, the personality, and an inner beauty along with those damn extraordinary looks and legs. Her eyes got to him first. He was captivated by their deep forest green color with those long black lashes. Her skin and exquisite shape made his head spin. He even liked her southern American accent. No doubt she had gotten under his skin and in his heart. But his world was one she didn't know and she sure as hell didn't need to know. He couldn't live his life with her because she wasn't the type of woman to share a bed with a man and then not want to share his life. This was why he couldn't respond when he heard her declaration of love. He had been lost in his thoughts of how to tell her the truth about him. He should have told her, dammit! Instead, he had let her assume the worst.

Mad at himself beyond control, he kicked the door

open into the hallway and then went after her in the castle. He needed to let her know he loved her too. He needed her to hear what she needed to hear. He got to her door and then heard the low sounds of crying inside. He tried the door. It was locked. The tears swelled up in his eyes. The last thing he ever intended was to cause her such pain. He was hurting inside so much that he wanted to tear the door down and run to her. Knowing Leigh Reid like he did now, though, he knew she wouldn't listen to him right now. He would wait, then, let her calm down, and then he would tell her everything in the morning.

It was a little after 7am when Geoff opened Leigh's door to find her maid cleaning up. "She's gone? What do you mean, she's gone? Geoffrey roared in the hallway outside her door.
"She's not there, My Laud." The maid was obviously scared. Ms. Daniels was walking up the hallway as she heard his loud questions to the maid. She never knew the Duke to look so upset. The maid was trembling. Ms. Daniels asked, "Shall I check with Simpson? He may have seen her leave."

"No! I'll check outside myself!" He stomped out of the hallway and she heard every footstep until the large front door closed.

No sign of her anywhere. The gates hadn't been opened. Leon, the gatekeeper, was sure. No horses missing. He even checked down in the broche and boathouse. She had vanished into thin air. How could she have gotten away so quickly?

"My God! What have I done?" He was talking out loud as his fear was growing. He went back inside and went to the study. Sitting down at his desk with a keen ear and eye, he looked around for any sign she had been in there. Under the library desk there was an envelope with his name in feminine writing on it. He reached down and grabbed it. Thank God! Maybe this will explain why and where she's gone. He tore it open with shaking hands. The note read: "Geoffrey, I will send you my final report on Princess Melinde's murder in a few days. Do not try to contact me as I have everything I need. Know that I meant every word I said to you last night. But I know now that you feel differently, and I won't be back to participate in any other humiliation, so I am leaving. Last night is something I shall not ever need to discuss again with you. Good luck with your life and give my apologies to Gabriella for not being able to see her again, either. Regards, Leigh."

Geoffrey dropped the note and it floated silently in the air to the floor of the study again and by the time it landed, he was nowhere in sight. Running through the inner recesses of the castle, his mind was in fast gear. There was no time to wait. She can't go back! Damn that strong headed American! She may just have walked into her death trap. And damn himself for letting her!

....

Her eyes hurt, but she opened them anyway. There was nothing but dampness, silence and darkness. Her hands and feet were tied together with a rough rope. She had some sort of gag over her mouth. She was lying on what felt like a cot or small mattress. She was totally immobile. It was cool wherever she was and she began to shiver. They had taken the blindfold off her when they left her here some hours ago. She wasn't sure how many hours had passed, though. Her eyes had adjusted to the darkness by now and she could tell there were no windows in the room she was being held in and there was only one door. She was waiting patiently for the first set of questions. She hadn't been spoken to by anyone since they took her. How they got her out of the lodge she wasn't sure, but she must have been knocked out or drugged. She came to when they laid her on the cot. If they had searched her room, they would have found the code. Why take her, then? She had no more information for them. They must think she was smart enough to know what was on the coded disc. Too bad she wasn't, and she just bet she wouldn't be able to convince them of that fact. Smiling wryly under the gag, she knew this would be the beginning of a long and not so pleasant encounter with 'them'.

Suddenly and groggily, the thought of Geoffrey and the way it had ended with him. The pain was sharp in her chest. She had never known what a heartbreak felt like, not until now. She was so upset over allowing herself to fall in love with a dream. That's the way she preferred to look at it, too. A dream, a very sad and gut wrenching dream. In fact, she knew in her heart that she foolishly entered this dark abyss of emotions of her own free will. She hadn't ever imagined herself as the type that any man would really want, anyway. She was strong-willed, assertive, and she made things happen. She managed to excel in what had traditionally been a man's world. She raised a son on her own and she conquered the effects of a divorce and the loneliness that single mom life offered her. Except for Kevin, she had not let herself get next to any man. And the feelings for Kevin were unlike those she had with Geoffrey. She was so disappointed with herself that she didn't feel like she could face herself, anyway. She had fallen so hard with an unrealistic hope that Geoffrey could have the same sort of feelings for her. She felt so very childish, stupid and now very hurt. She was possibly facing the same fate that had befallen the man in New Orleans when he tried to hide the coded disc. Well, the way she was feeling, death seemed a much more appropriate choice than living. The sharp heartache and physical chest pains gave way to more tears. Maybe her captors would drug her so the pain would go away. Away to a great beyond where there were no heartaches. Now that sounded good to her. "Geoffrey," she whispered quietly to herself followed by another endless set of aching sobs echoing in the room.

CHAPTER TWENTY-NINE

"He's the Duke of Dalroch, Commander." The Sergeant was repeating.

"I know that, but what has that got to do with her being with him?" Kadar was perplexed. They traced her trip back from the Dalroch Castle by train and then by cab. "She would have no connection to this man normally. There are no family ties. What would she have that he needs? Get me answers, I want to know if he knows anything about the code. I want to know the connection they have."

Kadar was prepared to go to any lengths at this point. He already had been seriously called on the carpet by Sahib. He had to explain that he was so close that Sahib would be pleased to know the code was well within his grasp. He had to make those words ring true. Sahib was not beyond hiring someone else at this point and Kadar could smell the remaining money he was due for his efforts.

As he entered the dark room where she was being kept, he switched on a small light. After her eyes adjusted to the small but powerful light, she looked at him. His face was that of a cool and calculating man. He was her captor. She knew immediately. His rough and scarred skin was pale in the dim light. He had cropped blonde hair. He was smiling, but it was a smile full of evil. He took her gag off her face and took her bound hands in his and started with the obvious nice approach. "Ms. Reid. I am sorry we have had to meet like this. I had no choice, really, since you planted that dummy code in your lodge. We were not too happy to find that out. It would have been a lot more pleasant for you if you had not done that."

This was a shock to her. A dummy code? Was that what she had? A planted copy of some other disc? Good Lord! For all the effort she already had gone through and apparently was about to go through for a fake?

Kadar was continuing calmly, "Now, I can save you a lot of pain if you will just give us the location of the original disc. You have been evading us for days and I don't like having to chase you down. I prefer my women come to me on their own accord." He grabbed her hands and stroked them methodically. He was smiling invitingly at her.

He was obviously a sociopath as well as a paid soldier. She believed that he could do anything to her and would. She opted to try to talk to him rationally. After all, she really didn't believe she would make it out of this alive. But she would try if only for her son, Jarrod. She swallowed trying to find her voice. "So that's what this is all about! You know, I do not know anything about that code or any 'dummy code'. But I am tired of having to run and hide because of it. I am not up for it anymore. I'm very tired. You have me. But you have someone that hasn't got what you need. If I had anything like what you are asking about. I'd give it to you. All I know is a friend of mine had something that was the subject of a murder in Louisiana. He called me to tell me about it, and I met him, he gave me a legal brief. Then he calls me to tell me he has slipped me a disc and wants me to see about getting it to the Federal authorities. That's all. The next thing I know, you guys are on my tail. If what you found was a dummy code, I know nothing about that. I haven't turned it over to anyone, and I haven't told anyone about it. I just kept it. I only had that one disc, no more. You should know this if you searched and trashed my house in Mississippi and the lodge here. What is it about this thing anyway? Why is it so important? Never mind, I really don't want to know the answer to that question, now do I? Knowledge is dangerous in some situations, such as this one."

He smiled, "Ah, Ms. Reid. I am not in this to play silly games with you. Since you were such a promising prosecutor of those who commits such terrible acts as murder, you are right to assume that sometimes people are killed for their information. Now, let me be clear. If you don't tell me what you know, I will have to kill you. It is that simple. And, no one will ever know I did it or where to find your body. I am good at what I do, Ms. Reid, or shall call you 'Leigh'? Quite frankly, I would rather not kill you, Ms. Reid. I would rather have you beside me." He squeezed her hands tightly as he added, "as my lover." He smiled an evil smile again and at that moment she believed that part of what he was saying. He added, "I have been in your bedroom at night and have watched you sleep, Leigh. I don't mind saying that sleeping in the nude suits you well. I enjoyed my nights seeing all of you."

Bastard! She wondered if it was true. She tried not to show her emotions.

She tried to be as calm as he was. She said, "I can't play your so-called 'games' when I know nothing about the disc. I will not give you what you want, because I quite simply don't have any knowledge about it. I'll tell you this, though. It does have some symbols that are from some ancient language." Tell him something he wants to hear, Leigh, she said to herself. Your life depends upon it.

"Leigh. Thank you for admitting some truth. Yes, it is coded with symbols. The symbols however on the planted dummy code in your lodge have been decoded and they mean nothing. Now, shall we try this once again? Where is the original disc?"

"Whatever you found in my lodge is all I know about. You have decoded it, then you know more than I do. If I knew the information myself, and it was so important, then do you think that I would leave something that is apparently so important in an obvious place like where I stay? Really, give me a little credit."

"Oh, I do, Leigh. I really do. You have evaded me for many days. I was surprised by your clever tactics. I'm not accustomed to having to look so hard for someone, especially a woman. Be that as it may, I don't have a lot of time left to retrieve the actual code and I need answers right now. Do you want me to pick one these nice serums I have?" he said as he opened a small leather pouch with syringes in it, apparently all loaded with a variety of different colored liquids. Leigh was sure they had more than serum potions in them.

"Try what you think you need to. I don't have any other disc and I don't know where one can be found. But, before you stick me with one of those, maybe you could put me on a lie detector test. I'm game for that, too. I have nothing to hide." Why not volunteer at this point? What did she have to lose in the grand scheme of things?

"Trust me, my serums are much more effective, Leigh. Well, I'll let you think about it a little while longer. For now, can I get you some water or some food?"

"No thank you. I'm fine." Probably had some of his scintillating drugs in it anyway.

'I will see you later then Leigh. Try to rest, as you will need it." Emphasis was on 'will'.
He put her gag back over her mouth and rubbed his hand across her forehead smiling. Chills ran up her spine at the touch.

The light was turned off and she heard the door open and close again with a locking sound. She couldn't believe that the coded disc had been a plant from the start. Why would this charade be going on over a fake? Was she being used as bait by someone? Well, the proverbial fish was hooked now. What was next? She could only speculate that a long ordeal was ahead of her and quite frankly, her own death. Well, she didn't have too much to live for, that was for sure. Except Jarrod but she knew he was old enough to make it through this and go on to be the man she always knew he would be.

Damn Geoff for giving her the bliss she felt for a little while but jerking it away almost instantly! Damn him for being so – so, well, it wasn't his fault that he was the most titillating and spell-binding man she'd ever known. It was certainly not his fault that she fell in love with the bastard! It was, quite simply, her own stupidity! She could've stopped herself from her growing attraction to the man, but she chose not to. She then thought about her captor, the devil incarnate. What would he do if he thought Geoff or, God help her, even Gabby had knowledge about the coded disc? How could she let either of them suffer because of own stubbornness in keeping the damn thing in the first place?

With a renewed strength to fight, Leigh finally resolved what she had to do.

CHAPTER THIRTY

Geoffrey called the University first. Gabby hadn't seen her. She received a really nice gift from Leigh, though. It had been delivered by someone at a local jewelry store. Something about a borrowed gown and riding clothes. Did he know anything about that? Geoffrey had trouble remembering anything but her being in that gown in the study and the moonlight coming through the gown and showing the lovely outline of her body. Jesus, she had been so distractingly seductive. Gabby was adding, "Professor Flackerty has not heard from her since early Monday and she is scheduled to be in a big meeting that she scheduled at the University tomorrow with some senior law enforcement officers."

That did not help because she had placed that call before she had come to Dalroch so she could continue her work for him. He called her Kilconquhar lodge again with no answer. He called the reception then and inquired if she had been in. The lady said not since she was in Tuesday morning early. She had left in a hurry when she was told about that nice German man that had been looking for her. She had seemed a little upset when they had told her about it.

"Damn!" he exclaimed when he heard that. Now it was confirmed. The dreaded news he had hoped wouldn't be confirmed. The worst that could've happened had happened. He knew then that Kadar had her. He decided before to pull his own operatives off the surveillance of the lodge when he secured her presence at Dalroch. He thought she would be there until he located Kadar. That was a mistake and a half! He had to put things right quickly.

Geoffrey was down in the cave below Dalroch. He was irrational and plagued with guilt. Not to mention sick with the thought of what Kadar and his sick band of thugs would do to her. How could he have been so ignorant? He had let her go without knowing how he felt about her, too. Now he may not ever have that chance again. And it was all his fault. Had he not used her as bait, she wouldn't be in danger of losing her life. He could have told her the truth, should have, he argued with himself. If she died, and he knew there was a good chance of that happening. Well, he couldn't think about that now. He wouldn't let that happen. He was the Keeper, the leader of the best intelligence organization in the world and right now he couldn't think of how to find her. He had to clear his head. He was beating it against a wall and not getting the job done. Her safety depended solely on his thinking clearly and using all the skills he had. The first lesson always in trying to find someone or something was to put yourself in the place of the person hiding. Learn all you can about them, their tricks and their trade, then try to think like they would. Act as they would.

Geoffrey started with what he knew. He knew Kadar wanted the code, needed the code for final payment from Sahib. He had the plant that Geoffrey switched with the original in Leigh's closet and he had apparently found out it was a fake. Quicker than Geoffrey had thought he could. His mistake, and now he and Leigh were paying for it. Kadar is probably figuring Leigh has the original too or has passed it off to someone else. He has her and is asking questions. He will resort to anything to get answers. He knew how Kadar and many like him worked when they needed information. Unfortunately, Geoffrey knew all too well.

After the way he treated Leigh, he knew deep down that she wouldn't mention their relationship unless she was forced to by some drug or blackmail technique. Kadar couldn't trace her back to Dalroch, or could he? How did she get back to Kilconquhar? That's it. Her transportation back would have been by rail or by bus and by taxi from the castle. Well, then Kadar does know she's been here. Geoffrey slammed his fist on the desk in front of him and his eyes narrowed with the thought.

How absolutely ironical! Dalroch was the one place that Geoffrey had hoped to keep her safe. It was also the one place he had tried to keep secret from so many prying eyes for so long. Damn that code! He had already lost Raven, one of his finest US operatives, in New Orleans after Raven retrieved the disc from another dying operative in Cairo. Geoffrey wrote and prepared the code for the Cairo operative and passed it off to him while being watched by one of worst terrorist insurgent groups ever infiltrated. He gave it to the agent in Cairo as a last resort for sanctuary when he had been being closed in by the radical group. The operative, unfortunately, was tortured into telling the terrorists what the code signified, that is, the operative's sanctuary. What the agent didn't know, nor did he get a chance to activate, was the unlocking code for the information. That would have only come with a phone call into the cave. A series of beeps would have had to be transmitted to the agent to be entered by computer on the disc. After that, the code would have been broken and the information his to see. But, the terrorists had, in turn, placed it on the Black Market for the highest bidder, thinking it would be a gold mine for global terrorist information and security-related issues. That is when Geoffrey learned that Sahib hired Kadar. From Cairo, Raven retrieved it and had plans to get it back in the Society's hands via a large detour to throw off Kadar. But the plans changed when Kadar closed in on Raven on board a freighter in South America. Thus, the New Orleans stopover and the unfortunate murder of Raven. Geoffrey now wished he had left the damn thing in Leigh's lodge. Kadar could have decoded it and then he would have just sat and waited on them. They would have come, he knew, because the symbols, once decoded, spelled out the exact location of the storage facility and sanctuary for all the Society's operatives: 'DALROCH'.

CHAPTER THIRTY-ONE

"Ah, my dear Leigh. And how are we doing now?" Kadar came in with a glass of what looked like water.

Taking the gag off once again, Kadar cocked his head smiling at her.

"I'm fine. But, when can I go? I have a pressing hair appointment." She was caustic in tone but trying to be humorous.

"That's a feeble attempt at humor, I see. Very funny, Leigh. Now, have you given my questions anymore thought while I have been gone?"

"Yes, as a matter of fact, I have. Yes, I have thought and thought, and I just really have a problem coming up with anything but the same answer as before. Honestly, I think that maybe someone planted what you called the *dummy code* just to get you off their track. Anyone else you know that might want it?"

"You are a bright one, I will give you that. Yes, I have given that some thought, too, but they are not here with me now, are they? I have only you. I think you know more than you are saying about the information on the disc. Now what am I to do with you so I can find out the information?"

"You could try using me as bait. Apparently, I have already been used once that way with this so-called "dummy code" you keep referring to! Maybe they also want it and are watching you right now."

"Well, it's an intriguing twist, I admit, but you see, I

don't believe they know I am here with you as I am very good at hiding. And, I seriously do not have time to flush out the others that might be trying to get the code. I was hired to bring it back, the original. My time to do that is running out, too. And, quite frankly, you are expendable to me once I know if you have it, have passed it to someone else, or even if I believe you don't have it, you probably know what it means. Your life is in my hands, Leigh. However, I do have the discretion to let you go if I find out what else needs to be known."

"What else would you need to know?" Like, right, you'd let me go, she thought..

"For instance, who have you discussed the code with? The professor of Criminology in St. Andrews? How about your Duke friend?" That hit a nerve. She cringed inwardly at the thought of Geoffrey. She hoped that didn't show. She wouldn't bring Geoffrey and Gabby into this soirée. Damn, this creep already knew she was connected with Geoffrey somehow.

Obviously, she must have given a visible reaction, for the man smiled very broadly this time. "So, Leigh, just *what is* your connection with this Duke?"

She answered quickly. Perhaps too quickly. "I am employed by him. He knows nothing about this code thing. I am working as a consultant on a family criminal matter. Please do not involve him or his family."

She wished she had kept her big mouth shut. The minute the words were out, she knew that this man would focus immediately on Geoffrey.

....

Joe was on a British government plane, courtesy of MI5. His repeated prayer across the ocean was that his sister would be at the Embassy as instructed. Since the call from Kevin, a voice from the supposed dead, Joe did more snooping into the matter regarding the murder case in New Orleans.

He learned from his source at the FBI that there was a 'need to know' lock on a limited amount of information regarding the recent discovery of a body in Lake Ponchatrain. It was purported to have been the one who was murdered at the Fram warehouse. The deceased was confirmed to be a former CIA agent who disappeared several years back right into thin air within days after retirement. In addition to this death, though, the FBI source said that there had been several early retirements at the FBI, CIA, MI5 and Interpol that were some of the best agents each respective agency had. They all seemed to disappear right after retiring and drawing out their retirements in lump sums. They all had some connection in their disappearances, and that connection, the FBI was convinced, was that they all were recruited into an underground private intelligence group. The coded disc that was in New Orleans had something to do with the location of the missing early retirees and probably a lot more, but currently the FBI only knew about the militant group trying to get it at this point. After the murder in New Orleans, the FBI were following the warehouse worker until he met with the Mississippi prosecutor. When the prosecutor came up missing, there was a renewed effort to locate Kevin and the witness. Once located, they learned about good old Sam, the witness. The only other thing they learned was that it wasn't any of their men, nor any of the other US Intelligence agencies, who were there at the time of the murder. The mercenary hunt was then on.

 Well, that was all well and good, Joe was thinking, but they better lay off Leigh. She didn't have a criminal bone in her body. Quite the opposite. She was always, since a little girl, wanting the bad guys to get punished. It wasn't the FBI he was worried about, though, as far as finding Leigh. It was the ones who killed the man in New Orleans. His source admitted the mercenary group they thought were involved at the time were based out of Germany and the leader had several identities, evaded authorities with expertise, and had been tied to several murders. Contract murders. Professional mercenaries were Joe's pet peeve. They got paid a lot. But more aggravating was that usually governments paid them to get trained for their private and profitable work and then they go haywire working for the criminal enterprises.

The plane was making a final approach into Edinburgh airport. If Leigh wasn't there, he planned to get Ml5, and everyone else he could muster, actively involved in the search for her. Please God, let her be at the Embassy, he silently prayed again.

CHAPTER THIRTY-TWO

Kadar was not the least put off by Leigh's denials. He thought from her reaction to his question about the Duke McKennah, though, that there was more going with him than she was letting on. In fact, he was convinced he needed to search the Duke and his home. She very well could have left the original disk there.

Well, then, first things first, though. He would give Leigh a nice little serum and see if she gave any more pertinent information first. He may get lucky with that. Then he would have to move fast before this Duke knew she was missing. If he had knowingly been given the code, he could get it to the local authorities quickly with his title and rank there. He prepared the syringe and took it to his lady prisoner.

Knowing her limbs were tied tightly, but trying to loosen them anyway, Leigh already determined that the next move made by her captor would be the drugs. His face had been so full of anticipation when he brought that little pouch out. She had a little basic knowledge about the more common potions from her forensic training. In serological profiling, there were several combinations of natural and chemical compounds that could be used to render a person with an inability to control the truth coming out. She knew that some could be beaten with a strong will power. Would she have such a will? As far as self-preservation went though, probably not at this moment in her life. In fact, she really wasn't particularly sure she could face the world again, much less her own reflection in the mirror. The pain of the rejection from Geoffrey had been the proverbial straw that broke the camel's back with her. Maybe if she hadn't been through the recent shock of having found out her DA boss and the Judge were crooked, corrupt, and into buyoffs, maybe if she had not been on the move for days trying to avoid this, ah, getting caught. Maybe if she had just said no to keeping the disc in the first place. Maybe if she never even existed, huh? What was her problem? Maybe, crap, she thought. She did not want to cave in. This self-pity was for the birds, she thought. When it came to protecting innocent bystanders like Geoffrey and Gabby, she figured she did have a better will power than she thought. In fact, she saw her son, her brother, her home and horses. Hell, she even saw her new job with the University as something to live for. She'd give it her best shot. In fact, by the time Kadar came in, she was mentally disconnected from the real world. Her fantasy world was forming n her mind. She would focus very hard on it and keep the real world from distracting her. After all, now it really was a matter of willpower.

The needle went in and immediate warmth went throughout her body. The bagpipes were playing in the background and it was that haunting tune she heard that first time stepping foot on Dalroch's grounds. The heather was blowing in the wind on the hillside. The sun's warmth felt so good as she was lying in the grass on the top of the hill. The air was flowing through her hair and the sensation was warming her all over. The castle was so pretty from this viewpoint. She closed her eyes and let the music lighten the darkest corners of her mind. She was oblivious to anything but her peaceful warm place on the hillside.

"What is your name?" Kadar's voice was asking. No answer.

"What is your name?" He asked again knowing the serum had been in long enough to initiate a response. Silence. Her eyes were closed and, what? She was smiling. This was supposed to cause a different effect. It was not a mood enhancer!

He paused for a few seconds, and then asked again, "What is your name?"

Her horses were there with her. Cerces was gaily prancing in the grass and tossing his head. She walked up to him and rubbing his seek coat. The warmth of his breath on her hands was so real. "That's a good boy. Now go and play."

Hearing her says these words, he yelled at his compadre, "Give me the other syringe." Kadar was getting frustrated by the lack of a correct response. She was actually smiling with her eyes closed. Was she trying to insult him? The serum would have inhibited conscious reactions other than that of responding with the truth to all questions.

Another shot of warmth. This time a huge fire was crackling in the fireplace in the study at Dalroch. She had a large cup with hot buttered rum in it, sipping it slowly and feeling the warmth go down. She looked up and smiled at Geoffrey who was sitting across from her with a book in his hands. But he was looking at her, not his book. He was asking her if she was ready to start the planning of the big party they were hosting for the National Trust Board of Directors. Gabby is coming in. She wants Leigh to help her with the entertainment details for the party. They are happily discussing the plans as the fire gets warmer and the rum gets hotter in her hand.

"What is your name?" No answer again from Leigh.

A pause for a few minutes. Then again, "What is your name?"

"She's not responding. She should have by now. She is trying to beat my concoction here. Give me the last one. It is the strongest I could find on the market."

"But, with the others, it may send her into a permanent unconscious state, Commander."

"Just give it here!" He was not about to let her beat him at what he knows best.

Another feeling of warmth. There's Jarrod! Her sweet

son. He is four. His small voice is so young and precious sounding to her. "Momma! Hold me!" he is saying with his arms outstretched. She reaches down and picks him up and he puts his arms around her neck and hugs her, '" I wuv oo, momma." She holds him close and feels his soft warm body clinging to her in his innocent love. She smiles and drifts off into the warm darkness.

"Now, let us try again. What is your name?" Kadar saw her go limp and then cursed loudly in German.

He furiously looked at his Sergeant standing next to him quickly concluding, "We'll have to move on that Duke's castle, Dalroch, since I can't determine what role he has played in this," he told the Sergeant.

A couple hours later, Kadar finished making the necessary plans. In a room full of his mercenary minions, he was explaining the mission.

"After I call the Duke and inform him that I have her captive and that she has important information about him and his family, I will demand two million Pounds. I will threaten making the information public and imply that it will ruin his family. I will give him instructions to make the drop point in Calais in order to get him out of the castle. We will make the simultaneous return of Ms. Reid to the castle and search the obvious hiding places. When the ransom money is in hand, as per the word of the Sergeant, who will be supervising the drop, I will terminate Ms. Reid. The group of anxious soldiers all nodded in unison to his directive.

"There should be no one at the castle since this Duke will be told that the castle must be abandoned totally for the drop of Ms. Reid. Since you will be in charge of the money drop in Calais, Sergeant, you will need to set up a satellite feed directly to the drop place. If the code is at the castle, it is probably hidden where only she knows its location, since I don't believe she would have told him about it. I will tell the Duke that she will be safely deposited in his castle when the money is confirmed to be in your hands. I'll be in radio contact to confirm my location and status. He can talk to her if she has regained consciousness. Otherwise, I will video her presence via the satellite link up. It will look as if she's fine. When we are through searching, she becomes expendable to me, and I won't have but one other avenue to explore with her." By the smile and look on Kadar's face, the Sergeant was immediately convinced he was planning on having his way with the lady before he murdered her.

Kadar was continuing, "He is a public figure with money, and I believe he would pay, as anyone in his position would, want to avoid a public scandal. Even if he knows of no scandal, she has been consulting with him on a criminal investigation. We'll make him think it's damaging information, He will play this little game and I will have a chance to search his property. Now that I have been around her and seen how she lives and acts, I am confident I can think like she does and find it. If it's there. If it *is not*, we have the ransom money to take as a contingency plan. Sahib will not pay us without the original code; but, I am betting the remaining fee from the way she reacted to my questioning her about this Duke, that the original is safely tucked away at this place called DaIroch. Get me a map. We will start out immediately. Secure the copter, gather this woman and let's be off."

"What are you going to with her now that she's out? She may be nearing a coma state."

"I will use our taped sessions. I'll play one of them initially for him to let him know we are serious and she's alive. They always demand to hear their voices, don't they?" He smiled at his plan. This Duke won't know what hit him. It was a perfect ruse to get in and search and to make a small fee. After all, if he couldn't find the code, he would need a little extra cash to go back underground for a while because Sahib would have his head and chop it into little pieces if he can't produce the coded disc. That was, *if* Sahib found him. Amazingly, his little American prisoner had done just what he would have under the circumstances. Hid the code in an innocent person's secure location. Dalroch Castle was probably the answer to her prayers of where to hide it. Too bad she got caught. Now it would be the answer to his prayers; that is, if he had been the praying type.

CHAPTER THIRTY-THREE

Geoffrey was frantic. His operative in Edinburgh relayed a message that Leigh's brother was at the Embassy and raising a raucous. Well, if her brother knew she was missing, did that meant he was aware that she was trying to carry the coded disc with her? He probably had no idea how much danger his sister was in, but law enforcement agents were on alert and word was out that a manhunt was to go down starting at Leigh's lodge. Maybe, just maybe, they could find a lead on where she had been taken. But Geoffrey knew better than to rely on them. Leigh would be found at this point only if and when Kadar wanted her to be found. He looked at the clock above his desk. She had been missing now for 36 hours. My God, what had been done to her by now? Something inside him told him that she was still alive, but he knew she wouldn't be for very much longer. But, then again, she was a stubborn, assertive, and inventive woman

His thoughts reverted back to her. She was successful where so many in the same position would not have been. He remembered the first time he saw her. She was working in that courtroom in Mississippi. Her head was held high and she was so confident acting and sounding. She didn't let that Judge in Mississippi get away with that insult about the docket, either. Geoffrey smiled. He had been there watching and she had in fact looked right at him in his rogue biker outfit. He thought that when she came to Scotland and met him the first time, she might have remembered some similarities between him and his biker disguise, but she didn't. Thank goodness. Then he remembered seeing her in Hattiesburg the night when the other prosecutor friend of hers apparently gave the disc to her. They had embraced, he remembered. He had not thought too much about that at the time. But now, he wondered what exactly their relationship was. He'd seen her again at her home, and walking in the woods, and with her horses. He admired her then, but it was when he looked into those eyes of hers for the first time in the shelter by the sea that he had lost himself to her forever. He knew it now, looking back. He was attracted to her from the first time he started tailing her, but it was definitely when they made that first eye contact that he was gone. Even if he had a choice, which he did not, he wouldn't have been able to resist her after that one captivating moment. He silently prayed and hoped beyond hope that she would hang on until she could be found.

"There's a phone call for you, My Laird." It was the castle intercom system.

"Put them through." Everyone in the castle knew he had his own private extension, but no one knew where the extension went.

He picked up the phone. "Yes?"

"Leigh Reid's got information that could hurt you, Mr. Duke, and your family name."

Finally! The voice of Kadar. His stomach was instantly tightening up.

"I am listening."

"Two million untraceable British pounds. Small bills. You have four hours. You personally bring the money to Calais. The railway station pay phone will ring at exactly 10:00 pm for more instructions. I would advise against trying to trace this call. No law enforcement is to be involved in any way or she dies. She will be delivered to your castle when the money is in my hands." So, he was trying to pass this off as a kidnapping for ransom. Okay, he'd play. It was his only choice.

"I want to know she is alive and well before I accept the

terms."

"Listen, then." A pause for a split-second.

Then he heard Leigh's voice. "I'm fine." That was all. Just those two words.

"Leigh? Leigh?" Geoffrey got no answer.

"Two million. Four hours. Leave your castle deserted or no exchange. Understand?"

"Yes, I understand."

Geoffrey hung up and checked the call back function on the phone first. Of course, untraceable.

He thought quickly. Two million would be easy to arrange. But he couldn't let Kadar in his castle. It was too close to the target that Kadar and Sahib were blindly seeking. He knew Kadar wanted something here by asking the castle to be abandoned. Geoff felt sure it was the code. He must have believed that Leigh had hidden it here. A safe assumption. But Geoff destroyed it after retrieving it from her closet at Kilconquhar. If Kadar was believing it here, he wondered if Leigh gave him some information after being tortured? The thought of that made his stomach nauseous. She wouldn't have known that he had the code. She couldn't have! Therefore, Kadar is taking a risk and using her as bait to get in and search. Well, that's what Geoff did, wasn't it? He'd used Leigh as bait to try to lure Kadar out. Well, if Kadar only knew that he would be in the one place that his employer, Sahib, would have readily spent millions more to be in! The caves below had the Society's storage rooms, computers, and most of the past and present world secrets.

Then Geoffrey thought of Leigh. Her voice hadn't sounded normal enough. He played the conversation back and increased the background noise when Kadar had said "Listen". There! A clicking noise. It had been taped. Of course! That would mean Kadar was under the mistaken assumption that Geoffrey was just a Duke. Not the Keeper. Kadar wouldn't have pulled such an amateurish ploy with taping her voice if he knew otherwise. He would have known that the Keeper would have the technology to check out the authenticity of her voice. Good, a more even playing field. That placed Geoffrey the driver's seat for the finale of this all too close to home mission. But if it was taped, was Leigh really all right or even alive at all? No. Dammit. He had to be prepared for the worst. She may not be alive.

Breathing deeply and attempting to clear his head of that thought, he surmised if she was alive, he better be clear-headed from here on out as her life may certainly be depending on it. Geoffrey called on his nearest operative who lived nearby and told him he needed him immediately.
He assured Geoff that he would be there in fifteen minutes. Geoffrey smiled. It helped to have a McKennah clansman on his operative team. There were several McKennahs close by, but his cousin, Kenneth, would be perfect for this job and he was die-hard loyal.

Calais, France

The money was ready in a large aluminum briefcase. The Sergeant placed the call to the railway station at 10:00 sharp. The Duke picked up the pay phone in the almost empty station. "Hello?"

"Do you have it?"

"I have it," was the response.

"Go to the bar across the street, Tres Bon. I'll expect you to go to the men's toilet and leave the case in the last stall on the left. Then leave."

"I will not leave the money until I know she is all right."

"You will be able to look in the monitor set up in the bar. I've linked a video of her. If you are satisfied, then leave the money and leave the bar. The proprietor is a friend and will not help you answer questions. You have ten minutes. Starting now."

"Fine."

Ten minutes later he went into the bar and looked up at the television monitor above the bar. The local TV station was playing, but there was an interruption, then a two-second shot of Leigh. She was lying in a lounge chair. She looked alive, but not well. "Did you get that?" the supposed Duke asked into his hidden microphone to Geoff. "Yes, Proceed. It's a go," was the response from the Keeper.

The Sergeant smiled when he saw the 'Duke' get in a cab and leave the bar. He radioed his men to make sure the Duke's cab was out of the area. Then he went in the toilet area, grabbed the briefcase where it had been left according to his instructions. He opened it quickly and made a swift count of the bills. How sweet it is, he said to himself. He picked up his radio and said, "It's all here, Commander."

Then he turned to leave with his bounty. The next thing the Sergeant knew, he was surrounded by three men all dressed in black with automatic weapons. There was no time to warn Kadar that it was a trap.

CHAPTER THIRTY- FOUR

Dalroch Castle

  Kadar and four men dressed in military drab exited the copter after landing outside Dalroch. They immediately secured the area, looking for signs of anyone left on the premises by the Duke. One was posted as a guard and the other three had pre-assigned areas to search according to the maps Kadar retrieved from the local museum. Even though it was a large castle with many rooms, prior to the trip they used an experimental metal scanning system via satellite with a special tracking device that captured and pinged the metal used on media discs like the one already in Kadar's possession. It not only identified the metal, but it calculated size and shape. It was a simple process once the dummy disc had been retrieved. Loading in the metal composition and then analyzing it was done by a special lab Kadar had access to in France. The disc components were set into the satellite imaging software and a command to scan and search was added. There were only six such locations inside the rooms of the castle. The scanning equipment narrowed the search to a smaller area, one that could be canvassed easily and quickly.

  While the men navigated the castle to the pre-determined locations, Kadar entered carrying Leigh in a blanket. She was still unconscious. He had given her several amphetamine shots to try to bring her back around. But it didn't look very promising. He wasn't sure she would awake in time to capture her image to send to the bar in Calais. He took her in the large reception hall and laid her on a lounge chair. As soon as he did, he went to join in the search. They were quick and thorough. After they had been there for about an hour, the fruitless search was called off right before 10:00 and Kadar waited for the Sergeant to contact him.

Leigh was finally beginning to react to the dosages and awaken from her slumber state. Kadar took the camcorder and took a shot of her while her eyes opened for a few seconds. That would be his relay shot to Calais. Two million from the Duke versus five million from Sahib. It wasn't a fair swap, but then again, as he smiled at Leigh, he thought that it wasn't truly over yet.

He got out another syringe. This one had enough poison to kill her within five minutes. But he was waiting for the money to be in hand. Then he would finally have his way with her just before she paid for his monetary loss. His lust for her had grown into almost a vengeful need. He was used to taking what he wanted from women, and she wasn't going to be the exception. Especially after what he would lose for not having the disc in hand to give to Sahib. No, he knew he would have her shortly. She would be his before he killed her, he promised himself.

The voice of his Sergeant broke the silence, "Patch the link up now. He is here. He wants to see the bounty before he leaves it."

Kadar smiled. They always want to see them before they give up the money, don't they? It was a good thing she opened her eyes a minute ago. He plugged in the camera to his laptop. The infrared hook up with the satellite took only a few seconds. Two seconds was all the Duke would get. Then he removed the camera and packaged up the computer.

"It's all here, Commander." The Sergeant had retrieved the money.

Music to my ears, Kadar said to himself, as he went to her. Her eyes were slightly open,

"Now, Leigh Darling, I have just been successful in completing my alternate plan. We will celebrate, just you and I, before you go back to dream land." He unbuttoned her blouse and ripped her bra off with a delighted look on his face.

"My, my, how sweet they are! This will be so worth the wait." He put the syringe in her arm and gently pushed the poison into her. It was halfway down when he thought he would wait on the rest so he could watch her enjoy his caresses and his forceful taking of her. He then put his face down to begin to caress her nipples with his tongue.

....

Leigh was just beginning to come out of a long blackness. The first thing she saw was the reception hall at Dalroch. She must still be dreaming. She blinked a couple of times and decided she wasn't dreaming. It was too real. How could she be here? She couldn't think clearly. There was a dark fog in her brain. She had no memory of how she could've gotten here. She thought and thought. She must still he dreaming and the drugs she'd been given were playing tricks on her. She couldn't raise her arms or legs. In fact, she couldn't feel anything. She was trying to make sense of things when she saw her captor come near her. He had a camcorder and was taking her picture. Why? Why couldn't she make her mouth move and talk? Still convinced it was a dream, she closed her eyes again. Then she heard him saying something. It was coming in bits, but she opened her eyes and saw him unbuttoning her blouse. She still couldn't talk or move. Her dream had turned into a nightmare. He was tearing her bra off and then she saw in horror as his evil face was coming toward her breasts with a sinister grin. No, please, no! Let me wake up! Please! This is a nightmare! Then she saw the needle in her arm. "God, help me!" she screamed. But there was no sound. He was licking her nipples with his tongue. Why couldn't she stop him? Nothing would work, her legs, her arms. Nothing. Oh God, don't let me die like this! Then she was aware of something else happening in the room. There was the sound of doors being opened. She was trying very hard to turn her head. Suddenly, someone else came into the dream. She saw her captor raise up and get a kick in the head from a boot. Then she saw a sword being placed at his neck. She tried very hard to raise her eyes to see who it was. She used all her strength to look past the sword to the hand and into the face of who held the sword. There, with every ounce of strength she saw him. No, it wasn't. Then, she saw him very clearly for a second. Oh, yes, yes it was! Geoffrey McKennah! The Duke of Dalroch himself in the flesh and in full warrior dress. His face was full of rage. He said something but she had no clue what it was. Maybe it was a Highland warrior of the McKennah ancestry, she thought in her drug-induced state. After all, this was her nightmare and her savior could be a warrior from the past, couldn't it? She heard him scream at her captor. Then, suddenly she saw the man who she just tried to fight off fall to the floor and she laughed to herself as she thought she saw his body was headless. There now, she said to herself sleepily, her dream had a happy ending. Her Duke, or his ancestor who looked like him, had rescued her in the nightmare. Her dream was not ending up in her death. That's good, she thought. She had lived through enough real nightmares lately. She quietly passed back into the blackness again. Safe from the world, knowing her life had been spared in her unreal world of dreams.

CHAPTER THIRTY-FIVE

Geoffrey was in the cave when the chopper landed. His outside security cameras sent the signal down to the cave. He was also monitoring the situation in Calais. He wasn't sure Kadar would really produce Leigh, but his agents already were strategically placed in the secret inner recesses of the castle. He watched with pure hatred as Kadar brought her out of the chopper in the blanket. When he saw this, his stomach felt as if it was in his throat. Her arm fell limp out from under the blanket. The fury that had been smoldering inside him was at the point of igniting. But he told himself to hold back his feelings so he could concentrate and remain objective with the mission. She looked so lifeless, though. He will pay dearly for hurting her, Geoffrey promised. There were four men with Kadar and Geoffrey relayed their positions to his men inside. They, in turn, advised where Leigh had been taken to the reception hall.

Back on the computer monitor, he watched from the hidden camera that was mounted in the collar of Kenneth McKennah, his look-alike cousin, as Kenneth entered the bar. The monitor showed her quickly in the reception hall.

"Did you get that?" Kenneth asked over the microphone.

'Yes, proceed. It's a go." Geoffrey was off and running at this point through the underground tunnel back up into the castile. He planned to take Kadar down personally now. His men in Calais would grab the pickup man for Kadar. Now, he had to get to Leigh. The picture on the monitor clearly showed she was very ill. His radio rang out in his earphone. The agent in the reception hall was whispering, "He's got a syringe. He must be giving her some drug. What do you want me to do?"

This agent was in the stairwell above Kadar and was quickly making his own way down.

"I am at the door. Come down and cover me." Geoffrey demanded calmly as he came through a hidden door right outside the reception hall. He cocked the Glock in his hand. Then he saw the McKennah Clan battle sword on the wall. He grabbed it and had it in his other hand, when he heard his agent say the words that finally succeeded in igniting the rage that had been building up inside since Leigh had been captured.

His man whispered again, "Sir, this sick bastard is tearing off her clothes and he has a syringe. Do you want me to – "

At that very instant, Geoffrey lost control and stormed through the reception hall doors. He saw the putrid sight of Kadar groping Leigh's breasts and licking them. Operating on pure primal instinct, he ran to Kadar screaming, "Get off her, you *bloody bastard!*"

Geoffrey kicked Kadar with the force of a one-man army. Kadar was so caught up in his own sick selfish sexual desires, that he didn't hear or see Geoffrey until it was too late. He felt the blow from Geoffrey's boot and was thrown a few feet from the chair where Leigh was lying. Geoffrey was on him in an instant with the sharp point of his sword placed on Kadar's neck, "What have you done to her?" Geoffrey hissed.

Kadar smiled, and even though he had been caught off guard, he calmly asked, "Who are you and what's it to you?" Then he realized he was facing the rage of someone who was tied very much to Ms. Reid. "Oh, right. I get it. You must be the Duke. And, I assume since you are here and not in Calais, that someone else posing as you gave my men the money. So, she is much more to you than your employee, isn't she? Well, then you can't even imagine what all have done to her. She's very sweet and loving. It's all been so satisfying too!" Kadar put his hand between his legs making it clear to Geoffrey that the monster mercenary had violated her. Kadar then attempted to reach for his weapon. But he never got the chance.

It took less than a second to shoot Kadar in the heart from his gun hand. The Glock had armor-piercing rounds that shattered anything they penetrated. But while Kadar still breathed, a bloodcurdling yell from Geoffrey was followed by a swift movement of the McKennah Clan battle sword as it sliced Kadar's head off with a neat precision. Geoffrey watched it bounce and roll on the floor to a sudden and then very silent stop.

CHAPTER THIRTY-SIX

 Geoffrey barked off the order to move in on Kadar's men inside the castle and then he went to Leigh's side. He gently took the syringe out of her arm. No telling what this is, he thought. Damn his own rage. He should have tortured the truth out of Kadar about what was in the syringe. But he couldn't help himself with the urgency of his McKennah blood fury and the need to kill. He looked at Leigh's face, arms and body. There were bruises, needle marks, and rope burns all over her. She was wearing nothing more than a rag with her breasts showing all bruised and battered. His eyes watered at the sight. His very precious Leigh was so marred and so hurt. For every injury he saw, he felt the pain she must have felt. He was to blame for her getting caught, he reminded himself. He tried to open her eyes, but they were almost dead looking when he lifted her lids. Tears came down as he realized she was near death. She had been brutalized in all senses of the word. But there was some hope. She was still breathing and that meant she was barely alive.

 He stood up and yelled into the transmitting radio he wore on his wrist, "Get the medical trauma team in Inverness on their way. Tell them to bring the best toxicologist they have. Call the Embassy and get word to Joe Reid, Ms. Reid's brother with US Customs, that she's here and he can ride with the medical team up here." Geoffrey was back in charge now and he meant to do anything and everything in his power to try to save her. He just didn't know if that would be enough.

....

Joe was escorted from the embassy in Edinburgh to Inverness, where the medical team requested by the Duke of Dalroch was being loaded onboard an emergency helicopter. Kevin, who dropped everything after his call to Leigh and flew to Scotland, arrived just in time to board the copter with Joe and a member of MI5. The search for Leigh had been called off, but Joe and Kevin were full of questions. Why a medical team? Where were they going? What has happened to Leigh? The MI5 agent had very little information but he knew that the Duke of Dalroch was well respected amongst the government officials and when he asked for something, there was never a question about why or how high to jump. Kevin and Joe were so caught up in their own worries that it seemed the flight to Dalroch was over before they started.

Geoffrey carefully moved Leigh to a room easily accessible for the medical team. While they waited for the arrival of the doctors, one of his agents took a sample from the last syringe he had pulled out of Leigh's arm and tried to isolate the toxic compound in the makeshift lab down in the cave. The Society kept a workable lab to test potentially hot viruses found across the globe. He was in hope that they could save the doctors some time.

After about an hour, the agent reported that the compound was a complex set of chemicals with a highly lethal toxin, along with some mood enhancers. That evil son of a bitch had planned all along to kill and ravage her, Geoff confirmed to himself. He was glad he had reacted as he did when he killed him. He didn't deserve to live one more millisecond. Geoffrey had her hand in his stroking it. If she lived, he wondered how much Leigh would remember. What did she see, or feel when Kadar was on her? Did she see him kill Kadar? So many questions. Where are the damn doctors, he asked as his fear for her life was overtaking his rational thoughts yet again.

Two hours passed after the doctors and their equipment were rushed into her room. The lead trauma doctor came out of the room only once during that time and told Geoffrey that she was indeed comatose. He had no way of knowing if they could reverse the poison advancing into her system. If it got to her nervous system, she would die immediately. He said that if the toxin had not been isolated by Geoffrey's friend at the lab close by, wherever that was, then they wouldn't even have this fighting chance to save her. The toxicologist initiated the antitoxin immediately that would stop further spreading of the poison into vital organs, but he had to wait for another more specific compound to be flown in from Edinburgh before he could determine if the damage was truly stopped. The compound arrived by copter not long after this report and was quickly administered.

The doctor came out for another report and said it was a wait-and-see few hours before they could analyze her blood again to see if they were successful in stopping the toxin.

It wasn't but a few seconds before Joe Reid came storming in ranting and raving where Geoffrey was waiting in the ante room outside the room where the doctors were working on Leigh. "What *the hell* is going on here? Where is the owner of this place? I want to know how my sister is!" He looked at Geoff, asking loudly, "Who are you and where is my sister, Leigh Reid? Is she in there?" he asked pointing to the door the doctor had just gone back into. "Somebody better be talking or I'm going in and getting her *right now*!"

Geoffrey stood up and offered his hand. "I'm terribly sorry. Please let me introduce myself. You must be Leigh's brother. I'm Geoffrey McKennah. This is my home. Yes, I asked that you be flown up here. Please sit down, and I will let you know what is happening." He motioned to the settee nearest where Joe was standing in his rage.

"Your sister is a--," he stopped, sighed, and then finished, "Friend and a consultant for my family. I am so sorry, but she was kidnapped because of her working association with me. I'm afraid they tried to ransom her for two million pounds. I am so very sorry, but they apparently tried to use several torture drugs on her, and she is gravely ill. I have seen to it that the ones who were responsible have been turned over to the authorities. Leigh is now fighting for her life. They intended to kill her upon the delivery of the money, but I was fortunate enough to get to her before they got the full amount of a poison in her system by the use of a syringe. I have the best medical team in Scotland working on her. I *am* sorry, but there is the possibility that she may not pull out of it." Geoffrey's eyes were watering as he watch Leigh's brother look on with almost as much fear as Geoff felt. He couldn't hold back his reaction to his own words. He turned away and said, "I am sorry. You can wait in here if you would like, but I must excuse myself."

Joe did not let the emotional response of the Duke go unnoticed, even in his own despair. He was sure there was more to the relationship of this man and his sister than just friend or employee. He saw a deep sorrow in the man's eyes and face.

"Please let me do something! I cannot sit here and just wait!" Joe's voice cracked and he stopped and then he swallowed hard. How could such a seemingly docile research project have turned into this? It wasn't fair. He had so many more questions. He couldn't lose her. They were all each other had. Both their parents died when he and Leigh were in high school. Then he thought of Jarrod. God, what and how would he tell Jarrod if Leigh doesn't make it? He sat down in a chair and placed his face in his hands and cried.

Geoffrey was overwrought himself, but he was trying very hard to keep from showing his feelings. He eased out of the room with his head down and his hands in his pockets. He had been taught by his father and his father before him never to show his emotions in public. So many generations of Dukes had been here and been taught the proper things to say and do for so many years. He was close to losing it, though, when, as he was walking down the hallway, what looked like an American cowboy was walking toward him with fear on his face. Cowboy boots, jeans, a vest and a cowboy hat made the man look particularly out of place. Then he recognized the face. It was that lawyer friend of Leigh's. Kevin Johnson. Geoffrey recognized him despite the apparel. What in the world was *he* doing here?

Kevin looked at Geoffrey first and then said, "Dammit! What does one have to do to get some information about Leigh Reid around here?" Kevin was feeling so guilty himself because he was scared she was now in danger because of what he had given her that night in the Blue Parrot. No one had told him why she was here, how she had gotten here, and he was near the breaking point in despair. He wanted to hear she was ok, and that she would be up and going in no time.

Joe heard the commotion and came out to see Kevin. "Kevin. Calm down, man! It is not good. This is Mr. McKennah, Leigh's friend, who tells me she has a slight chance to pull out. The doctors are working on her now. She had been kidnapped apparently because of her work. He is the Duke we were told had found her like this and called the doctors."

Kevin walked back and forth a couple of times in the room and then spurted out, "I'm going in to see her! I can't let her go like this! She has to know." He was frantically trying to get past the doorway to get to where the doctors were working. Geoffrey and Joe both caught a hold of his arm and pulled him away from the doorway. Kevin jerked away from their grasps.

"Damn all of us if she dies!" He had turned fighting mad and was trying to get through the door again when it opened and two doctors came out.

One of the doctors looked at the three men with anxious faces. "We have stabilized the toxins in her bloodstream. We know now that it was very close to killing her. Her liver almost shut down. Another minute more, she would have died. We have pumped her stomach and initiated a charcoal treatment into her digestive tract to absorb what is left of the toxins. What we don't know is whether or not she will regain consciousness for any length of time. She apparently was given some other drugs that, in excess, can cause permanent comatose states in patients. Neurologically, she appears to be fine, but we will not know for certain about that until or if she becomes conscious. She has been through a lot. Furthermore, she hasn't eaten in several days. We have nutrient drips ordered. In addition, her bloodstream will have to be flushed of the drugs that are in her before we know much else." This doctor looked at Geoffrey and said, "My Laird, you saved her life, but I cannot say what kind of life that will be." The doctors turned and went back in the room where Geoffrey saw Leigh lying on the bed with an ashen face and no sign of life other than the beep of the heart monitor.

CHAPTER THIRTY-SEVEN

Three days passed. There were no signs of Leigh coming back into the waking world. The three men that loved her most were taking turns sitting with her. All but one of the doctors had returned to Edinburgh. She had more color in her face since the drugs had been flushed from her system and the nutrient drips were slowly working on nourishing her body.

Geoffrey would not leave her side for very long, even when Joe or Kevin wanted to relieve him. He would only be a short distance from her. He took time to check on the progress of locating any more of Kadar's men, and he was monitoring the interrogations that were taking place of the Sergeant in Calais, who was indicating he wanted to cooperate. Although he didn't have much information about Sahib's weaponry, he did know how to pinpoint where Sahib's headquarters was in the Middle East. Money was being offered for his information. The murder in New Orleans was witnessed by the Sergeant as well as the torture of Leigh Reid. All in all, the post mission briefings were promising for the Society's interests. Of course, Geoffrey's main goal was to secure the chemical weapon storage facility. That would come in time, he knew. But, he also had a personal agenda with Sahib. Kadar was given full authority to murder anyone who stepped in his way by Sahib. It was Sahib who would also pay for what had happened to Raven and Leigh.

Gabby, who was none the wiser of her father's other life as the Keeper, came home to learn of the kidnapping only and was also staying with Leigh as much as she could. She saw her father's sick and disheveled looks and knew Leigh had to be weighing heavily on him not only because of the kidnapping but because of the relationship they apparently began to share with each other. Gabby wasn't blind to the fact that her father was showing the first signs of interest in a woman in years. And she adored Leigh herself. Who would have believed that the case Leigh was working on for her father had been the impetus for the kidnapping? She was terribly distraught over the fact that she had suggested Leigh for the job in the first place.

Jarrod was flown in courtesy of Geoffrey. Arrangements were made for tickets to be issued for first class flights from Boston to Glasgow and then for a train ride to Inverness. Gabby picked him there on her way home from St. Andrews and brought him to Dalroch. He and Gabby were joining Joe and Kevin in the anteroom, awaiting any new word on her condition from the doctor.

Jarrod finally got a chance to go in to see his mother and was so upset that he left and cried. Gabby found him crying and took him down to the castle kitchen and tried to get him to eat.

"Your Mother is one of the strongest women I have ever known. She will pull out of this, Jarrod. She will. I believe if anyone can, she can. Now you let us feed you so you will be well enough to help get her back on her feet when she wakes up!" Somehow, having Gabby there made it easier for Jarrod to cope. They consoled each other and quickly became friends while doing so.

Geoffrey was glad they had each other because he was unable to console anyone in his own state of guilt and grief. The only thing that made him feel better was the fact that he had been able to save her from dying. But, like the doctor had said, if she doesn't regain conscious, what kind of life would it be? Even if she did, there may be permanent brain damage.

CHAPTER THIRTY-EIGHT

One week had now passed. Leigh was still unconscious. The doctor examined her earlier in the morning and told Geoffrey that there was a good chance now that she would go on in this comatose state indefinitely. Her external wounds were healing fine, except for the rope burns that would eventually go away. She lost a lot of weight during the kidnapping and recovery period, so the doctor was very concerned about heightened inability to ward off any infections. He suggested that a full-time nurse stay with her and to limit exposure to infection by only allowing short visits by the family. After another few days, he suggested that she be transferred to a long-term care facility in Edinburgh. Geoffrey agreed about the nurse, but reluctantly told everyone the news. He knew he would have to limit his time with her so her family would have a few more extended visits with her in case they needed to carry on with their lives. He also knew that he had a lot of guilt inside himself for her predicament. He could not stand to stay away from her for very long. He wasn't sure he wanted her to be moved anywhere else, but then her brother had the last say on that.

After announcing the doctor's recommendations about her being relocated in a few days and reassuring Joe that he would see to her every financial need, both Joe and Jarrod thanked him shaking his hand. They both agreed with the doctor's recommendation. Geoff offered to bring in private around the clock care at Dalroch for her, but Joe was sure she would be better off in a facility geared to watch her and have specialists available. They all agreed to take a few days to say goodbye before they would head back to the United States to their separate lives. They also wanted Geoffrey to know they did not blame him for her condition.

"My sister would be very happy to know how well you have seen to her every need. She wouldn't blame you, Geoffrey, for her condition. I know her. She would have done whatever it took to help you and not looked back on her decision. It is unfortunate we have no real hopes that she would regain consciousness. But, we don't blame you. If it hadn't been for your quick actions, she would not even be alive. Please believe us when we say we owe you our gratitude."

Kevin shot up hearing all this and said, "I am going in first if this is how she's going to be indefinitely. Before I go, I have to see her one more time. She's got to know something and I can only hope that somehow she will hear me." He said the last few words mainly to himself but they were audible to all, especially to Geoffrey, who was standing right beside Kevin and the door to Leigh's room. Geoffrey felt a sharp pang of jealousy. He watched Kevin go in and then stood unabashedly at the door and listened as the doctor eased out of the room.

Kevin was talking low, but Geoffrey heard every word.

"Leigh, my sweet, sweet Leigh. Please hear me, I am begging you. Please, come back to me. I love you. Always have, you know, Kiddo. We were really meant to be together. We just didn't know it at the time when we were together before. Well, maybe you did, but I didn't." He was patting her hand. "But I should have married you then. I was an arrogant idiot for not asking. I just wanted to know in my heart that you were not on the rebound from your divorce. That is why I began to see so many married women after you. It was my twisted way of showing you that I was hurt when you didn't want to see me again. Leigh, please hear me, my life has been so shallow and empty all these years. I want you to marry me now. Please, listen. I have a new horse ranch and a prosecutor job in Cody, Wyoming. Horses, Leigh! You and I can breed and raise horses together. Wouldn't you like that? We could even have children, too. We are not too old, I don't think. Wouldn't it be grand? A family, horses, a whole new life together. I want you, Leigh. Please wake up and say you will marry me and come back with me!"

Geoffrey turned and left the doorway, not really seeing anything in front of him. He exited the anteroom and then he left the castle for the first time in days. He took Lomond and rode at a fast gallop up to the hilltop where he and Leigh had eaten their picnic lunch that day. He saw her laughing and enjoying herself, and then thought of what he had done to her and how she looked now all drawn up and quite likely, a vegetable for the rest of her life. All because of his damned Society obligations and his hesitancy to let her into his life and world. And this, this Kevin fellow, the cowboy, he was so in love with Leigh. Geoffrey had managed to screw not only his only hope of happiness with Leigh up, but it looked like he had interfered in another love of Leigh's and her future with Kevin. It was too much to bear.

There on the hill he sat for a long, long time with tears rolling down his face, and his sobs echoed down the valley so loud that even the ears of ancestor Highlander clansmen could have heard and would have had no choice but to cry too.

Four Days Later--Dalroch Castle

Somewhere down deep in the pitch black darkness, a light the size of a pen was visible. Leigh felt something or someone stir near her. Who was it? It was so very dark here. She wasn't aware of anything but the darkness and the light. It gradually grew from a small dot to a larger round ball, and then it suddenly turned into a room of bright white light. It almost hurt to see this white light. Then, an image came into the light. Who was it? "Who is this in my mind?" she wondered to herself. The form took the shape of a woman with long black hair and holding an infant in her arms. What is this? Who are you? Leigh tried to talk but couldn't. But the woman's beautiful face smiled and walked closer to Leigh. Her voice was accented and the minute she started talking, Leigh did not know why but she knew who this woman was. The woman said in English with a heavy Spanish accent, "You have come so close to helping me find peace with my child. It has been so long since I have felt hope. My murder has gone unsolved for so long. I have wandered here for centuries waiting. Please come back with me and finish what you started. You know the truth. Make it known, and we will finally know peace. You must go back to where they are in the light. Try. You must! Please, Leigh Reid. Hear me and come to the light, come with me now. Come! Come! Come!"

Leigh remembered something. This woman was someone needing her help. Yes, of course! She's the Melinde who was murdered! She needed Leigh. Her brother, Joe needed her, her son, Jarrod, needed her. Her home, Marlowe, needed her! She needed to find this light the woman is wanting her to go to…..yes, she thought, she was needed and she was coming, if she could. She even felt a strange sensation that somehow she knew that Kevin needed her, too.

"I am coming," she began to shout to Melinde, who was walking away into the bright light. "Wait, I'm coming back with you!"

A strange tugging sensation began deep within her body. The darkness became lighter and lighter. She was being drawn back into the light once she got to it. Melinde turned and smiled with her infant in her arms. Then, she disappeared as Leigh began to hear noises around her.

At first, after hearing noises, she felt her legs and arms jerking. Then, she heard voices, but she couldn't open her eyes. Those were voices she knew and they were very close to her as they seemed loud. Someone said, "Well, thank the stars above, miracles do happen. I believe she is actually coming around!"

Leigh heard that and tried harder to open her eyes. Soon they obeyed and she felt her whole essence being deposited back into her body and reality was knocking on her consciousness. When she could finally focus, she saw the loving and smiling faces of Joe, Jarrod, Kevin, and even Gabby. Gabby? What happened, where was she? Why was Gabby here? She tried to open her mouth but it was too dry.

"Give her some water and see if she can talk." She heard this voice and looked around. There was a doctor and a nurse in the room.

She drank and it felt so good going down. She tried to talk again. "Am I in a hospital?" she asked in a small hoarse voice.

"No, dear, you are in a room in Dalroch Castle where you have been now for three weeks." She looked where the voice came from. It was Joe.

"Hi, brother of mine," she managed to scratch out the words hoarsely but with a smile. "What on earth are you doing here? What has happened? Why am I here and more importantly, why are all of you here? Did I miss something?" She asked him very weakly. But he looked at the doctor as if he didn't know what he should tell her, and the doctor said, "That's enough for now. Welcome back to the land of the conscious, Ms, Reid. You have defied the laws of probabilities more than once, so I think it would be best if you rest now. Then we can get some real food in you and you will begin to feel a lot better. Your memory will slowly come back, so don't worry now if you are having trouble remembering. Just rest."

With that the group was escorted out, and Leigh closed her eyes, this time smiling and she rested.

....

The hilltop was aglow in sunlight. Geoffrey was refusing to leave it. For two days he left Leigh's room only to come here. He wouldn't talk with anyone or participate in any of the meals. He insisted on everyone staying a few more days before the transfer to Edinburgh but he wanted to stay out of the family visits with Leigh and with each other. He didn't feel like he should be with them since he had caused Leigh's condition. His only solace in being up here where he could let his mind clear bit by bit.

He was struggling for reasons that had led him to this, his fate. He had to know that his role on this planet had been worth losing her. It was a unique and necessary position that had developed from ancient times when the need to keep intelligence on the potential enemy had started among the tribal nations in Scotland. For centuries, his family played an integral role in this process by having Clan meetings to gather information. He had just begun to feel the weight of the responsibility of his leadership though only in the last few weeks. It was bothering him to the point of truly questioning his role. There had been several global war threats diverted since his grandfather had begun the Stenness Society. That was something he was proud of, too. Very proud. He completed dangerous missions all over the world. The Society lost agents before in the line of duty, but he had initiated updated training and fine-tuned the technology needed so that they were always equipped and ready for action. The Society was now one that could cope with the ever-changing highly explosive political world. All of it run from the little cave headquarters down under Dalroch, with no one the wiser in his family, other than his operative cousin, Kenneth, who had taken the look-alike role to nab Kadar's Sergeant in Calais. No two ways about it, the Society's work had to go on. It was not something that he could stop. He had never questioned it before. Not even when he married, then divorced, and then taken on the responsibility of a single parent with Gabby. He was questioning it now for it was the one thing that he would always blame for Leigh's condition. It was because of the Society that he caused the pain to Leigh when he had the chance and didn't tell her how he felt about her. Need to know basis, be damned. It was his organization, after all, or well, his family's legacy. But, he truly should have told her how he felt, brought her into his world and that of the Society's. And, he should have never, ever used her as bait.

Well, he was destined to be alone now. After knowing how it felt to be in love with her, there would never be another woman. No one would move him the way she had. He didn't even know how it happened, it just did. No woman in the world could do what Leigh had done to him. Opened his heart, his soul, and his mind to a world which he closed off for years.

Then he mentally replayed the scene in Leigh's room when Kevin had been telling her how much he loved her. That made him ache inside, too. Namely because he knew he could never have the chance to tell her the same thing. He had been given the one opportunity he would ever have and he had plain and simply blown it. It was too late now. The doctor had given her no chance of reviving. She would always be in a coma. And he had himself to blame for her being in that state. If he had only gotten to her sooner. If he had only told her how he felt. If. If. If. The world was just too full of 'ifs' to suit him at the moment.

So he decided just at that very point that he would have to leave Dalroch for a while. He knew it would mean he was running from his hurting. But, he knew he needed to be alone and sort through his emotions for a while. His Society duties were still there, after all. He could make plans to do what was needed next. Only then would he have any chance at being himself again.

Since Kevin stayed on after confessing his love to Leigh, and waiting for the transfer to the long-term care facility, Geoffrey was getting too fed up with seeing Kevin sitting by Leigh as if he could magically wake her up like Prince Charming did Sleeping Beauty. He couldn't watch, and yet he couldn't stand leaving her at the same time. But, with no chance of her coming back to him, he made his exit plans in his mind while trying to get the energy to get up and head down the hill.

Suddenly he heard the sound of a horse at a full run coming up the hill. He turned and saw Gabby heading toward him on her pony. She was smiling and yelling. The wind caught her voice and brought it to Geoffrey before she got up the hill.

"It's Leigh, Father. It's a miracle! She's back! She's awake. Isn't it great? Come back with me and see for yourself! Hurry!"

His heart flipped over at the news. First not believing it, he stopped Gabby's pony by holding the bridle.

"What do you mean? She is awake?" He almost didn't want to hear the answer in case the wind had it wrong.

"Father! You won't believe it. The doctor doesn't believe it! I don't believe it. But, she is wide awake and knows all of us. You have to come back with me. Here, take my pony. I'll go get Lomond there and ride him back."

Geoffrey jumped on as soon as Gabby slipped off and took the pony down the hill at a fast pace. She was back. How incredible! How wonderful. He wanted to yell out to the mountains but thought he might scare the neighbor's miles away with the echoes. Laughing out loud to himself at the thought of neighbors! Not any for many miles…

Before Geoffrey went in, he consulted with the doctor on her condition. His heart was pounding inside at the thought of seeing her with her eyes open, but the doctor was saying she was to rest. He said, "The young man in there now wouldn't leave her side, though, and I made an exception for him. You can sit for a few minutes with her after he is through, but no more than a few minutes! She will regain strength and her memory soon with rest and nourishment."

"Thanks, Doc. This is a great day, is it not?"

Smiling, Geoffrey went to the doorway and eased in.

The room was dark except for a small night light. He couldn't be seen so he stood there and watched what was going on. He wanted to sit there with her himself and tell her everything. He had a chance now. Her life had not been taken from her and she was back. He wanted to tell her how he felt. He wanted to give her his world, his life, his home. She already had his heart and soul. He wanted his chance to set things right. She had to forgive him, that was the first step. Then, he had to tell her about his role with the Society and how that lead him to following her, meeting her, trying to use her to lure out Kadar, and ultimately how that lead to her being kidnapped and tortured. That would be a lot to swallow, so maybe he should just settle for telling her he loved her for now.

"Leigh. I've been a fool for so long." Kevin was saying as he was sitting by her on the bed, holding her hand in his. "You were always the one for me, I love you dearly, Lady. Please let me love you and take care of you forever."

Geoffrey lowered his head and put his hands in his pockets. Dammit! The man obviously adored her. They must have really had a serious relationship at some point as he recalled the confession given earlier. He was offering her his heart. Who was Geoffrey to stand in the way of this? Dammit! He had been the one who had used her as bait in an espionage mission, gotten her kidnapped, tortured and almost killed. He was not the one to come with an undying declaration of love to her. It was not meant to be, he thought. He turned to walk out but not before he saw Kevin gently kiss Leigh on the lips. She looked so frail and so beautiful to him. No, she would never forgive him for his hurting her emotionally or for using her. He wouldn't forgive himself for that, so how could she? He had been a cad. Loved her and used her, at least in her mind. Best to leave it that way. She was not to be his. He didn't deserve her after all. The irony he thought was that the fate that brought her to him, the Society's coded disc, was taking her away because he couldn't be with her after using her as a means to an end. These were circumstances he could not reverse. Let her go with the cowboy have a happy life, you fool, he told himself resigned. Don't interfere. Leave them alone. He eased out and closed the door ever so slightly but not before he heard her sweet voice saying, "Kevin, I love you, too."

CHAPTER THIRTY-NINE

"Kevin, I love you, too," she said very weakly and then paused as her head was still spinning and aching from the waking up. She repositioned herself and then continued. "But, not in the way you are claiming you love me after all these years. I love you as a friend and as a confidante. I admit I did have deeper feelings for you at one time. You remember how you told me you were not ready for marriage? I was hurt over that, sure, but I got over it. Don't you think that you're misinterpreting your feelings toward me possibly because of your guilt for getting me involved in having the disc and murder problem?" Before he could answer, she continued. "But, I don't blame you. I should, mind you. But I never will. You don't have to fake affections for that, Kevin. You did what you thought best, and I was the stupid one. I should've given it to Joe like you said. You know, after all I have been through, I still don't know what that damned thing meant. Do you?" Kevin had been given the same story that everyone else had been told by the Duke. That she was kidnapped for ransom money from the Duke. He knew only what the FBI knew and what Joe knew.

"I didn't hear you say 'no' to my proposal, Leigh. Please think about if before you answer. I don't care if you don't love me like I do you. That was my fault years ago. I didn't want you on the rebound from your ex. I thought you needed time to make sure of your feelings. But when I saw how hurt you were, I guess I just turned to those other women. They were a safe haven for my heart, because it belonged to you, dear. It was my fault for giving you all that time hurting and not telling you how I felt. But, I knew I'd hurt you and really didn't know how to approach you again. So, I just worked and stayed away from any other serious involvement. As for that disc thing, just forget it. If you haven't given it to Joe, please just do so. I really was worried that all this happened to you because of it, not because of your criminal investigations for the Duke's family. You do still have it, don't you?" He wouldn't tell her anymore about the FBI's concerns for the missing agents and the competing organizations looking for that code. He had done enough to hurt her by getting her involved in that blasted thing already.

"No. I don't have it anymore. It was stolen from me." That was at least what she thought had happened. She still had the symbols scanned into her laptop probably, but she was not sure if the captor had gotten it, too. But she didn't have the disc itself. Someone had taken that and planted the dummy one in her lodge, so this captor had said. She wouldn't let Kevin know the code was the reason for her abduction. Apparently, everyone believed it was the criminal case she was investigating for Geoffrey that caused her to be kidnapped and tortured. If Kevin knew that was the real reason, he really would feel guilty.

"I hope who ever stole it will now leave you alone. You have been through enough, dear lady."

Well, she did know one thing. Her captor will leave her alone. He is no longer alive, she decided from something in her memory. She was now remembering seeing her captor with a sword on his throat. He was bleeding all over. Someone got to him before he got her. She could see the last few seconds. Someone very familiar was standing there with the sword on her captor. Someone very special. Geoffrey! It had been him with the sword? What had happened at the end? Why was she even here? She still couldn't sort all the details out. She thought that seeing Geoffrey at the time had been a dream, something caused by the drugs she was full of. She could not distinguish between the cloudy memory and reality.

She began to frown and hold her throbbing head. She had to know what happened. She had to talk to Geoffrey. Why had she been recuperating at Dalroch and she hadn't even laid eyes on Geoffrey? Where was he? She couldn't remember seeing him since she awoke. There were so many questions that only he knew the answers to. She looked at Kevin again and said, "I'm very tired, Kevin. I need to talk with the Duke now. Can we please talk again later?" Leigh was not sure why she wouldn't just say yes to Kevin's proposal. Before she met Geoffrey, maybe Kevin's declaration of love and his pained explanations for the past would've moved her to the point of considering the proposal. But, after loving Geoffrey, she wasn't sure she would ever love anyone again. She only knew she wanted to see Geoffrey and she needed answers to what had happened to her before she talked with Kevin about his proposal.

"I will come back this evening, Leigh. We can talk again then. But you know I am leaving as soon as possible. I have to try to arrange flying back to Wyoming tomorrow. If you can get up and get going with me that would make me the happiest man alive.

Then as he was turning to leave, he said, "Oh, by the way, did you know that your ex-DA Boss was indicted by a federal grand jury? I heard that from my old colleagues before I flew out here. It seems he and the Judge and an assistant district attorney were all charged and apparently going down. They told me that a Federal witness flipped, and they got the goods on money laundering and other various federal code violations. You were right to leave them when you did! I hear it's pretty nasty down there right now. Well, I'll see you later this evening." Kevin walked out leaving Leigh to ponder the news.

As if she could just picture the look on all their lovely

faces, she laughed out loud for what seemed like the first time in a very long time. The news brought closure to at least one of the traumatic events she had suffered through in the last couple of months. Smiling, she thought that life sure has its ups and downs. One day you're flying high thinking you can't be touched, and the next, the Feds are knocking on your door and serving indictments on you. She was thrilled to know that at least sometimes, crime didn't pay. She only hoped Cheryl would make it through the fallout that was surely coming for the office there. She would call her in a couple of days to make certain she was okay. Leigh also wondered how good old Garrison Roberts had fared in his trading information for leniency. She hoped he had not been given too hard of a time or 'time'.

Then it struck her that she would have to eventually go back and take care of her affairs there. She hadn't had time to give her future much thought since the kidnapping. But one thing was for sure. She wouldn't have a life here in Scotland. She loved it so much here. Or was it she was 'in love'? Well, Geoffrey surely didn't share that emotion with her. That was made perfectly clear to her in the most poignant way it could've been. She was sure she could finish her research within a few months, and then she could go home and might possibly even think of running for District Attorney herself. After all, the post should be open within a few months. Give them enough time to force a resignation or two, or three, she smiled to herself. That thought gave her hope that her life could start again. No matter what had happened here, especially after the ordeal suffered at the hand of the mercenary captor, she still had her family and her home and her horses.

There was a soft knock at the door and she was greeted by her son, then Joe, and then Gabby. They were all so good to see and she tried very hard not to tell them the real reason she had been kidnapped. Joe and Jarrod were ready to take her home, but she still wanted answers from Geoffrey so she told them all she would be ready in a day or so.

Geoffrey was in his study writing out specific details for the running of Dalroch while he was gone. He made several lists for staff and for Gabby. There were castle tours already scheduled for the next few months and Dalroch needed to be back in ship shape for them. He was ready to leave as soon as he had everything in order. He was making himself focus on the mission ahead in order to keep from thinking about the pain he felt seeing Leigh with the cowboy and hearing her declaration of love for him.

There were Society details to take care of, too. Geoffrey was confident that his cousin, Kenneth, could hold down the fort. Geoffrey would personally be in charge of overseeing the continuing interrogation of Kadar's right-hand man in Paris, the Sergeant. He wanted to talk more but for more monetary incentives. The stalemate would be easily remedied by Geoffrey. This Sergeant wouldn't want to make Geoffrey any madder than he already was. Within a few more hours, the location of the chemical weapon lab and the location of the hiding area for the weapon would be known. Geoffrey was to meet with several Society agents in France and the plan was to take the lab and Sahib's headquarters within days of knowing their location. He felt sure that Sahib would be wary now that he could not contact Kadar.

Geoffrey's yacht, the Kelly Reefer, was being shined up and readied. His journey would take him straight from Dalroch into the North Sea where he planned to anchor and then take his chopper to Calais. He hoped that he could continue to concentrate on what lay ahead for him. He needed this focus so it would take that still so bittersweet taste of Leigh out of his mind.

As he was finishing his lists, he called for Gabby. While he waited for her, his mind flashed to seeing Kevin and Leigh again. He heard her say she loved him, too. That sharp and deep thrust of pain went through his heart taking his breath.

He remembered her saying that fateful night that she had never loved anyone like she did him. Then her note she left for him said that she meant every word she had said the night before. Funny thing was that he still believed her. But, he also now knew something happened before with her and the cowboy. He reconciled himself to believe she loved Kevin. She deserved to be happy. Kevin had more of a life to offer her than Geoffrey, anyway. He ran around all over the world in dangerous situations. He knew she wouldn't be entertaining any dangerous situations for a long time after what she had just gone through. He also knew it was not a life she would want.

Gabby came in cheerful as usual, "Hi, Father, What's up?" She plopped on the large sofa. "Did you want to see me especially for some reason?"

Geoffrey was at the desk still and looked over at his beautiful daughter. "I've been so busy lately with everything going on around here that I haven't had time to talk with you. How are you, dear?" He wanted to be with her a few minutes before he sprung his trip on her.

"Daddy, I am just so relieved about Leigh. She is looking better, don't you think?"

"I haven't seen her much since she awoke. How do you like her son, Jarrod? I haven't seen him much either. But, since you are of similar age, you two seemed to have hit it off. Is he a lot like her?

"He's a super guy. Yes. He's smart, ambitious, and he loves his mother immensely. He's not a bad chap to hook at either." She winked at Geoffrey when she said this. "Besides, I was really hoping I could go back with him when he leaves." That brought Geoffrey's eyebrows up. Laughing, she continued, "I meant to Harvard to visit the University. You know I want to advance my degree there after this year."

'Yes, yes, I see. But, could you be more interested in Jarrod than in Harvard, though?"

With feigned shock on her bright face, she said, "Father I have hardly gotten to be around him at all except while everyone has been so scared for his mother. You know I am careful with guys. But, I do want to see Harvard and Jarrod has offered to show me around. I will stay in a hotel for goodness sakes!" She laughed at her father's stern look.

"I have to take a trip myself, my dear. I am going away for an extended holiday on the Kelley Reefer. I really need you to be here while I am away. And, I don't want to worry about you being in America, right now. Could you postpone this trip for a little while? There are several tours to arrange here and I cannot leave it all on the staff's shoulders. "He knew he was asking a lot, but he was too focused on getting away to take no for an answer.

"When are you leaving? You know Leigh is being released by the doctor. Father, you're not going to leave before Leigh does, are you? I thought, I mean, I really hoped, well, I -- " She got up and walked to the bookcase and turned around and then said with a little apprehension, "1 was so sure that you two were beginning to feel, well, I guess I thought there was something between you two. Or was I imagining it? I wouldn't be against that, you know. I liked her the moment I met her and well, we are friends. I never thought any woman you were around would be like a 'friend' to me." She stopped and then walked towards him. "Well? Was I wrong to assume such a thing about you and Leigh?" She had made her way back to his desk. He stood up and turned away. The hurt was self-evident on his face.

"Leigh is in love with that cowboy. He's asked her to marry him. I assume they will get married soon. I am not too thrilled with seeing the two together here. I choose to be away until they are gone." Then he turned to see her reaction as he felt like he spoke words that would shock her about the marriage.

It suddenly dawned on her as she watched him. "Father! You are in love with her! I knew it! Well, I hoped anyway!" She was almost giddy with delight. "She loves you, too, you know. I know she does because of the way she looks at you!" She paced a few seconds and then said, "You can't go away tomorrow without telling her how you feel. I don't for one second believe that she would rather be with this cowboy! You just cannot let her believe you are leaving without a word!"

Geoffrey was surprised at Gabby's intuitiveness and her outright acceptance of his feelings for Leigh, but he said, "I don't think that it would matter now. She has been through a lot of trauma and sickness and I am to blame for a large part of it. Don't worry, Gabby. I think it's for the best that she does not hear anything from me." He puts his finger out toward her and shook it saying, "And not a word to her about my leaving either, you hear, young lady? I am leaving in the morning. I'll be in touch, and I really would appreciate you looking after things around here."

Gabby sighed resigning herself to the fact her Father was giving up too easily. She came up and hugged him with tears in her eyes. "Father, I don't want you to leave. You're hurt, and I think you should stay until you and Leigh have talked. Anyway, I won't leave until you get back. Where exactly are you going?" Gabby learned years ago not to ask too many questions of her Dad since he never gave her a straight answer.

"I'm taking the Kelly Reefer out for a while. I really don't know when I'll be back."

There, just like always, the evasive answer. Well, she had learned to not ask more questions when he would leave. "I love you a bunch, Father! Don't leave in the morning without saying goodbye!" She walked out of the room feeling like her Father was torn between leaving and staying.

Geoffrey shook his head. That girl was the only thing he had that was real. He hoped she wouldn't be hurt about Leigh's marrying Kevin. She was obviously fond of Leigh. It would have been nice for all of them to be together as a family. That was a stupid dream on his part now.

He sat back down dejectedly in his chair. Then he thought how much he was losing with Leigh. Not really, though, not yet. Damn! He stood up and then kicked the chair and watched it roll over the floor to the window. Then he threw his paperwork on the floor. For the love of the McKennah name, he would be damned if he would go without seeing her one more time! Gabby was right in her mature young mind. He was going to set the record straight at the very least. Leigh did need to know that he loved her. He marched up to the bedroom where she was. He was going to throw anyone out that was in his way, too. After all, just like Gabby, he was a McKennah, too, and when they set their mind to something, they don't let anything get in their way!

CHAPTER FORTY

Leigh was asleep and dreaming. The music was tantalizing. The bagpipes were playing the song she had heard Geoffrey play the time she found him in the balcony. It was so moving, that tears were in her eyes. She smiled and in the dream she saw Geoffrey. He had that same intense look in his eye. She wanted him. But she knew she couldn't have him. His figure faded from her dream. She cried out, 'Geoffrey! No, don't go! Please come back! Please don't leave me again." Her tears flowed down her cheeks.

Geoffrey was so overcome by hearing her calling out his name as he was coming in, that he ran to her side and placed her face in his hands. 'Leigh, it's me, I am here. I've been here all along. I will never leave you. You are dreaming, please wake up, now." He kissed the tears on her face gently and lovingly.

She opened her eyes and saw him there. She felt his kisses on her cheek. Was it really him? "Are you a dream, too?" she asked weakly.

He stroked her hair and grabbed her hands. "No, I am very much real. How are you feeling?"

She was too stunned to talk. He said he had been here all along. Why hadn't he come to her before? Then reality came with her doubts. He was here, but she must have been dreaming what he said to her. It was not real, just her foolish mind playing tricks on her stupid and tortured heart. Like a stab in the gut, she felt the rejection from the night that she had been with him. Her head ached with another sharp pain. She remembered how he had not spoken that night. Remembered it all too well. What did he want with her now? She was suddenly very wary of him and straightened herself up. Trying to get a grip, she took her hands away from his. She wasn't about to get caught up in that same emotional roller coaster she had been on with him before. He had been oh so very clear about what he thought about her, in the most basic way. Hurt consumed her again. No damned way would she believe she meant anything to him.

She cleared her throat and tried to talk with confidence, "I am fine. I have been waiting to see you since I regained conscious. I have some questions for you. And, I also have to get back to work. I am not use to being down like this. Now, first of all, why was I kept here at Dalroch after I was found? What kept me from being put in a hospital? Why was I here in the first place? And, who found me? The last thing I remember is being tied up and questioned by someone in a dark room. They took me from my lodge. Then I remember being here. Yes, I think, and my captor was with me. That is the last thing I remember, except" she closed her eyes and tried to remember what had happened next.

Geoffrey caught his breath and waited.

"I remember. You were there at some point, weren't you?" She was still in a misty state of mind but she saw Geoffrey again with a sword going after her captor.

He watched the change in her expressions as she was trying to remember. He hoped she couldn't remember everything. And she was obviously remembering how he'd treated her. It was disappointment he read on her face. But, hadn't she had cried out for him in her sleep? She thought he was a dream when he had answered her. Now the aloofness. She was obviously fighting her feelings. He didn't blame her for her responses. She deserved answers to not only her verbalized questions, but to those that her heart asked. Then he thought that it must be her engagement to Kevin that was keeping her from opening up to him. After all, she had a wedding to plan, didn't she? But that still didn't mean she didn't care for him, too. His heart was being tugged to tell her everything but the aloofness she was showing threw him off.

'You are here because I insisted you stay here. After what you have been through, I dare say moving you would have set your recovery back. As far as why you were here in the first place, well, it was because I -- "He was cut off by a knock at the door and Kevin eased into the room.

"I hate to interrupt, but have you got some time to talk Leigh?" Kevin asked gently as he openly sneered at Geoffrey sitting on the bed by her. "I think we should finish our conversation from earlier."

Leigh looked at him and back at Geoffrey. Geoffrey's answers were so business like and aloof sounding. He was certainly trying to keep the conversation from getting to a personal level. But, he did kiss her tears earlier, did he not? He did say he would never leave her again or did he? Oh, she was so confused, it must have been part of her dreams.

Waiting for him to say something, anything, she held on to the slight hope he really cared for her. An awkward silence began. Kevin was shuffling his boots and trying to remind both of them he was still there. Well, here we go again, Leigh thought. That non-responsive non-personal demeanor. Damn him! He didn't care for her any more than he had before! She began to flush red and got angry. He was only there out a sense of obligation to her because she was in his house and in his care. He must have been ready to apologize for the kidnapping being his fault because of the family's criminal investigation. That was all, she concluded rather severely and with all the hurt all over again piercing her heart.

She looked at Kevin and said, "Sure. We're apparently finished here, aren't we, My Laird?"

Geoffrey felt dismissed. He had more to say, but he began to get mad too. Kevin wouldn't leave her alone. By damn, he better. Geoffrey hadn't finished what he came to say. He stood up and stared at Kevin.

"I think we still need to have a few more moments, Mr.

Johnson."

Leigh had let her hurt and pain control her and now having a distraction to boot, she said, "Oh, I believe I am quite through, My Laird." The attentions of Geoffrey had only been as a result of their business relationship. She continued, "You must have a lot of business to tend to, and I really have already taken up way too much of your time. I'm sorry that I have been a burden here but Kevin can help me get going, so I will be out of your way. Don't worry about my work, I have almost finished." Her voice was breaking up as she finished, which did not go unchecked by either man who was standing there.

Geoffrey conceded. It was not going to happen. He couldn't tell her his true feelings. He felt Fate's blow and got up without a word and left the room to let the betrothed couple make their plans.

A little after midnight, the sleek 75 foot Kelley Reefer eased out of its berth in the boat house below Dalroch and into the Bay of Frith heading due north. The crew of five, a group of men he kept on standby in the nearest small village had stocked the cruiser with plenty of food for the coming weeks. Geoff took a few minutes checking the various instruments in the captain's navigation room. He then went from stem to stern with an eye for the slightest of details being tended to. With a heavy heart, he gave the captain a go ahead and the engines roared into life and picked up cruising speed. Sitting quietly in the dark of his master cabin, Geoff watched out the window as the last glow of the castle's lights faded into the night. With the horizon now in another direction, he knew it was time to put the painful scene from earlier behind him.

Before Leigh left Dalroch, the sense of needing closure drove her to complete her last report on Melinde's murder. She knew Geoffrey had left because Gabby and Jeremy both came in her room to tell her. Gabby was very discerning and frowned heavily as she asked, "So, did you and Father get to visit before he left? I had the impression he had something very important to discuss with you."

Leigh was still hurt and couldn't bring herself to even see the implication of the question from Gabby. She just said, "He came by but was obviously very busy getting prepared for this, this 'trip'."

Gabby's face showed a clear disappointment, but Leigh was sure it was more because her Father was gone than for the fact that Leigh and he hadn't visited very long.

Jeremy was fidgeting and got up from his chair and asked, "Well, Mom, if you're going with Kevin to Wyoming for an undetermined time, do you want Joe and I to go and check on things at Marlowe? I have a few more days before reporting back to school. We can head on out tomorrow and let you know how things are there as soon as you and Kevin get to wherever you're going."

Leigh was not concerned about Marlowe, since Della had things under control, but she felt like Jeremy needed some focus in light of the near fatal events and the fact that she wouldn't be going home from here. "Sure, that'd be great, son. Yeah, I'll be in touch real quick as soon as I can. Don't let things at Marlowe bog you down, though. School's numero uno priority."

"Yea, yea. I know. I just think you'd feed better when you know things are good in Mississippi too. Well, then, I guess we'll finish packing." He turned to go, but then came back to Leigh's bedside. He leaned down to kiss her and said, "Don't ever do this again, you hear?"

She saw a tear in his eye as he kissed her on the forehead and then he left the room. Gabby quietly followed.

The next morning, after a very tearful goodbye to Joe, Jeremy and Gabby, Leigh knew it was time to finish her time there, too. She got Kevin to agree to go sight-seeing and she wandered around a couple more days getting her legs back in shape and thinking on the murder. The drawing sensation she felt at the display on the landing since that first day at Dalroch lead her back to that location several times. She finally asked Ms. Daniels to open the cabinet so she could look closer at the items.

Several jeweled daggers were lined up on purple velvet in the center of the display. Leigh picked up the one in the middle and examined it closely. There, she said to herself as she looked in between the colored jewels on the handle. A dark stain! An 'aha' factor! This had been used at least once, she said to herself. Not wanting to get too excited though, she decided to send it by courier to the chemist that extracted the two sets of DNAs out of the blood stain in the broche. He insisted if it was for the Duke, he would analyze it quickly and get back a report ASAP.

A few hours before her flight out with Kevin, the chemist called and confirmed that the stain on the dagger had the very same DNA as was in the stains found and analyzed earlier for her. He was most accommodating and assured her he would have his report faxed to the castle and the dagger would be couriered back to Dalroch within the day. Asking if she needed anything else, she answered, "No, but thank you so much on behalf of the Duke and his family." Hanging up the phone, she said to herself, no, she needed nothing else to confirm her suspicions.

Taking time to write out the final report, she gave her conclusions to the Duke formally. She had every indication that Melinde was pregnant at the time of her murder. Leigh knew that it would've been a big time social taboo to have a child out of wedlock back then, even though the marriage to the Marquis of Dalroch was already planned. But, from the ranting and ravings of the maid in her journal leading up to the murder, Leigh was sure that the maid had been in love with the Marquis. She had indicated, by numerous phrases, that she knew Melinde was with child. The maid was not only jealous of Melinde, but she was crazed over the pregnancy, and not wanting the Duke to suffer through any scandal over the baby being born before the appropriate nine months. Leigh was sure it was she who had plotted and planned Melinde's murder. She was the one who called her to the broche that night. She had easy access to the dagger in the Heritage Collection, and she would make certain Melinde would not scar the McKennah Marquis' name or reputation. The clincher was that seemingly indescript reference in the journal that day before the murder. She had said, 'No one will have reason to say the house and all the occupants were not clean. My mundane job is hard sometimes, but it is all going to be worth the effort, especially when it comes to the Marquis. He will always have the reputation of being clean. I will see to it, no matter what it takes."

CHAPTER FORTY-TWO

SOUTHERN AFGHANISTAN

In the desert sun, a jeep traveled at a fast pace stirring the sand up behind it as it moved into the seemingly endless sea of sand. The remote concrete bunker was a few more miles and the driver was hot and tired, but he was mostly very apprehensive. He was bringing a dreaded word to his master, Sahib. Kadar was dead and his mercenary group captured. It would not please his master, but the implications of having anyone know where the insurgent group might have a stronghold was even more disturbing. The chemicals and the lab were Sahib's pride and the steppingstone for his move into the leadership role he wanted and deserved. The driver smiled knowing he would be right along Sahib's side when he overthrew the American-loving governments in the Middle East one by one.

CHEYENNE, WYOMING -NOVEMBER 1998

Leigh had to admit the sky was big and glorious at night here like she always heard. There was a distant sound of a coyote yelping and a couple of whinnies from the barn. Other than that, though, the night as quiet. Leigh was upstairs at Kevin's log cabin lodge. She was sitting on the wooden deck in a lounge chair with her flannel gown on. She was soaking up the crisp cool air. The wind gently blew her hair around her shoulders and away from her face with a cleansing sensation. Her thoughts were blank, and she tried desperately to remember the astronomy she attempted to learn in college. "Attempted" was the operative word here. She recognized the Big Dipper, but she wasn't really sure about even that one. A shooting star eased across the sky making a stream of instant light and then fading just as fast. Make a wish, she said to herself. Maybe wishing on shooting stars was silly, but she really had a need to have one wish come true. And that was she would make the right choices in life from here on out. That really was not too much to ask now, was it? She hadn't made too good of choices in the past that was for darn sure. Sitting here right now, I feel nothing, want nothing out of life, want only time to myself to learn to feel again, she thought. She remembered the words Kevin had implanted in her brain upon her moving to Wyoming with him.

"You don't have to commit to me or a life here. All I ask is that you give in to coming and resting. I don't need anything from you but a 'yes' and I will give you anything you want to make your stay comfortable. No pressures, no responsibilities, Leigh. I know you don't love me the way I love you, and I am willing to give you all the time you need to sort through your feelings for me. If you find you can't make your stay permanent, I will understand. Just give me a chance to show you how I feel. When you are ready to make a step forward in our relationship, I will be here. Otherwise, whatever trauma you have suffered through will have a chance to heal while you are here. Deal?"

Leigh though about his offer throughout the long flight back from Scotland across the Atlantic. She knew she couldn't stay at Marlowe because she was afraid of putting the farm in danger by her presence. She wasn't sure if her captor had any more friends still wanting something from her again that she didn't have. She knew she was paranoid about it, but deservedly so.

So, Mississippi was out for the time being. Scotland was definitely out, needless to say, and she wasn't about to go down that emotional road for a long, long time. So, she had agreed, by default, to take Kevin up on his offer. She moved into his cabin in a guest bedroom and Kevin had been sweet as cotton candy to her since that point. He saw to her every need but gave her room for her own personal time and space. He was working as the Chief Assistant District Attorney in Cheyenne and was obviously happy doing so. His ranch consisted of 100 acres with Santa Gertrudis cattle and a few prize paint horses. It was on a grassy plain with a backdrop of the mountains. It really was a peaceful place and despite her fairly catastrophic emotional well-being when she arrived, there was a healing process beginning.

Her days so far were slow and melodic in nature. She had no obligations and no stress. She would ride out on the ranch in the mornings and then tended to the horses for Kevin in the evening. Kevin bought her a small SUV and told her to go wherever she wanted whenever. She became so lazy she felt she might just have to do something meaningful or she would start vegetating. She refused to think about her kidnapping and torturing as it was strictly too painful along with the hurt she suffered with Geoffrey. She refused to think about her job at St. Andrews, as that was something she had been enjoying before everything else happened. Kevin relayed her situation to Alan Flackerty who was most understanding and willing to put Leigh's research project on hold for a few months to see if she was up to continuing it. So, she had refused to think about Scotland as a whole and Geoffrey in particular. Anytime a fleeting thought of him would try to infiltrate the barriers in her mind, she would shut them out with a viciousness that only someone with major emotional baggage could do.

All in all, though, her decision had been a good one and what Kevin had offered was timely and therapeutic for her.

One slow afternoon, while trying to find something new to occupy her time, she contacted her former secretary in Mississippi, Cheryl.

"You okay?" were Cheryl's first words. "Not a word from you for several months!"

"I'm fine. I'll tell you where I am if you won't jump to conclusions and promise to keep this to yourself."

"Well, oooh-kay," Cheryl said skepticism in her tone.

"I'm in Wyoming with Kevin Johnson. He's working here now and has a ranch. I came with him a couple months ago. I live with him, but I'm not WITH him, in case you're wondering."

"What? I thought he was dead! What in the world?" Cheryl sounded shocked and Leigh, quite frankly, had forgotten about the circumstances surrounding Kevin's disappearance before her exit to Scotland.

"Oh, well, it's complicated, but he's fine now. I'd tell you more if I could, but I just can't."

"Well, it sounds mysterious and very hot! Yeah, right! Living in the same house with that hunk? Not WITH him. Uh-huh! Well, if that's how you want to portray it, I'll believe you. Ha!"

"You doing okay after what happened to Mike and the Judge?"

"Dammit, Leigh! You have no clue what this place has been through! It's like a vault in this office. No one is allowed in and we're barely allowed out. FBI agents took over for a while. It was crazy, I'll tell you! Crazy! I was worried about going home at night since there was an obvious snitch on the case and I thought I'd be the one Mike would suspect. Finally, I've been given clearance to work with this new fellow. He's a gubernatorial appointment from Jackson, but he's moved here now and going to run for DA. I don't particularly like him."

"Who is he?" Leigh asked wondering if it was anyone she knew.
"Charles P. Dickinson, the third." She said with an attempted British accent. Leigh smiled as she could just see Cheryl's face as she animated his name.

"He signs everything that way and wants it known he is from an old line political family. He's more like a spoiled brat, if you ask me! Hey! Why don't you come back and run against him? You'd probably beat his pants off."

"Not really thinking about coming back anytime soon. Maybe someone else will come out to run against him, though. Someone you could enjoy working with."

"That's what I'm hoping, too. But, yeah, sure not going to be anyone like you! So, when will you be coming back? Sometime before the end of the century?"

"Not sure, really. Kinda on neutral and hoping for a little more of that for a while."

Leigh then changed the subject and asked about the Judge's race. Cheryl was going to get back with her on that, since she truthfully hadn't heard much on it. There was a bit of Leigh that was enticed by the thought that she could go back and run for that office, but she owed Kevin an opportunity to see how things would work with him after what all he'd done for her. She hoped to give him that chance as soon as she felt she was healed enough inside to do so. Agreeing to keep in contact with Cheryl, Leigh hung up and went back up on the deck where she spent a lot of time just sitting.

The door to the deck opened and Kevin walked out in a pair of grey jogging pants, tennis shoes and a t-shirt. He was perspiring like he had been working out.

"Well now, what's a pretty girl like you doing in a place like this all alone?" Kevin smiled as he pulled another chair up beside her, and Leigh couldn't help but smile at him.

He continued as he wiped his perspiration from his brow, "I thought you might need a little company other than that pack of coyotes out there. Am I wrong?"

Leigh did want Kevin to stay and talk with her. She was feeling very alone all of a sudden, and said, "Sure, Kev. I hope your sleep wasn't disturbed by my rambling up here. Or have you been working out?"

"Yeah, on the weights for a while. I did hear you moving around and thought I'd come up and tell you about your surprise. I was trying to wait until in the morning, but I'm too excited to wait." Kevin's face looked like the bird that swallowed the canary.

"What surprise?" Leigh asked wondering what he was up to now. He had been bringing her little surprises ever since she'd come back with him. Flowers, clothes, little bottles of perfume, etc.

"Well, you'll have to put your robe and slippers on to come see this one." He got up and pulled her up by her hands, "Don't daIly, now, Lady!"

A few minutes later, Leigh was looking from the window of Kevin's pickup through the fence panels of a holding pen at a pure white Egyptian Arab stallion. He was magnificent and his white coat gleamed in the moon light. He moved with such grace and she felt as if he was magical. She couldn't say a word. She got out of the truck and eased into the pen where the horse was, "He's beautiful, Kevin," she whispered as she stood and waited for the horse to come to her and smell her. He had huge black eyes and his black nozzle blew warm air into her hair as he got acquainted with her. Leigh was mesmerized by the beauty of the gorgeous animal in front of her.

"He's broke for English and Western Pleasure. I got him from a couple going out of the horse business. He was their herd stud and they were really sad to sell. I promised breeding rights if they ever got back into the business. You think you'll like him?" Kevin had made a seat for himself on the top rail of the pen while he was talking.

"Like him? Kevin, he is magnificent! But I couldn't accept him as a gift. It is way too much.' Leigh walked back toward Kevin and the horse followed her. He nudged her shoulder as she was talking to Kevin.

"He seems to think otherwise, Leigh. Look, he just followed you," Kevin was amused.

"What is his name?" Leigh asked turning to pat the horse's head.

"It's some sort of Egyptian long name on the registration papers, but they called him 'Gypsy'."

"Wow, Gypsy, I think you need to come back to the barn with me and have a snack of sweet feed, don't you?" Leigh was talking to the horse while Kevin jumped down and came and put his arm around Leigh's waist.

"If you want, I'll bring him into the barn paddock tomorrow morning, and you can get to know each other better." Leigh's body had frozen at the touch of Kevin's arm around her. She hadn't felt physical contact, nor had she wanted to feel any since she left Dalroch. Then, she eased up and thought that Kevin's arm around her was more like a chummy gesture rather than sexual, so she laughed nervously and said, "That'd be great Kevin. He's an extravagant gift, but I love him already. Thanks so much." She looked up into Kevin's handsome face and he smiled and tightened his arm on her waist.

Then letting go, he said, "Let's get you back home and maybe we can have some hot chocolate before bed since it is rather nippy." He started walking while whistling back to the truck.

Leigh was flabbergasted at the gift of Gypsy. She was beginning to think that Kevin really had her interests at heart by go out and finding her the horse. He must have known she needed something of her own to take care of while she regained her momentum. She knew even in a distress sale, a stud Egyptian Arabian would be pretty pricey, and she was worried about the expense, but seeing how happy he was, she thought she'd leave it alone for now.

Smiling, she patted his right hand on the seat and again said with true appreciation, "Thanks, Kevin. That was the best gift you could've given me."

He smiled back and grabbed her hand saying, "Yeah, well, I thought you'd like him. I couldn't help myself, especially since I knew how much you missed your horses in Mississippi."

Leigh smiled and eased her hand out of his. Then, she quickly picked it back up and held it until they got back to the cabin.

CHAPTER FORTY-TWO

WESTERN PAKISTAN

Sahib dealt with mercenaries before in his attempt to rise to power. He paid the best and gotten the best results. It was risky having Kadar and his men trying to retrieve the code. But it supposedly contained the type information that would be worth the money he paid thus far. However, Sahib's efforts were apparently waylaid for the moment. Learning about Kadar's demise didn't bother him much at this point, but something else did. There were some holes in the intelligence he had received, things that didn't add up too nicely. He knew Kadar retrieved a dummy code prior to his being killed. The reason for Scottish royal involvement wasn't clear, nor was the location of Kadar's other men. Sahib was confident that he was protected since Kadar's men hadn't been cleared with the little information, he'd given Kadar about his terrorist group and their base location. That was the agreement anyway. However, to be safe, Sahib relocated his lab and his operations center from if's previous location. It was a matter of time before he learned the last location of the code and a new paid soldier would be hired to retrieve it. He was willing to sit and wait for that information to surface. His only problem at the moment was trying to find more chemicals for his lab. His power was dependent on his arsenal being complete and ready to deploy.

CHEYENNE, WYOMING-APRIL 1999

Leigh had now been in Wyoming for six months. She was sitting and reading large novels to pass the time when she wasn't out with Gypsy riding or grooming him and the other three working cow ponies.

It was a Friday night and Leigh was busy in the horse barn taking out the blankets for the horses and hooking them on because it was forecast to be a very cold night. She closed the last stall door when Kevin surprised her by coming in the barn.

'How's the equine family tonight?" He asked as he came in and leaned up against the stall door. He was dressed in rather tight-fitting jeans with a large silver buckle on his belt. He also wore a western shirt the color of sand with a brown leather jacket over it. He obviously dressed this way after coming in from work.

"Everyone's fed, watered and blanketed for the night," Leigh said as she looked at his western wear. "How was your day and why are you dressed for a 'Hoe Down'?" Leigh asked as the aftershave aroma and soap smells drifted from his body. They seemed to have their desired effect as Leigh looked at Kevin for the first time in a long time, really looked at him.

"Well, since you asked, uh- I was planning on celebrating this evening in town with a steak dinner and a little 'Two-step' with my favorite girl. That is, if she would do me the honor?"
Leigh became a bit embarrassed at the way she must have been staring and she turned to put a bucket back in the doorway to the feed room.

"Well that depends on who your favorite girl is, I guess. But, it sure sounds like fun to me! I would love a good steak! What are you celebrating?"

"Course it is you, crazy girl! And, I am celebrating –"he stopped and offered her his arm as they started walking to the house together. It was dark outside already and the night sounds from the crickets started. Kevin continued, "Well, we got a conviction today on that corrupt son of a bitch that stole from the county coffers. You know the one that's been in the news. We've been wanting to get him for the longest time."

"That's great, Kevin. I know you were hoping to get the conviction. How long was the jury out?"

"About thirty minutes. Was beginning to sweat it out, but isn't it great? The Judge sentenced him to 10 years and boy were we happy! The whole office is going out."

"Yeah, I do miss that feeling when the jury announces that word: 'Guilty'. I'm glad you won the case. Congrats."

"Well, if you miss the work, why don't you think about coming to work at the DA's office with me? We have an opening coming up when one of the ADA's goes out in a month. He's retiring after twenty years there."

They had reached the house and Leigh stopped at the front door. She turned and said, "Thanks, Kev, but I don't think I want to consider going back to the position I was in before in Mississippi. It was too disillusioning to have everyone up top being bought and sold. I appreciate your asking me, though. And, I don't mean to imply your office would be like that. You know, it was just that I worked really hard, enjoyed it and was looking forward to retiring there. Then, the corruption, the murder case blowing up, well, you know it just leaves a very bad taste in my mouth still."

Kevin shrugged and said, "Okay I understand. But, if you change your mind, let me know."

"Thanks, I really appreciate you thinking about me for the job." She smiled and turned to go up the stairs saying, "I'll just be a few minutes getting dressed, Kev." Leigh headed up to her room and started to change. She felt a sudden need to please Kevin. She actually wanted to look good for him tonight. Maybe it was because he had been so kind to not push himself with her and maybe she thought she was becoming attracted to him. Silly me, she thought, any normal red-blooded woman in her right mind would be attracted to him! But she remembered the last time she fell for his charm. She pondered the new feeling as she applied her make-up and jewelry. There was no time to ponder much as Kevin yelled up the steps, "Leigh! I'm dying from starvation down here! How long does it take for someone already beautiful to dress up for God's sake?"

Leigh laughed and threw on her best pair of brown corduroys and riding boots. She pulled a tight knit red sweater over her head and placed a brown shawl down on her arms. The long turquoise dangling earrings caught the sparkle in her eyes, and she smiled pleased with her looks.

"Whoa, there, Little Lady! I'm not up to having someone gawk at my date! You look, ah, well, fantastic! But you may want to stay close to me when we're on the dance floor so none of those rowdy cowboys will try to steal you away. You hear me?" Kevin was putting her coat over her shoulders and he turned her toward him. "I'm serious. You really are a temptation for the Gods!" Leigh felt something stir inside as he touched her cheeks with his warm hands and said, "Let's go, how 'bout it?"

They were out until 2:00am. Leigh took in more fun that she could've imagined as she was whirled and sashayed around the dirt dance floor in the saloon they were in. She had one too many white wines from the bar and was feeling a bit fuzzy headed as she climbed out of Kevin's car back at the cabin.

"Are you all right, Leigh?" Kevin grabbed her elbow and helped her up the steps inside.

'I am perfectly fine, Kevin, just cold. Boy, it must have really dropped down tonight!" She let him take her coat off and watched him get a fire started in the large fireplace in the den. The fire was instantly warming, and Kevin brought her a cup of hot chocolate with Irish cream in it.

She took a small sip and savored it. "That feels so good going down, Kevin. Thanks, and thanks for a wonderful evening. I can't remember when I've had that much fun." Leigh sat down on the sheepskin rug in front of the fireplace and stared at the fire as it leaped to the top of the firebox.

"I'm glad you had a good time. I sure did. It made me proud to be toting you around town tonight. I felt like I won some sort of contest or something!" Kevin said as he sat down beside her and hugged his knees.

"Man, I didn't even know how to Two-Step before. You made it easy and I felt like I was floating. That was really fun! What a great band, too!"

"Yeah, they're a fav of mine. I've been there a couple times before. Say, we can practice some more if you want. Then we can start entering those dance competitions! Are you up for it?" He looked at Leigh and then without waiting for a response, he jumped up to go put some music on. Leigh was still feeling the effects of the wine and Irish crème. She didn't feel like she had a care in the world. Sure, why not dance some more? She found herself laughing at the thought of being in a dance contest.

Kevin grabbed her hands and helped her up. The music was slow, and Kevin pulled her close saying, "Two-Stepping to slow music is fun, too," he said as he ran his arms down her back. They began swaying and then moved into a slow two-step. Leigh was so caught up in trying to make the right steps that she didn't notice her foot getting caught in the rug. "Oops!" she said as she tripped while taking Kevin down with her. They landed on the floor with Kevin on top of her and both laughing. Then it just happened. He quite naturally put his lips on hers and kissed her. And she let him. She felt funny about it at first, but then he pulled away and she felt as if she was going to die if he didn't kiss her again. Something had stirred inside her. She grabbed his head from the back and ran her fingers through his hair and pulled him back down to her. They kissed long and hard. His tongue found hers and she thought of nothing but wanting a physical and sexual release with him. He pulled her sweater shoulders down to reveal her strapless bra. Before she knew it he'd reached behind her and had it off in an expert second. She wanted him to look at her and that he did, with a lustful and longing look. He buried his face on her breasts, licking and massaging her nipples with one hand while unzipping her jeans and pulling them down with the other hand. He rubbed her panties with a soft hand and as she felt her wetness pouring, he pulled them off. Then she stopped and said, "Leigh. You are so beautiful. Damn! I want to take you now. Are you sure you want that too?" He stood up and unbuttoned his shirt revealing his taut chest and muscular arms. Leigh could only stare and think she needed him inside her to satisfy her burning desires. He didn't wait for a verbal response. He pulled his jeans and briefs off revealing what looked to Leigh like desire personified and it was all for her. She was about to lose all restraint when she looked into his face and the face she saw as her eyes traveled up his torso was that of Geoffrey McKennah! What am I doing, she asked herself, but she was too caught up in the fuzzyheaded desire and needs that she let him come into her with a blast of hurt and pleasure that lead to a quick release for them both.

She lay in Kevin's arms for a while afterwards. He was sleeping peacefully while her mind was frantic. She lost the emotional battle that had been plaguing her since she'd made love to Geoffrey. What should've been an enjoyable and satisfying experience with Kevin was forever marred by the burning images of Geoffrey making love to her. She saw his hands running the length of her flaming body. She saw his intense blue eyes soaking in every inch of her being. She imagined it was him inside her while all along Kevin was the one making love to her. She frowned with the realization that she would never be able to put him out of her mind and heart. Kevin was a good man and she honestly thought she could make herself forget Geoffrey, but tonight brought the truth out so poignantly. She only had sex with Kevin, when she had truly passionately made love to Geoffrey. She felt an odd sense of guilt to Geoffrey, all well knowing her love for him would always be unrequited. But her true guilt was for being with Kevin when she was only thinking of being with Geoffrey.

Kevin stirred and tightened his arms around her with a smile on his face. Leigh couldn't stop the trickling down of the tears in her eyes.

MARLOWE
TWO WEEKS LATER

Today, after all the days and nights that have passed since Leigh and Geoffrey were together, she had no idea how to erase his image from her mind, her heart, and her soul. Every time she listened to any type of music, she heard the music of the bagpipes. Every time she looked out across her pasture and hills, she thought of the Highland mountains, and when she would spend time in her barn with her horses, she thought of being with Geoffrey in the heather-topped hills above Dalroch. God help her even during the intimate time she had been with Kevin, only Geoffrey's body did she want to be feeling next to her and inside her. It was too much for her to cope with. She needed to distract herself from all relationships, the one with Kevin and the one she would never have with Geoffrey.

While walking among the tall virgin timbers on her property several days after arriving home, and after hearing from several former colleagues' words of encouragement to talk with the local political backers about her running for Circuit Judge, she thought that maybe she would entertain the idea. She ran away from her job there before when she felt betrayed by the District Attorney and the Circuit Judge. She knew now that the Gubernatorial appointees that were in those positions were hoping for an easy win in the upcoming elections, but she also knew that a campaign might be what she needed, win or lose. If she lost, she would have more name recognition in the county and could open her private practice here with a good solid base of clients. If she won, well, she would not get hopeful just yet.

She bent down and took a twig lying in the path and sat on a fallen tree log. She drew out a heart shape. Inside she wrote 'Geoff'. The sharp pang that hit her chest was followed by a big "X" being drawn over the name. This was her signal to her own heart to put the thoughts of past, present and even future romances behind her. She would from this day forward focus on the reestablishing of her self-identity and self-worth. Nothing like getting back into the real world and quit romanticizing. Her life and her work were more important that worrying about a love life.

She knew she would have to answer Kevin's offer to her of marriage, though. He had proposed the morning after they'd been together. She asked for a little time to think it over and in the meantime wanted to go home and see her house and horses. She had no real sense of direction, but just came to realize her feelings for Kevin would always be clouded with her feelings for Geoffrey. There was no other way she could protect Kevin from a life with someone who could never return the same genuine love he showed her. She would call Kevin tonight and tell him she couldn't go through with any commitment right now. It was the best she could do at this point, but she knew what the call would do to Kevin. She would lose him, and she would never be able to have his love again. But what was his love if it wasn't returned in the true sense of the word? Her friendship with him was all she could ever be able to give him and a false sense of security with her lovemaking. Geoffrey would always be in her, not Kevin.

She slowly walked back to her barn where the late evening sun was setting and casting an orange glow in the horse stables. She felt a sense of peace easing back in her as she looked at her horses, her property, and her left hand, that slowly was shed of the diamond engagement ring that Kevin had given her when he proposed. She placed it gently in her jacket pocket and wiping the tears again that were streaming down her face, she walked back to her house with a new sense of purpose.

CHAPTER FORTY-THREE

EASTERN PAKISTAN—June 1998

There was a loud explosion. It was an unexpected cannon blast that surprised the small Society Groups infantrymen. Someone had seen them coming, unfortunately. Geoffrey, dressed in desert camouflage, with a scarf over his mouth and nose, motioned his agents to press on through the growing dust storm. They couldn't risk the mission going sour just yet. Sahib's men would be onto them and they would uproot their base of operations again. It already had been long enough for the Society to pinpoint them again. Geoffrey was sure that the chemical weapon processing lab already started back up and the product quantities were growing.

They advanced into the building but were met with defensive fire from at least twenty uniformed men. Geoffrey had twelve men with him, but odds not being in his favor were replaced by the skill set of those recruited for this job. Advance intelligence was sparse, but it was enough to plan the attack. They were armed with the most advanced hand weaponry and fire grenades that were on the market. Two agents already had entered the building from an underground entrance. They had radioed that it was secure as well as the tunnel to the main concrete bunker. They were now entering the leader's suite of luxury accommodations. Geoffrey's plan was to bring Sahib out alive to make a show of his capture to the remaining insurgents. He continued to return fire while talking into his wrist radio. There was another explosion, but this one was expected since it would have been the planned demolition of the arsenal room. Geoffrey smiled at the perfectly timed bomb. But he was supposed to already have the building in his control by now. So, he was off by a few seconds. What difference would that make? Normally, he was such a stickler for precision work, but he felt confident that the building was theirs now that Sahib was in custody and on his way to Geoffrey.

Sahib entered the large room full of boxes and crates. His hands were restrained behind him and two agents were on either side standing with automatic rifles pointed into his sides. Sahib ordered his men to drop their weapons in Arabic. The men turned toward him and stopped firing. They dropped their weapons. The agents went in and secured the men and weapons.

A quick search of the building yielded the mother lode of mission objectives. There were more written plans for chemical processing and manufacturing, lists of potential purchasers for the weapons which were like a laundry list of the known terror cell leaders Geoffrey and the Society already knew, and there were rooms full of precursors for the weapons.

Thirty minutes later, the Society brought the terrorists and their leader out of the building. They then set off another explosion that took the rest of the building down.

Sahib was finished. The word would go out that he was alive but captured. The Society would follow up by turning him and his remaining soldiers over to the World Court at The Hague for war crime prosecution.

Geoffrey, feeling a little relieved that this part of the mission was over and thus meeting the goals of his forefathers yet again, walked over to Sahib.

"My friend, Raven, died because of your hired gun, Kadar." Sahib laughed and spit into Geoffrey's face.

Geoffrey wiped the spit off with disgust. He bent toward Sahib's face and with a venomous voice whispered, "And, the woman I love was tortured by Kadar, you piece of filth!"

Before he lost his temper, though, he stood up and turned to walk away. He didn't see the grenade that roiled onto the ground from the bottom of Sahib's pants until it was too late.

DORSEY COUNTY COURTHOUSE-JUNE 1999

Leigh's informal mediations were becoming her signature way of handling the large amount of mass tort cases in her court district. As the new Circuit Judge, few attorneys would turn her down for settlement conferences. She cleared the backlog of cases that gummed up her court docket before she took office. In record time, most of the older cases settled. Many of the litigants just wanted someone to tell them why it was in their best interests to settle. Sometimes it was because Leigh knew the defendant was on weak grounds for a trial. Other times she could see the plaintiffs were so close to breaking financially that they would cave in under the pressure and settle for much less if they went to trial. The latest pharmaceutical tort cases had been filed and pre-trial conferences set at the time of the filing of the complaints. She set the trial date and dared anyone to try to tell her they couldn't complete discovery on time. Her tactics kept defense attorneys fuming at the lack of time they could bill their corporate clients on discovery extension motions. Plaintiff attorneys fumed at having to get experts in and paid for so early in order to be ready for trial. All in all, it seemed to work nicely. Both sides were ready to talk today. Leigh insisted the attorneys have their clients in the room when she set these informal mediations. That way, they were there to accept or decline any offers that were made during the day.

There was a break coming up while each side discussed numbers and Leigh headed from the conference room to her office. Cheryl looked up from her new desk as the new Court Administrator for the new Judge and said, "How's it going in there? Any progress?" Her phone mike was in front of her mouth and she was typing on the computer at the same time while talking to Leigh and someone on the phone.

"Should be. I think the numbers are getting closer to everyone's palatable amounts. Anything real important happening?" she asked as she unzipped her robe.

"Yeah, there are a couple of important phone messages for you. You got time to return them or should I call them back and tell them to wait until tomorrow?" She handed the phone slips to Leigh.

Garrison Roberts and Joe. She hadn't talked with Garrison Roberts since before then, well, the trip to Scotland. She had received a couple of donations from his legitimate businesses when she was running for Judge. May as well see what he wants, she thought.

"I'll return them, Cheryl. Thanks.'" Cheryl nodded as she carried on with her phone call and typing.

Inside Leigh's new 'chambers', she took the judicial robe off and wandered to the window overlooking the front of the courthouse. She probably should call Joe first, although she knew she would hear the same 'are you sure you're all right?' that he said every time he called. She never told him about the kidnapping being because of the code and for all he knew, just like Kevin, it was all to do with some family murder mystery of the McKennah Clan.

"Joe, it's me. Yes, before you ask. I'm sure I'm fine. What about you'?" Leigh listened to Joe tell about his latest cases and then he told her he was flying in with someone he wanted her to meet, someone very important to him.

"Is she the one, Joe?" Leigh asked, knowing if he was bringing her home, then she must be the one.

"Looks that way, sis. Now don't you go making any snap decisions there. There is someone good enough for me in this big old world!" He laughed and Leigh told him to bring her home.

Her next call was to Garrison Roberts. She wondered, from the phone number, which was local, if he was out of federal prison.

"Leigh Reid! Or should I say 'Your Honor?'" Garrison's voice was loud and boisterous.

"Well, thanks to a few really timely and necessary campaign donations, yes, I am the Judge. But you knew all about that, didn't you?"

"Yea, well, I wanted to have some influence with the new Judge," he said with a note of humor in his voice. "Ha! You certainly know better than that, don't you?" she laughed at the thought of being influenced by anyone.

"Yeah, I know. I just am proud of you and after that Federal inconvenience of mine, I'm going the straight and narrow. I just wanted to see how you were doing and make sure you know if you ever need anything, that I'm available."

"Well, thanks, Mr. Roberts. I hope I don't get in that position, but one never knows what's around the next corner. I am enjoying the work, albeit a huge amount of it!"

Garrison said, "You'll do just fine, I'm sure. Well, take care Leigh Reid. I mean, 'Your Honor'!" and he laughed and then was off the line.

Leigh smiled as she hung the phone up. She knew who he was and what he was, but damn if he hadn't been a friend to her and helped get rid of some of the corruption in her home town. Funny how things can happen that sure surprise you.

She sat down in her high-backed leather chair and sighed. Wow! Sometimes it just got to her that she was actually a State Circuit Court Judge now. The weeks that had rocked by since her return home were like a blur in her memory banks. The decision to run was already made for her by several business leaders when they heard she was back. It took no real amount of arm twisting and she was all of a sudden on the baked chicken and English pea speaking tours throughout the district. Her only opposition was the gubernatorial appointee and he already was suffering from a pretty bad reputation of being a loose cannon with cases. The local attorneys came out in support of Leigh and carrying the distinction of being the first woman judge in the district, she was sworn in two months ago. Hiring Cheryl from the D.A.'s office was her first official duty and the job was off and going. The days of being on the opposite side of the bar were over and her prior experience as a prosecutor, as well as her pure life experiences gave her a fair mind and an obstinate nature for getting things done.

She looked at her calendar on the desk and her eyes wandered to the wall where one photo she had saved from her Scotland travels was displayed. It was of the worn torn Victorian bath building on the edge of the North Sea. She made it on one of her walks there while the sun was rising one morning. She had it blown up and then framed and put it on the wall to the right of her desk. It was the only photo, but it was the most significant one she could have. It was the first place where she'd met Geoffrey. As she thought about that day, her eyes immediately watered and she unconsciously wiped the tears as they started down her cheeks.

"Ah, Judge?" was the voice on the intercom from Cheryl. "You ready? They are."

Coming back to reality from her Scottish moments and drying her eyes, she pushed the intercom button and said, "Coming."

CHAPTER FORTY-FOUR

BOSTON—July 1999

Jarrod Reid was up late studying in his apartment just off the University campus. The last exam of his senior year at Harvard was supposed to be easy, but he was finding it hard to concentrate. He had his music on and a small desk light warmed the area on the table where the book lay open. He went to the fridge to get yet another bottle of water and then thought he'd make tea. While the water was on, the phone rang.

"Jarrod. It's Gabriella McKennah. How are you'?" was the bright and cheerful voice that greeted his hello.

"Well, now, how about this? Where are you, Gabby?" Jarrod was pleased to hear her voice since he hadn't heard from her after he came back from Scotland. She visited with him while he was there at Dalroch about possibly coming to Harvard for graduate work.

"I am in Boston. I just got in. I know it is late, but I'm going to tour your college tomorrow, and thought we could get together for dinner tomorrow night. How about it?"

"So you are really still thinking about graduate work here? That's great and sure, I'd love to see you. Where are you staying? I'll pick you up."

"At the downtown Hilton. Could you call on me about 7?"

"Will do. And boy will I be ready to celebrate. I have my last exam tomorrow. Great timing. Can't wait to see you."

"Good luck, ole boy! Look forward to visiting with you tomorrow too. Cheers!"

Jarrod smiled putting the phone down. He liked Gabby and enjoyed her chipper voice and accent after not hearing it for so long. He hoped to help her with any advice on Harvard and the surroundings. She was just 'cool' to him.

Hearing the teapot begin to whistle, he sighed and prepared to launch back into his studying.

…………………………….

There were very few people in the pub, and the fire in the fireplace warmed the surroundings. The aroma from the kitchen was tantalizing as Jarrod and Gabby sat in a booth close to the fire. They visited for at least an hour about college life there before the conversation finally turned personal in nature.

"How's your Mother doing, Jarrod?' Gabby asked as she sipped her after dinner hot cider.

"That's a good question. I think she's fine, but I haven't really gotten her to talk too much since she went through that ordeal over there."

"Yes, it was such a bloody shame that she suffered at the hands of some terrorizing criminal like that. I still don't know why she was kidnapped for ransom and tortured like that, but then I never get too many answers from him. I do love him, though, and know when not to ask certain questions. But we all felt so bad that we had any part in that horrible time for Leigh." She was thinking about her encounter with her Father over his feelings for Leigh prior to his departure from Dalroch months ago. She had only received occasional emails from him and notably no phone calls, since he left. The National Trust tours ended two weeks ago, leaving her free to leave and come to Harvard for her tour and hopefully approval of admittance.

"Yeah, I know what you mean. Mom's usually more open, too, than lately. Ever since she got back home to Marlowe and poured herself into the Judge race. I think she's trying to forget it. You know, the kidnapping and all, so she buries herself in work."

Gabby's eyebrows raised up. "I'm sorry, did you say 'back at Marlowe'? I thought she and that cowboy, Kevin is it, were living in Wyoming? She's a Judge now? What happened?"

"No, she came back home several months ago. Alone. I don't think it worked out between them, but she doesn't want to talk about it." He shrugged his shoulders. "I really don't ask anymore since it must not have ended well."

Gabby was confused, "But, they did get married, didn't they? Does this mean they are divorcing?"

"No, they didn't get married. Really, I don't know much about it, Gabby. I know Mom is not a very happy person now, though. When she works so hard that she doesn't call me regularly, I know she's hiding something she doesn't want me to know. We've always been so close that I guess I just know these things."

Gabby was already moving on in her mind. Jarrod didn't need to know about it because Gabby wasn't sure how she would pull it off or whether it would work. Leigh's not married is basically all she heard.

They finished their visit and then she promised to be in touch with Jarrod about her plans to start the University in the Fall. They hugged quickly as she ran back out into the blustery wind and towards her hotel. She was, most assuredly, preoccupied with getting back to Scotland and finding her Father just as soon as possible.

CHAPTER FORTY-FIVE

DALROCH-October 1999

After several weeks in a hospital in Cairo, Geoffrey had been moved back home. Things were not real clear to him about his last few weeks, but he remembered having surgery on his right hip after the doctors were hesitant to try the surgery. It was an experimental surgery at best involving some reconstruction of bones and rearranging a couple of connection points in the hip joint. He was currently unable to work at all and the prognosis was not very promising that he ever would. The other injuries he suffered from the blast were mending slowly because of the surgery. He had burns on his right shoulder and cuts that shrapnel caused all over his body. Some would leave scars; others were minor and had already begun to fade.

The castle had been made ready for his arrival in a wheelchair. Ramps were installed and an elevator up to a bedroom that was easier to negotiate than his in the tower wing.

Today, Geoffrey was trying to get his mind clear of the foggy haze that was caused from the pain medications he was administered constantly from a stay-at-home nurse. The pain was easier to take than the unclear head in his estimation. He was in his library going through some of the paperwork and correspondence for the castle that piled up since he left. The emptiness of the room was pushing in on him to the point that he needed to get out. As he put some of the files back together, he ran across the handwritten note that Leigh had left the night she ran away from him. The note was in between other papers and the sight of it startled him as it reawakened the memories of Leigh. He didn't want to read it again, but he was drawn to it by some force beyond his control. The words were igniting a fire inside him. The emotions that permeated his entire being were too much for him to handle.

Ever since the last mission, he made himself focus on his work so as not to let his feelings for Leigh interfere. The note reminded him of his foolishness and guilt over Leigh. She had been in his home and in his bed. He had been so caught up in his mission as to let her believe he didn't care for her. Enough of this, he said to himself. No trying to rehash the events. It was never to be: He and Leigh! Ha! She was by now married and living the non-complicated life that Kevin could provide. He wasn't ever going to see her again. Although with the flick of a mouse or the pushing of a button, he could find her and see if she was indeed happy. He did think about doing this several times but each time he chose to just leave it and her alone. He was heartbroken and now physically broken. He tried to erase the thoughts of Leigh by throwing the note in the trash. He then wheeled himself to the main landing and glanced at the Heritage Collection. With a blissful sigh, he remembered how Leigh sensed things and found the answer to Melinde's murder. He remembered how she was so quick and thorough in her work. Then he thought of the times he watched her when he was trying to figure her part in the Sahib plot to uncover the Stenness Society. Damn his feelings for her! He suddenly realized his life was so shallow now having known her and then having to watch her go away from his arms and his home.

He wheeled his chair through the passages and then to the locked area that only he could enter. Then he made his way to the cavern home of the Society. Inside he found Kenneth McKennah busily watching several surveillance cameras sending signals to the cave. Kenneth was manning the helm there ever since Geoffrey was injured. He turned to

THE OGHAM CONNECTIONS

a computer monitor that kept cryptic satellite links with the operatives. Geoff watched as Kenneth expertly typed in commands to the world media computer that scanned major stories in every country and in every language. The lights in the dark control room blinked and flashed while sound bites were being downloaded from all over the world for storage purposes. Kenneth looked up as he saw Geoffrey wheeling into the room.

"Hello, Cousin. How goes it today? You look better than you have been looking, mate." Kenneth was smiling at Geoffrey as he helped to maneuver the wheelchair. Geoffrey was sure that Kenneth was just trying to be polite and that he really didn't look any better.

"Thanks, Kenneth. You should know I am going to have to relinquish my position until further notice. I want you to initiate protocols with the field agents and advise them that they are to answer to you until further notice. I am not up to much, I am afraid." Kenneth was not pleased with this news, but he had been expecting it because of the injuries and because Geoffrey seemed to have lost all the incentive he always maintained as the Keeper. Of course, he loved being at the top of the organization, but he also loved his cousin and he saw he was slipping away from the vital man and leader he had been.

"Sure, but only until you are back and ready to take it. And that will be soon, I know. Shall I report in daily upstairs?"

"Yes, I am sure that is fine." Geoffrey was busy picking through the Sahib/Kadar file and computer printouts that he amassed during the complete mission. This is quite a compilation, he said to himself. Kenneth went back at the monitors. Geoffrey picked up the first photo he made of Leigh and stared at it. She was getting into her car at the Blue Parrot in Hattiesburg right after she was slipped the disc by Kevin, her now husband. She was so beautiful to Geoffrey. Her very soul he connected with during the mission and then he felt the immense pleasure of knowing her intimately. Even if it was only one time, it was unforgettable and even if she looked like a troll, she had captured his heart and he only saw the beauty. He wanted to reach into the photo and touch her now, to hold her and to finally get to claim his love to her. He wished so much to have that night back. But it was not to be, he realized for the thousandth time, as he put the picture down and slowly wheeled himself out with his head hung down low.

Kenneth McKennah watched him go silently and then went to the stack of documents he had been looking at. He saw the photo of Ms. Reid. Man, he thought to himself, Geoffrey McKennah, cousin, you sure have it bad for this woman. He watched the wheelchair disappear, shook his head in sympathy and went back to his seat at the Society monitors.

CHAPTER FORTY-SIX

DALROCH-November 1999

Weeks had gone by at the castle. Mrs. Daniels was trying to get the Duke to eat, but the last few days he was leaving his plates full when she would come to pick them up. She felt almost helpless with the slow deterioration of his physical and mental well-being. He was giving up because of his injuries. She couldn't get through to him no matter what favorites or new concoctions the cooks were trying.

In addition, there was no gaiety in the house at all. There were no tours planned, no parties, and the castle seemed to be dying as the Duke sat silently in his saddened world. He had taken to staying inside his room day and night. The staff was constantly asking if there was anything they could do to cheer him up, but he would wave them away. He even refused to begin the physical therapy sessions for his leg. He was losing weight and drying up to nothing.

Today, the kitchen helper came in to pick up his plate. The curtains were drawn even though it was a beautiful day. Geoffrey was sitting in his wheelchair staring at nothing. The helper asked if she could start a fire for him in the fireplace. He just motioned for her to leave the room.

She went down to Mrs. Daniels afterwards and told her the Duke hadn't eaten again as he did every day now. Mrs. Daniels just shook her head and said, "That poor man is dying a slow death, he is. Nothing good will come of this if he doesn't eat something!"

The front gate phone rang in the kitchen and Mrs. Daniels picked it up. She knew they were not expecting anyone, so this must be someone unexpected.

She hung the phone up and looked at the chefs and the helper, saying, "I think we have just been given the medicine My Laird needs. Gabriella has returned! Quickly, let's get her some of her favorite dishes started. Great! I'll go and greet her at the door."

Gabby was prepared by Mrs. Daniels for the state of her father, but she still gasped out loud when she entered the room. Then she swallowed very hard and said, "Father. How are you? It's Gabby. Father?" She knelt beside his chair. He inched his head up frowning and speaking with a bare whisper, "Who?"

"Your daughter, Gabby! What's the matter, Father? Can't you hear me? Are you ok? You look a fright I must say Father!" She almost choked out the words.

"Gabby? I didn't know you were coming home." He opened his glazed over eyes and tried to focus on her by squinting. His voice was weak, and he looked so much older.

Gabby's tears were fixing to be shed, and she tried to hold them back so he wouldn't see. "Father I didn't know you had been injured. Mrs. Daniels said it was an accident. She said you walked onto a live explosive device while touring in Egypt. Why on earth did you not let me know?"

"There was nothing you could do about it, dear. I am sorry, but I have not recovered too well, I cannot walk and I'm not up to trying. I cannot get enough energy to do much."

Gabby then got just plain mad. She said sternly, "Father, listen to me. I don't know who you think you are to pull one over on your own flesh and blood, but the Duke of Dalroch I know is not one to let things get him down so easily. You have too much of the McKennah strength in you to let this injury get you down. Now, you mind me because I am going to be ordering you to get some food in your system so I can take you out of here and get you back into living your life again. I need you, your staff needs you, and this castle needs you." She waved her arms to show him how big a responsibility he had. "Look at you! No self-respecting McKennah would be seen looking like a wino with nothing to live for!" Gabby was not the preaching type, but she knew he needed to get back into the swing of things somehow. He was so frail looking and actually acted as if he didn't care if he took another breath.

"My dear, thanks, really, but I am not hungry. I will be all right. You go and have a good time now tending to things around here, since I haven't been able to. No parties, though. I'm not up to much of anything." He tried to smile, but the lifelessness in his eyes was so overwhelming, Gabby almost gave up and left the room to go sob. Then she thought of the reason for her coming back from Boston so quick!

"Father. Are you listening to me?" She took his shoulders and shook them. "Look at me. While I was in Boston, I visited Leigh Reid's son, Jarrod. You remember him, don't you?"

The sharp pain stabbed what was left of his emotional well-being when he heard her say Leigh's name again. He tried so hard to keep thoughts of her out of his lifeless mind lately. Please don't tell me anymore about her, he wanted to scream to Gabby. Instead, he didn't say anything.

Sensing that he was not in the mood to hear what she was about to say; she went ahead because she knew he would want to know. "Father, he told me that Leigh is not married. He said that it didn't happen. They did not get married. She is back home in Mississippi, alone. Jarrod swears that she doesn't have any dealings with that Kevin guy anymore. He also said she is still very unhappy, although she is now a Judge. Do you hear me, Father? You need to know Leigh did not leave here to go marry the cowboy!"

"Not married" was all he managed to hear, and it made him jolt awake almost instantly.

His eyes widened and his eyebrows lifted with disbelief. "What do you mean? I thought they were in Wyoming and living "happily ever after". Are you sure, dear? Is this true?" The beginning of a light entered his eyes as he asked her again if she was sure.

"I am as sure as I am a McKennah, Father. You know you still love her. Why don't you go and see her?" Gabby was seeing the reaction that she had hoped for. He was thinking about her question. Bingo, she thought to herself. He showed immediate signs of life returning to his mind.

He straightened up in his chair, rubbed his face with both hands as if to wake himself up and then with a stronger voice, said, "I want you to get Mrs. Daniels in here immediately. I need her to contact my physical therapist to set up those sessions he has been trying to schedule. We will start this evening. Tell her to get you and myself some coffee first, then I want the best the cooks have to offer for supper. Then, my daughter, we will sit and talk some more. Now, you go and get yourself rested after your trip, and I will see you at supper." He smiled at her and this smile told her she had gotten through to him. Whatever happened now was up to him, but she felt satisfied she had done her part in waking him up to the possibility of not only seeing Leigh again, but of living again. She ran to him and hugged him and without a word walked out of the room with the tears of joy now running down her face. She heard her father barking more orders over the intercom as she headed down the hallway. Yes, maybe this was just what the doctor ordered.

CHAPTER FORTY-SEVEN

MARLOWE - Early December 1999

Leigh had been riding Cerces this morning and was back in the stable washing up him down after the workout. His coat was glistening with soap and, as usual, she ended up with as many bubbles all over her as on him. She was laughing and talking to the horse as she cleaned him. She had on cutoff blue jeans with a white Ole Miss jersey that was quite soaked. It was warm for December and the sun was bright as it shown into the hallway of the barn. The radio was blaring out country music as she continued with her rinsing. She was contented with her Saturday morning ritual as it brought her peace after the long weeks sitting on the bench listening to the pains and tribulations of those seeking fairness and help from her. Life wasn't perfect, but she was content. Kevin surprised her earlier with a transport truck with Gypsy in it. There was a very sweet note in the shipping papers saying Gypsy was hers and Gypsy needed her, too. She then bought a new carriage and hired a trainer to teach Gypsy to pull it. She took it out on late Sunday afternoons just before the sun set to enjoy the country and her property.

She was reaching up to grab the shampoo from a shelf when she noticed a shadow down at the entrance to the barn. The morning sun glared so much though that she couldn't make out who it was. She was expecting her Ferrier that morning to trim the horses' hooves, so she thought it must be him.

"Bob? Come on in! I'll be done in a moment with Cerces. You can set up at your normal spot." She continued to wash, but she didn't hear a response. She thought he would've said something to acknowledge he heard her. She stood up straight and tried to focus on the man walking toward her. She put a hand over her eyes to try to block the glare.

"Bob? Is that you'?" she called out again. There was no reply.

"I 'm sorry. But you aren't Bob, are you?" She was a little perplexed, but not scared like she would have been a year ago. There were often times deputy sheriffs and police officers showed up to get warrants signed.

"Hello?" she asked wondering who this person was.

A voice calmly stated, "I am definitely not Bob."

Leigh leaned a little forward looking over Cerces at the figure as he came closer. That voice! It was familiar. Accented, and most definitely not Bob's southern drawl. As he came into focus out of the sunlight, she caught her breath and felt a tremor go up and down her body. No, it can't be. But he sure looked an awful like that someone from her not-so-distant past.

"Hello, Leigh," he said as he came forward seeing it was dawning on her that he was there. He took in the sight of her and his eyes soaked up every inch.

"Geoffrey," was all she could muster her not so cooperative voice to weakly say. She saw he was in blue jeans and a crisp blue jean shirt. His hair was back in that ponytail. He looked ever so handsome. But he was thinner and drawn in the face. However, she had no doubt it was definitely the face of her Geoffrey. His unmistakable blue eyes were looking at her with that twinkle and intensity that she remembered so well. Neither of them spoke until she realized she hadn't taken a breath for a while. She saw his eyes rest on her chest where the wet sweatshirt outlined her nipples very distinctly.

Finally finding her lost voice again, she said, "I am, uh,

well, surprised to see you! What are you doing here of all places in the world, My Laird?" She was totally off guard and trying to recover from the shock. She became self-conscious about her wet shirt and tried to look around for another sweater or something to cover up with, but her eyes wouldn't leave his sparkling eyes.

"I should think that would be obvious. I came here to see you. What else would I be doing here? Please, I am only here so we can we talk a bit. Would you have time right now?" His eyes were very serious all of a sudden.

Trying to sound as if she was a normal human being instead of a bowl of shivering jelly, she said, "I can have Della make us some lemonade and lunch, if you will stay long enough." She broke the stare she found herself in and saw a sweater hanging over the top rail of the stable and quickly put it on while trying to take deep breaths.

"I am not interested in anything but talking to you, Leigh. But if you insist, I will indulge in whatever your hospitality results in serving up." He smiled and with that she melted all the way down to her knees and her toes became numb with the physical reaction to him.

This will not do, girl, she said to herself. Get a grip here or you will just cave in.

"I'll just, uh, call Della and we can, uh, head up to the house? How did you find me, Geoffrey?"

"I have certain relatives who know certain relatives of yours." He laughed at her frown. "Gabby and Jarrod saw each other some time back in Boston."

"Oh," she said and finding her normal voice again, spoke into the barn phone about the lemonade and lunch. Then she walked toward Geoffrey making a wide berth away from his physical presence in hopes to get control of those uncontrollable physical reactions.

Well, she thought to herself that would explain his knowing where she was. But, why had he come after their last encounter at Dalroch? She felt they had parted not on good terms. As she passed him, she noticed he had a cane and was limping toward her. She hadn't seen it before. Her heart jumped quickly as she wondered how he had been injured.

"Geoffrey! What happened to you? You're limping and you are so much thinner than you were! I best get Della to make a larger lunch than usual." She went back without waiting for an answer and picked up the phone again and this time Geoffrey heard her say, "The fixings."

As he got next to her when she walked by, he reached out his free arm and grabbed the top of her shoulder. A shiver went through her as she felt the contact of his hand on her.

"It is really good to see you, Leigh," he said in almost a whisper.

Leigh was so electrically charged that she almost went into his arms and unabashedly hugged him. But she checked herself with Miss Reason and Miss Rational sitting on her other shoulder, saying: 'Don't rush this. You haven't heard what he has to say. It is good he is here but wait to hear him out. Don't be a fool and react on your emotions."

"It is good to see you too, Geoffrey. Right this way to the house." She broke away from his touch. She walked on ahead of him.

Geoffrey almost said, "Yes, I know the way to the house. I know every inch of this place from running surveillance on you before." But he kept his comment to himself for the time being. He was a little shaky on his leg, but his emotions were even shakier as he watched Leigh walk in front of him.

"Bob! There you are!" Leigh was saying to someone who just drove up in front of the barn. "I left Cerces tied up drying. You know the rest that need trimming. Just leave your bill on the barn office desk when you're done."

While Leigh was talking to the man, Geoffrey watched her and could hardly keep his physical attraction to her at bay. She looked so damned good to him, that he wanted to grab her ass, take her clothes off and made passionate love to her right then and there and in that spot. But there were more important things to be done today. He didn't want to ruin this chance. He was going to tell her everything and leave nothing out. He was coming clean finally with her. He needed to do it more than anything else in the world. And, whatever happened after that, well, that would be up to her. He also wanted answers to his questions about Kevin and her feelings toward that cowboy who took her away from him. But most importantly, he wanted her forgiveness for the position he put her in because of his mission with the Society.

"Della!" Leigh called out as she and Geoffrey entered the back door of the house with the screened door whining shut. She turned to him after getting him seated at the breakfast table. "Geoffrey, I'll just get changed and then be right back. Della! Please get Mr. McKennah, I mean, the Duke, or should I just say, My Laird?" she looked over with her rusty and less-than--royal-expertise look and asked him with such sincerity.

Laughing, he said, "Geoffrey is just fine, Leigh. I am not in my country and certainly thought we had gotten past formalities."

"Right, well, Della, get Geoffrey, some lunch and lemonade. We'll eat in the study after I change." Della came in and was watching with interest as the guest had Miss Leigh a bit upset it seemed.

Leigh turned back to him and said, "I'll join you in a bit," Leigh walked to her bedroom door knowing he was watching her walk, with her heart still racing. She entered with as much grace as she could and closed it. Then she fell up against it after it closed trying again to catch her breath and slow her heart rate down. Damn her body for being so treasonous to her! She wanted to not show how much she cared, and she feared she had given a lot away. Get a grip, girl, she ordered herself again. That is the guy who broke your heart and left you in emotional pieces. He may be here to see you, but don't go flattering yourself that he cares any more than he did when you made love to him. Remember that night?

The voices of the Misses Reason and Rational got her

attention again, finally, as she jumped out into and out of the cool shower, put on some new, if not prudish clothes and kept reminding herself: Keep your grip, girl!

She found Geoffrey was now sitting in her favorite wingback recliner with some lemonade and a bowl of fresh fruit at his side.

"I'm sorry to keep you waiting, Geoffrey. Just what exactly did you travel so far to see me for? Did I not wrap things up on the murder of Princess Melinde to your satisfaction? I was very glad to have found the probable answer to her murder mystery." Leigh sat on the sofa across from Geoffrey and tried to appear aloof.

"That's part of the reason I'm here as a matter of fact. You didn't stay long enough to get your paycheck for your work, Leigh. I have brought the funds in US dollars for your efforts." He brought out an envelope and put it on the table beside him. "But I have something more important to discuss with you." He looked very serious again. "It is about why you were kidnapped and why you almost died." He sighed heavily and looked straight into her eyes saying, "It was not just for the Melinde potential scandal for my family. Quite the contrary. It was indeed all my fault for letting you serve as bait in an international terrorist hunt."

CHAPTER FORTY-EIGHT

Leigh was speechless as she looked at him. What was this he was saying? She was bait? An international terrorist hunt? What did that have to do with her? Or him, for that matter. There was no way he could accept the blame for the real reason she was kidnapped and tortured. She knew the code and her having it was all her fault. Definitely, it wasn't his. Maybe he was meaning bait to flush out the family blackmailer, her captor. Well, he was a terrorist, that's for sure. She wasn't really sure what to say.

"Geoffrey, I certainly don't blame you for anything. I was told that this man had been holding me for ransom for the murder scandal. Isn't that what happened?" She began to feel fear inside her as she asked him this, knowing it must be something more to what had happened to her and why. The topic of her kidnapping already was bringing up old painful memories. She did not want him to know that she had been taken to try to get the whereabouts of the coded disc from her.

"No, it is not what happened. That is what everyone else thought. Other than me and my agents."

"Agents?" Leigh asked thinking something really ominous was about to be known. The Duke should have servants, staff, aides, yes. But not agents as that implied to her some sort of underground spy group or law enforcement.

"Leigh," he stood up and limped over to a window overlooking the green pastures. He could not look at her while he told her. He knew what he was about to say would be a shock.

"I have another job other than Duke of Dalroch. I belong to an organization that keeps tabs on terrorist groups around the world. We are a 'watchdog' group basically. We have agents that are based all over the world. We also have to resort to espionage and intercede with force on occasions with insurgent groups that are too powerful for the government to subdue. My agents are highly trained and skilled in all manners of combat, weaponry, and tactical support. We also kill when necessary." He looked over at her face, stoic as it was. He continued, "I have known about the coded disc you were given by Kevin Johnson ever since he gave it to you. It contained code information that, if broken, would give away some of the major secrets of our organization. My family has been the keeper of the secrets for years. As such, I am in charge of the safety and security of those secrets."

He limped back to the wingback chair and sat down and tried to look at her, but she was not watching his eyes, she only stared into space as he continued. "You were caught up in something that was way over your head. I knew it, but I used you as bait to try to catch the man who kidnapped you. He was known as Kadar. He was employed as a mercenary soldier by a Middle Eastern terrorist group lead by a very evil man. They were manufacturing chemical weapons and planned to use them for his own personal and pecuniary gain. I had to find him and his weapons. But I never ever meant for you to get kidnapped and tortured, I swear. I was a fool to let it happen. I am so, so sorry. Sorrier than you will ever know." He stopped and waited to get her to look at him.

Leigh was shocked and confused. She was also in wonderment at what Geoffrey was saying. He was the one who lead her into this whole thing! He watched her from the beginning and even met her under total false pretenses. Her mind began to swim in a puddle of memories. The meeting at the bath house, the hiring for Princess Melinde's case, the memory of the sword at Kadar's neck! The whole time she was involved, it was incredible that she was trying her dead level best to keep him from knowing about her having been in the mess with the code, and now she's finding out he knew all along she had it and he used her as bait?

"Leigh, before you say anything, please let me finish. After you came out of your coma, I left to go and bring down the terrorist leader and his group. I didn't want them to try to find you again, and I had to act quickly in order to catch them before they knew I had killed Kadar."

Killed Kadar. That meant she had not dreamed seeing Geoffrey come to her rescue that night. It had happened, the memory was real.

"I was successful in my mission, Leigh," he was continuing and looked down at his leg. "However, I received a few unexpected injuries in a grenade blast. Thus, my cane and my limp," He was tiring as he was talking, but he went to sit beside Leigh. "Please understand, Leigh, I never meant for you to know about this. And I risked the sacred rule of secrecy for our organization by disclosing its very existence to you. I needed to get to you and let you know this for a while. After I got my strength back, at least. I want you to know that I trust you to never divulge this information. I wouldn't have told you now, though, but, well, I was going full speed ahead with my plan to use you as bait in the mission until I, well, until I," he reached for her face and turned it toward him. "Until I met you and began to care for you. I have always been taught to not mix personal feelings with business. But I did and that's why I hired you on the Melinde murder so I could get you closer to me. But when you left Dalroch that night, I lost control when I knew you were caught. I am so very sorry for all the hurt caused you. In more ways than one." He finished and then waited for her response.

She got up this time trying to digest the revelations he had just made. Her face drew into a pensive frown complicated by the small amount of anger she felt personally about his treatment of her feelings that night at Dalroch and now by the revelation that he had let her walk right into Kadar's clutches knowing all along that it was what he set out to accomplish. But then, she left that night unbeknownst to Geoffrey. She left the castle then out of anger and pain. It was her fault she walked away, but who could blame her? It was too much to digest all at once. Her heart was screaming that she should be happy to see him after his almost getting killed apparently trying to keep more terrorists from coming after her. She knew he must care for her enough to come this far to apologize. Yet he was so intense about the use of her as bait in the mission, she felt she should try to give him some sort of reassurance about that. She turned to see him standing up again in front of her.

She put her hand on his hand. The electricity from that small touch sent shockwaves throughout her. She almost lost all control again with the betrayal of her senses towards the contact. Dammit, she cursed herself. She couldn't stay close to him without the magnetism drawing her in. Looking him in those deep blue eyes with all her strength she had, she said softly, "Geoffrey. I got involved in that code thing innocently. But I stayed in it of my own choosing and free will. I could've turned it over to the FBI, CIA, or whoever. But, at the time, I was at a loss career-wise. I needed something to focus on in life. The opportunity I had at St Andrews was just a way to a means. It was to give me a new focus, and time to learn, if I could, what the coded disc meant and try to find out why Kevin almost was killed over it, why another man had been killed in New Orleans over it, and more importantly, why someone wanted to follow me. I don't blame you for my getting caught up in that mess." She walked away from him and then turned and said, "I left Dalroch that night on my own accord. I am sure if you had known I was leaving, you would have tried to stop me. Regardless of why I left," she almost choked at the words, "It was not your fault that I did and was captured. And, I believe you saved me from my own foolishness, did you not?"

She crossed her arms and looked at him trying to keep

her distance and yet trying to make her point. "You can be rest assured that I will never reveal what you have told me today to anyone. I don't blame you for the position you are in and the position you put me in. As for that night at Dalroch, well, I guess I need to try to put that in perspective of what you just told me." There was a sense that she should say more, but, quite frankly, she felt he wasn't ready to talk more about the personal side of their past.

Geoffrey sighed a long sigh. He was so relieved to hear her words. But he wasn't sure what else to do or say. He started, "I really wanted you to have the opportunity to know the truth. And, I want you to think about what I have told you carefully. It is a lot for one to swallow. You may think things through and not ever want to talk to me again. I really wouldn't blame you if that is your decision. I came here today to tell you the truth and to ask for your forgiveness."

That being said, Leigh was glad she didn't have to talk anymore about her heart and her feelings toward him. Maybe it was best to take some time to think about everything like he suggested.

"I will give it some time, Geoffrey. Thank you for telling me. It means a lot that you would share the secrets and that you would travel so far to ask me to forgive you. How long are you in town for? Could we talk again tomorrow?" She was sure right here and right now that she wanted to see him again. It didn't matter. Anything he said to her just now wouldn't change how she felt about him. It had never changed, and she also knew it never would.

Geoffrey was turning and limping with his cane out of the study and toward the front door. "I have to leave this evening, Leigh." The thought that she just got to see him again was still sinking in and here he is leaving as suddenly as he came? After coming so far. She screamed 'No!" to herself and wanted to pull him back to her but kept her anxiety in check. He looked very intensely at her and said, "But, I left something else in that envelope for you other than your paycheck. After you are sure you may want to visit Dalroch again, I would like you to use the airline tickets in the envelope to come in December to meet the heirs to Princess Melinde's family. There will be a Christmas Ball and a ceremony between the families. Of course, the invitation is yours to accept or decline. But, after all, it was your work that helped to mend the fences between our families."

Before she had a chance to say anything, he noticed there was no wedding or engagement ring on her left hand. That was enough to confirm what Gabriella told him and for him to think he had some sort of chance with her. With that he smiled and opened the front doors, walked to the rental Jeep Cherokee and got in. He nodded to her and drove out of the driveway without looking back.

DORSEY COUNTY COURTHOUSE—-December 12, 1999

The bright lights and monotonous routine sounds of the courtroom caused Leigh's mind to drift off for a few seconds. The proceedings before her only called for her input when an objection was made. She had one ear on what the attorneys were saying, but the other was tuned into some other dimension where she was fantasizing about what her upcoming visit to Scotland would be like. She had been over and over the reasons for her not to go, but she always ended up with the 'what have you got to lose, your heart?' question that was always answered with the 'my heart was already lost to Geoffrey" reply. She envisioned several self-serving scenarios of what could happen when she saw Geoffrey again. She tried to imagine herself back on the hills above Dalroch in the heather with Geoffrey's arms around her and her telling him she loved him again. She couldn't imagine that he would ever feel as much for her as she did for him, and she wondered if he would react the same way as before. He could ostensibly be involved in some other super-secret matter that prohibited his personal life from becoming intertwined with anyone. He could tell her he cared for her a lot but wouldn't get seriously involved with anyone because of his other 'job'. He could tell her that he was glad she came but he had someone else serious in his life. Or, he could possible tell her he cared deeply for her as a friend and he is sorry but he can't care anymore than that.

But why did it mean so much for him to come to her and ask her for her forgiveness? Didn't that mean he cared? Well, of course she preferred the scenario that she daydreamed which ended in the "I dos" being said, but that was pure fantasy based on nothing other than an invitation to a Christmas Ball. Her pen at the bench was drawing circles as she concluded she was crazy, but she was going. Then, she fantasized that she was with Geoffrey and he would grab her and hold her tightly while saying he was as much in love with her as he had ever been with anyone and she should stay with him forever in his castle and in his arms. Well, a girl can dream can she not? She smiled at the blissful scene in her mind. Her face must have shown she had such pleasant daydreams because the attorney in front of the bench was almost shouting: "Objection, your Honor! That is hearsay within hearsay, and I would ask the court to instruct the jury to disregard that entire statement!" The defense attorney was red faced and livid. Jerking back into reality from her dream state, Leigh leaned forward with her most judicial look and said, "You don't have to shout, Counselor, because I am right here. Now, having heard this statement before in pre-trial motions, Counsel, and without any objection to it then, I find there is a basis for the exception to the rule under prior inconsistent statements. The statement will stay in, your objection is overruled, and please, move along." The attorney looked at his client, then the jury, and quietly said, "Nothing further."

Leigh said, "Well, then sit down. I'm recessing for lunch. Be back here in an hour." She got up as the bailiff said,

"All rise," and she smiled all the way back to her chambers thinking the same pleasant thoughts as before. Well, she knew one thing that if she didn't take up the Duke's invitation, she would drive herself crazier thinking about it.

CHAPTER FORTY-NINE

SCOTLAND- December 19, 1999

It was late afternoon as Leigh arrived in the Village that was down the mountain a few minutes from Dalroch. It was small and quaint with just a few retail stores and a pub. There were sprinklings of snow that gave an ethereal glow to the Christmas lights and candles all along the street running through the town. Leigh was entranced again with the beauty of the country as she asked the taxi driver to stop in front of the jewelry store. She ran in and grabbed a small bracelet that she wanted to give as a small gift to Gabby when she saw her again. She had the clerk wrap the box and as she was leaving, she noticed a leaflet pinned to the door as she closed it.

It was red and green with greenery borders and read: **CHRISTMAS AT DALROCH! OPEN HOUSE BY SPECIAL INVITATION OF THE DUKE – TONIGHT. FESTIVITIES BEGIN AT 7 PM. BRING THE KIDS AND WEAR YOUR DANCING SHOES. ENTERTAINMENT AND FOOD WILL BE PROVIDED. COME SHARE THE JOYS OF THE SEASON WITH US. MULLED WINE AND SPECIAL MUSIC BY THE DUKE AND HIS FAMOUS PIPES.**

Leigh was overcome at that very moment with the almost silly hopes that she was coming to Dalroch for anything more than a chance to meet Princess Melinde's heirs. The novelty of the fantasizing moments before were now replaced with an almost dread looming in her stomach. Who was she to think she was even good enough to have someone like Geoffrey, a Duke, for God's sake, care for her more than as a friend? Geez, you dummy, she said to herself, you really are crazy. She sighed and the rest of the drive into the mountains toward Dalroch was filled with so much anxiety that it made Leigh nervous to the point of almost turning the taxi driver around. Geoffrey didn't know she was coming after all. She hadn't called to let him know. She hadn't even told Jarrod since she had simply been fighting herself over coming up until the last second.

As the taxi got closer to the castle, she was regretting her decision. She could just head back home and then send her regrets at not being able to come. Yes, that would be easier, now wouldn't it? Then she thought of the effort she had put in the Melinde murder case and the feelings that she had for the Dalroch castle. She even remembered the fact that she thought Melinde was trying to persuade her to come out of the coma and back to help her and her unborn child. Well, she would keep going, but she knew if Geoffrey was there with someone else, as in, female in nature, she would say her pleasantries and leave as soon as she could get back out. Just what have you done by coming here, she asked herself.

....

There were no lights on and dusk was settling in. The castle was getting darker by the second. Inside the large entryway, the entire staff of the castle was standing along with Geoffrey, who reached for a light switch and calmly said, "Let the festivities begin!"

He pushed the switch and the whole castle entryway was instantly aglow with thousands of tiny crystal lights. It was a magical sight appreciated by the loud group of sighs that followed. The large Christmas tree in the middle of the room rose almost thirty feet to the ceiling and was dressed in the most formal of Christmas attire. There were ornaments from generations of McKennah Christmases before, plus fresh candied and frosted fruit slices, garlands from the greenery around the castle grounds, and lovely poinsettias from the conservatory. The stairwells were decorated as well with live white poinsettias and garlands with twinkling lights. Gold and purple satin bows were placed all over the room on vases, lights, candelabras, and mirrors until the room was full of life and light.

The staff clapped at the results of their hard work and Geoffrey thanked them with Christmas bonus checks. Then he told them that after the Melinde Ball, which was in a few days, they would all have days off.

Mrs. Daniels was the last to be given her envelope and she hugged him sheepishly saying, "You have made this place a fine home again, Me Laird. I am so glad to see you wanting to celebrate and doing what you do best. I am very happy to be serving you, and I hope this will be the best Holiday Season Dalroch has ever seen. Just let me know what else we need to do for the Ball, and we will all be eager to do it, Me Laird."

"Why, Mrs., Daniels, you are going to make me blush. I think we all deserve some festive times and hopefully come the night of the Ball; we will all see the grandest party ever thrown behind these great walls!"

The staff dispersed and Mrs. Daniels started to head out too. Geoffrey said, "Mrs. Daniels, have all the invitees responded yet?"

"Yes, Me Laird. All, but your friend, Ms. Reid from America. I haven't heard from her yet." She noticed the obvious disappointment in his face and continued, "But, it is still a couple days away and anything can happen, right?"

Geoffrey would be very happy indeed if Leigh accepted the invitation, but at this late date, he was assuming that she was not coming. But he did have the local villagers due in any moment for the Open House, so he chose to focus on having a good time this evening. He headed to get his bagpipes ready for the night's activities.

Moments later, the taxi pulled through the open gates at the gatehouse. Leigh thought it odd the gates were open, but probably for the Open House, she surmised. The long drive up to the castle from there was spotted with several lighted Christmas trees in the woods. It was certainly enchanting to see them glow brilliantly in the darkened woods especially with the snow glowing around them.

She paid the taxi driver the hefty fair from Inverness and took her small suitcase up to the entry door. It was already open and several staff members she didn't recognize were milling around putting out food trays. She didn't ask anyone anything and eased up the main stairwell.

She instantly was drawn again to the front of the Heritage Collection showcase and just seeing it calmed her nerves as she remembered her initial feelings toward the collection and then learning the dagger was in there that ended up being the murder weapon for Melinde. As she was staring at it, the whole business of her employment for the McKennah family took on new importance and her confidence started coming back, at least a bit.

Geoffrey was taking the stairwell by leaps and bounds in an effort to get to his room for a shower and change before the first guests arrived. He stopped short when he saw the legs. Those legs! He would recognize them anywhere in the world, Mississippi, New Jersey, or Scotland! His eyes wandered up the legs to the tailored skirt and jacket to the brown bob of hair on the one person he had hoped would come to Dalroch. He was so shocked at her unannounced arrival, that he couldn't find his voice, so he just folded his arms and leaned back on the stairwell staring at her. He watched her as she placed her hand on the showcase as if she was still trying to figure some new mystery out like she had before. He wanted to grab her and hold her tightly and never let her leave Dalroch again. He knew as soon as he saw her that she belonged here, permanently, with him. However, in his exuberance, he thought he might better see how she was feeling about seeing him again, especially since he wasn't sure how she took what she had learned during their last encounter.

"You came," was all he could finally say when he found his voice.

Startled, but very aware that it was Geoffrey's voice behind her, she turned and smiled at him with a warmth that told him she was glad to see him.

"Oh! Hi! I am sorry. I just came on in. I didn't find anyone to let me in. I hope you don't mind?" She gave him a once over and noticed his rugged looks were sharpened by a much healthier face and he seemed to have gained weight to the point of being just perfect again. Her heart ached to let him know how much she was feeling just seeing him again, but she knew not to start anything that she couldn't finish when she didn't know how he felt about her. At the moment, his twinkling eyes were a good sign, but she was worried that they might be joined at any minute by some lovely sweet young thing that Geoffrey had as an accompaniment for the evening.

"Right! Well, the staff and caterers are all trying to get last minute bits and bobs ready for our Open House tonight. I am afraid I am quite a mess myself and was just heading up to redress for the evening. You look grand, Leigh. Did you have a nice flight?" He eased up to face her.

"Yes, I did. Thank you. I must say you look much better yourself. It looks as if you've made a full recovery from your injuries. Are you well'?" Leigh was so thrilled inside to just look in his eyes that she was, once again, having a tough time focusing on the mundane chatter.

He smiled at her. "Thank you, Leigh. Yes, I am much better. My limp is about gone now. I am very glad you made it. I wasn't sure you would darken the doors here again after our last visit."

"I thought it was very kind of you to invite me for the Princess Melinde Ball. I also had a certain curiosity about the heirs and wanted to meet them. Thank you for asking me,

Geoffrey. Shall I call for Mrs. Daniels for a room or do need to book a room at the village?" Say 'You can stay' she silently said or prayed. "I mean, if you have overnight guests for the Open House and Ball, I certainly would understand, especially since I gave you no warning of my coming."

Geoffrey's cemented feet finally got free and he went to Leigh and grabbed her elbow "Leigh, you must be kidding! You will stay here, of course. I will have Mrs. Daniels get your room ready." He smiled and she melted again. Her room. How sweet. He remembered.

"Sorry, I must run and tend to changing, Leigh. Duty calls. But, please join us downstairs when you have rested. I'm sure you're exhausted from traveling, but we'll have a fun evening, I promise." With that, he reached over and kissed her gently on the cheek and then he ran down the stairs calling for Mrs. Daniels. Moments later, as Leigh was still touching the cheek where his lips brushed, Mrs. Daniels and a young boy came up the stairs with Leigh's luggage. "Miss Reid! I am so glad to see you again! You will be staying in your regular suite. We can have a fire going in a jiffy and linens are already freshened, so please follow me!

Leigh smiled as she followed the two to her suite. The gaiety of the place was toxic and contagious. When she got inside her suite, she waited for them to start the fire, deposit her suitcase and then close the door before she lost her cool and ran and jumped into the middle of the grandiose bed and laid there with her eyes scanning the room. It looked the very same as her many memories of it, except for the Christmas garland on the fireplace mantle and the floral arrangements with the candles lit on nightstand and side table next to the chaise. Her room! How wonderful it felt in here and how cozy! She realized she was so much at home here. She got up and walked into the dressing area and bath. Yes, it was also just as she had remembered, too. She thought many times that she must have imagined the whole place and time, but here it was. Here she was again. Wow! She really was so happy, she forgot that she needed to unpack and try to find something to wear for the Open House.

She pulled her clothes from her suitcases and placed them in the closet and drawers. She chose a red satin fitted chemise that she picked up at Neiman's in New Orleans before her flight out. She wanted to really dazzle him tonight even if Geoffrey had a date. She filled the big marble bathtub and soaked in the warm bubbles for a few minutes. She was just out with a turban towel wrapped on her hair with a white terry robe wrapped around her when there came a knock at the door.

Opening the door slightly, Leigh saw a young maid with extra towels in one hand and a couple of small gift-wrapped boxes on the other.

"May I come in, Miss? I have some fresh towels and these presents are for you from My Laird."

Leigh let the maid in. She handed the boxes to Leigh and went to the bath area with the towels. Leigh waited until the maid left before she opened the boxes. She examined them and saw a card on the top of the smallest box. Handwritten apparently by Geoffrey the card said: "Leigh. To welcome you and thank you for coming, Geoffrey". She smiled at the gesture. She opened the small box first and after pulling back soft cotton padding, she saw large ruby stud earrings in a marquis shape. Whoa, this must have set him back a few, she thought instantly. How sweet! It would go with the chemise she was going to wear. The other box was a little larger than the first and as she opened it beneath the padding shown a brilliant jeweled necklace which literally caught her breath. It was choker length with marquis-shaped rubies and emeralds dangling from the gold chain. This was way over the top, she thought. Maybe she should return them to him as being too extravagant. But then she thought the jewelry would be the icing on the cake with her dress. Decisions, decisions! Maybe she would wear it and then return it. No, that would probably be rude. She lay the boxes down. She was getting into her dress and began to get the jitters about seeing Geoffrey later. The thought of being close to him and the way that always affected her, she wanted to discipline her body from making too much of a fool of herself. She remembered all too well the last time she had run from this place and that was enough to get her guard up for the evening.

As she finished placing her hair up and spraying perfume on her neck, there was a slight knock at the door. Leigh caught her breath because she was scared it was Geoffrey. That hesitancy was brought on by not knowing if she was truly dressed right for the occasion coupled with her nervousness from not knowing if she would say the right things. She waited a few long seconds before opening the door.

She opened the door slowly and saw the maid again. She said, "I am sorry to disturb you, Miss, but My Laird asked if you would join him in the study. He would like to escort you down to the Open House."

Leigh took a deep breath and said, "Thank you. I think I remember my way there. I'll be there in a few minutes." The maid smiled, nodded and walked away. Leigh closed the door and took one last look at the mirror. She was pleased with how she looked, but it was only Geoffrey she really wanted to please. With that thought, she put the luxury jewels around her neck and on her ears and headed down to the study.

The door loomed in front of her. She had made it to the study without getting lost, she congratulated herself. Whew! It was very intimidating to be back here in the vast home! But, surprisingly, it really was all so familiar and it felt almost normal to be wandering around a castle dressed for a party. But, definitely normal to be scared to death to be escorted by a Duke in Scotland! Taking a few more deep breaths, she started to knock on the study door when she heard a woman's voice behind the door. Then she heard Geoffrey's voice, but she couldn't tell what was being said. Oh, boy, she thought. Here she is thinking that he had no one else in his life and what a fool she is going to feel like if she opens that door and sees he does have someone else. Getting apprehensive again, she almost turned around to run the other way when it dawned on her that he had asked to escort her to the Open House party. Right! But it would not be so hard to believe if there was someone there with him. He was, after all, a very eligible man! Good looking, rich, and needless-to-say, a Duke for goodness sakes! Well, that would entice just about any number of good-looking, young vibrant women to his house, wouldn't it?

But she countered to herself still waiting to knock on the door, he did have some feelings for her, did not he? He bought her these gifts, invited her here for the ball. But then, that could all be out of gratitude and guilt. Gratitude for her solving Melinde's murder and guilt over her plight with the code.

Trying to get up the nerve to continue her knock, Leigh started to knock again when the door suddenly opened. Staring at her was a beautiful woman. It was like looking at a ghost! Leigh's first thought was that this woman was the spitting image of Princess Melinde!

CHAPTER FIFTY

"Excuse me, I did not know anyone was at the door," the beautiful woman said with a bit of a Spanish accent.

Leigh was in shock momentarily and couldn't do anything but stare at the woman. Geoffrey came up from behind the woman and saw the look on Leigh's face and then said, "Leigh, I can tell from the look on your face, you are thinking the same thing I did when I first saw her. From the only painting we have, it would seem this woman is Melinde's twin."

Leigh just nodded in the affirmative.

Geoffrey went on, "Please let me introduce you two, Princess Jessica de Limale, heir to Princess Melinde of Spain, please allow me to introduce you to Leigh Reid of Mississippi in the United States."

The woman gracefully extended her hand and Leigh shook it with still wonderment in her face.

"I- I am glad to meet you," Leigh stuttered.

"You are the crime solver, then, that Geoffrey has told me so much about. I am so happy you could be here for this occasion." The woman's fluid movements and speech were certainly mesmerizing, and Leigh did not miss the familiar reference to "Geoffrey" rather than Duke, My Laird, or anything else. She also noticed Geoffrey's eyes watching the Princess and Leigh assumed he was probably thinking how attractive she was.

"Well, I must be getting back to my room to change for this evening. So nice to meet you, Miss Reid. And I will see you later, Geoffrey?" The question was left in the air as she glided down the hail with a scent of flowers trailing her.

Leigh did not miss a thing. Geoffrey was obviously admiring the Princess and the chemistry she exuded with him indicated there was something between the two of them. Leigh also noticed a bit of sizing up by the Princess. It was as if she was trying to decide if Leigh was good enough to be in the same room, if not castle, with Geoffrey.

Leigh looked at Geoffrey and as his eyes met hers, she smiled and said, "Wow! I was not expecting that when you said Melinde's relatives would be here. She is definitely related!"

Geoffrey said, "Yes, I know it is most telling, the line. Leigh, you look stunning! I hope you like the gifts. They are quite lovely with your dress. And, did you find your accommodations all right?" Geoffrey raised his hand to her elbow and guided her into the study as he was talking.

"Yes, they are wonderful, just like the last times I have been here. Thank you and Geoffrey, the jewelry, they are magnificent, but too extravagant. I feel like I am wearing something as valuable as my house, home and horses all put together! You really should not have spent so much on me!"

Geoffrey's smile went straight to her heart as he looked at her intently before saying, "Those jewels have been in the family for years and haven't been worn for any occasion by any family member that I can remember. They are yours as a gift of appreciation for your help to the family. I won't hear another word about it, you hear? Now, shall I pour you a glass of mulled wine or would you like to go down and order from the bar in the banquet hall? I know people are beginning to pop in for the Open House."

Geoffrey conveniently skipped over the topic of the lovely Spanish lady, but Leigh wasn't about to let it be skipped over.

"Geoffrey, is this Jessica the only relative that is here representing the heirs?"

"Yes, she just arrived with an entourage the size of the Queen Mother's! They are all staying in the west wing. I didn't have any idea that she was so much like Melinde's picture, but then, I have never met her or any of the family. I have only corresponded with her father. So, what about that drink?" Obviously, the subject was closed for now. But only for now as far as Leigh was concerned. She wanted to know if Jessica was competition for Geoffrey's affections or if Geoffrey was even contemplating the idea.

The farthest thing from Geoffrey's mind at the moment was Jessica. He had known plenty of beautiful women in his life and dismissed the advances that Jessica already made in their first meeting. He was holding all his emotions for the one and only woman he intended to ever be around, if she would have him. His predicament, though, was that he didn't know how she was going to react when he told her of his love and the life, he wanted her to be a part of. He hadn't dared even think he would even have the opportunity to try to work something out with Leigh until a couple of hours ago when she showed up. He intended to do all he could to make her feel comfortable with him before he approached the subject of his feelings for her. He still was not real sure she would open up to him after all that had happened.

Geoffrey handed Leigh a glass of mulled wine and she sipped it. Her hopes had been dashed with the arrival of the Spanish diva and she was feeling a bit like she shouldn't even be there. Hating that feeling and not giving him the benefit of the doubt, she looked at Geoffrey and saw he was watching her closely. Not quite knowing what to say, she smiled and said, "Ah, tasty."

Geoffrey was dressed in a black tuxedo top over the traditional McKennah tartan plaid kilt. His face was softened by the firelight and glow of the table lamps in the study. The way he looked at her, Leigh almost melted again. He reached out with his arm and grabbed her arm as they stood in front of the large fireplace. He was about to say something when the door came open with a flurry of noises and in stepped a large man in the same sort of dress as Geoffrey. He bellowed out a

Scottish, "Hello, My Laird! How are things in the Dalroch Castle? And, where can a man get a real drink around here?"

Geoffrey smiled at Leigh and let go of her arm and said, "Cousin Red, you old bull you! So nice of you to come tonight. Things are just fine here. May I introduce you to my friend from the US? Leigh Reid, this is my cousin and sometimes neighbor, Red McKennah. Red, please meet Leigh."

Leigh extended her hand and the large robust man with a large red tuft of hair and a thick red beard grabbed it and kissed it gallantly. 'My, my Geoffrey, my boy, you do have a way of attracting the lovely women. Yes, I can see things are fine here! Indeed! And what do you do, missy?" The man put his arm around her shoulders as he asked her this.

Before she could answer, Geoffrey stepped closer to them and said, "She is a tough Judge from Mississippi. Puts people in jail a lot. You know I daresay she could straighten a few people around here out if given the chance. So you better watch your step, Cousin." Both men laughed together. Geoffrey wanted to take Red's arm off of Leigh, but said, "I hired her to solve the Princess Melinde murder. You are coming to the ball this weekend, are you not?"

"Why of course I am! Wouldn't miss it. And thank you, little lady, for your work on that. Our family is indebted to you. Now, would you be saving a dance at the ball for Ole Red here? I can jig with the best of 'em and you'd be dizzy with the after affects!"

She instantly liked this gruff Scot and smiled, saying "Well, I am My Laird's escort, so you'll have to ask him."

"I could show you around town, too, while you're here, if you want. Yep, I got me one of those new American SUV's, the Hummer, and can take it out in the wild out here without worrying about getting stuck. Now, what about tomorrow? You have time to wander around here in my Hummer?"

Realizing Geoff was letting this conversation continue without interrupting, she smiled at the man and said, "I would be delighted. That is if Geoffrey thinks I won't be missed around here." Leigh looked at Geoffrey the whole time while she talked hoping to see some sign of feelings. His face was one of stoic expression.

"If you will promise to bring her back in one piece. I think we could spare her, but I do want to have some time with her myself before the ceremony." He smiled that wonderfully warm and hypnotic smile and Leigh became lost in his eyes again. She forgot Red was even in the room as she returned his smile.

"Well, it's settled then, little lady. I could pick you up tomorrow morning and we could make a day of it. There are the normal tourist spots, you know, but then there are the not so normal, secret spots that we can prowl around to. I will make sure she's back in one piece, Cousin." The man was very likable and seemed harmless enough to Leigh. But she really didn't want to leave Dalroch, especially while the Spanish woman was here. Even though she knew she couldn't stop the advances the lady would make on Geoffrey, if that was what was starting earlier. What she hoped was that no feelings would be returned by Geoffrey. Her being here wouldn't stop that, she knew. If he had the propensity to respond to the woman, then she might as well let it happen and she would know how she stood with him as well.

"I'll be ready by 10:00 m. Is that okay with you, and shall I call you Red?" Leigh gave her most charming smile and batted her eyes at him.

"Red it is and always will be, little Mississippi Southern Belle! Cannot help the genes there!" He pointed to his hair and laughed a big belly laugh. "I'll be here at ten, then. Wear some clothes to walk in, since I expect to take you into some wild areas!" He laughed and patted Geoffrey on his back "Now, where's the food and libations?" He walked out of the study and Geoffrey cocked his head smiling at Leigh.

"You may wish you hadn't agreed to spend the day with him. He could take you to some unsavory places, Leigh. But he is harmless enough, I suppose. You will be careful, won't you?"

Geoffrey walked toward her with those eyes that she felt were seeking her soul.

"Sure, Geoffrey. I hope you didn't have any plans made for me tomorrow that I am to miss?"

"We'll catch up tomorrow evening when you return. Really, I am going to be busy with the last preparations for the ball and I probably wouldn't be able to spend much time with you anyway during the day. Shall we go downstairs now? I need to greet my guests and warm up the pipes." He placed his hand under her elbow and escorted her out of the study and then downstairs. Feeling very special, indeed, she beamed with his touch all the way.

Leigh spent the next several hours enjoying meeting the local villagers and several more McKennah Clan members and their families. After Geoff's initial bagpipe concert, the dancing music was performed by a local Celtic folk music band. The gaiety of the place was contagious by the time the Duke finished playing and the true Scottish dancing began in the banquet room. It wasn't the formal ballroom dancing she expected. It was more folk dancing; a combination of the Irish River dance and what Leigh would refer to ask dancing the jig. Everyone was happy whirling around to the music. Geoffrey spotted her several times during the night and smiled as if she was the only one in the room, but she wasn't able to visit with him much. Red spun her around a few times before he became too intoxicated for Leigh's taste.

Jessica came down late in a swoosh of crème-colored silks and taffetas. She was immediately surrounded by all the gentlemen in the room who were asking to get her drinks and food. She was beautiful and she obviously knew it. Leigh watched for Geoffrey's reaction, but he acted as if Jessica was only another guest. That was comforting, Leigh thought. She hoped that it was going to stay that way!

Christmas songs on the bagpipes played by Geoffrey again began and the crowd calmed down and quietly toasted the Duke every few minutes. Some of the songs Leigh recognized, but many were foreign to her, but beautiful just the same.

As the late hours drug into the early morning hours, there were still guests dancing and visiting with Geoffrey. Leigh hadn't danced one time with him, but she was exhausted and decided to take her leave from the party. She looked to see if Jessica left yet and when she didn't see her, she walked toward Geoffrey to tell him goodnight. Geoffrey saw her coming and tried to break away from the group he was talking with. "Excuse me, friends, I won't be but a moment." He walked to Leigh and she said, 'I think, My Laird, that I have reached the end of the day for me. I thank you again for the gifts and the lovely time."

"I am so sorry, Leigh. I wanted some time with you on the dance floor! Damn duties sometimes interfere with personal choices. I know you must be exhausted from your travels today and this. I'll find you tomorrow after you return from your outing with Red. Don't let him keep you away too long! Goodnight, Leigh. We will visit more tomorrow." With that he bowed and went back to his conversation group.

Leigh felt a small let down at not having Geoffrey to herself, but she was so tired, she thought he would think her a bore if she stayed up any longer with the gaiety in the castle.

She went to her room and took off her dress and underclothes in record time. Then, with a shiver, she fell naked between the sheets and slept like a baby all snuggled in and very happy to be there.

It was 4:30am before the last guest left and after Geoffrey said his goodbyes he eased up to Leigh's room. He cracked the door open and walked to her bed. She was sleeping peacefully and in the light of the waning fire, and her face and body beckoned him. He was aroused just looking at her. "Sleep well, my love. I am so glad you are finally back here," he whispered softy to the sleeping woman who had his heart. Tucking her comfortably over her shoulders, he leaned down and kissed her softly on the cheek. Then, he quietly put more coals on the fire and eased out of the room.

THE NEXT MORNING-December 20, 1999

"Well, don't you look a sight, Miss Leigh Reid of Mississippi!" Red's boisterous voice boomed as he walked into the stairwell area. "I think you and I will have a grand time today, don't you? And you are dressed for the occasion!" Red was dressed in a tweed jacket with a tan turtleneck and khaki pants. His huge voice and his big body reminded Leigh of a red-headed Santa Claus. Leigh was coming down the stairs dressed in her brown suede pants, brown wool sweater and faux mink collared jacket.

"Now doesn't it look like the party must have been a success?" Red said as he looked around the room at the leftover menagerie of glasses, cups, food, etc. "I left early, about 3:00am, but there's not many stirring around here now, so must have gone on later than that! Now, let's get going 'cause there's a lot to see, Miss Reid. The earlier we get a goin' the more you can see." Red escorted her to the Hummer outside and she smiled as she got in thinking it wasn't the black horse-drawn buggy she had been up in the hills in, but it was a really nice vehicle. Quickly checking for any sign of Geoffrey, and seeing none, see settled in for the nice day promised by Cousin Red.

Hours later, and many miles and a few pubs later, they returned to Dalroch. Red had been a perfect gentleman and shown her some truly neat parts of the Highland area. She wanted to see several places she had read about, but hadn't taken the time before, small wonder! Red also spoke very highly of Geoffrey as Chief and head of the McKennah Clan. He obviously was very close to Geoffrey and Leigh thought they must have always been close judging from the amount of childhood stories about their growing up in the same family and area.

He was the perfect guide, taking her to some out-of-the-way scenic areas that caught her breath. He explained historical events, pointed out plants, birds, and other indigenous wildlife as they went. They hiked up a hill into a cave where Blue John jewels were still found after a mine had closed there years before. He found a nice stone and cut it out to give her with a sheepish grin. She was warmed by his big teddy-bear way.

As they were coming back in the Castle, Leigh spotted Jessica and Geoffrey apparently coming in from a horseback ride near the stables. Her perfect day was ruined at this sight. Some 'ball' business, Geoffrey! It was obvious that the business had turned into a social engagement for Geoffrey. Just whose idea was this? She figured Jessica had encouraged it, but Geoffrey could have said 'no'. Jessica was dressed in equestrian 'extraordinaire' clothes and holding her arm through Geoffrey's with a big smile pasted over her face as they were walking toward the castle. Leigh noticed Geoffrey was smiling too and before they could spot her, she turned quickly to Red, politely thanked him for the day, and then ran upstairs to her room to put distance between her and the happy 'couple'.

"Miss Reid? May come in?" The voice was not familiar to Leigh. She was groggy from the nap she made herself take after taking her anger and jealousy over Jessica out on the pillows on the bed. She wasn't really sure what to do about the woman or Geoffrey at the moment.

"Come in," she answered.

Another young maid came in and handed Leigh a small package wrapped in Christmas paper. Leigh looked at her quizzically wondering what Geoffrey was sending her now. The maid just bowed and left closing the door behind her.

There was no note on this gift and she thought maybe Geoffrey was sending her another thank you gift. She wondered if he knew that she saw him and Jessica together earlier and it was a guilt gift. Whatever, she thought, smiling as she opened it. The box contained a small book. It was titled 'Royal Niceties'. She skimmed through it and saw it was a guide on etiquette required when meeting and conversing with members of Royal Families in the United Kingdom. At first, she thought it was a helpful thing seeing as she was not well versed in this area. Then she thought, who would have given it to her? Geoffrey? Not likely without asking her first if she wanted to learn more. Who else? Red? Maybe, but it was a little too bold to send someone he just met. Hmmm, then she thought, Jessica? Yes, that was it! She thought Leigh might need to brush up on these types of things since she was a country 'hick' from Mississippi. What an insult if it was from her! Leigh became enraged by the assuming gesture. What audacity! Well, she thought indignantly, as she threw the book down on the floor. I will just deal with Jessica in my own way. Boy, she hoped Melinde was not still hanging around the castle. She would be horrified at her heir's temperament and audaciousness.

Leigh thought for a few minutes and then went to the phone.

"Mrs. Daniels? This is Leigh Reid. Could you join me in my suite for a few minutes? I have something to discuss with you. No, everything's fine. I just need to ask some advice from you." With that she hung up and waited to talk to the woman who knew more about what was going on in the castle than anyone else other than Geoffrey.

Leigh was dressed in a winter white pant suit with a rather low-cut front on the jacket. Her hair was twisted into an updo with a mother-of-pearl comb in it. Donning white leather boots and a simple bracelet of pearls on her arm, she thought she would ease down to the study first before heading down for supper, just to check on 'things'. Geoffrey said last night that he would find her after her tour with Red, but she hadn't heard from him all evening. As she neared the open study door, she heard voices again that sounded like Geoffrey's and Jessica's. Well, that could be why she hadn't heard from him! She came into the room and saw them standing at the fireplace with drinks in their hands.

Before they saw her, she said, "Good evening. I hope I am not interrupting something important?" Her very best courtroom non-emotional smile was on.

Geoffrey put his drink down and instantly came and grabbed her elbow to direct her toward the fireplace. "Leigh! You certainly brighten up this room. How was your day of touring?" Geoffrey's smile looked genuine to Leigh, but she wasn't buying anything just yet.

"Quite nice, thank you. And yours?" she asked still in an extremely distant but polite tone.

"Well, Jessica insisted on a horseback ride. We went up the hills for a short tour also. I've shown her the broche and the castle, so I would say it's been a busy day, wouldn't you, Jessica?" Geoffrey looked at Jessica a second and then returned his gaze to Leigh. Leigh noted Jessica's eyes and thought she saw the not-so-jolly green giant looming in them.

"Why, Geoffrey, you have been such a sweet host to me today," she said almost too lavishly. "Yes, it was busy, but I was quite frankly having such a good time, that the day was over before I knew it! Geoffrey is such an entertaining escort," Jessica said as she swished in her voluptuous pink gown over to Geoffrey and put her hand on his arm as if to say, "He's mine, all mine."

Well, there was no mistaking that gesture, Leigh thought to herself.

"Great, Jessica, I'm sorry, may I call you 'Jessica'?" Bitch, she wanted to say, but checked her tongue. "I'm glad to know you are enjoying your visit here. Yes, I received the same treatment my first time here and I agree it made so much more fun with the Duke's personal touches on the tour." Leigh smiled sweetly at Jessica and then turned to Geoffrey.

His eyes were questioning her every word and movement, "Well, I shall leave you two to your conversation. Shall I see you at dinner, Geoffrey?"

Geoffrey put his hand back on Leigh's arm as he wiggled from Jessica's clutch. He moved her to the other side of the room while saying, "You don't have to leave, you know. I could fix you a drink and you and Jessica could get to know each other better."

That's not going to happen, she said to herself. "Why, that's very kind of you, My Laird, but I need to touch base back home with my Court Administrator before the time difference gets too late. There's a case I am especially interested in following in my absence. No, you and Jessica get to know each other even more than you have already." She smiled sweetly at them both through her clenched teeth.

Walking to the doors, she turned and said, "I'll see you at dinner or whenever." The 'whenever' was the only word that had a tonal change and she knew Geoffrey caught the inflection. He either thought she was being too polite or very angry. She left him to decide the answer to that question as she went out of the room. Standing where she couldn't be seen, and with the door ajar, she listened for the conversation to start up again with Jessica. There was a silent period of about a minute before she heard, "Geoffrey, are you all right? You look a bit pensive. Why don't you come over here and let me massage your neck? My fingers have been known to work wonders on tension and stress. Come here and let me help you relax." Leigh was disgusted enough to leave at that moment, but she heard Geoffrey's response first.

"Jessica, I need to tend to some other matters right now. I will see you at supper. Please have your guests join us in the dining room at 7:30 pm." With that dismissal, Leigh hurried down the hall to hide. Geoffrey came out of the study with a definite purpose in his walk as he went past her and headed down the stairwell.

Leigh nodded and she decided right then that it was Jessica pushing Geoff as she thought already. And, thank goodness, Geoffrey wasn't taking the bait. At least, not yet.

Having already been reminded by Mrs. Daniels during

their 'woman to woman' talk earlier of where the 'west wing' actually was, Leigh took the hallway to the west wing. The Spanish entourage was staying in several rooms down this hall, but she didn't know which room was the Princess's. She quietly eased into an unoccupied room that apparently adjoined a sitting room where several of the traveling servants were grouped and obviously visiting in their down time. She eased to the door and heard some chattering by female voices, but her Spanish was too rusty to make it out. One voice finally said, "We must practice speaking more English as Miss Jessica asked." There were some affirmative responses, all of them female. "What do you think this one's worth?" one asked. "Several million I should think," another responded. "When do you think she will have her hooks on him?" another said laughingly. There was more laughter and then, "She better hurry since she tells me that she is running out of her inheritance and cannot afford to keep all of us on much longer." There was some general 'sis' and 'yeses' and then the room got quiet. Jessica must have entered the room.

There was some loud ranting in Spanish from Jessica and then Leigh heard in English, "You all need to be on your best behavior tonight and please dress formally. The Duke and I will be very busy together. I want to make a good impression on him again. I am so in love with him! I intend to have him for my very own by the time the ball occurs this weekend. Now, do not do anything to embarrass me. And, again, you need to speak English tonight."

Leigh eased back out of the room and down the hallway back to her room. Yeah, she's in love with him all right. In love with his title, property and money. Mrs. Daniels was right. 'A gold-digger ready to strike gold' is what she said. Leigh was not about to let Geoffrey get ensnared by this woman. Regardless of how he might feel about Leigh, she was sure he didn't need that type woman in his life. But she was going to need some additional help pretty quick.

CHAPTER FIFTY-ONE

Leigh decided not to join the group for supper. She didn't really have to check on a case in Mississippi. She wanted time to think about what to do. She called Mrs. Daniels again and asked her to pass along the word that she was busy with some overseas work and wouldn't be appearing for supper and the Spanish Conquistador's road show. Mrs. Daniels laughed in agreement about the road show and insisted on bringing her supper to her room.

While Mrs. Daniels was in the room, Leigh called Red. He agreed that Geoffrey was in for a ride if he accepted any affection from Jessica. Besides, he told Leigh there was something to that look Geoffrey gave Leigh that said his cousin was hoping for more than 'friends' with Leigh, and his bet was on Leigh. He said he would be very happy to help Leigh and Mrs. Daniels rid the McKennah clan of the woman. Leigh explained a proposed role for his part in the plan and he assured her he was in for the simple fun of it.

Below Dalroch, Geoffrey was sure he had some intelligence on the woman who was trying her dead-level best to distract him with her advances. He didn't think she was in the espionage business, but something else was stored in the Society's media clips he was sure. He brought up the archives of the files that were kept on the Spanish royal histories and current profiles. Scrolling through the headlines, he spotted an article or two from the Madrid newspapers that confirmed his suspicions about the woman. "Heiress Jessica to Wed", followed by "Heiress now Widow but Seen with New Beau".

Reading more, Geoff learned she was considered a wild child and extravagant spender since teenage years. She was now 35 and it looked like she had been seen recently with an IT tycoon from the United States, but the relationship had gone sour. The papers reported she just about exhausted her inheritance. That was why she was so eager to have Geoffrey's attentions then. He smiled as he congratulated himself on confirming his conclusion that she was no good for him. He usually could smell the fortune hunting women. The problem was that he wanted to get the Melinde Ball over with and boot Jessica and her entourage out immediately but had no way of tactfully doing that. He thought how she had monopolized his time away from Leigh. He hadn't even been able to ask Leigh how long she was staying after the Ball. He had to know because of his definite agenda for her after the ball. He wasn't letting her go back home without the knowledge of how he felt about her. Well, he decided as he got up to head back to the castle, he would just have to figure out a way to make it known how he felt before the ball and get Jessica out of his castle and off back to Spain.

DALROCH--December 22, 1999
    Now Leigh wasn't a person that stooped to interfering in the natural order of things. Her only problem with that stance was that the natural ending of the natural order usually left her on the short end of the natural proverbial stick. This time, she knew her duty lay in making sure Geoffrey was left unscathed by the Spanish harlot. Leigh wanted Geoffrey, more than life itself, and although she still had no real idea if she had a smidgen of a chance, she was dead intent on having the opportunity to find out. She wasn't going to let Jessica take that chance away from her. Feeling like a schoolgirl with an attitude, she promised herself that she would have at least the opportunity to find out before she left Dalroch again.
    The morning started early as Leigh dressed for a horse-

back ride. She called to the stables and asked for Lomond to be saddled. Her last ride on him had been such a delight and she was ready to have another opportunity to ride him. She looked forward to a vigorous run.

As she approached the stable area, she heard voices and recognized Geoffrey's immediately. She came around the corner and saw him without his seeing her. He was dressed in brown riding cords and a brown vest and jacket. His riding boots gleamed in the Highland morning sun. His hair was back in a leather tie and his very presence absolutely took Leigh's breath immediately. She had that giddy feeling that he always gave her, and she started to turn and run when she heard the stableman say, "Miss Reid! Lomond is ready. He's already been warmed up by My Laird."

Geoffrey turned and looked at her. His eyes went from head to toe and back to her eyes. His stare was positively possessive, and he walked toward her without glancing away.

"Leigh. I missed you last night. Were you so busy that you couldn't join me at supper?" He got close to her and she could smell his distinct manly smell.

"I am sorry Geoffrey. I did have some pressing matters." Pressing to the point of making me lose precious moments of time with you while trying to figure how to rid our lives of Jessica, she wanted to say.

"Well, we had an early evening. I have been up for a ride already, but I would love it if you would join me for another. Breakfast is buffet style this morning so we should have time for good ride. What do you say? On second thought, don't say anything. Just come with me, please," he said with a smile and he grabbed her hand which made her chest flip again.

Just as she was about to say 'yes', Jessica came waltzing into the stables with her million dollar looks and her talons all out for Geoffrey. She slinked like a snake up to him, put her arm in his and said, "Good morning, Geoffrey!" She looked over at Leigh with a look of disdain and then back at Geoffrey.

"I was hoping for a few minutes of fresh air with my favorite Duke this morning! You did tell me you would take me riding again, didn't you, Geoffrey dear?"

Geoffrey looked at her and with what almost looked like a forced smile and then looked at Leigh. "Well, I was just going to take Leigh out for a trip."

With an obviously fake pout Jessica said, "Oh, you don't have to cancel plans for me, dear! Although, I am so worried that I may get lost on my own. Maybe I should just sit this one out, then. But, you know, I am only here for a couple more days and then off I go to other parts of the world. You don't want me to leave feeling like you cheated me out of this last ride with you, do you Geoffrey?" Batting her long eyelashes, she eased into his shoulder and continued to pout with such an effort that Leigh wanted to put her finger in her open mouth to gag.

Instead she relented by saying, "I will just wait and ride some other time, Geoffrey." Leigh said matter-of-factly. "I think your guest is in much more dire need of your services as host than I. I practically can get around here like I live here anyway." Leigh smiled at Jessica with that comment and started to walk off but then turned again and said "I'll see you later Geoffrey. Jessica." Geoffrey started to reach out for Leigh, but Jessica grabbed his arm and started walking him toward the horses. "Oh, thank you, Ms. Reid. Geoffrey, you will make this day have such a nice start by going with me now."

Leigh gagged at this exchange too. She knew Jessica was mesmerizing to most men, but Leigh felt Geoffrey wasn't taken in by her too much judging from the look on his face which reminded her of a wild animal caged. Well, Leigh's job was to make sure he wasn't taken in at all!

CHAPTER FIFTY-TWO

Red arrived mid-morning and he and Leigh spent some time together laughing and talking in the kitchen with the cooks. Red was to be the 'extremely-rich' cousin, which he already was, who would try to steal Jessica's affections by any means necessary, only to dump her as quick as he could. He planned to come over this evening for a drink and give some special 'blow hard' tales of his money and adventures that would be sure to at least turn part of Jessica's attentions toward him, like a 'back-up plan'. He made Leigh laugh so much as he made up some pretty horrendous tales that were pretty unbelievable, like his owning the largest diamond mine in Africa and how he would get a minimum 6 carat diamond for all the girls he had dated. Leigh was laughing so much that she found herself having a great time plotting and planning. Red told Leigh he would make Jessica his date for the Ball or at least keep her away from Geoffrey by promising lots of material things worth lots of money. Leigh hoped she wasn't getting him in over his head! Somehow, looking at the burly red-head Santa-Claus standing next to her, she thought he would be able to manage.

"Good luck, Red. Thanks so much for the help and the laughs. I needed both." She reached up and kissed his cheek, which turned immediately as red as his beard. "See you tonight!"

Knowing she had to be on her best behavior also, she went up to her suite to review the etiquette book Jessica had so kindly given her so she would be ready for tomorrow night.

Later in the afternoon, Leigh got a call from Geoffrey on the phone in her room. Hearing his voice startled her out of an almost nap.

"Leigh, will you join me for a drink in the study before dinner? We haven't had any time to talk since you got here. I know it is all my fault with all the busy plans for the Ball, but I think we need to talk." Geoffrey's voice was even and unemotional.

"Well, Geoffrey, I know you have other guests to worry about Geoffrey," she said but added to herself, "and you better be worried about that bitch whore-dog, fortune hunter of a guest!" Instead, she continued, "I have been fine, but I would like to visit you too, a bit since I did come a long way to be here." She wanted him to know it was him and not his Ball she was interested in, but she would not elaborate over the phone.

"I'll have a mini bar brought to the conservatory upstairs rather than the study. I think that would be more private, and I will instruct the household staff to direct any inquiries as to our whereabouts to Mrs. Daniels. She will be discreet enough to leave us alone for a while. How does 5:00 pm sound?"

"Fine with me, but, Geoffrey, I don't remember how to get there from here. Can someone show me?" She really had forgotten where the stairs were to the rooftop conservatory at the castle.

"I will come and get you. Just stay there. See you at 5:00!" Geoffrey sounded a bit relieved and Leigh was definitely relieved that he wanted to spend time with just her. But then she thought maybe he wanted to go over the Melinde murder again with her before the Ball so he would be up to date on the events that lead to the resolution of the matter. Shoot! That probably was it!

At any rate, she decided to get the smart short black cocktail dress she brought with her to wear. And, yes, she said to herself as she put it in the dressing room, it does have lots of swing and curves and reveals the tops of her breasts. Well, she thought, as she put the finishing touches of her make up on and put a jeweled comb in the back of her hair, she would make herself as presentable as possible and hopefully tempt him into more than business talk!

There was a knock on the door and Leigh's heart stopped a second. She wondered if it finally was him! She opened the door. Instead of the handsome Duke she was expecting, she saw Mrs. Daniels.

"I have a message from My Laird. He said that I'm to fetch you to the conservatory and he'd be along in a bit." She shook her head negatively and then added, losing her prim and proper English to the Scottish brogish words, "I'm sorry, but it's dat woman agin. She called him up to her suite to come check on her ankle she swore was wrenched in the saddle when day went a ridin dis morning.'"

Leigh's eyes widened and then narrowed into a squint as she started to get mad, too. Then she thought about Red's debut as the gentleman caller. "Has Red McKennah shown up yet? He was coming to make a call on 'dat woman' you know tonight"

"Oh, I haven't seen him, Ms. Reid, but I'll make sure she gets a visit from him when he arrives! If there's anythin' else I can do to get dat woman away from My Laird, I will!" She clucked and fussed as she was taking Leigh up to the conservatory.

"Just go interrupt them and tell Geoffrey he has an urgent message from me. Tell him I'll not be available but for just a few minutes if he wants to talk with me. Maybe that will break them up. I'm afraid she'll drug him or worse if we don't do something quickly. She wants him and his money and power very badly and time is running short for her. Now, quick, give me the rest of the directions to the conservatory and get to them as soon as possible!"

"Thank you, Miss Reid. I surely will. And by da way, you look smashing, you do!" She gave her a wink and the directions to the conservatory and then ran down the hall she had come from.

Leigh made her way to the conservatory and as she entered, she noticed the mini bar had been placed inside the sitting area. She smiled and thought again how Geoffrey was at least having good intentions on seeing her if not for Jessica. She got a glass of chilled white wine and sat in the cushy loveseat to wait. After about 35 minutes, when she already finished two glasses of wine, she decided that Geoffrey was going to be detained indefinitely. She poured another glass and wandered around the large trees that had grown into the tall recesses of the room. She felt a cold chill even though the room was toasty warm in the room. She wondered if there was a break in the windows, but she did not see one. It was very quiet in the room and Leigh got a bit edgy with the long wait. After another 30 minutes had passed, she left the room and went down to her suite, this time remembering the route. It was obvious now that yet another day of her visit here was going to end without seeing Geoffrey. She called Mrs. Daniels' extension.

"What happened? I've been waiting a while and I just decided you didn't get the scene broke up!"

"Well, Miss Reid, it was quite funny, actually," she said almost giggling. And that was saying something for the once dour-looking Ms. Daniels, Leigh thought. "Master Red McKennah came and I sent him up to where Geoffrey and dat woman were. Next thing I know Mr. Red is insisting on taking her to the emergency clinic down in the village. Wouldn't take no for an answer, he wouldn't, even though she's insisting that My Laird escort her instead of Master Red! They just left a minute or so ago. Master Red, he's just going on about how he can afford anything she needs to get her comfortable and feeling better. Dat's while they are getting in his car! Both My Laird and I were most grateful Master Red showed up when he did, we were, for sure!"

"Oh! Goodness, well, I am back in my suite now. Could

you let the Duke know I'm here?" Just then a soft knock was on her door.

"Thanks Mrs., Daniels, a bunch!" Leigh hung up and eased the door open. Geoffrey was standing there in his black tuxedo with a flower in his hand. A large white rose! He smiled and said, "I'm so sorry to leave you at the conservatory after I made the arrangements for us to be together. Can you forgive me?" He handed her the rose and smiled with blue eyes twinkling.

"Oh, well, I assumed you had gotten tied up again. I did have a couple of glasses of wine already, so that took any edge off the wait. Please don't feel too put off. Would you like to come in?" She opened the door and Geoffrey came in without a wasted moment. He closed the door and then looked over the room and said, "Have you been comfortable here? I mean, I haven't asked you if everything was still to your liking. In fact, I feel as if I have ignored your presence here, totally. I certainly am glad you are here though, Leigh. How long are you going to be able to stay?" He wandered to the fireplace and took the poker and moved the coals around aimlessly.

She didn't answer him and he turned to look at her, this time really look at her. She was beguiling in her dress, so much so that he felt as if he might lose control if he got very close to her.

Leigh watched him give her a once over. She sat down in one of the high-back chairs by the fire and coyly enjoyed the eyes on her. "Well, I have some important cases in court coming up right after New Year's Day, so I had planned on leaving as soon as possible after the Ball."

He looked at her seriously and said, "Not without a proper visit, you won't! I mean, I intend to have this castle cleared out by late Christmas Day. The staff will be going on holiday then and even though we may have to fend for ourselves some, I really want to have some personal time with you. Besides, Gabby is coming home Christmas Eve. You really have to stay long enough to see her. She would be very upset with her old man if I let you leave before she gets to see you again."

Laughing and blushing, she said, "Okay! Okay! You talked me into it. I'll stay a couple of days after Christmas, but that's about all I can afford." But only because you used the words 'personal time', she added to herself. She smiled and got up and went to him. "When is the Spanish entourage leaving?"

"As soon as the Ball is over, I hope. They have just about been more trouble than they are worth. Now, how about I escort you to dinner?"

He held out his arm and they walked down to the dining room together. He spoke of his physical therapy and the progress on his leg after the doctors hadn't given him much hope. Leigh was enjoying his sharing this but had a very hard time really listening as the touch of his hand on her arm was enough to distract even the staunchest of listeners. Had Jessica met them this time, Leigh was ready to fight like a junkyard dog to keep Geoffrey's attentions tonight.

The dining room was decorated in more lavish Christmas decorations. There were candles lit all over the room with berries and holly leaves all around them. Leigh's mood was lifted tremendously by the sight. Geoffrey pulled her chair out for her and then he sat right across from her. His face was so very handsome in the candlelight. He was dressed tonight in a full black tuxedo and his whole demeanor was lighthearted and charming.

"I think we actually will be dining alone. Cousin Red has taken Jessica to the village clinic to see to a small sprain." Geoff said this and smiled with his whole face. His eyes were alight with the glow of the candles.

"Really?" Leigh acted shocked but not sympathetic. She almost laughed.

"Yes, so no interruptions, I hope. Would you like another glass of wine with your dinner?"

Leigh was still staring unabashedly at Geoffrey's face

and almost forgot to answer, "I, um, would, uh, sure. Another glass would be fine," Embarrassed, she looked away. Then she thought about Red taking Jessica in his car to the hospital and smiled again hoping he was able to distract the woman for a while. She didn't for one-minute think Jessica's so called injury was real. It was a sympathetic ploy to get Geoffrey's attentions, she was sure.

'Well, let's see what Krista and company have cooked for us, then." He opened the silver-domed large tray. "Ah-hah! There's roasted gammon and yams, so I would suggest a sweet white wine, then." Geoffrey was watching Leigh closely hoping she wouldn't bolt and run at being alone with him after he hadn't made time to see her in several days. He certainly had more to deal with than just the usual guest. That blasted woman was monopolizing his time and he was ready to personally pack her up and send her on back to Spain and even cancel the Ball if it meant he could spend more time with Leigh.

"Whatever you suggest, Geoffrey, I'm sure it will be fine." Leigh's eyes would not leave his. Realizing that having Geoffrey to herself was heaven after being here several days and wanting to be with him, she also knew the time would come, at some indefinite point, for her to find out what his feelings for her might be. She was cautiously optimistic that his wanting to share alone time with her could mean he cared for her, and she also realized he could never have the same intense feelings she had for him, or he would have never let her go that night. But right here and at this very moment, she was just happy to sit at the same table with him.

After dinner and desserts were served, Geoffrey asked the staff to leave and he came to Leigh's chair and helped her up. As she stood up, he ran his hands ever so slightly, if not by accident, up her bare arms. The electricity would have lit the whole country of Scotland up for a whole decade. It was as if a bomb had been smoldering in her stomach ready to burst out at any moment. She tried to keep calm as he backed up and asked if she would like to walk out to the grounds for a few minutes. She thought that would be a start at trying to cool her entire body off since it was freezing cold outside. He grabbed two overcoats from a hallway armoire and slid one over her shoulders. His smile was so sweet. Please, don't let anything interrupt this, she prayed to herself. They went out through the now quiet kitchen exit and walked in the starlight and the crisp, cold, clean air hit her face immediately. She took several deep breaths and felt cleansed.

"It is so cold, but refreshing, Geoffrey. And, look at the night sky! It is beautiful."

Geoffrey put a protective arm around her shoulders, and they didn't say anything for a period of time. She was enjoying his closeness, but realized he was very quiet, almost too quiet.

As they got to the garden area with the cliff to the ocean on the side of the castle, he turned her toward him slowly and looked very seriously at her. She didn't know what to expect but was suddenly apprehensive. This is it, she thought. He's going to tell me something very profound. I know it. Like probably how he is so glad to have me at his house and all that jazz, but that he was too busy for a relationship. Or, he is going to say how grateful he is for her helping the family and forgiving him for his putting her in harm's way because of his work with his secret group. Or quite simply, he just really wanted to be 'friends.

His mouth opened to say something and fearing the worst, she quickly put her finger over his lips. She smiled and said, "I don't know what's on your mind, Geoffrey, but I am really enjoying just being with you. I mean, being alone with you. I have a lot of things I could say, but I'm not sure you want to hear them or would welcome them. Especially after the last time I spoke to you about my feelings."

Geoffrey looked quizzically at her and said with a smile, "Leigh, I don't know what you have to say, but I really, really need to tell you how I feel about you. I don't know when we will get another chance. Please, hear me out before you say anything else."

He turned and looked up at the sky. Then he slowly turned again and said, "I have been a fool. You remember when we made love?"

As if that burning video hadn't been replayed 24-7! She was cautiously nodding.

"I have wished so many times since then that my job hadn't gotten in the middle of our relationship." He came to her and lifted her chin. He was going to do what she had wanted him to do ever since the moment they had made love that night so many months ago! She closed her eyes and her mouth was ready to feel his lips, when suddenly a shrill cry went out from the house.

"What the blazes is going on'?" Geoffrey was like an animal, swift and sure. He bounded over the hedges in the garden and was gone in the dark, leaving Leigh breathless and nervous at the same time. Her head pounded at the suddenness of the scream and Geoffrey's quick movement back into the castle. She waited a few seconds before deciding to follow Geoffrey. She headed to the kitchen door when she heard out of the darkness behind her, a voice snarled "Leigh Reid!"

Leigh turned and faced a figure wearing dark clothes and carrying what looked like a pistol. It caught the gleam of the moon and she then knew it was a gun. The voice had been decidedly female and accented, but Leigh had no clue who she was. She was quickly coming to her senses, though, and asked, "Who are you, how do you know me and why the *hell* have you got a gun pointed at me?"

The accented voice said, "You are in the way." Leigh was listening but was watching the surrounding area to see if there was a way to quickly hide. She saw an opening in the hedge but wasn't sure where it went. She tried to continue talking to the woman with the gun. Surmising it wasn't Jessica, but someone ordered here by Jessica, she said, "You let your boss talk you into murder? She is in way over head and you will be taking the fall with her if you shoot me. She's not going to give you any money for this. She's broke and she cannot give you anything. So, don't do this, Think about it. You are on your own."

"Shut-up, bitch! I will be well rewarded. I have been promised a large bonus. My boss is going to be rich really soon."

Leigh noticed the aim of the pistol dropping a little as the woman talked. As it did, she took the opportunity to jump through the opening in the hedge, and she found herself flying down a long incline. It was a few seconds before she heard the pistol fire several shots and then she felt the icy hands of the water grab her down into it and the darkness enveloped her.

CHAPTER FIFTY-THREE

Edinburgh, Scotland
December 25, 1999

Leigh woke to the soothing voice of a nurse that was looming over her, "It is all right, Ms. Reid. You are in the hospital in Edinburgh."

Leigh let her eyes adjust to the light in the room and then focused on the woman in white standing next to her bed.

"You should know you had a nasty fall. You almost died of drowning and exposure."

Trying to remember what the woman was referring to, drowning?

"There's someone here who hasn't left your side, Miss, and I believe he saved your life. He really wants to see you. Are you up to a visit?"

Leigh just nodded as she was remembering the jump from the woman with the gun.

"You had a lot of folks worried there little lady!" Boomed the voice of Red McKennah. "Now don't you worry, I'm going to tell you everything you don't remember, but first cousin Geoffrey is beside himself. He just now stepped out and is occupied with a constable. He will be right in. How do you feel?" He sat in a chair beside the bed.

"Like I've been in a refrigerator for days. What happened? I saw nothing but darkness after I fell into the water. What happened to the shooter and to that Spanish bitch that hired the shooter?"

Red laughed loudly. 'You called her right. missy, I've never run across such a manipulative, mean-spirited, bloody self-serving viper in all my life! Well, to answer your question, she's in the brig and her hired gun is being treated for multiple gunshot wounds. My cousin sure didn't 't dally around when he figured the fix was in on you. He went after the shooter while I held on to Ms. High and Mighty. It wasn't until the shooter realized the witch boss wasn't going to fess up to hiring her to try to kill you that she told us that you had fallen into the ocean. Geoffrey jumped in and swam until he found you. I don't know how he did, mind you. It was pitch black down there. It's a miracle he did, though. And I am mighty grateful you are still with us, Leigh," Red said with a bit of wetness in his sweet eyes. "You know you have warmed yourself into the hearts of several around this old country."

Touched by his comments, she suddenly wondered what day it was. "What's today? How long have I been here?" Leigh's voice was weak, and she couldn't help thinking she was not really here or that she was in some sort of major foggy dream.

"Well, now don't you go a worrying about that. You just be glad you are still alive," He reached for her hand and patted it.

Leigh was groggy headed, but she wanted to know what day it was since the Ball had been planned for the day after the night she fell. She felt her eyelids getting heavy and she closed them for a few seconds. The next thing she knew, her hand was being kissed. She threw open her eyes and saw Geoffrey sitting beside her on the bed with his hands holding her left hand. He was still dressed in the tux and his beard was heavy. His eyes were red and swollen. He had such a gentle smile and said, "How are you, my dear?"

"Fine, Geoffrey. Just a little groggy. And you? Why don't you get some rest and change clothes? You look quite tired."

"I am not leaving here until you can come home with me," he said this so authoritatively that it sounded like something she wouldn't ever be able to argue with him about, and more importantly, even with her foggy head, she knew it sounded as if he thought his home was hers.

He smiled and quietly said, "By the way, Merry Christmas."

"Is it Christmas, really?" Leigh was horrified that so much time had passed. "Oh my, I've been out for three days?"

"Yes, and it is my Christmas gift that you are still with us! And," he said as he reached into his jacket pocket, "I have a little something for you."
"I actually have had it for, well, for a while. It is time to open it. Right now, right here." There was a small box wrapped in Christmas paper in his hand. He put it in her hand.

"But, Geoffrey, I don't have you anything. I wasn't really prepared for Christmas. I didn't plan to," She was stopped by Geoffrey's finger on her mouth this time.

"You don't have to say a word. Just open it." Leigh was not about to argue with this man who had apparently saved her life, yet again. Who hadn't left her side in several days and who was very anxious for her to open the box.

Leigh's shaking hands took the paper on the box and unwrapped it slowly. It was a gold velvet jewelry box. Without looking at him, and with extreme hesitation, she opened it. A large teardrop gold solitaire diamond ring was staring at her glistening in the light. She looked up at him with her eyes asking what her mouth found a hard time doing.

Geoffrey took the ring out of the box and held it between his thumb and forefinger. "I was interrupted the other night when I planned to give this to you, of course, if you had said 'yes'. I wanted to ask you if you would consent to stay at Dalroch a little longer than just New Year's Day. I really want you to stay forever. With me. That is, if you will have me." He stopped and his eyes were watering, "I almost lost you twice now, Leigh Reid, and I don't intend to let another second go by in my life without asking you to be my wife. In case you don't know it, I am very much in love with you and I have been crazy over the thought of losing you these last few days. I would have asked you in Mississippi that day, but I was honestly scared to ask you after what I told you about my life. I am not going to let another day go by without you in it if you will stay here and marry me." His voice broke a little as he continued, "Leigh, please say you will give us a try. I promise to try to make you very happy. You may not be able to control a courtroom here, but you could be in charge of my life forever. I want you; I need you and hear me: I love you! Please say you will be my wife."

Leigh was sure this must have been a dream. It was not truly happening. The pinch test would not do. Not this time. She shook head and closed her eyes a couple of seconds. Then when she opened them, he was still there, and the ring was still in his hand. She swallowed very hard, realizing this was real and it was happening to her in this place right now. Not noticing the tears coming down her face, she said, "You already know the answer to that. At least you should. I told you the night we made love that I would always love you. That hasn't changed. My heart has been yours since that time." She wiped the tears again coming down her cheeks and sniffed, "You know, I couldn't even fake any feelings for Kevin other than friendship. Not even after I thought you had intentionally broke my heart. I did try to see if my feelings for you would change, but it is impossible. It will never happen. I am yours for always, Geoffrey McKennah! Now that I do know you want me, I can say with my whole heart that yes, I will marry you. Now, kiss my cold lips and see if you can warm me up, My Laird."

Forgetting that the room had more people in it than just himself and Leigh, including Red and Gabby, Geoffrey bent over Leigh and sweetly kissed her lips. A whoop and holler went out from Red and a clapping noise from Gabby that sent the nurses in to quiet the occupants down. But when they were told the news, the nurses were clapping too.

Leigh and Geoffrey wiped each other's tears off and laughed at the same time. They were together finally after all that had happened, and that was certainly something worth shedding a few tears over!

CHAPTER FIFTY-FOUR

After the proper Christmas meal, even if a little belated, Leigh and Geoffrey curled up in front of the crackling fire in the study on the thick sheep skin on the floor. The door was locked, the staff was all away, and even Gabby had the good sense to make plans out of the castle for the night.

Geoffrey's skin glowed in the fire light. His hair was loose, and his ruggedly handsome face had nothing but love written all over it as he held Leigh close with both arms squeezing her every few seconds.

"Geoffrey? I know we need to make plans, but, I am so happy right now that all I want to do is to stay just like this forever!" He smiled and squeezed her soft body again closer to him as if to make the two into one.

"I do want to ask you something, though. How'd you find me in that dark water? I mean, you didn't have a flashlight and it was pitch black as I recall. I don't think I had anything on that was luminescent and it minutes had passed before you knew I was even there."

Geoffrey had been waiting for her to ask this. He swallowed hard. He knew she wouldn't question his response, either. "Well, I guess you could say I had a personal guide. There was nothing there at first, but I was frantic and I wasn't going to give it up, so I prayed as I swam looking. Then there was a light. A light that was in the hands of an angel. A true winged floating angel. I believe it was Melinde. No, I am sure of it. It was she who lead me to you."

Somehow, Leigh knew this to be true. Chill bumps crawled over her skin. Yes, Melinde helped her to come back to life after being drugged by Kadar. Leigh believed Melinde was with her earlier that evening in the conservatory, before she was shot at. Melinde was a friend in the afterlife, obviously. Even though Jessica was Melinde's living heir, apparently Melinde knew danger was afoot with Jessica.

Geoff said, "I think we have a resident guardian angel. She didn't want you to die and she knew I would come looking for you. I think she deserves the credit for our being together, don't you?"

Yes, Leigh thought as she felt her body shiver all over again. "You know, she helped me back from the coma I was in, too."

"No, but I am not surprised!" Geoff kissed her gently on the lips.

Melinde helped, but it was that dammed coded disc that actually, as fate would have it, was the true reason they had met and found each other. Thank God that was over with, she thought. How special this moment was, though. Knowing how Melinde helped keep them together.

She looked up adoringly at Geoff and said with a crooked knowing smile, "I love you and Melinde had known that apparently since I first came here. It's not disconcerting, though, to know a ghost has brought us together. Shouldn't it be?" She looked at him smiling as Geoffrey shrugged his shoulders.

She continued, "You know, I hope the Society has no special plans for you for quite a while. We have a lot of catching up to do." She brought his face and lips to hers again and the warmth that resulted made the room, the castle, and nearby hills lose the icy chill for a few blessed hours.

CHAPTER FIFTY-FIVE

Leigh positioned the shaking coffee mug on the table beside the recliner. The boat was drifting to a near stop and the evening sun was beginning to touch the clouds. In purple, red, and orange hues, the sky announced that the day was now officially over. She had finally completed the dreaded task of the recommended therapeutic recall. The therapist Geoff hired, or rather insisted upon, was a gentle soul and after several sessions, Leigh was beginning to believe that she was over the worst of the anxiety that the past events caused her. The recall must be a successful venture, she thought, as she was feeling like she could finally accept the trauma, the monumental changes and the twists and turns her life had taken in such a short period of time.

From the days of handling more than her load of criminal cases in the Dorsey County Courthouse, she faced some quite dramatic decisions that resulted in significant life changes and events. She survived the ordeal of running with the Ogham code. She learned from Geoff the code was based on the ancient Druid priests' Ogham symbols, but they were cleverly scrambled enough to be almost impossible to decode. But, once decoded, the Society's headquarters could have been found and once found, the data that the Society kept would have been compromised and the identities of agents uncovered to those who do them harm. She also learned the man who was murdered in New Orleans was Geoff's friend and agent known as the Raven.

Leigh survived Kadar's ultimate torture and kidnapping. Her life was turned upside down by the discovery of her feelings for Geoff and then by his apparent denial of those feelings. Unfortunately, she then had to realize her feelings would never die for Geoff. That was an expensive lesson as she still felt guilty from hurting her close friend, Kevin, in her attempt to move on. Finding she had a chance again with Geoff, though, after restarting her career, running and winning the campaign for Judge, she had then ventured back to Scotland where she was the target of the jealous Jessica's plot to wed Geoff, barring no others.

But now, thank the Lord, she was well on her way to making a new life in Scotland, with her very attractive husband whose family was rich in history and traditions. And, yes, there were new challenges. Even though Geoffrey wasn't out of the Society business totally, he turned over much of the day-to-day affairs to Kenneth. He was, however, prone to visit with Leigh about his ventures down under the castle, and she was worried for his safety often, but confident of his skills and experience as the Keeper.

After Jessica was escorted back to Spain in total embarrassment and handcuffs, the gift to Melinde's family was sent to a museum in Madrid with a condition that it never be sold unless the Duke of Dalroch had the first right of refusal. The gift was the painting that Melinde painted for her betrothed. It had hung in the balcony area where Leigh first listened to Geoffrey play his bagpipes. She remembered how she admired it then, especially since it looked so much like Geoffrey, but she didn't know it was painted by Melinde. Geoffrey told her that it had always been a special painting as it depicted the castle from its most complimentary view behind the Marquis.

Leigh smiled to herself as she picked the coffee mug back up, this time with no shaking. That recall thing has some merit apparently, she thought smiling as she saw there were no more trembling fingers.

Geoffrey and Leigh were spending a month on the Kelly Reefer down in the Mediterranean. The wedding occurred on New Year's Day in a quiet chapel in the small village of Ogden, near Dalroch. There was very little fanfare, as Leigh required, but there was an unmistakable curiosity of the whole affair by the media. News articles printed a couple of days after the news broke in Edinburg made Leigh an immediate celebrity. This was something she wasn't really thrilled about. She wanted private time with Geoffrey, but she knew after the 'honeymoon was over', the responsibilities and burdens that went with that kind of notoriety would begin and it scared her a bit.

Their respective children were delighted with the union. Joe and Jeremy made it to the wedding, due to a little help from the Duke's private jet. The few days following the vows were spent entertaining guests and local McKennah relatives.

There were other loose ends that needed tidying up, such as Marlowe, her horses, and her Judicial resignation, but for now she was extremely content with the emotional and physical bond that tied her to Geoffrey and he to her.

EPILOGUE

In the days before their departure from Dalroch on the Kelley Reefer, Leigh stole away in the middle of the night to the broche by the water where Melinda had been murdered so many years before. She sat in the broche literally with tears streaming down her face, crying for Melinde and her unborn child. The feelings running through Leigh were genuine and prompted by the complete happiness she felt with Geoffrey as compared to the tragic ending of Melinde's life and that of her unborn child.

Geoffrey awoke to the cold and empty side of the bed and somehow knew he would find Leigh in the broche. He brought a flashlight and entered listening to Leigh's soft cries in the dark. Sitting down beside her, he grabbed her and held her close saying, "Leigh, you sure don't need to be sad for Melinde. She was given a great gift by your solving her murder from so long ago. She can go in peace now."

"Yes, but she hasn't gone. She was there to guide you to me when I almost drowned. Is there something I missed in my investigation? What could keep her here? Do you think she is here now?"

"Maybe she left and came back as our guardian angel, my dearest. I owe her your life, you know. I am so glad she was there. Quite frankly, I would hate to see her go. She's actually become a part of this place now."

"I know, but I feel like if she is still around, that something else will happen to one of us. Or do you think angels just hang out when they want to?" She looked at Geoffrey's sweet expression and sighed. "Oh well, I am sorry to have disturbed your sleep, Geoffrey. I'm being silly, I guess." She leaned her head onto his shoulder and closed her eyes.

A few minutes later, while Leigh was breathing evenly and sleeping on his shoulder, an ever so slight beacon of light eased out of the floor in front of them and then slowly moved up into the inner recesses of the broche. Geoffrey watched it and smiled knowing at that moment that they would always be watched over by Melinde.

After a while, he gently helped Leigh awaken.

"We have a honeymoon to plan on the Kelley Reefer and you need your beauty sleep."

She smiled sleepily as he slowly guided her steps out of the broche. Geoffrey heard the sound of the waves breaking below on the shore. But there was another sound that seemed to be in unison with the falling waves. There, in the distance, a soft far away beating of drums. After all the miracles he experienced with finding, loving, saving and now finally holding Leigh, he believed the drums must be those of his Highland ancestors in the majestic protective hills above. He heard the sound before on occasions but tonight he knew they must be signaling to the McKennah Clan far and wide that, once again, all was well behind the great stone wall of the ancestral home of Dalroch. Squeezing Leigh's shoulders protectively, he smiled at her and then took her to the warm fires inside their home, where they would once again and eternally ignite with love.

Made in the USA
Columbia, SC
28 April 2025